# BATTLEFIELD 4
## COUNTDOWN TO WAR

# BATTLEFIELD 4
## COUNTDOWN TO WAR

Peter Grimsdale

First published in Great Britain in 2013 by Orion Books,
an imprint of The Orion Publishing Group Ltd
Orion House, 5 Upper Saint Martin's Lane
London WC2H 9EA

An Hachette UK Company

1 3 5 7 9 10 8 6 4 2

A CIP catalogue record for this book is
available from the British Library.

ISBN (Hardback) 978 1 4091 4889 0
ISBN (Ebook) 978 1 4091 4887 6

Typeset by Input Data Services Ltd, Bridgwater, Somerset

Printed and bound by CPI Group (UK) Ltd, Croydon, CR0 4YY

The Orion Publishing Group's policy is to use papers that are natural,
renewable and recyclable products and made from wood grown in sustainable
forests. The logging and manufacturing processes are expected to
conform to the environmental regulations of the country of origin.

www.orionbooks.co.uk

For Martin

# 1

## Chinese–North Korean Border

The wall of wire stretched 880 miles. It was twelve feet high, supported every hundred yards by a concrete post that split into a Y near the top to make a double row of razor. The message was clear: do not cross.

Kovic wished he hadn't.

He watched the border disappear under them, barely visible in the darkness, the condensation on the inside of the Sea Hawk's windows already freezing. Olsen, the lead Marine, pressed the mic close to his mouth, his face a sickly green from the instrument lights.

'Maybe you'll start the next Korean War.'

Olsen's look said all he felt about the CIA.

This was supposed to be the Station Chief's big play. 'Do this right,' Cutler told Kovic, 'the White House'll be calling to congratulate you in person. *Highbeam*'s our biggest coup since Bin Laden.' How many times had he heard *that* one? Cutler was new to the region, impatient to make his mark, China just a stop on the elevator to Langley's seventh floor. 'It's all fixed with Beijing, they're right behind us. First ever Sino–US covert; too bad we can't tell the world.'

Kovic knew the Chinese would have vetoed that. They preferred it backstage. Beijing had pitched in, giving them the forward position with refuelling for the helo and arranging for a power cut to black out a corridor thirty miles into North Korea ten minutes before they hit the LZ.

He picked at the ice on the window beside him. A piece slid away exposing the dark nothing below. A few wisps of low cloud flashed by. The Sea Hawk bucked as it swung hard left, slinging the

Marines out of the flimsy picnic chairs they'd brought along for the ride. The pilot let out a whoop.

'Go easy, Tex. This ain't the rodeo.'

Kovic had wanted this done with his own assets hand-picked out of Shanghai, but the Chief vetoed that. '*Highbeam's* expecting John Wayne; he sees a bunch of Chinese riding into town, he could panic.' What did Cutler imagine this was, a meet and greet? With all their kit on plus the amount of light they'd be shining on him, their man wouldn't even see them; they might as well be Klingons. But Cutler wanted it his way, never mind if it was the best way, and that meant Marines.

'Ten minutes to LZ,' came Tex's voice over the headset.

A sudden updraught silenced him and tossed them all out of their chairs again.

'Hey, Mr Pilot – you want my breakfast all over your nice clean chopper?' shouted Faulkner.

'This joyride better be worth it,' said Olsen, looking at Kovic.

'You bring my boys back in one piece,' Garrison, their commander, had warned Kovic when he heard he'd be leading the mission. He had reasons for saying so that neither of them ever wanted to go over again.

Kovic gazed at them. Even in their body armour, they all looked too young to be there, though he knew that he was, by their standards, middle-aged. The trouble with experience was you knew all the things that could go wrong.

He decided it was time to put them in the picture; Cutler had insisted he wait until they were airborne. He flicked on his mike.

'Listen up, guys, this here *Highbeam* wrote the Dear Leader's entire missile launch protocol, source code – the whole shebang. He is *the* man behind North Korea's nuke capability. Defectors don't come much higher up the food chain than this.'

Hype didn't come easily to Kovic. His default mode was blunt truth, in a plain wrapper, no ribbons or bullshit, but he needed these guys enrolled.

'Fuckin' A, man!' Deacon, the baby of the group and the noisiest, was the first to react, as if to make up for his youth. 'We goin' make his-sto-ree.'

'That's the plan, bro,' nodded Kovic, hoping it would be the right kind of history.

Eight hours earlier he had watched them step out of the Sea Hawk at the base outside of Xian, all tough guy banter and rap star swagger, and thought to himself how foreign they appeared – another reminder to him of how used he'd gotten to China. They looked every inch an invasion force, standing guard over the machine like they'd just put down in Mogadishu, eyeing all-comers as if they were hostiles, even the ground staff preparing to refuel. The Chinese weren't big on manners, but if you wanted the place to work for you, you needed to show some respect.

'He's a high value catch so you treat him good, make him welcome,' Kovic added, knowing that after six months on pirate deterrence in the South China Sea they needed to reset their attitude. The six of them packed themselves into the Sea Hawk's cramped airframe, encased in all their kit: high molecular polyethylene helmets, ballistic plates and fleeces under their tunics, an M4 and a Beretta M9 each – typical Marine overkill – plus the new-issue four-tube NV goggles. Deacon and Kean were playing with theirs, like kids at Christmas. Tex the pilot had brought a customised M79 grenade launcher with the barrel cut so short it looked like a musket out of *Pirates of the Caribbean*.

'I can't shoot for shit, so this kills everything in a ninety-yard radius without I even open my eyes.'

'Yeah, he shoots better with his eyes shut, dontcha, Tex?'

Kovic kept it simple, just a pair of two-barrel NV goggles and his Sig Sauer P226 with a Nightforce scope, suppressor and five or six clips.

'Smooth, man.'

Deacon admired the P226, still nodding in time to whatever was coming through his earbuds. Faulkner was absorbed in a game on his phone. Kean was curled up like a cat, out cold – though it didn't stop him from farting, which he did often.

'Hey, Kovac.' Faulkner glanced up, waving a half-eaten Hershey

Bar. In his enormous baseball-mitt hand it looked like a matchstick.

'Kov – *ich.*'

'This make you homesick?'

He shook his head. Somewhere along the way he'd lost his taste for American candy, and a lot of other things American too. He thought about what he could be eating now, like the special prawns with abalone at Mancun's. If home was anywhere now, it was Shanghai. Everything he needed was there, everything in the world: imported or knocked off, in the malls and the movie theatres and along the sidewalks, where every kind of delicacy could be found, in delicious, steaming dishes. And then there was Louise, neither American nor Chinese, whom Shanghai had unexpectedly brought into his life. What was she doing now – apart from wondering where the fuck he'd gone this time?

Faulkner bit off a chunk of chocolate, talking as he chewed.

'So, Jason Bourne, how come you sitting in a Hawk full of Marines, 'stead of jumping across rooftops somewhere?'

It was a good question. He could easily have passed on this one. His infil clearance had expired, he hadn't used a weapon since Afghanistan, he was out of shape plus he had plenty going on in Shanghai. Every bone in his body had told him to stay away, but he knew he needed to make some sort of show for Cutler if he was going to stay in his post. They hadn't exactly bonded. 'Watch your back,' Krantz on the desk back at Langley had warned him, 'Cutler's looking to China to make him King of the Hill. Stroke his dick a little, on account of your résumé's got a bit more meat on it than his.'

It was true, Kovic had done more than his share of hot postings: in Lebanon disrupting Hezbollah, in Liberia to sting an arms dealer, a stint undercover in Grozny posing as a Chechen returnee, two long tours in Iraq and then Afghanistan. His colouring and pronounced cheekbones meant he could pass as local pretty much anywhere from Vladivostok to Venezuela. Shanghai was supposed to be a reward, 'a chance to reinvent yourself' Human Resources had claimed. The first two years he'd hated it, struggling with the language and trying to crack the mysterious codes by which China operated. Now he couldn't imagine living anywhere else. If he had any say in it, he would die in the East – though not in North Korea, and not tonight.

Price, the tall quiet one, chipped in.

'If this screws up, who we call?'

Olsen shut him up. 'Hey, kid, no one's gonna screw up, okay?'

It was about time Olsen spoke some sense. He and Kovic knew full well that if they did screw up, they'd be on their own. This one was a deniable. The others didn't get that, but who could blame them? They were serving soldiers with rules to play by. In the CIA rule one was don't get caught, because no one will come for you.

'It gets to daylight, we outta here, man,' said Price. 'Package or no.'

Kovic nodded. As they got closer to the LZ some bravado was wearing off. Sometimes the ones who looked the toughest had got boot camp confused with the gym.

'For sure. But no package, no bonus,' said Faulkner.

The talk of money woke Kean up.

'No bonus means I gotta do 'nother tour, or the old lady's lawyer's gonna have my ass.'

He's more concerned about his alimony payments than getting his balls blown off by the North Koreans, thought Kovic: easier to fear the devil you know. They'd all volunteered like good patriots, but it was the money that fired them up. He didn't have the heart to tell them that the fabled spec-ops bonus was discretionary, down to some anonymous bean counter in the bowels of the Pentagon.

'And I ain't gonna get no Chinky tail tomorrow.'

'Ain't that why your old lady's got her lawyer on you in the first place, on account you can't keep it zipped up?'

'Yeah, baby! They don't call it The Beast for nothin'!'

Kovic smiled. A million Pentagon directives on the use of appropriate language and these guys were using the same terms his father had. It must be true what they said, that travel narrowed the mind. When he had once dared to warn Cutler about some xenophobic slight, the Chief looked at him over his glasses. 'We're not here to make friends, Agent Kovic, we're here to get even.'

That was US foreign policy in a nutshell, and from the mouth of one who had made a career out of missing all the big and ugly shows. Kovic despised desk jockeys like Cutler, who in turn was threatened by Kovic's field record. That was what irked Cutler most about him, Kovic figured, and explained his need to remind him who was boss. And God help you if it was an election year.

Kean was in full flow now, spurring on the others.

'At Susie's Bar in Ningbo they got these twins—'

'They ain't *real* twins, jerk-off. They just all look the same to you. They show you a girl and her grandmother you'd think they was twins.'

'At least I don't gotta *pay* for it.'

'Deacon, you're a virgin, man! You don't even know where to put it.'

Another ripple of laughter shook the picnic chairs.

Olsen growled.

'Enough already. Change the channel, will ya?'

'Hey, Kovic: I been wonderin' – do they really got them straight pubes?'

Olsen gave Deacon a look that silenced him. There was a lull. Tex was slowing down. He turned briefly and gestured at the ground.

'Whoo-yeah! Santa and Rudolf twelve high!'

Snow. The supposedly state of the art meteorological imaging from Fleet Command had confirmed clear skies. They might as well have gone with Pyongyang TV's weatherman, whose forecast had to be approved by the Party. Wouldn't you know, thought Kovic: this job just keeps on getting better and better.

What he didn't know then was that the snow would save his life.

# 2

The Sea Hawk's engine note changed to a heavy drumming pulse as the rotors flared and brought it to a hover. Kovic slid the door open and the icy gale blasted away the warm human fug that had built up on board. He scanned the barren moonscape below. None of what he could see remotely resembled the satellite images. Cutler's information had been thin. All he'd said was that *Highbeam's* vehicle would be parked up north of a cluster of concrete blocks imaginatively referred to in the brief as a 'deserted village'. 'Just swoop and scoop,' he'd added, smirking at his great new catchphrase.

Kovic spotted a dark-coloured station wagon pulled off the road. Better be him and not some young lovers seeking a commodity even rarer here than food – privacy.

He switched to the troop net, went over the drill again.

'We surround the vehicle, one at each corner, no closer than ten feet, weapons down but ready. We don't want him thinking we've come to kill him. Once I've confirmed ID, he gets out the car, we frisk him. If he has luggage I have to check it. We're on the ground ten minutes. No more.'

'You the boss,' said Kean.

Olsen cut in. 'My information was two minutes.'

'We leave when I say; when I'm good and ready.'

There wasn't time to go over just why Olsen felt like he did about taking orders from the CIA. Kovic knew all too well. He and Garrison went right back. He knew about their unfinished business. Right now he just needed Olsen to get the job done. They weren't going on vacation together – just in, out, and home. No friending on Facebook.

'You want to get out of here sooner,' he told him, 'get on and tell your men who goes at which corner.'

Olsen sighed then assigned each man a corner. Kovic didn't care which of them went where; he just wanted a clear chain of command.

'Okay, Tex, put us down.'

As they descended, Kovic flipped down his NV goggles, blurring the snowflakes into clumps like bright white cotton balls. Fucking useless piece of kit. The frozen hillside looked barren and empty; he preferred working in crowded places with a multitude of distractions. Out here there was nowhere to hide.

The snow was coming down thick and fast now, transforming the locality into an unlikely Christmas card scene in March, not to mention a white carpet of light which would show them up like figurines on a wedding cake. But they weren't doing stealth tonight. The Sea Hawk's clatter saw to that.

There were no new cars in North Korea, just as there were no new washing machines or TVs. If you saw a beat up old Nissan like the one they were looking at cruising your neighbourhood in America you would call your kids inside, here it was quite likely to be the personal transport of the nation's top nuclear programmer.

The wipers made a single sweep and through the screen Kovic could just make out a lone figure at the wheel. In his experience defectors could often be a pain in the ass. Some had an over-inflated sense of their own value and tried to strike last-minute deals, or showed up with loved ones they'd decided they couldn't be parted from – girlfriends, boyfriends, mothers and other assorted hangers-on hoping for a place on the American magic carpet out of whichever hellhole they'd had the misfortune to be born in. One guy Kovic had lifted in Beirut tried to bring his dog. Some, fearing reprisals, had a last-minute change of heart. Those were the emotionally tough ones. There were gulags filled with the extended families of these people – everyone they had ever loved or given birth to, mere hostages in waiting.

Tex set the Sea Hawk down on the road.

'We have now landed in the Democratic People's Republic of Korea. Set your watches back fifty years.'

'Keep her running, Tex.' Kovic jumped down and ducked under the rotors.

'I'm going to walk up this left side of the road until I'm parallel with the driver's window. Olsen – move your men into position when I start talking.'

The snow was gathering thickly on the ground. Kovic approached the car, stopped twenty feet away and trained his torch on the figure at the wheel: high forehead, hollow cheeks, long upper lip, slight break in left eyebrow – check. He was wearing a suit that was much too big for him, the cutting edge of DPRK couture no doubt. He had an unnatural grin on his face. And he was shaking so much the lapels of his coat were vibrating. Kovic quietly cleared his throat and switched his brain to Korean, running a quick mental check that he'd got the guy's real name right.

'*Shun-kin, I bring greetings on behalf of the government of the United States.*'

The man at the wheel continued to grin but didn't move, didn't even look round. Deacon, Kean, Faulkner and Price took up their positions, one at each corner, with Olsen at the back, bookending Kovic. He wanted *Highbeam* to see the men; give him a sense of security and reassurance that this was for real.

Kovic kept his NVs flipped up so he looked a bit more human and stepped closer to the driver's window. The interior smelled of ashtrays and sweat. There was a large fake leather suitcase on the back seat, much like the one his grandparents had brought with them to America back in the thirties.

'*Are you ready to take these brave steps to freedom?*'

No words, just a series of rapid nods.

'*It's okay, you can speak to me: I'll understand.*'

Kovic's flair for languages was another thing that spooked Cutler who preferred to do all his talking through interpreters.

Still the inane grin and the shaking. And still *Highbeam* didn't move. Kovic took another step towards him. In Pakistan he'd had to strap one guy to a stretcher and carry him after he passed out from fear.

*'Shun-kin. Please step out of the car. We are taking you to America. You understand? We are taking you now.'*

What was it that rooted him to the spot where he sat? Last-minute doubts, fear of the unknown? The realisation he could never return home?

Perhaps the sound of a Yank speaking his native language was too disconcerting. This time Kovic tried English, and a little more urgency.

'Hey, Shun-kin, time to go, okay?'

The Korean opened the door and stepped tentatively out into the night. Despite the cold he was gleaming with sweat. The inane goofy grin didn't make him look too bright either. Close up he looked so young – too young. Either the guy was a child prodigy or—

As Kovic reached forward to shake his hand, the Korean jumped to the left and started to run. Kean, who was nearest, blocked his path.

'Get away from me!' he screamed in clear English. He pushed at Kean, his narrow frame making no impact on the solid, stocky Marine. 'You must get away from me! They've—'

Kean almost had him in a bear hug.

Then Kovic suddenly understood. He screamed at Kean.

'Run, man, run! Drop him! Go! Go!'

The first detonation, an igniter, came from somewhere on the guy's chest. Kovic caught sight of it just as he turned to run. The second explosion turned night into day and lifted him off his feet as the force propelled him halfway back to the Sea Hawk. He slammed down on to the road and rolled in the snow.

Shun-kin was gone, vaporised in the blast. The car was on fire, setting off a third explosion as the gas tank caught. Kean lay fifteen feet from where he had been standing; one arm gone, his face a mask of blood. Deacon, dragging one leg, got to him first. Kean reached up to him, then flopped back. He was gone. Deacon's face was frozen in shock.

Tex was at the controls, yelling into the net.

'Kovic, talk to me!'

The blast had temporarily knocked out Kovic's hearing, but his mind was in hyperdrive. Shun-kin had tried to run; he hadn't detonated the device himself. It couldn't have been on a timer as there was no knowing their exact time of arrival. So someone else with sight of them had triggered it. He whirled round and shouted to Tex to lift off, get out of range. On the ground the helo was a sitting duck and they needed eyes in the air.

'Go round; tell us what you can see.'

Snow and gravel whipped around him as the Sea Hawk ascended. 'Hey, back here, now!'

Olsen was yelling and waving, as if Tex would see him in the dark. Kovic moved past him and caught sight of Deacon curled up in a semi-foetal position, holding his chest as if the contents would spill out if he let go. Kovic rushed to him, ripping a tourniquet from the side pocket of his fatigues. His whole torso was a mass of blood.

'Steady now. Don't breathe so hard.'

'Fuckin' suicide—'

Kovic knew Shun-kin wasn't a suicide bomber. He had tried to warn them, even though he knew he was done for. He had probably saved Kovic's life.

'Hey, look!' Faulkner was pointing. The 'deserted village' was alive with men moving toward them.

'Fucking ace,' Olsen spat.

Kovic grabbed Deacon and hauled him behind what was left of the station wagon, then went back and got his M4. His goggles were gone, swept off by the blast, and his eyes were full of dust. The temptation was to squirt a lot of bullets around and hope some made their target. Better to resist that, try to think, he told himself. He peeled Deacon's NVs off his helmet and put them on. There were maybe a dozen North Koreans, just black silhouettes against the whiteness, armed with their standard issue Russian RPKs. At least those would be hard work in the dark and snow and he guessed they wouldn't have NVs or lasers. On the other hand the RPK's drum magazines would have seventy-five rounds, good for spray and pray. There were no more than thirty rounds in Deacon's

M4; he was going to need every one of those. Seeing movement ahead and to the left, he jumped up and loosed off half a dozen shots. Three Koreans sprawled in the snow with head wounds, pools of blood merging into a huge spilled snow cone. If they were going to get out of this at all, there was going to be a lot more blood.

Kovic saw a sniper run towards them, then vanish into the shadows. He aimed into the spot, fired and heard a scream.

'Where's Faulkner?'

He was staggering towards them in a daze, clutching his shoulder, his weapon dangling uselessly from his smashed hand. Kovic ran and pushed him to the ground while Price covered them. He pulled a bandage from his kit and tore Faulkner's sleeve away with his teeth before wrapping the arm as best he could. There was morphine in the kit too, but something else now grabbed his attention.

Olsen was shouting on the net to Tex.

'The fuck you doing? Cover, for fuck's sake.'

'We gotta be outta here.'

'Negative.' Kovic didn't need this right now. 'We got to neutralise all this first. He comes near, he's a sitting duck.'

Olsen wasn't listening. Kovic gripped his shoulder and spun him around. 'They take one shot at him we are lost, got it? No one comes for us.'

Olsen shook off his grip, his face contorted by rage.

'You took us straight into an ambush, you fucking moron. You were set up. Your intel was shit. It was fucked up from the off. I'm getting my guys outta here. This mission is officially fucked. I'm taking my guys out and *you* – can go fuck yourself.'

Kovic lunged at Olsen but he dodged and slammed his knee into his balls. Then Olsen landed a boot in his stomach, sending him sprawling in the snow.

And then they heard the deep thrum of the chopper. Barely visible, a grey blur behind the snow like a half tuned television image, the Sea Hawk moved above them. Tex was bringing it back.

'Sayonara, assholes.' Tex yelled over the radio. It was as if the whole covert thing had gone to his head. His side window was slid back and he was waving his grenade launcher where he thought the

NK were positioned. He blasted it as he made his second descent.

But as Olsen gestured to Price to help Faulkner towards the LZ the Sea Hawk lurched sideways, as if grasped by a giant unseen hand that had reached out of the cloud. The engine revs shot up to scream level as the nose tipped up as if struggling for altitude. The whole machine started to slide sideways, the tail rotor combing the ground right where the Koreans had taken up position. One of the main blades snapped free and catapulted end over end away into the night. Then the helicopter started a slow motion barrel roll and finally slammed on to the ground. Kovic threw himself over Faulkner and Price and Olsen stumbled behind the remains of the station wagon as the helo exploded in a fireball, spraying the area with clumps of disintegrating machinery before erupting into a mushroom of fiery smoke.

There was nothing to say. They were thirty miles into North Korean territory, their ride home gone, their advantage of surprise non-existent, with a column of flame and smoke rising into the night to alert anyone else in a ten-mile radius who still didn't already know they were there. Alone, Kovic could maybe have gone to ground, evaded any patrols and tried to make the border. But with two dead and three wounded—

Olsen looked at him full of contempt. 'Another one for the CIA Hall of Shame.'

Kovic was past anger. 'You're the one told him to turn back.'

Olsen jutted his jaw towards Kovic as if to say, 'Oh yeah? Bring it on,' and his mouth opened. For a moment Kovic thought Olsen was forming his next insult, but then he twitched, his eyes swivelled upward, his rifle dropped from his hands and he slumped forward, face down in the snow. Price rushed towards him.

'He's hit!'

'Sniper! Cover!'

It had come from high ground to their left, almost invisible behind the snow. Blood gulped from a gash in Olsen's thigh; if the femoral artery was severed he didn't have a chance. Price tore at a first aid pack. Kovic ripped the already shredded remains of Olsen's fatigues, made a makeshift tourniquet and bound the thigh tight.

'Here.'

Price gave him the morphine. Then they mounded snow over the wound to constrict the blood vessels until they were ready to move him.

Muzzle flashes and wild revving announced a large open jeep-like truck coming at them down the hill, with a second close behind.

'The fuck's that?'

'Border force. Kaengsaeng-69, that's Korean for piece-of-shit-mobile.'

None of them moved. They were overwhelmed.

'We are so fucked.'

Kovic watched as both vehicles drew to a halt. 'Not yet. I want those wheels.'

He figured he had one advantage; these guys were conscripts, not Special Forces. Nothing like this would have happened to them before. The best he could hope for was to pick off whichever he could and scare off the rest. He aimed the M16 infrared at the driver in the first jeep. Bullseye. The driver flopped out of his seat while his passengers jumped for cover. Kovic followed them through the sight, picking off two more. He might be out of shape but his aim hadn't deserted him. The remainder jumped into the second vehicle, which took off, fishtailing in the settling snow.

Kovic ran to the abandoned jeep and jumped in. The engine was still running. He stirred the shift until he found first, brought up the clutch until it bit, then manoeuvred towards the group behind the burned-out station wagon.

'I got you in here; I'm gonna get you out, okay?'

'How?'

Olsen was barely conscious. Faulkner was better but in shock from his pulverised arm. He closed his eyes, waiting for the morphine to take effect.

'Plan B: we go through the military crossing.'

At Kovic's insistence, the Chinese had agreed a back-up overland escape route via a disused mountain border post.

Price helped Kovic load the wounded into the vehicle. He was shaking with fear and shock.

'Now, let's get out of here.'

The snow was coming down harder and thicker now, a wind sending it straight at them. Kovic killed the lights and relied on his NV goggles, even though they made the flakes look huge, as if they were driving through a huge, exploded quilt.

'This speed we're not gonna make it,' observed Olsen, uselessly.

'Wanna get out and push?'

In the rear-view mirror, Kovic saw the second jeep had turned and was now in pursuit, gaining on them. So much for scaring them off. He tried to find a higher gear. There wasn't one and in trying to up-shift he had lost speed.

As the second jeep drew closer Kovic yelled at Price to fend it off. But none of his shots deterred them. The road was still climbing but it was straight as far as he could see – which was not more than about two hundred feet. The other jeep was now almost alongside. Kovic wrenched the wheel. There was a screech of contacting metal, but the other jeep stayed obstinately on the road. Kovic swiped the jeep again. This time it veered off its path. Its nearside wheels caught in a ditch and it toppled off the road and rolled on to its side.

The first rush of relief didn't last. A bend loomed out of the snow, a sharp left with a treacherous negative camber. He pulled hard on the wheel but momentum had got the better of the jeep. It wasn't going anywhere except straight off the road, where it bounced, rose and bounced again, spilling all of them into the snow before coming to rest in some trees.

This is so not my night, thought Kovic.

He flattened himself against the bank and peered at the other jeep. The occupants had righted it and were back on board. The engine fired. It was coming his way. Kovic ducked out of sight as it went by, skidding in the slush. The NK hadn't seen them go over the edge. He sprinted forward, slipped in the snow, recovered, vaulted into the back of the moving jeep and took aim. The suppressor on his Sig meant the two in the rear seats were gone without the guys up front even noticing, but then the vehicle lurched as it bounced through a pothole, throwing Kovic on to the driver and knocking his weapon out of his hand. The other man up front struggled to free the barrel of an RPK that was trapped between his knees. Kovic smashed his left elbow into the side of the soldier's head and lunged for the weapon before he could raise it. But the driver, distracted by Kovic's sudden arrival, let go of the wheel. The vehicle slammed into a post, the impact throwing Kovic head first into the footwell, mashing his chin against the muzzle of the gun. He tried in vain to reach his gun that was now wedged under the pedals. The passenger freed his machine gun and loosed off a spray of fire into the sky that blasted inches from Kovic's face, numbing the side of his head so that for a second he was sure he had been hit. What an unholy mess, he thought, as he struggled in the tangle of trapped weapons and writhing limbs. He grasped the barrel of the PRK, the heat searing through his gloves, and wrenched it in the direction of the driver just as its owner fired another volley. The bullets perforated the driver's neck, so many and at such close range that his head almost entirely detached itself and flopped on to his chest. The passenger's eyes bulged in horror. Kovic saw how young he looked and felt a flicker of pity before he seized the gun from his grip, jammed the butt into his chest and knocked him out into the snow.

There was still work to do. The semi-decapitated driver's boot was still wedged firmly on the gas. Kovic seized the wheel – too late to stop the jeep slamming into a low wall and sending him airborne, tumbling over the hood and the wall and into an icy ditch. His nose smashed against a rock and he heard the crunch of splitting bone. On the way down he cursed Olsen, cursed Cutler, cursed the Agency and finally himself for being fool enough to accept the mission at all.

For a full minute he was immobile. Almost blinded by pain, he struggled to stay conscious, but could feel his brain giving up, shutting down. In this ditch, hidden by the wall, he could just remain and maybe the bad guys would go away … the snow could cover him and he'd never be found. It would be so nice and restful. He felt himself sinking.

Someone was screaming. He snapped back into consciousness, lifted himself a few inches and peered over the parapet where the jeep had come to rest. It was empty. If he could get it moving it was theirs. He climbed back over the wall and jumped in. The wheel was slimy with blood and brain matter. He wiped it cursorily with his sleeve, fumbled with the controls and found the ignition, turned it and pumped the gas. It fired hopefully, then stalled. He turned it again; it fired and stalled again. Price was struggling towards him in the snow pulling Olsen and Faulkner. Together in the swirling snow they already looked like ghosts.

Kovic finally got the engine going, then revved it and rocked it back and forth until it found grip and reversed towards them.

He pulled out his phone. There were three agreed text codes: *Alpha* was mission accomplished, *Beta* was abort, *Gamma* was land exfil. He was about to text *Gamma*, which would alert Cutler to confirm the border crossing – if they made it.

'Fuck this, we're blown anyway,' he told himself.

He dialled Cutler.

He picked up straight away. 'What happened?'

'Blown. Two men down plus the pilot. It was a fucking set-up. *Highbeam* had a surprise vest on.'

Silence. All he could hear were Cutler's short quick breaths coming down the line. Kovic wanted to chew him out but that would have to wait. There were more pressing issues.

'We're twenty miles inside the DPRK. I have wheels, but we need that border post confirmed open. Otherwise we're talking six dead Marines plus one of yours – on the wrong side of the wire, copy?'

'We're on it. Go carefully.' Cutler hung up.

The Chinese were their only hope now; they better have that border crossing open. But Beijing would also have gone into damage limitation mode, while Cutler would be busy figuring how this was going to play back in Langley and how to cover his ass. But rage wasn't going to get Kovic anywhere. The cover that the smoke from the burning helo had created was already drifting away.

His anger gave him a fresh surge of energy. They were going to get in this thing and get the hell across the border and Olsen and Faulkner were going to live, never mind the snow and however many NK were headed their way.

He helped them into the jeep, which had stalled again.

'Where we goin', man?' Faulkner was vague with cold and pain.

'Home. We make the border in this thing, someone Chinese side will scoop us up.'

No one else spoke. The sight of the two dead men and the burned up Sea Hawk with Tex inside it was fresh in their minds.

Olsen groaned. 'Garrison warned me about you. Oh yeah, I know all about—'

Kovic cut him off. 'Save it. I got you a ride out. We get over the border, we never have to so much as look at each other again – but until then we gotta make like we're a team and look out for each other. That way we have more chance of staying alive. Right? Try and keep each other warm. We got a thirty-minute drive ahead.'

He didn't wait for a response. He rammed the shift until he found first and the jeep jolted forward. The road was completely hidden under a carpet of white.

When it was this bad, the only thing was to think about the other bad times he'd gotten out of. The time in Sudan, captured by child soldiers high on smack who'd pushed the muzzle of a rifle up his ass and were arguing about who got to pull the trigger. In Kurdistan, the aggrieved knife-wielding hooker who thought he wouldn't pay up because the Taliban commander he'd recruited her to sting turned out to be gay. And his first month in China, when an Indonesian arms dealer hung him by his heels from a high rise because he thought he was a rival …

He didn't want to think about Garrison's son, though.

With each minute the snow thickened and the wheels lost even more grip. He slowed to below twenty, which was still too fast. The track met the border on the slope of a mountainside. The jeep protested furiously at the gradient. The clutch was shot, but he managed to force the shift out of second gear and back into first. He was following the contour of the hill but the negative camber on a right-hand curve tugged the vehicle sideways. He applied more gas but the wheels just spun. Then the revs climbed and for a time it looked as if they would make it. Kovic squinted ahead, focused with all his will as he replayed his memory of the map and sat-photos, how the track narrowed as it rounded a sharp hairpin, and where some landslip had spilt over the surface. He kept the gas steady as the jeep bucked over the uneven surface, but the gradient defeated the transmission until a sudden metallic crack under their feet told him the drive shaft had snapped. He stood on the brakes but the wheels were already locked. They were sliding backwards, the engine released from its burden revving to a scream.

'I can't hold it. Bail!'

They jumped out, Kovic pulling Olsen and Price holding Faulkner before the jeep disappeared over the edge of the track and turned on its side, displaying its broken prop shaft like a dangling limb. The engine was still idling but the vehicle was clinically dead.

'Okay. We walk from here.'

'How far?'

'A mile.'

A mile on the flat in this was twenty minutes minimum, uphill twenty-five. Carrying a wounded man each …

Kovic hauled Olsen on to his back, while Price hooked Faulkner's good arm over his strong shoulders and half carried, half walked him. Faulkner was the biggest but Olsen felt like a steer, his weight seeming to double every few yards. Kovic dug deep into what resources he had left, forcing his mind to separate itself from the fatigue. The cold had slowed the seepage out of Olsen's thigh but he was getting paler. Kovic felt the cold biting deep, freezing his face, gluing the hairs in his nostrils together. In Afghanistan during the winter of 2008 he'd come upon an oddly shaped mound in the snow. Curious, he'd dug into it and found an entire family huddled together in a last desperate search for warmth. Their corpses were fused together, frozen solid; they had become their own memorial.

'Hey, see that?'

Price, who was a few yards ahead, stopped and pointed into the gloom.

'Fence.'

'Hey,' said Faulkner. 'We're almost there.'

Kovic fired a distress flare which the snow clouds swallowed whole. The wind coming round the hill sharpened and drove into them, slowing their progress further. Kovic started to count his steps, just for something to focus on other than the cold. With each step he imagined another dish on the menu at Mancun's, promising himself double everything if he ever got out of this. Out here in the bleak white nothingness, brash, brittle Shanghai seemed like heaven on earth.

The checkpoint was deserted, but the giant mesh gate was unlocked. Something had gone right, though somewhere inside him he had hoped fancifully for a Chinese welcoming party. He climbed up the watchtower and found the phone in its all-weather metal box. There was no dial, no buttons: just lift and wait for an answer. Hopefully someone in the border HQ would pick up. He looked down at Price, his arms around Faulkner and Olsen, trying to shelter them from the punishing wind that was itself now a weapon, whipping them unrelentingly.

The phone line crackled. The voice sounded as if it was on the other side of the world. Kovic tried to speak. The frozen air ripped at his windpipe. The sweat from heaving Olsen had frozen on to his face like a glaze. He sank to his knees, his muscles going into shutdown, his memory too. What in the hell was the Mandarin word for help? He searched the recesses of his brain, feeling his consciousness receding as the cold claimed him. Finally, after what seemed a lifetime, it came. He tried to move his lips but they would hardly obey him.

'*Yu-cheng* ... Help.'

He dropped the phone and lurched towards the steps. His only hope was to get back to the men, to share their dwindling warmth before it was too late for them all. He found a footing, lost it, tried another, and then fell the ten or so feet on to the snow that had drifted round the base of the watchtower. He landed softly, completely encased in the fresh snow. He had done it, got them back over the border. Now exhaustion overwhelmed him. Maybe he would stay here forever, just let go. Yes, why not? Didn't he say he would die in China?

What's the last thing you want to think of before you die? They tell you to fix on something special and precious, someone you love.

20

He saw her coming towards him. *There you are. I was wondering when you'd show up.* Louise's face, looking down on him, shaking her head, her hair floating. She was laughing and holding out her hand. *Come on, come to bed. Come on ...*

He was woken by what sounded like a couple of dull thuds, possibly thickly booted feet jumping down from a vehicle, he imagined. He heard the sound again. He opened his eyes but everything was dark, even darker than before. There was something in front of his face. He blinked and felt wetness. He was buried in the snow. How long had he been lying there? He blinked the snow away until with one eye he had a view of part of the scene in front of him.

The huddle that had been Olsen, Price and Faulkner was gone. There was an SUV. Help had come. Two silhouetted men were loading something into the back of the vehicle. He thought he could feel the heat coming off it – warmth, comfort, safety. He struggled to move, found he couldn't. He saw a third man standing over a heap on the ground, an arm raised.

There were two more thuds, accompanied by tiny flashes. Then the two men from the SUV joined the gunman. One took off his glove and reached for a cigarette packet, his hand bright white against the rest of the darkness, three marks like arrows jutting from the cuff. They stood over the body for a minute, smoking and talking, wisps of smoke and condensation floating away from them. Eventually two of them bent down and lifted the corpse by an arm and a leg, as if it was a fresh kill from a hunt, and dragged it to the SUV. It was Olsen.

Kovic closed his eye. Didn't move again.

# 3

Commander Garrison looked over his glasses at the young radioman.

'Let me stop you right there, son.'

He knew the kid meant well, but right now he looked like he wished the deck would swallow him up. Bale took a couple of breaths to try and steady his nerves. He knew the Commander had an obsession with plain English, he'd heard him chew out an intelligence officer for talking about 'delivering information-centric capabilities'. He glanced at Lieutenant Duncan, but she was concentrating very hard on something on the tip of her boot. Garrison felt sorry for the kid and tried to throw him a lifeline.

'Just imagine you're explaining it to your—'

No, that would sound sexist. He had to watch that these days. He glanced at Duncan, a tiny smile just visible on her lips, then his gaze drifted to the first purple of sunrise off to the east.

Bale pressed on.

'Sir, it's just there's this algorithm stack and for the last three hours it's – our reflex monitors—' Bale's sentence faltered to a stop, like his engine just ran out of gas. Garrison failed to stifle a chuckle.

'Bale, when were you born?'

'In 1991. Sir.'

'You know where I was in '91? Right here on this ship, in the midst of the first Gulf War. Now when we're at war we have to tell it like it is. No bullshit, no jargon.'

Bale wished to Jesus he'd kept quiet. He shouldn't even have been scanning north at this time. But the signal, if it was a signal, was like none he had seen before. He had shown it to Ransome when he came on duty, who'd dismissed it as random noise. But Bale was sure there was something to it. It was much too sharp, plus there was the way it pulsed. He had stepped out of the control room straight into the path of Garrison on his daybreak walkabout and, well, he couldn't help himself.

'Give it one more try.'

Bale took a deep breath.

'Take it slowly.'

'There's a communication stream emanating from a point on the Chinese land mass.'

Garrison nodded. The sunrise was turning the glassy sea a spectacular pink.

'Okay, I'm getting that. Keep going.'

'It started at 0410 and lasted thirty seconds. There was another at 0550 from about half a degree south. They were bounced to a receiver fifteen hundred miles away into the Chinese interior.'

'Okay, I'm receiving that. Any decrypt yet?'

'That's just the thing, sir. There's no way into it. It's like plain white noise. No contours.'

'And the receiver?'

'None that's on our data. It could be it's just come on stream, but it doesn't show up as anywhere near any known military or intelligence facility.'

'Can you – capture it?'

Garrison wasn't sure what you did with stuff like that, so he went for a familiar word.

'That's the other thing, sir. It won't. It has no – it's like a vapour trail. It just melts away.'

'Nice analogy, Bale. Write it up and we'll get our intelligence people on to it.'

Garrison squeezed his shoulder. He didn't want to squash the kid's initiative, after all that was just what ... Shit. His thought stopped in its tracks as another jumped into focus.

'Where in China did you say?'

'On the border with North Korea – a mountainous region with—'

Garrison was on his feet.

'Get me the exact coordinates – *now*.'

# 4

Garrison moved swiftly through the ship, men stepping out of his path, saluting as he went. He nodded to each of them, because that was his custom, but right now they were almost invisible to him. He'd told Olsen to signal the minute they were clear. It was gone 0700 which meant Olsen was late, and there was nothing from Cutler. A satellite had picked up a suspected aviation fire close to their sector on the border. He needed answers.

'It's all ready for you, Commander. Langley's China desk online and waiting and the Pentagon are listening in.' Duncan held the door for him.

'Thanks, Lieutenant. Afraid you'll have to step out for this.'

'Understood, sir.'

Whatever he was about to hear he wanted to digest it alone first.

He closed and locked the door. The room smelled stagnant. A month had passed since anyone had used it. Duncan had put out a pitcher of water and a glass and had fresh coffee sent up. Too bad he had to do this without her in the room. He always behaved better when she was around. But he needed the others to level with him and they might clam up if they saw her alongside him. He patted his tunic and helped himself to something stronger from Jack's silver flask. He typed in his personal code and hit Enter. Two screens sprang to life.

'Sir, good day.' It was Krantz on the China desk at Langley. 'And we have Colonel Benskin at the Pentagon with us at this time.'

'Hey, Roland.'

'Hi, Brad.'

It was all over their faces, thought Garrison. Krantz's eyebrows were raised as high as they could go, desperately seeking upsides.

Benskin looked more grizzled than ever, a desk warrior carrying twenty more pounds since they'd last spoken.

Garrison sat and faced the screens.

'Okay, gentlemen: give it to me.'

Krantz launched in. 'So here's what we have so far, sir. We have ground reports China-side of a downed aircraft within the assigned corridor, plus thermo images confirming likely aviation fire smoke coming up through heavy cloud.'

He looked at Benskin.

'Doesn't look good, Roland.'

'That's it from the Pentagon? "It doesn't look good"?'

The Colonel nodded gravely. How many times had they been here before? He'd lost count. He turned to Krantz. 'Where's Cutler in all this? It's his show.'

'He's on it, sir. He's talking to Beijing right now.' Krantz picked up his cell. 'Hold one minute, sir, I might have more for you.'

'I don't give a shit about Beijing. I want my men back.'

God, how he hated covert action. The men loved it, loved the mystery, the bending or even breaking of the rules, the relief from the boredom that inevitably infected them on routine manoeuvres. Marines were built for action; inaction was the next worst thing to death. But covert was invariably problematic. Command chains were confused by the interaction of different agencies, and conflicting agendas. Langley was the worst. Too many last-minute missions, planned on the run. Throw men at a problem and deny everything when it turns to shit. Garrison felt his cool ebbing away. This stuff didn't get any easier. In fact it was getting harder. That was why they retired men younger than him. He tried to get the words out at a sensible volume.

Krantz squirmed in his seat.

'You understand the sensitivities, sir?'

'Yeah, *I'm* fucking sensitive, that's what I understand.'

Benskin raised a hand.

'Roland, everyone's on it. We think the weather was against them, unscheduled snow.'

'That pilot can fly through molasses. You're gonna have to do better than that.'

Krantz was scratching around for something he could use to put Garrison on hold.

'Sir, the White House has been briefed. There's a blackout on this one until they come back to us.'

Garrison killed the screens, then sat staring at nothing. He felt the ship moving under him. He knew there would be no point trying to find someone to blame. Blame achieved nothing. But this time he would get answers. He would get every detail. He felt for a cigarette, then remembered he'd given up – again. He would have words with Cutler as well. And now that other name had come back to haunt him – one he would have been glad never to have heard again in his life.

That name was Kovic.

# 5

## Chinese–North Korean Border

Kovic stayed in the snowdrift until a dirty grey dawn gradually spread over the hills. He had either fallen asleep or lost consciousness and become rigid with cold, proof that you could succumb to rigor mortis without actually being dead. The drift provided some insulation from wind chill, but the heat of his body melted the layer of snow immediately around him, keeping him soaked through. He was desperately thirsty, but knew better than to try to eat the snow. He allowed himself one swig from his hip flask, then emptied it out and refilled it with snow, which he'd allowed to melt first with his body warmth.

He had heard the SUV pull away. He had strained to listen to any of what the executioners said to each other, but the wind made that impossible. Although their faces were uncovered it was too dark to make out any features. The only detail he had absorbed was a mark on the hand of one who had pulled off his glove to extract a cigarette from a packet. A scar or maybe part of a tattoo – three lines with what looked like arrowheads poking out from his sleeve. The casualness of their movements, some laughter even, and the manner in which they had moved the corpses, like it was just another day's work. *Who were these men?* There was nothing military about them. His phone was gone so he had no GPS, no compass, but there was no question he had made it across the border. The SUV had definitely moved off to the west. He was on the Chinese side.

He pushed more of the snow away and started the tortuous process of trying to move. The sky was brightening, the snow clouds gone. Visibility was growing by the minute. Further down the mountainside there was less snow and he could see the track that led from the border post snaking away west. Still he waited, watching and listening, to be sure that he was alone. He didn't feel like trying the phone in the watchtower again. Was his call what had brought the men in the SUV?

He had to fight the impulse to stay put and let exhaustion take over. Limb by limb he tried to straighten up, and then attempt to stand. Just take your time, he told himself.

His progress down the track was pathetically slow, but he made it to the point where it met a wider road. He realised he had forgotten about the cold – which was a sign of his senses shutting down. This wasn't going to work. He dropped to his knees. And then he heard it, not four hundred feet away, coming from the east. If the SUV guys were coming back, there was nothing he could do.

Only when it was close could he make it out, an ancient pickup. The driver slowed so he could stare at the unexpected presence, but wasn't intending to stop. Kovic, anticipating that, stepped right out in to his path. The driver swerved and slowed, not quite to a stop. He wasn't taking any chances with the strange figure on the road. Kovic reached out and grabbed the bar that held the door mirror and got a foot on what was left of a running board. He had some sympathy for the driver, avoiding a blood and mud caked figure with a smashed face and a *lǎowài* – a foreigner. He immediately stood on the gas, but Kovic had a fifty-yuan note ready to thrust against the window, which assuaged the driver's fear. He wound down the window, letting some precious heat escape. Kovic would have given much more: his watch – a kidney – just for half an hour in the wondrously warm truck cab. He didn't even mind the fact it smelt strongly of goat.

The pickup came to a halt.

'Good morning. Thank you for stopping. I need a ride to town.'

Kovic tried to smile. His face wouldn't work, but at least his Mandarin did. The driver reached for the note and gestured for him to get in. The relief! Kovic quickly improvised a story about getting lost on a hike and falling down a ravine. It was the sort of mad thing that a Westerner might do in these remote hills.

The driver moved off, still staring at him, weighing Kovic up.

'American?' He revealed a single long brown tooth.

Kovic shook his head. It didn't feel like a good nationality to be today.

'French. You know – the Eiffel Tower?'

The driver's face came alive. 'Paris! Good! My son studying neuroscience there.'

Okay. Welcome to modern China, thought Kovic.

'I'll look him up and tell him what a good man his father is.'

The driver suddenly looked fierce. 'You see him you tell him from me to stay away from French girls. Bad for his study.'

Kovic nodded gravely, hoping the opposite for the young neuroscientist.

The driver dropped him by the railhead at Longjing, a grim monochrome place. A smelting plant dominated the skyline, belching out sulphurous smoke that had settled a coat of grey dust on the entire town. The streets thronged with manual workers starting their day, all in the same grey tunics. This was how all of China used to look under Mao, Kovic knew; Chinese capitalism, rampant as it was, hadn't completely obliterated the past.

He should call in, but he couldn't risk briefing Cutler down an unsecure line. And even an email from an internet cafe could expose his location. China was his patch. Now it suddenly felt like enemy territory.

He was in survival mode now. Risk nothing; get out of the locality. He had lost his phone on the North Korean side where it was probably still giving out a signal. For all Cutler knew, he hadn't made it out but died along with the others. And this had been his show; he could easily find his fast track to the seventh floor suddenly cut short.

Kovic was hungry and a glance in a window reflection told him he looked a mess. Next to the railhead was a sprawling market. Whatever the mission he always carried cash, lots of it. He took a seat at a stall and ate a bowl of fried pork and noodles while half a dozen rail workers stared sullenly at his swollen foreign face. His beet coloured frostbitten fingers couldn't begin to operate the chopsticks so he slurped the contents of the bowl straight into his mouth like most of the other diners were doing anyhow. China wasn't big on table manners. At another stall he bought a plain blue suit and shirt, and got directions to the public baths. How easy China made this process; imagine trying to do it in America without getting arrested.

The shower was tepid and pressureless, like being pissed on by a small animal, but it felt like the best he had ever had. The water that ran off him was a red brown from all the detritus he had accumulated overnight, the blood, some of it his, some the Koreans', some the Marines'. He stared at it as it puddled around his feet. How little human beings amounted to, after they were gone. He stepped out, dried himself on a small damp towel. In his fresh clothes he started to feel more like a person again.

He found a cab to take him to Yanji airport. He gazed out of the window, life carrying on as normal. He could never get over that about the world, how all kinds of shit could be happening in one place and a few miles down the road it was business as usual. He had once observed a refugee ship trying to land on the shore of Beirut with hundreds on board near starved, while all around it surfers enjoyed the breakers.

The airport was brand new, like so much of new China. When he paid the driver he frowned.

'What's the matter? That's a good tip.'

The driver pointed. 'Your face – it looks bad.'

In the airport he bought a baseball cap and some foundation make-up and went to the restroom. The cab driver was right. It wasn't so bad in the town where everything looked dirty, but here in these bright shiny surroundings and despite the new suit, he looked a wreck. He applied the make-up generously over his smashed nose and a gash on his forehead, then added the cap. It would have to do.

All the time he had been in China he had mostly felt at ease. Not today. As a precaution he used the South African passport he always brought along on missions. He bought a ticket with cash – not many places in the world you could still do that – and joined a queue of men in suits headed for Security. In Departures he logged on to one of his email accounts and sent Cutler a do-not-reply coded message with no details other than confirmation that he was still alive.

Never had the inside of a plane seemed so welcoming, and as he slumped into his seat he wondered, not for the first time, at the madness of his chosen profession. Just before he closed his eyes he glanced up at the TV screen in the seat back in front of him. Breaking News: *US Forces killed in North Korea.*

# 6

## USS *Valkyrie*, South China Sea

Commander Garrison looked over his glasses at the Lieutenant.

'Shouldn't we wait on confirmation, sir?'

Garrison looked at Duncan. Why was everyone querying his orders today?

'Marion, I don't have to remind you of all people that we are living in the age of instant messaging. We don't control the news agenda; it controls us. I want to talk to each wife, mother, girlfriend, next of kin *before* they see anything online. I want them to hear it from *me* that they are missing, that we are doing everything ...'

Everything – like what? If it was down to him they would have scrambled search and rescue, and the airspace above the NK border would now be alive with US Navy hardware. He would be on the line to Pyongyang delicately discussing the mutual benefit of their working this out together. But it wasn't down to him. He was a walk-on in this goat-fuck; this was the CIA's play and they had a habit of handling things their own way. Langley would be publicly and vociferously denying all knowledge, claiming it was another of the DPRK's paranoid fantasies. Pyongyang was always protesting that their airspace or waters or territory had been violated by one 'enemy aggressor' or another. Meanwhile, the State Department, the Pentagon and the White House would all refrain from comment 'pending investigations', which was Washington-speak for multi-agency ass covering, as the story gradually withered for lack of substantiation.

Duncan felt her cheeks redden.

'I completely understand, sir. I was out of line.'

He looked at her. She was about the same age as his son when—He swatted the thought away.

'Just get their files, Lieutenant. I'll make the calls.'

He knew all about those calls. He hadn't just made them. He'd received one. It was right here at this desk eight years ago when word reached him about Tommy. A big enchilada from the Pentagon, as high as they could get, on the line.

*'Commander, I regret to inform you—'*

He had guessed even as they were putting the call through, already pictured the headline – *First serving Naval officer to lose a son in Afghanistan*. But when they were done with the massaging and spinning, what the press got was a hell of a long way from the down and dirty CIA mission Tommy had stepped up for. And there was nothing about the CIA's man who got out without so much as a scratch.

Duncan returned from registry with the files of each of the men. She noticed his eyes looked a little pink, but knew better than to show it.

'Sir, do you think there'll be any survivors?'

His look said it all.

# 7

'We have to talk.'

Kovic stepped back from the mirror as far as his broom closet-sized bathroom would allow. His dark brown hair, thick and short, was plastered off to one side at the front by the gash he'd sustained, as if gelled into place by a particularly inept barber. Under the unforgiving fluorescent light his complexion, so useful for disguising his origins, was a lurid mix of zombie and nicotine. Should he try that foundation again? He shrugged. In the cramped, crumbling *shikumen* in Shanghai's French Concession where he chose to live, he stuck out a mile anyway; he was a good few inches taller than everyone else for starters. With the bruising, he just looked like your average Westerner who had strayed too far from home, fresh from a dispute over drugs or a woman.

He picked up the sunglasses and gently lowered them on to his nose, where they perched ridiculously above the swelling so that the bottom of the rims cut right across his vision. He put them back on the shelf. Who gave a shit anyway? He was no Brad Pitt in the first place.

'Are you hearing me?'

Louise was leaning against the doorway, arms folded, in the classic female defence position.

He'd known this was coming; it was only a matter of time.

'I know, I look a "right hooligan".' He turned and grinned at her. 'As you Brits would say.'

'Don't.'

Cliché though it was, she unquestionably looked extra desirable when she was cross. Her midnight blue eyes were so dark they looked almost black and the angle of her eyebrows gave her a kind of feline aggression that took him right back to the first time his eyes fell on her.

He opened his arms to her but she kept her distance.

'I'm real sorry about your birthday. But hey, you should have seen the other guy.'

Another day, another lie. Once he thought it would be fun to lie for a living. It came naturally; his mother had told him so and his high-school principal said the same. 'It may even be the *only* thing you're good at,' he'd told him. Never had he imagined what a rare commodity the truth would become. Louise gave him a sour look.

He'd given her the knotted silver and amber earrings she'd admired when they passed the antique market in Dongtai Road. But just in a box and without the dinner and champagne attached, they hadn't had quite the desired effect. She turned and took the two steps into the equally tiny kitchen.

The fact that he had just disappeared into thin air for four days was nothing unusual. At first she had taken his sudden absences in her stride and accepted his vague excuses of impromptu business pitches in Shenzhen or Beijing. But vanishing over her birthday, he'd crossed a line. And then there was the state in which he'd come back. As well as the face there was the deep graze on his shoulder left by Korean shrapnel. He told her it was down to a drunken fall down the back stairs of a club. And the nose – well, that he could put down to his impressive arsenal of Mandarin insults; Louise knew all too well that his patience shortened with every drink. In fact, with her encouragement he had been dry for weeks, so he would have to claim a lapse. As for the frostbitten hands, well, they were shaping up into a nice swollen purple and would pass for collateral damage, proof of how useless fists were as fighting tools.

But then he thought, *who am I fooling? She's looking at me like I'm a slow-motion car crash.* And that was the way it had to be. His apparent benders were the ideal cover, no matter how much they disappointed her. No way could he share with her any of the events of the last thirty-six hours. She could never know what he did – or even his real name.

'I'm afraid this is just not working for me.' She sat down at the kitchen table, opened a compact and started to do her face.

He tried some contrition.

'Honey, truly, I know how you feel. It was a serious mistake and I'll make it up to you.'

No reaction. There were only so many 'vanishing tricks', as she'd started to call them, that any woman worth respect would tolerate, and only so many silences or shrugs. That was the price of trying to have a relationship in the field. As soon as it went anywhere, the problems started. He imagined Cutler's wife was safely contained in some suburb off the Beltway back in Virginia, her curiosity smothered by Prozac and the belief that there was something patriotic about her dumb, unquestioning subservience. Louise was different. She deserved more and better, he was starting to realise, and that was a problem.

He watched her putting her war paint on. God, he wanted her.

Being a good liar was what had got him the gig. Once you joined the CIA, the truth was quarantined, a no-go area. What had ever led him to believe he could be different? Lesson One on Day One of training at the Farm: thou shalt have no god but the Agency. Lesson Two: whoever you were no longer exists. Lesson Three: your personal life can go to hell, so stick to one-night stands.

He'd given Louise quite a detailed sketch of dull State Department work; Commercial Liaison, he'd called it, lots of schmoozing with Chinese businesses and banging the drum for Uncle Sam. Her career, teaching English to men in suits so they could talk to other men in suits – and tell Western hookers what they wanted – was turning out not to be absorbing or unpredictable enough to keep her distracted from wondering why he kept disappearing.

Before Louise he didn't have much understanding of women. Mastering Mandarin had been a breeze compared to fathoming female thought processes. You could study for years and just when you thought you'd graduated, they threw you a curve ball and, just like that, you were back in third grade. But she had provided a crash course and brought him up a level. Now he owed her something for her effort.

She snapped the compact closed and glanced up at his battered face. 'And you know what else? Even when you do show up, half the time you're not really here.'

It was true even now that his head was elsewhere, the cold-blooded execution replaying itself like a nightmare from which he couldn't fully wake up, the questions stacking up about what just happened and why.

He looked at her, feeling like a fraud.

'It won't be like this forever. I'll change.'

For different reasons they both knew that wasn't going to happen. She nodded at the coffee left on the table between them in no-man's-land. He downed it quickly and held the cup out, half hoping she might reach out to take it and he could hold her. The thought of her body temporarily obliterated all other thought. But then she shook her head in disappointment and the cup hung there between them, untaken. The bottom line was that they had both started to care for each other too much. He had naively thought he could keep it on a level, but she was too good for that and he owed her more, far more than the job would allow.

He'd had a buddy in training at the Farm whose wife had left him without warning. Eight years of marriage and she'd gone one Sunday morning while he was out jogging, '*Enough*' squirted in Olay hand cream across the kitchen table. It was only the writing medium that was unusual; officers' relationships failed all the time. They should have another memorial wall at Langley to commemorate all the marriages the Agency chewed up.

He watched her as she continued to get ready for the day in sullen silence. She wasn't even going to dignify his promise with a response. She was right; he wouldn't have either.

It had started so well. They were both fugitives from their own countries. She had no interest in America, which was all right by him. Shanghai with its collisions of cultures, the ongoing duel between past and future, amused her as it did him. Being with her made him feel even more at home and even less like going back to where he had come from. She'd told him from the get-go she didn't do housekeeping or nurturing. 'You can get that from a local girl who wants to go and live with you in America,' to which he'd shot back, 'Who wants to live in America?' He'd surprised himself about that; the place had got under his skin, detached him from home like no other posting had done.

Her bluntness surprised and pleased him. The first time, a mere thirty minutes after they'd met, at a sports bar in Pudong, she'd said, 'We could go to my place and fuck, unless you'd hate yourself in the morning.' Soon he was hooked. It made a refreshing antidote to the wearying coyness of the local girls; even the ones for hire behaved like Mormons. That and her wavy blonde hair, like a beacon in the sea of straight black; he could see her coming a mile away. When the sun shone there were little glints of copper in it like it had been forged from some rare alloy used only in the most hi-tech weaponry. And the sex, of course, not just how it felt physically but the way it opened up a space in which he could be someone other than Kovic the liar and sometime killer. Someone better than he dared imagine he could be.

He made a move towards her. He couldn't help it.

'I'm late for work.' She took a step back, scooped up her bag and hoisted it over her shoulder. It looked heavier than usual. But she was wearing the earrings. *Come on, Kovic. Give it a try.*

'Look, I'm not much use to anyone right now; I got a shitload of stuff to deal with. Why don't we talk later? We could ride out to Zhujing, to the place you like by the lake.' It was frequented by young courting couples getting away from their relatives, none of whom had their own bedrooms, let alone apartments. It was just that, the very romantic corniness, that she liked.

He stepped aside so she could get through the narrow doorway.

'I suppose a blow job's out of the question?'

The crack nosedived, crashed and burned somewhere in the space between them. The door closed behind her and was gone. Fuckwit, he told himself. Last night he hadn't counted on finding her there. He assumed she'd waited at the restaurant the first night, then gone back to her apartment, then when there was no word, stayed away. Maybe she'd even been worried; let herself in, waited up, then finally, with her fine slim hand still marking her place in her book, had gone to sleep. When he got in he'd been on the move for thirty-six hours. Boy, had he been glad to see her – a beacon of humanity after the carnage on the border. But now, looking round the apartment, he noticed the few things she kept there – her hair drier, a coffee pot, her birth control pills – were gone.

His backup phone buzzed with a text from Cutler. *Get in here, now.*

# 8

Garrison was on the bridge in his grey leather swivelling chair. *Wow, just like Captain Kirk in* Star Trek, Tommy had exclaimed, aged eight, on his first visit to a control tower. These were the most coveted seats in the navy and when he was counting up the pluses in his life Garrison tried never to forget that. Sure his ascent to that lofty position had probably cost him his marriage, but this ship was his kingdom and this was his throne, as long as the Pentagon allowed.

To his left, Merrick, the Boatswain's Mate, steered four acres of US sovereign territory on its course across the South China Sea, the charmingly archaic wooden ship's wheel a single concession to history in an otherwise twenty-first century machine. Beside him, Danes, Quartermaster of the Watch, kept track of navigation. Usually there was a lot of banter between them, but they had read Garrison's mood, as had the other personnel up there. The heavy silence was broken only by the E2C Hawkeye on the deck a hundred feet below, blasting off on its routine sweep of the other fleets in the sector. The computer screens around Garrison teemed with constantly updated information, all you needed to wage war anywhere on the planet at the tap of a key. But right now he wasn't looking at any of them.

All this mighty hardware and all he could do was stare helplessly at the images on his phone. There was no disputing their identities; whoever took the pictures made sure the faces were in full view. They had even dragged what remained of Tex out of the chopper. Tex the whooping cowboy was the most popular; Price, reserved, a gentleman in the making; Kean, a heartbreaker that boy; Faulkner, solid, built to last; Deacon, little more than a kid. And then Olsen, on his last tour. He was the one Garrison felt worst about. He had sent him to watch out for the others.

Once there was a time where images such as these were vetted, censored and filed away, never to be seen. They even relied on the news agencies to destroy any that could cause offence or upset. All that was gone. Every man and woman on the ship would have seen them by now. One face was missing though. Where was Kovic?

# 9

## French Concession, Shanghai

Standing by his kitchen window, Kovic rehearsed his questions for Cutler, and which piece of his mind he might want to give him. Louise's departure had further darkened his mood, but he was determined not to lose it, tempting as it was. At least he would get some answers about what the fuck had just happened.

In the courtyard below, an argument was under way about a washing line that had snapped, dropping some of the laundry on to the ground where the next-door neighbour's dog had peed. He listened to the vicious exchange between the two elderly women who had shared the same subdivided apartment for forty years, but only ever traded insults, usually about each one's dead husband's infidelities. The guilty dog started barking and then someone turned up their radio to drown out both the dog and the row. Louise said she didn't know how he could stand living with all the noise. The truth was he hated silence. Silence made you listen out for sounds, so it was harder to switch off. That was another thing he liked about his adopted home. All over Shanghai, quiet was in short supply.

He slid his laptop into his backpack, tried the sunglasses one more time, tossed them away and shut the door.

As he emerged from the stairwell the old ladies suddenly stopped screeching at each other and looked at him. They waved tentatively then started another exchange in lower tones, clearly about him. They took particular interest in him whenever Louise was around. They would have seen her leave. Perhaps the change in her expression had given them a hint that something was up. Despite their nosiness he liked them. He generally engaged them in conversation about the minutiae of Shanghai life, the pace of construction, the smog, the recent scandal about infected pork, bidding them farewell just as they edged the conversation towards his 'beautiful friend' and 'future plans'. Any sign of increased intimacy – or the opposite – and he feared he'd be inundated with the vast reservoir of marital advice that all elderly ladies seemed to carry around with them, whatever the culture. Louise charmed them as well, asked about their grandchildren and even more important their ailments, and they liked her. And Kovic also humoured them because they were the next best thing to CCTV. Anyone looking for him, checking his door, they'd be the first to notice and tell him, in officious, concerned-but-nosy tones.

He gestured at his face.

'She's very cross with me.'

They thought this hilarious. The row was forgotten.

He stepped out of the courtyard through the main gate of the *shikumen* and into the narrow street. Two cars, a Chery and a locally made Audi, faced one another like bucks in a clearing, the drivers both resolute, determined not to give ground. This would take some time. Shanghai's planners couldn't have dreamed of the automotive revolution that would wreak havoc on the narrow one-lane streets, and bring out the worst in its newly automated citizens. Just the other day they'd passed a similar stand-off, and Louise had said, 'I wonder what the record is?' And he'd told her.

'One pair went through the night. A local restaurant brought them both breakfast.' And she'd smiled. Whether it was true or not, he couldn't remember, but it made a good story.

He took a right into the even narrower street where he garaged his Buick, a grudging concession to American flag flying, but also a popular import so it didn't stand out. He didn't use it much but today he felt a little fragile for the scramble of the Metro. The sanitation truck parked across the garage door was no surprise. A group of hard-hats were bent over a hole in the road from which a pungent smell was drifting.

His backup phone buzzed. Cutler was getting impatient. *How long?*

He texted back: *Traffic. ETA 40.* He wanted the meeting, but he wasn't going to be hurried, probably another thing about him that got up Cutler's nose. Above all, he needed to be on the front foot. He knew how these things usually played out, and he was damned if he was going to be made to carry the can for any of this.

He gestured at the blocked garage door. 'How long?'

'Two minutes,' replied a hard-hat without much conviction. Kovic thought about having a cigarette, remembered that he had given up – at Louise's suggestion. But there was a still a packet in his jacket. Try to do one good thing today, he told himself.

He had checked the morning headlines some hours ago. Characteristically, Beijing was 'unable to confirm' reports of disruption on the border. They could keep that up to eternity and beyond. North Korea's news agency had put out the usual risible nonsense: '*Foreign insurgents have been repelled by the valiant populace.*' No one was going to take that seriously. But Washington was a different matter. US press and TV would already be all over the White House, demanding their version of the story.

What bothered Kovic right now wasn't what the media would say, but what had actually taken place. He reviewed what facts he had. There were far more unknowns. He couldn't even be a hundred per cent sure that *Highbeam* was a plant, only that he had been turned into a human bomb against his will. What wasn't in question was that it had been a set-up, a trap they had walked right into. But whose trap? There was nothing considered or elegant about the ambush. Mounting an ambush with machine-gun toting conscripts was a recipe for chaos – they were more likely to kill each other than have any impact on their quarry. There was no evident chain of command; the officers who were supposedly in charge had tried to flee the scene in their jeeps. Even by North Korea's pitiable standards it was a mess.

But what happened after that was in another dimension. Kovic picked over his memory of what he saw from the snowdrift one more time. By his reckoning the assassins weren't military, not even coverts. It wasn't just their lack of uniform; the perfunctory executions, then their casual attitude around the corpses, smoking and joking, and the way they heaved them into the SUV as if it was something they did every day. And what bothered Kovic most was that they were inside China. Who where they? And who had sent them?

And what was supposed to be the outcome: lure Americans into a trap on one side of the border and then have them killed on the other? None of it made sense. If he had been cleared to hire his own team locally, would it have ended differently? Maybe not – but it wouldn't make international news. In the hierarchy of news events, American deaths ranked a lot higher than Chinese or Korean.

'Hey,' he called out to the sewage men. 'I got to get moving!'

One of them left the group round the hole and moved towards the cab with a studied lack of urgency.

How was this going to play for Cutler? Kovic knew he better be prepared to navigate all the swift and lethal currents of Agency ass covering that would be going on. One thing he was damned if he was going to do was have this hung round his neck. It was the Chief's show, his plan, and the corrupted intel on which the whole fateful mission was based had come from his own sources.

The thought flashed through Kovic's head that maybe today was the day to bail, tell Cutler where to stick the damn job. For sure, that would be an end to all the lies with Louise. But he knew it was impossible. No one left the Agency voluntarily. And even if you went, you didn't actually *leave*. Anyone who did was guaranteed to be a source of suspicion in perpetuity. There was another problem; he didn't do the future. That was the place where no matter how much analysing, modelling, war-gaming, and downright worst case scenario imagining you did, stuff happened. Not only stuff you had overlooked, stuff you couldn't have dreamed of in the nightmares lurking in the deepest recesses of your own twisted subconscious: Pearl Harbor, the Bay of Pigs, Lee Harvey Oswald, the Iran hostages, Bin Laden, the Boston Marathon. Maybe it was another sign of his enduring immaturity, that he had developed a taste for living in the moment and couldn't give it up, not for Louise or anybody. Or maybe it was just a natural fear of the future.

The shots played themselves over and over, without warning, the pictures in slow motion. The straight arm rising to aim, the shot, the move to the next man lying half frozen and exhausted in the snow.

The guy in the sewage truck turned the ignition, it almost fired then stalled. When he tried again the starter was in its death throes. Kovic sighed, lit a cigarette, then called Wu.

# 10

'Agent K! How are you?'

'Stranded. Where are you?'

'Look up.'

He looked and saw the BMW X6's lights flash as it advanced with a low metallic beat from its profligate eight cylinders. That detail was one of many Kovic had managed to absorb from Wu's exhaustive enumerations of his prized machine's attributes. He had had it wrapped in matt black with tinted side and rear lights. Wu called it the stealth look – surely a contradiction in terms, Kovic thought, more like 'Hey, look at me. I'm a drug dealing gangsta!'

Growing up in Detroit had given him a deep distaste for the automobile. Its giant plants had lured his grandparents to America and enslaved them and their children, only to spit them out a few decades later into a half-deserted wasteland. But Kovic hadn't burdened Wu with all that as he fawned over his precious toy. Foolishly, he had even conceded a mild admiration for German machinery, which Wu had fatally misread as an invitation to kill him with detail. Sure, the five on-board cameras that gave an almost complete view of what was happening ahead, behind and even above could be handy for surveillance – if the car hadn't been so damned conspicuous.

Grinning, Wu opened the passenger door while still in motion, like a getaway driver grabbing his accomplice from a heist. A deafening blast of Bruce Springsteen – a Kovic favourite though not at that volume – hit him like a wall, the sound waves causing the shop fronts to shudder.

'Take it down a bit, can you?'

'What?'

'TURN IT *DOWN!*'

Wu grinned. 'These are nine channel, 825 watt amps with sixteen speakers and exclusive neodymium magnet drives to produce crystal clear acoustic fidelity.'

'You're talking to yourself, man. Just drive.'

Where he had found or borrowed the million plus yuan for this sleazemobile Kovic didn't want to know. It couldn't be what they paid him. He climbed in and inhaled the aroma of leather.

'Why are you here anyway? I didn't ask for you.'

Wu was Kovic's security detail, which might have seemed ridiculous since Kovic was both taller and more heavily built. One of the few perks of the Shanghai posting was supposedly the local muscle. Initially, Kovic was having none of it. He didn't want anyone shadowing him and attracting unnecessary attention, and preferred to take care of any pursuers himself. The candidates on offer were all lumbering thugs who had come out of sedentary jobs in the military, liabilities in any kind of fight. Wu was different, and his own choice. Lean, bright, committed, and an Olympic standard marksman, he had been invalided out of *Zhōngguó tèzhŏng bùduì* – the Chinese People's Liberation Army Special Forces – after an eye injury. Kovic happened on him when he was acting as security detail cum interpreter for a Russian arms dealer Kovic was hoping to turn. The sting went badly wrong when Kovic tried to apply some blackmail and in the ensuing struggle Wu, trying to intercede, inadvertently killed his boss. Impressed by Wu's defensive skills, as well as his remorse, Kovic had also witnessed his terrible shame. Without thinking about it he made him an offer. *Come and work with me and we'll never speak of this again.* How could Wu refuse?

Kovic eased himself inside. He was still feeling fragile. Wu frowned at him in awe.

'Oh man, your face looks like the fruit left at the end of the market that no one wants to buy.'

'To the Consulate – hurry.'

Music to Wu's ears. He stepped on the gas and the BMW surged forward.

'Zero to sixty-two in only five point four seconds!'

'And zero to ER if you don't take it easy, man: it all aches. And you don't want any of my bodily fluids on your precious black leather.'

Wu slowed right down.

'It must have been big, big hangover.' Any trouble was explained away like this, by mutual agreement.

Kovic looked at him and raised an eyebrow. Wu raised both hands off the wheel in surrender.

'Oh sorry. *A* big hangover.'

'Yes, a major hangover.'

Wu thought that was hilarious. 'Major Hangover. I like that very much! And Colonel and General Hangover even worse?'

'*Are* even worse. Yes, very much worse.'

The downtown skyline reared up in front of them, like a crazed architect's proposal for a city of the future, only this one had already been built, the tallest, newest and shiniest blurred by the low hanging smog. Even after six years it still took Kovic by surprise, the relentless drive skywards at a pace that put the US to shame. A century ago Detroit had experienced the same breathless progress. Would Shanghai suffer the same fate? It reminded him of plants in his father's greenhouse that had bolted in their eagerness for the sun, only to wilt, having grown too fast to support themselves. Under all the glass cladding there was something fragile about Shanghai's foundations.

'I'll take Fuzhou. There's a protest starting in People's Square.'

'What protest?'

Wu prodded the touch screen on the dash. The sat nav disappeared and up came local TV; an ad for a pet hair-perming product modelled by a shih tzu whose coat was frozen in tiny ringlets. The animal looked startled, as if electric shocks to its genitals had been part of the perming process.

Wu touched the screen again and got CNN. '*... since early this morning, gathering with slogans proclaiming outrage at what they're claiming is an American-backed incursion ...*'

The world outside became mute as Kovic zeroed in on the pictures: a hundred plus young men and women carrying placards marching in a circle, stony-faced.

Kovic reached out to pause the picture. They were all quite smart-ly dressed and young, just the type who usually loved all things American. He touched Play. '... *as yet unidentified Americans and Chinese thought to be among the dead* ...'

And Chinese? This was a new one.

'Yeah, some screw up.' He didn't want Wu to read the depth of his concern and get curious.

'A real screw up, yeah.' Wu nodded vigorously.

Though he had no reason to doubt Wu's loyalty, Kovic had said nothing about the border mission. Like Louise, Wu was used to his boss's sudden disappearances.

Kovic changed his mind and tapped the screen. 'Take me there. I want to see it.'

'But you can see on the screen.'

Kovic gave him his Nike look. They were already on the ramp up to the Yan'an Expressway, but locked in a near-static jam of cars. Without protest Wu selected reverse and amid a cacophony of hooting, forced his way across the traffic to the emergency lane and backed out. Wu enjoyed this kind of challenge – especially when flagged down by police, so he could brandish his diplomatic licence and enjoy the disappointed look on their faces as they waved him on. At the intersection he did a U and worked his way across town. Wu's grasp of the Chinese driving style – fluid yet restrained – was a matter of envy for Kovic, who was apt to get cross and then stuck. Wu's objective when behind the wheel was never to come to a halt, that whatever the obstruction, be it a pedestrian, a washing machine on the back of a moped or a red light, he would find a way past it without making contact.

The police had blocked off the end of Wusheng Road. A motor-cycle cop pulled up beside them and tapped on the side window.

'*Tíng chē* – stop. No way through.'

He frowned across at Kovic.

'It's not good for Westerners right now.'

Wu waved his licence, but today it wasn't going to do the business. Through the window they could hear the sound of the chanting bounce towards them off the sides of the buildings.

Kovic opened the door.

'I'm going in.'

'You'll be late for the Chief.'

'Fuck the Chief.'

The cop didn't like disobedience. He came round to Kovic's side and blocked his passage. Kovic knew that if the cop could avoid it he would prefer not to have to touch the *lawai*; foreigners were still thought by some to be as verminous as Shanghai sewer rats.

'*Tell the round eye he's not welcome today and to get his nose fixed,*' the cop shouted to Wu, oblivious of Kovic's grasp of Mandarin.

Kovic replied, '*Tell him his mother is*—'

'*Sha-bi,*' interrupted Wu. Only in China could 'stupid cunt' be something you could say in front of a cop.

'You meant him – right?' said Kovic. Wu smiled.

Another thing he loved about this country, the common currency of breathtaking insults.

A protester had climbed on to a US TV news van and was tugging at the satellite dish. Kovic had to take a closer look. Three police in riot gear leaped on the truck, grabbed the protester and threw him off. More of them were hammering the windscreen with their fists while the driver cowered behind the wheel. Another half-dozen protesters appeared from behind the truck, wrenched open the side door and pulled out a hapless young American TV technician and threw him on the ground. They were high on hysteria. For all Kovic knew they might stamp on the guy. He waded through the crowd towards them.

'American go home!' A kid who could have been no more than eighteen bellowed in his ear. Wu, right behind, put his hand on the kid's face and pushed him away. Another cop grasped Kovic's arm. 'No good here – go.'

'He's right, boss, we should leave now.'

But Kovic shook them both off and waded into the throng that was closing round the technician. In all his six years in China he had never seen such behaviour. Most Chinese, the young urbanites especially, hero-worshipped the States. He struggled towards the helpless American on the ground, though the crowd having decked him were now uncertain what to do next, as if they didn't quite have the stomach for full-blown violence. Who were these protesters?

'Please don't do this,' pleaded Wu, who was struggling to keep up, dismayed by the unexpected interest of his boss in this bit of local trouble. This wasn't in the job description. Kovic's duty was to stay out of trouble, to observe, analyse and report. Always report. Well screw that. He reached the group who were closing in on the technician who was on his back trying to shield his head. A youth tried to push Kovic back. He grabbed him and thrust his face into his.

'*Cào nǐ zǔzōng shíbā dài* – Fuck your ancestors to the eighteenth generation.'

The youth fell back. Wu looked horrified.

'Where in hell did you hear that?'

Kovic shrugged. 'Some phrasebook.'

It was enough to distract them. He pushed between them, seized the TV guy by the arm and lifted him back on to his feet.

'Jeez, thanks, man. This is cur-razy. Not seen nothing like this since Cairo.'

Kovic dusted him down then addressed the protesters in his perfect Mandarin.

'If you don't like America go bang on the Consulate gates. This guy's just trying to do his job – which is to tell the world about your protest, which you can bet your news services aren't doing. You got the wrong people here, kids.'

Kovic bundled the shaken technician back into the truck and shouted to the driver to get the hell out of there fast. Several more riot cops had arrived and were pushing the protesters back towards the square. Kovic wanted to see the numbers but Wu was using his surprising strength to pull him back towards the car.

'Please, boss, before it gets ugly.'

'Guess they've forgotten who gave them Iron Man and Lady Gaga.'

'I expect the Chief will have something to say about it,' said Wu as he performed his second miraculous reverse of the morning. Wu's faith in the authority of the Agency was as quaint as it was misplaced. But Kovic could see that he was shaken by what he had just seen. Even touching a foreigner was extremely unusual. Attacking property in public like that was also very rare; the penalties were severe – three years' hard labour – so the protesters had to be seriously motivated. He turned to Wu who began weaving through the traffic again.

'What do *you* think's going on?'

'Huh?'

'Yes, you; tell me.'

Wu was mystified. Kovic had never asked him anything like this before.

'Haven't you got an opinion?

'China and America ver— *are* very solid.' He took both hands off the wheel to clasp them together, and then swerved to avoid a bike with a tottering cargo of mattresses.

'I don't mean what you hope: what do you *think*?'

Wu was silent for a time, pondering the difference. He took his loyalty very seriously, which made it next to impossible for Kovic to drag an honest opinion out of him. In that respect he wasn't so different from those of his compatriots who believed the American way of life was the best, not because they'd tried any other, but because they hadn't. It made a refreshing change from his own cynicism, but right now he needed to get beyond it.

'Come on, just your view. I won't hold you to it.'

He looked suddenly very sombre.

'I think someone doesn't want China and America to be friends.'

A heavy police presence round the US Consulate building was another sign that all was far from well. They swung into the murky car park under the imaginatively named Commerce Centre Building next door. It was heavily populated with top of the range German automotive hardware. It also reeked of piss. They observed the attendant shamelessly taking a leak against a wall. So very Shanghai, thought Kovic; so reassuringly inconsistent.

# 11

Kovic told Wu to be back in forty-five minutes and took the elevator to the twenty-eighth floor. The sign on the door said United States Commercial Attaché, an unimaginative cover. He used it as little as possible. This was only Cutler's third visit since his appointment to Beijing, but he kept a room permanently booked out to him with his name on the door, as if marking his territory.

Kovic didn't know whether Cutler hated Shanghai or just hated him. Either way he never stayed long, which suited him. Before *Highbeam*, their meetings had consisted of Kovic being grilled about his expenditure, an indiscretion by one of his field agents that had got back to Beijing, or his lack of progress tracking down *Armistead*, the fabled super-hacker the NSA wanted closed down – or better still permanently neutralised. Kovic didn't do sucking up – or dick stroking; it just wasn't in his nature. Their meetings mostly consisted of Kovic giving monosyllabic answers to a barrage of questions about the minutiae of his work. Today Kovic was going to be asking the questions.

Mrs Chan glanced at him and looked away quickly. She was forty-two, her face a frozen mask of plastic surgery, her eyes surgically widened so she had a permanent look of dismay, as if she had unexpectedly been entered from behind. Her hair was permed into a brittle shell that looked like pieces of it would snap off if knocked. It amused Kovic to think of her as Moneypenny to his James Bond. She was easily embarrassed, and Kovic was embarrassing, which triggered her profoundly irritating, high-pitched tinkly laugh. He always addressed her in Mandarin, which she was entitled to feel was a transgression of office code and a veiled insult to her own very shaky English. Whatever he said to her to make her squirm, she had to take it, because he knew that she was accepting payment from the Ministry of State Security for any supposed nuggets of intel she could glean for her handler, with whom she was also conducting a torrid affair. Little did she realise that Kovic was keeping the affair alive with gossip that was almost entirely fictional.

'I apologise if my appearance causes you discomfort, Mrs Chan.' He bent closer. 'My military police informant was disappointed with his remuneration. The cocaine is making him very jumpy and paranoid.'

Her already wide eyes looked like they might pop out of their sockets. Kovic delighted at the thought of this rubbish going up the line and the police internal affairs department struggling to work out who Kovic's mystery 'mole' might be.

'By the way, may I say how pleasing you look this morning.'

She giggled her infuriating giggle. Despite her unease, she was partial to a compliment. He had checked out her past. He made a point of knowing as much as he could about everyone he came into regular contact with, however menial, and discovered she had been voted Most Physically Pleasing Female by the male students in her administration diploma class.

She looked at him for a second, wondering desperately if this was the moment she should do her handler's bidding and kiss him. But Kovic moved away and the spell was broken.

'Mr Cutler is waiting for you,' she replied in her clipped English, taking care not to trip over the 'L' in Cutler. She got up from her desk, tottered over to the double doors and tapped almost inaudibly and paused before she spoke at the door, as if she was allowing him time to finish his prayers.

'Agent Kovic is here, sir.'

The Chief was sitting at the large desk he had ordered on the Shanghai station budget for his infrequent visits. He had a short torso so the surface of the desk was a fraction too high for him, which gave him the look of a prefect sitting at the teacher's desk. Although he had just flown in that morning the desk was swimming with documents as if he'd been there all night. He was tapping furiously at a camo-covered field laptop, which must have had some sentimental meaning for him, or was just an awkward attempt to convince visitors that he hadn't always been desk-bound. In his crisp white shirt with sleeve garters and thin dark tie, he cultivated the image of a standard issue Langley suit, impossible to imagine dressed any other way. Kovic pictured him playing golf, standing behind a barbecue, screwing Mrs Cutler, all in the same, anonymous garb.

'*Zǎoshànghǎo* – Good morning.'

Cutler nodded, put the remains of a packet of Oreos into a drawer and finished his coffee, didn't look up.

'Sit down, Kovic.'

The Chief's cellphone buzzed. He pressed it to his ear and turned away.

Nice start, thought Kovic.

There were two kinds of Bureau Chief in his experience, doers and readers. Cutler was a reader. He measured performance by the weight of intel produced, so Kovic fed him raw data by the ton. Material Kovic should have just given salient lines from or have précised or even discarded, he sent whole; extremely verbose minutes of every district intelligence meeting he had bugged, endless transcripts of meetings with field agents, including the mind-numbing minutiae of their particular domestic gripes and tiresome pleas for more cash or other perks. But Kovic sifted what he sent very carefully, since he knew it was all opened and read by their opposite numbers in the Chinese Ministry of State Security.

Cutler showed no interest in mastering the language. 'I'm a generalist, not a specialist,' was how he justified it to Kovic, which was another way of saying he didn't want to get sidetracked on his way up the Agency's greasy pole. He ate at McDonald's or Pizza Hut wherever he was in the world, and ordered whatever he wanted online to avoid having to deal with local shop assistants. He was the type of Agency man who regarded all foreign influences as potentially suspect and was alert to the possibility of contamination at all times. Kovic was his absolute opposite; a nowhere man who submerged himself in whatever culture he found himself, who traded on his indeterminate complexion, playing the ugly American only when it suited him. He ate local, lived in the heart of real Shanghai and excelled at the language, all of which Cutler found deeply troubling – even un-American.

The Chief was listening hard to whatever was coming down his phone, his fingertips pressed to his forehead. In most other postings, there was the pervasive sense that America was the Superpower and called the shots. That's what made Cutler hard. Places in the world where they had removed governments and put in new ones were even known as 'off the peg' governments, where heads of state were there at the Agency's pleasure. But China was not one of them, and definitely not today.

For Cutler's kind, China was an insoluble Rubik's cube. Nowhere else on Earth could you find burgeoning capitalism twinned with an utterly unbending, centralised ideology. The Communist high command had taken a shine to the free market; only they'd left the 'free' bit on the shelf. However many McDonald's were opened, however many Buicks sold, they would never allow democracy. It only resembled Western society on the surface. Like the Prada knock-offs for sale along the Nanjing Road, it looked the part – but was from a very different place.

Cutler was listening very hard, nodding occasionally to the unknown caller. Just by his demeanour Kovic could tell it was someone more senior. Was he being chewed out, or were they talking damage limitation? For once Kovic had to admit he was out of his depth too. Nothing of this magnitude had happened in his six years here. And he didn't have a good feeling about what was round the corner.

Finally Cutler finished the call, pocketed the phone, looked up and frowned.

'You mean to say you've been walking around town like that?'

Kovic was in no mood to be lectured.

'Thanks for the welcome.'

Cutler patted the sweat off his brow with a napkin.

'Well, I just got in from Beijing so shouldn't you be doing the honours?'

Kovic couldn't help himself.

'I just got in from DPRK and a near-death experience; you arrived on the shuttle.'

Cutler looked hurt. Just cool it, okay, Kovic said to himself. The Chief stared at him for a second, then, as if he had just received an urgent directive from his brain, completely changed his tone. His face contorted with sudden concern, he rose up from behind the desk like a crane – despite the short torso he had surprisingly long legs – came round the desk and grasped Kovic's arm. He was about to shake his hand when he saw the swelling.

'Holy Jesus.'

'Frostbite actually.'

Cutler retreated to his chair, shaking his head with long pendulous swings as if admiring the width of his desk.

'I hope you realise how serious this is.'

Another of his stock features was his uncanny ability to state the obvious.

'I'm working on it.'

Cutler ignored the sarcasm. He bent over his laptop and pressed his fingers into his cheeks, forming white blotches. He had a large bald patch surrounded by greying hair, which contributed to his pious, monk-like demeanour. Kovic found himself propelled back to his schooldays, called yet again to the despairing principal's office to learn the punishment for his latest outrage.

'The Chinese are taking it pretty seriously too. I just came by People's Square.'

But Cutler wasn't listening. 'We have one hell of a problem on our hands.'

Kovic was familiar with Cutler's tendency to 'own' the seriousness of the situation – as if only he could determine the true gravity of events. It was the same with *Armistead* who Kovic was allegedly pursuing. Cutler had lectured him on the need to get him 'before it's too late'.

To begin with, Kovic's policy of drowning Cutler in paperwork had kept him at bay. But then there had been a change. Cutler had started querying briefs and character assessments of his assets. He was being more assertive, more inquisitive about Kovic's activities, and quick to find fault, warning him not to get too 'intimate' with his sources. Cutler was like a throwback to the darkest days of the Cold War; he mistook Kovic's empathy with China for brainwashing.

Cutler was still shaking his head. 'It's a real concern.'

'It's a real fucking concern that five men died, three executed.'

He winced; was it the expletive or the mention of the method of death?

'Okay.' He let out a long sigh. 'Take me through it from the top.'

He touched the dial of a recorder. Nothing less than verbatim would do. So Kovic took him through it all right, lingering on the executions he had witnessed through his peephole in the snow.

'And they definitely didn't see you? You're sure?'

Cutler looked down at the desk, pressed a forefinger on an Oreo crumb, lifted it and flicked it away.

'If they had, do you think I'd be here?'

Cutler studied the ends of his fingers as if they might hold the answer. Eventually he said, 'Too bad you didn't have any witnesses.'

Kovic thought about what this might mean. Ten years ago he would have considered his honesty was being questioned and possibly grabbed Cutler by the throat, a career ending choice. China had taught him to be smarter. To watch, listen, and wait.

'Means you're going to have to take my word for it.'

'You didn't want this mission.'

'I went, didn't I?'

'But you were critical of it.'

Kovic snorted. 'With good reason.'

Cutler glared. Kovic put his elbows on the desk.

Now he could feel his restraint slipping as pure rage forced its way up like coffee through a percolator. He jabbed the air between them with a frostbitten forefinger.

'I put my life on the line to get them back over the border, dragged them half a mile and then some guys came out of nowhere – or more precisely out of China – and assassinated them.'

'The snow was pretty deep, huh?'

Kovic nodded.

'Visibility pretty bad?'

Kovic nodded, wondering where this was going.

'So pretty disorienting – low vis, battle fatigue, unfamiliar landscape—'

'Where the fuck's this going?'

He could feel the tempting catharsis of losing it reaching out to him like one fateful drink to an alcoholic. *Go on, just deck him. You know you want to.*

Cutler sighed. 'I'm only preparing you for what may be ahead.'

He reached into an attaché case next to his chair and produced a manila folder. He flipped it open. Inside was a clutch of photographs.

'You better have a look at these.'

He pushed them across the desk.

The photographs were in colour, but because of the snow and the bad light, you could have been forgiven for thinking they were monochrome. Even the blood looked grey. It was the same vehicle, the shitbin DPRK jeep he had commandeered for their escape. It looked like it was in the same position as they had abandoned it. But in the photo it wasn't abandoned. Arranged inside the vehicle were the corpses: Olsen, Kean, Price, Deacon and Faulkner, but that wasn't all. With them were three others – judging by their uniforms, Chinese.

Kovic looked up at Cutler, who was staring intently at him. He looked down again, lifted up one still, angled it at Cutler and pointed at the Chinese.

'They're fakes.'

Cutler said nothing. Kovic felt his battered face heating up. He studied the pictures some more.

'These others, they're not the North Koreans. They're in Chinese Army fatigues.'

'Beijing aren't confirming. There seems to be some uncertainty …'

His voice trailed away.

'What *are* Beijing saying?'

'Nothing. It's pretty shaming.'

Shame, embarrassment, loss of face: the stuff of Chinese nightmares.

'Who took these?'

Cutler shrugged. 'They were uploaded overnight on to a photo-sharing site. Soon as they went viral the account was closed. We're assuming it's North Korea.'

Kovic looked again. He didn't feel like assuming anything. In the background, clearer in the daylight, were the border post and the fence. A flag was flying from the sentry box that Kovic didn't remember seeing. Someone had gone to one hell of a lot of trouble with these.

'And Langley's saying this is all North Korea's work?'

'That seems logical.'

'Except for the executioners who took off into China, which is very much not logical.'

Cutler studied his hands. 'Well, that's your recollection. We'll need corroboration.'

Kovic glanced at the recorder. This was turning into an inquisition. He wasn't having that.

'Either the intel was corrupted, someone wanted us to fail from the start, or the mission leaked. Which was it?'

Cutler looked perturbed. 'That's a matter for investigation.'

'Fucking right it is. Where did the intel come from? Who gave you *Highbeam*?'

He waved the question away. 'Langley have a team in Seoul looking into all that as of twelve hours ago.'

'That's not an answer.'

Cutler sighed. 'It's Beijing deep cover – I can't go into any detail.'

Kovic stared at him. He had been responsible for some of the Agency's best coups across the entire Eastern theatre. It was thanks to him that they had traced the mole in Langley who had been Beijing's entry into the CIA's mainframe. He had also busted Berkhoffer, the Silicon Valley ubergeek turned supposed philanthropist whose set-up in Shanghai turned out to be a front for ripping off patented US pharmaceuticals. And Kovic had his own networks of moles deep in the Chinese bureaucracy whose identity he alone knew, who would deal only with Kovic, whose product was sporadic but always dynamite and which he made sure was never seen by the Chinese.

But he knew that his disinclination to toe the line or to work out of a sanctioned office – he liked to stay well away from the Consulate – the toll of traffic accidents and occasional drunken brawls all rankled with Cutler and gave him ample reason to want rid of him. Worst of all Kovic, who had done more than his fair share of hot postings, who had lived and worked undercover, was a constant reminder to Cutler of his own lack of credible field experience – which set him apart from the other Agency brass.

Kovic studied the photographs again. He had seen three of them shot in the forehead. In the photographs there were no facial entry wounds. Someone had either patched them up or doctored the images because the injuries that were visible looked like they were the result of an RPG or some other blunt instrument of battle. Whether Cutler wanted it or not, Kovic was going to give him the benefit of his analysis.

'They were killed China-side – we need to look this end. You know what this is about – someone looking to drive a wedge between us and the Chinese, and judging by the protest outside they're off to a good start. You want to get on top of this right now.'

Cutler steepled his fingers and pressed them against his nose. 'Let's not get carried away with conspiracy theories. It's Langley policy to have someone neutral looking over it. Out of my hands I'm afraid. They'll want to talk to you at some point.' He put his hands behind his head and smoothed down what little hair was there. 'Meanwhile, I'm standing you down. Get a little R&R.'

He tried to grin. 'Chase some tail.'

The words seemed so unlikely coming from him; Kovic would have laughed had he not been so mad.

*Cutler thinks I'm complicit.* The thought flashed up in front of him. His mouth dropped open, but quickly he closed it. If that's what the Chief suspected, Kovic wasn't going to let on he'd guessed. Much as it would have gratified him to climb across the table and throttle him with his own tie, Kovic swallowed his rage.

Cutler shuffled some papers on his desk and glanced at his laptop. 'You know, just stay out of sight till this blows over.'

Kovic just glared until Cutler started blinking rapidly. Then just as it was getting awkward, he had one of his sudden mood swings, got up, came round the desk and held out his hand, then remembering the frostbite quickly withdrew it again, settling for a brotherly arm grip so awkward and so lacking in conviction that Kovic had to look away.

'You've had a bad time. You're sore – and I don't just mean the nose. This is complicated, but we'll get through it. I want you to take some time – take a break, go to Hawaii or Guam. Get away from—' He gestured at the window. 'All this.'

He clearly had no idea about Kovic's personal life. Kovic had never formally registered Louise as his significant other as he was supposed to do. Probably Cutler couldn't imagine him with anyone but a hooker.

'We'll get to the bottom of this and get it straightened out.'

Having stressed the gravity of it, he was now talking as if it was a minor road accident. But the message coming through was clear: butt out. At this moment Randall, Cutler's gopher and interpreter, stepped through the door without knocking.

'Zǎoshànghǎo – Good morning.' Randall grinned, hoping to show off more of his Mandarin, then realised he had misread the mood in the room.

Kovic ignored him, but Randall came right up to his chair and gestured at the door. Kovic turned to Cutler for an explanation.

'He'll see you out.'

It said everything about Cutler that he felt the need to have him escorted to the door. He was a loose cannon, a threat to be contained. He had come asking questions and got nothing. And since he had come back alive instead of in a body bag, with a story that didn't fit with what the pictures said, the finger of suspicion was pointing right at him, the sole survivor and sole witness. What really happened out there? Kovic needed his own answers, fast.

# 12

There was no sign of Wu when Kovic reached the parking deck. Straight away he knew why. Randall, who had escorted him down, looked sheepish.

'He's stood my fucking detail down, hasn't he?'

Randall sighed in commiseration. 'You know Cutler, he's big on *efficiencies.*'

'So what are we doing in this piss lake? I could have left by the front door.'

'Er, that's not deemed to be advisable at this time.'

Thinking Kovic might be about to deck him, he gave a swift wave and retreated into the elevator.

Kovic headed for the exit. If Cutler was planning to hang this round his neck he was going to regret it. He wasn't going to stand by and let that happen.

Trying not to breathe in too much of the stench of urine, he jogged up the ramp. The chemical sweetness of the smog was a relief. After an audience with Cutler, he always felt the need for something very Chinese as decompression. He walked a few blocks, found Songshan Lu, ducked under an awning, made for the crowded counter and edged himself on to a stool.

'*Shengjianbao!*' he shouted over the din.

The owner ignored him and continued to slice meat, his huge cleaver intermittently visible through the escaping steam. Beside him, his daughter presided over the *shengjianbao,* turning them in a huge vat of oil, while her husband chopped the veg. Only their little daughter sitting in the back watching TV turned and made eye contact. Kovic waved, she scowled and turned back to the screen.

Kovic had gotten used to this lack of courtesy, not hostile, just irrelevant to the hectic business of the day. The owner, thin, bald and with just one remaining tooth – hardly an advertisement for the food – tended to shake his head as if he was just closing or didn't like you, but if you stood your ground you would get fed eventually. He lit a cigarette while he waited – another good thing about China, he reminded himself; you could smoke anywhere. Then he remembered – another promise to Louise had just bitten the dust.

After a few minutes a bowl of crisp-bottomed dumplings appeared, with a tiny saucer of pinkish-brown liquid on the side. Kovic picked up the nearest, dipped it into the vinegar, bit into it and took out his cell.

'Wu, you've been fired again, I assume?'

'Yes, I know!' Wu had a habit of injecting every comment with enthusiasm as if every time he had a chance to use his English brought him unbridled joy. Being stood down by the Agency, which had happened on a previous Cutler 'efficiency drive' simply meant Kovic hired him direct, which, as well as having certain tax advantages, appealed to his vision of them as a daring duo, answerable to no one. 'Like Butch Cassidy and the Sundance Kid,' Wu had once said, to which Kovic responded, 'Yeah, pal. But remember how the movie ends?'

A luscious blend of pork and green spring onions flooded into his mouth, swept in on a tide of meaty broth. How they got the soup to stay in the dumplings was a mystery he had not yet solved.

'Damn that's hot! Are you nearby?'

'Of course, Agent K.' Wu had never been able to get his tongue round 'Kovic' and was a fan of the *Men in Black* movies, so Agent K it had become.

'Can you do something for me, Wu?'

'You bet, sir.'

Kovic knew he would eventually exhaust Wu's reserves of goodwill, which he feared were inextricably linked to his fantasy of living in America one day. 'When I get to America, I go on big road trip. Route 1, up California coast, Big Sur.' Both his parents were dead and being an only child meant he had none of the usual family obligations. But it bothered Kovic that the only important things in

Wu's life were his job and his car. He lived in a single men's hostel, never drank or smoked. Even when he was on the Langley payroll, Kovic supplemented his meagre wage with some extra cash out of the considerable slush fund he had salted away over the years for his assets and for the frequent bribes he needed to give without having to account for every cent with Langley and the likes of Cutler. It guaranteed Wu's loyalty and enabled him to outsource some of the less savoury jobs he was occasionally required to do.

In a world where everything was traceable, cash was a wonderful thing. It extended his freedom to operate under the radar and kept the CIA auditors at bay. There was something in his DNA that liked it this way. His Croatian grandfather had never had a bank account all his life. It was in his blood to run his own cash economy.

But whether he could grant Wu's wish and get him to America was another question, especially in the current climate. Better to stick to the here and now.

'Okay, go back to People's Square, find out who's organising the protesters. Sign up with them if you have to. Photograph the placards and get anything they're handing out like fliers – *chuándān*. And find out if they are students or workers, or what.'

'Wicked.'

'Well, maybe. Talk to me when you're done.'

Kovic killed the cell, took another dumpling and stared out at the bustling street. Two old ladies were unloading a crate of live chicks from the back of a Toyota people mover, while a third, who was sweeping the front of a shop with a broom made of twigs, barked instructions at them. On a balcony above, an unshaven man in shorts and a pyjama top with a cigarette stuck in the side of his mouth was hanging out washing. Above the washing line the strip of sky he could see between buildings was criss-crossed with cables festooned with advertising posters: for foot massage, traditional herbal medicine, smart phones, divorces, toothache remedies, martial arts, fortune telling, haemorrhoid cures. A smart couple in suits, like matching CEOs, came past, loudly blaming each other for the quality of their son's exam grades. They stopped, the woman slapped the man's face, and they continued. A young woman with orange ringlets walking a pair of yapping cinnamon-coloured Pomeranians stopped by a metallic yellow Range Rover and passed the dogs through a window to a man with silver dreadlocks. He got out and they started to study their phones as they walked away, descended the stairs into the subway. Kovic smiled. Nothing made sense in Shanghai if you wanted it to. Better just to enjoy the surprises, especially the past and the future crashing in on each other.

When Kovic had arrived in the city, many of the older people still dressed in the buttoned-up blue trouser suits of the Mao years and travelled by pushbike. Now it was a twenty-four-hour cavalcade of the latest and coolest fashions and gadgets from anywhere in the world, admired, copied and reinvented. China was in the fast lane, pedal to the metal, breaking all speed limits. Where it was all going, who knew, but he was enjoying the ride. Perhaps it had been the same for his grandparents arriving in Detroit, marvelling at the cars and the roads, telephones and flushing toilets. He shivered when he thought about what had happened since, that city like the set of a disaster movie, a place to escape from, like he had.

Wu was back, standing in front of him looking triumphant, brandishing a flier. Kovic snatched it, gestured for him to sit, shouted for tea and *xiaolongbao* – remembering Wu preferred the steamed variety.

The photograph was the same as the one Cutler had shown him, only cropped to emphasise the dead faces and leave no doubt that there were both Caucasians and Chinese.

*'American imperialist aggression has enmeshed the flower of Chinese youth in treachery against our brother neighbour,'* it said.

'Reads like something out of Mao.' He pointed at the Chinese uniforms. 'And what about these guys?'

'Chinese Special Forces; look.' Wu pointed at the insignia just visible on one breast pocket, the dagger with a lightning flash across it.

'Anyone you recognise?'

He shook his head.

'What do you have on the protesters?'

Wu took a deep breath. Kovic braced himself for one of his info-bursts.

'They are accounting students from Shanghai Lixin University of Commerce, an institution of higher education under the direct jurisdiction of Shanghai Municipal Government. As a part of Songjiang University Park of Shanghai, in which it is located, the university has an enrolment of over 9,300 full-time students, who study a variety of four-year degree programmes mainly specialised in the areas of commerce—'

Kovic put his hand up.

'Okay, back to normal conversation mode.'

'Okay, sorry.'

'It's okay.' Kovic turned over the flier. 'You did good.'

He examined the flier more closely. In tiny print at the bottom on the back was the name of the printer: Le-wou.

'Time for your policeman act. Make them tell you who placed the order.'

As well as being an incredible driver, Wu had another handy skill, which Kovic had stumbled on by chance one day when he'd imitated his landlord for a joke. The guy was an amazing actor. He took out his phone, searched the printer's name and called the number. Then he took another breath, frowned, and drew himself up to get into character.

'This is Police Superintendent Jin Tai!' he barked. 'You are suspected of distributing seditious propaganda against the state of a nature likely to inflame the citizens!'

It was uncanny. Wu, frowning hard, nodded and listened as the printer remonstrated. Kovic shook his head in admiration. The boy was a natural.

'Are you denying you are the publisher of this material?'

Kovic could hear the frantic printer on the other end, pleading for mercy, and – he hoped – giving up the name of his client.

'Yes, well, be more careful in future who your customers are. Be watchful at all times.' He finished the call.

'The company is called something like Panamvan – a Western name.'

His *xiaolongbao* had arrived.

'Parnham Vaughan.'

Wu nodded, his mouth full of shrimp.

'Thassit. What are they?'

'Turd polishers.'

Wu stopped chewing and stared at him.

'Reputation management. They rebrand you if you've fallen foul of the law and need to make a fresh start, or you've got something controversial going like bulldozing a town to get at some mineral underneath, or flooding a valley for a dam and you got to sell the idea to the locals you're tipping out of their homes. All the big companies have them.'

Wu was already searching them on his phone.

'Jin Mao Tower: very good address.'

'Yeah, probably a broom cupboard in the basement.'

'No. Eighty-eighth floor. Good number.'

The number eight was associated with prosperity. Evidently they'd gone up in the world since Kovic last dealt with them. He tucked some money under his plate and headed out into the street. The old man shouted something after them.

'I gave you a good tip, you old bastard.'

The little girl shot out from under the stall with the rest of Wu's *xiaolongbao*, packed neatly into a box.

# 13

## Huangpu District, Shanghai

Kovic slid the wad of chewing gum out of its packet and positioned it in his cheek, taking care not to bite on the micro-receiver inside it. As the elevator propelled them up to the eighty-eighth floor he felt the nausea rising. Either it was the altitude or the prospect of an audience with Victor Vaughan.

British by birth, playboy by nature, Victor Vaughan was in a Hong Kong jail by the age of twenty-six, his family inheritance squandered on a casino in Macau, which also made him an enemy of the triads, not bad for a waster with no discernible skills. All he had left was his inexhaustible British public school charm, and it carried him a long way. He befriended the cop who arrested him, Jack Parnham, a corrupt ex-South African Special Forces tough, and when Hong Kong was handed back to China they teamed up, moved to Shanghai and opened up a combined public relations and private security outfit, using Vaughan's British charm and manners and Parnham's muscle to schmooze the city's new rich. When their client list expanded to take in politicians, Kovic, then still new to Shanghai, took an interest. Parnham was easy: he fell for the gorgeous field agent Kovic had put on to him, who copied his SIM card, before both of them were unexpectedly murdered, poisoned by a vengeful girlfriend. So Kovic turned his attention to Vaughan, but there were two problems. One was the impenetrable, military-strength security that shielded his database. And the other was that his preferred bed-mates were young and male. The CIA's prudish streak meant it didn't run to bankrolling rent boys. Undeterred, Kovic decided to make a direct approach. If he couldn't hack him, he'd recruit him. With that kind of sexual preference as leverage, it shouldn't be hard.

Vaughan seemed only too happy to be wined and dined and listened patiently as Kovic laid out the tempting opportunities afforded by an association with the CIA. Eventually he leaned across the table.

'All very nice, but you've overlooked one thing, dear boy. Who needs America? You're not even on my dance card. This is China's century. The Yanks have got nothing I want.'

To make sure Kovic had got the message, that night his apartment was turned over by the Ministry of State Security. Evidently Vaughan's connections were even better than he had imagined.

The lift whispered to a halt and deposited them on the highly auspicious eighty-eighth floor. Kovic paused to take in the view in all its smog infused, high-rise glory. Perhaps Vaughan had been right, what did China need from America?

Down one side of the lobby was a floor to ceiling fish tank stocked with patrolling koi. A pair of antique Fu dogs stood sentry either side of the entrance. Despite the plush surroundings there was nothing subtle about the security. A pair of lumbering Mongolian wrestler-types stood guard. Genghis Khan believed wrestling kept his army combat ready. All these guys looked ready for was a nap.

Two women in black sheath dresses with identically swept back hair appeared and directed them to airport security-style trays to deposit all metal objects and then through an X-ray arch.

Kovic smirked at Wu.

'Welcome to Hogwarts.'

They waved detector wands over them.

'Sure you shouldn't be doing a more intimate search?'

There was no reaction. Wu also remained stone-faced, glaring at the wrestlers like a perturbed undertaker measuring them for coffins. The wand pinged as it passed Kovic's face. He bared his gold tooth.

At a vast marble desk a red-haired European woman frowned at Kovic's scarred face.

'I'm sorry, Mr Kovic, Mr Vaughan is in conference.'

'Tell him I'll wait – no, give him this.'

He took out the flier Wu had collected from People's Square, and on the photograph of the dead men in the jeep, drew a circle round the empty driver's seat and wrote *Kovic was here.*

'Pass him this if you would? Thank you. Then I imagine he'll find he's available.'

They were shown into an inner office containing a pair of pale blue leather sofas. The heavies lumbered behind, shooting their cuffs like they'd seen in the movies. Kovic sat, took out his chewed gum and flicked it into a plant pot.

After a minute the double doors opened and Vaughan appeared, fleshier than Kovic remembered, in a five thousand dollar navy chalk-stripe suit with matching pink tie and pocket handkerchief. The man had certainly gone up in the world. He glided towards them; in his hand was the flier, on his face a bemused smile.

'Agent Kovic, how delightful.' Kovic didn't get up. Vaughan put out his hand. Kovic kept his clamped together in his lap.

'Seems you've moved into contract killing.'

Vaughan oozed a thin smile. 'Really, I haven't the foggiest what you're on about.'

'Yes you do, otherwise you wouldn't have bothered to see me. Nice artwork, Vaughan. Lot of trouble you went to rearranging the dead, mixing in a few Chinese, putting them in the jeep. Too bad one of us slipped past your executioners.'

Vaughan let out a cross between a cough and a guffaw and glanced at his minders who dutifully snorted in unison.

'If you're looking for a scapegoat for your country's latest – faux pas—' He shook his head in mock dismay.

'Who's the client?'

'Ha, ha. I'm sure you'll understand it's certainly not company policy to reveal the identity of any client.'

The smugness of the Brit pervert riled Kovic. He wanted to stomp all over his balls and then he and Wu could make fools of the tough guys when they piled in. That sounded fun, but there'd still be the little matter of getting out of the building. Someone

on the front desk would no doubt press an alarm and all the elevators would stop. And by the time they got anywhere near the
ground floor the cops would be swarming in. He glanced at the
heavies. One folded his arms, exposing his meaty hands. A mark
on the back of one of them stirred Kovic's memory. He glanced
at Wu to check if he had noticed but his attention was all on
Vaughan.

Kovic got to his feet. He put his face close to Vaughan's.

'Here's what's going to happen, Victor. Not now, but very soon,
you'll find yourself telling me all you know about this.' He flicked
the flier in Vaughan's hand.

The Brit was still on his high horse. 'Are you sure your work hasn't
gone to your head?'

'I'm not here on behalf of the US Government. I'm here for the
men in that jeep. And their families. And I'll be back, I guarantee
it.'

There was an intensity in Kovic's look that left Vaughan in no
doubt that he meant it. Kovic turned and exited through the narrow
gap between the heavies, Wu following.

The receiver in the gum would work for about twelve hours. It
would search for all Wi-Fi signals within a fifty-metre radius, lock
on to them and suck up all texts and emails incoming and outgoing
to all devices in its range. Then, as its power waned, it would spit
the whole lot out in one info-burst before it died, its work done.
That was *if* it worked. The Chinese were in another league when it
came to the design of espionage micro technology, but they charged
a fortune for it and the kit wasn't always as reliable as its salesmen
promised.

In the elevator down two women were discussing a new kind of
Botox that had caused a friend's skin to go like orange peel. They
stopped talking when they saw Kovic's face. The elevator stopped at
the forty-second floor and a thickset man got in. Kovic clocked the
micro-receiver screwed into his left ear. On the back of his hand,
three tattooed snakeheads peeped out of his cuff, their necks joined
to form a trident. Kovic looked away, then back. His pulse quickened. Where had he seen something like that before? Kovic glanced

at Wu and quickly back to the hand so he followed his gaze. Wu nodded almost imperceptibly. The man was a different shape but there was no question where he had seen the tattoo – on the back of the assassin's hand.

# 14

When they got out into the lobby the earpiece man peeled off and disappeared through a fire exit. Kovic could see his lips moving and had a feeling that they hadn't seen the last of him and his snake-headed trident. They carried on out the building and down the broad concourse that led to the steps down to the public garage where Wu's X6 was parked.

'Hey, Jake, how's it hangin'?'

A florid American who knew Kovic by his Shenzhen alias, financial analyst Jake Coulter, shouted and waved across the throng moving into and out of the building, as if hailing him from a passing vessel. He was another one like Cutler, travelling the world in an American bubble, with loud exuberant movements that stood out awkwardly. Kovic raised a hand and kept moving, but noticed a young Chinese spat on the ground in his path.

Kovic touched Wu's arm before he could retaliate.

'It's cool. Leave it.'

Kovic focused on the throng, his eyes sweeping the sea of people in their path for pursuers. He crouched down and pretended to retie his shoelaces, then abruptly changed direction as they reached the sidewalk. To their left a man slowed then quickened his pace. How many more were there? He changed direction and Wu followed as they neared the two entrances to the car park, a ramp and some stairs. He weighed up abandoning the car and getting into a cab – anonymity versus mobility – and decided on the car. The right call? They would soon know.

Wu fired up the X6 and moved out of the space toward the exit ramp. An Audi pulled out in front of them and the driver leaned out and fed a ticket into the barrier. Then a second car, a

Corolla, drew up behind them. The barrier lifted and the Audi moved forward. The barrier came down again. Wu went forward and fed his ticket in, but the barrier didn't open. The Audi's reverse lights came on. They were sandwiched between the Audi and the Corolla.

'Go! Go!' Kovic yelled.

Wu looked at him, pained.

'I'll buy you a new bumper.'

Wu's face was full of anguish as his sense of duty struggled with his passion. Duty won, and he stood on the gas. The X6 shot forward through the barrier and slammed into the Audi, sending up a spray of splintered plastic. Wu kept his foot down and the transmission screamed in protest as they ploughed the Audi up the rest of the ramp, slewing it sideways. There was a narrow gap between the car and the Armco that lined the ramp.

'Go for it.'

'It won't fit!'

'Just do it.'

Kovic's first thought was that this was a hijacking, but it was soon clear they weren't bothered about taking him alive. The rear windscreen exploded, blasted by bullets from the Corolla behind. The X6 let out a graunching screech of protest as it forced its way between the Audi and the corrugated barrier. They roared up the ramp, bouncing over a speed bump, into daylight.

'Okay, I'll buy you a new car. Just keep going.'

'Where to?'

'I dunno – anywhere.'

Kovic tipped the rear-view mirror towards him and eyed the scene behind just as one of the Audi's doors flew open and the driver reached out to take aim with a suppressed QSZ-92 pistol, the Corolla helpfully slamming a door on his arm as it tried to follow. Kovic smiled; there was nothing like one bad guy fucking up another for you to help out. But he knew it had brought them only temporary respite. What was clear was that these guys had no fear upsetting the authorities or causing chaos, as if they had their own licence to cause mayhem.

Kovic thought he saw tears in Wu's eyes.

'I have this car three weeks.'

'I have *had*. Think about your grammar.'

'I'm thinking about my car!'

'Well then, think about your ass instead.'

The street was one way, the traffic solid, but the bus lane was clear. Wu, clearly resigned to more damage, swung left against the flow, scattering oncoming mopeds like skittles. He tore down the lane to the next junction and turned left into a narrow street, cutting a path through slow moving vans and bikes, horn blaring. A man with a ladder chose this moment to cross the road. The X6 clipped the back end, which swung the ladder 180 degrees, knocking a cyclist out of his saddle.

The cross street at the end was also choked with vehicles and the Corolla had caught up. Wu's survival imperative had kicked in; he forced his way between two cars, grazing both. The opposite lane was moving, so why not use that?

'Good job I disabled the Active Cruise Control,' said Wu as he turned into the oncoming traffic.

'Why?' Kovic asked. He thought he should humour him.

'It slows it down when the sensors detect a slower or stationary car ahead to maintain a safe distance from the vehicle in front.'

They found a clear path. Wu floored it.

'Okay, take the wheel!' he yelled, as he dived between the seats and reached into the custom-made compartment under the back seat that contained his guns. The lid was stuck.

'Step on it!' yelled Kovic.

As Wu struggled to get at the weapons, Kovic veered in and out of the oncoming cars, horns blaring as drivers dived for cover.

'Brake!'

Wu obliged. Kovic veered across the central reservation as a space opened up to the left of a bus then back again. The jolt tossed Wu back into his seat, the gun now in his hand. He threw it into Kovic's lap and took back the wheel just in time to wrench them out of the way of a wrecker towing a stricken van.

'Good work.' It was the Sig Sauer P226 Kovic had given him as a present but which he had yet to use. Guns hadn't come into their work in Shanghai – until now.

The sky, which was an angry grey, now split with a scrawl of lightning and as the crash of thunder broke over them the rain slanted down, melting the view ahead into an indecipherable blur of colours. Wu hit the wipers just as the screen exploded, showering them with glass and pink plastic boots. The people mover they had rear-ended had deposited the contents of its roof rack on to them. The wipers continued their ungainly dance as they swept thin air.

'The fuck?'

'This is so not our day.'

This time the hood of the X6 had broken free of its clips and sprang up like a shield, a second later it was perforated with holes.

Times like this I'd like nothing better than to have my feet up by a log fire and settle into a good book, thought Kovic. *Why does my head do this to me just when I need it most?*

'If it's not one thing—'

But Wu was in full survival mode now, long past protesting at the desecration of his until very recently immaculate vehicle. He slammed the shift into reverse, Kovic doubling up with the sudden surge of Gs, mesmerised by his partner's capacity for contortion as he observed him speeding backwards, two hands still on the wheel, but his torso almost facing the rear. He made a mental note to do some yoga when he had a spare moment.

'You see where those bullets came from?'

He needn't have asked. A bike drew level with them and blew out the side window, Kovic sensing the air parting as a bullet shot past his nose. He lifted Wu's Sig, aimed, and the biker gunman was no more, but less than a second later another bullet shot the Sig clean out of his hand.

Wu threw the wheel to the right and they ninety-ed into a narrow street taken up almost entirely by a garbage truck. There was no way out. The Corolla Kovic thought they had shaken off magically reappeared behind them. Wu slammed to a halt and the hood flopped back down in time to reveal another biker coming towards them from the other side of the garbage truck, the pillion rider taking aim.

'Abandon ship!'

Kovic threw himself out and came to rest on the drenched sidewalk at the feet of an elderly lady. Her mouth made a perfect O.

'Excuse me, madam. Bad day.'

He scrambled up and disappeared into a completely dark alleyway. He hoped it would lead somewhere. It didn't. The sound of the motorbike ricocheted off the walls as it followed him in. He hurtled through a doorway and up a flight of stairs into a workshop full of women at sewing machines and giant rolls of cloth. The women stopped and gazed at him without expression. He could hear the clatter of feet on the stairs. He took the next flight, across a room strewn with toys and small children, a nursery for the workers. There were no more floors after that so he slid open a window and looked down into the alley. A ledge ran beneath the windows to the end of the building where there was a drainpipe. It looked fragile, but several cables ran alongside it up to the roof, and there weren't any other options. He gripped the top of the window, let himself out and inched along the ledge to the pipe just as his pursuer put his head out of the window. Kovic kicked as hard as he could manage in the tight space and hit the guy's face, unfortunately not quite hard enough, as he snatched at Kovic's foot. He lost his balance. As he slipped he grasped at the cables – they would either hold him or snap ... and that would be that. They held, but sliced into his palm. He grabbed with his other hand, swung his foot again and smacked the weapon out of the guy's hand. It clattered on to the paving below. But the movement swung him away from the drainpipe, turning it into a giant pendulum. Several people below were shouting up at him now. He used the pendulum's momentum to swing himself to the window ledge of the neighbouring building, where two teenage boys in aprons were craning their necks out to watch, delighted with the show. A huge bald man loomed up behind them and slapped their heads just as Kovic's feet arrived on the ledge.

'Mind if I come in?' was all he could think of saying as he landed on the floor of their workshop like a beached marlin. The bald man attempted to stop him getting up, threatening him with a long pole. Kovic wrenched it out of his grip.

'Just let me get to the roof okay and I'll be out of your hair.'

One of the boys behind motioned at the skylight that the pole was used for opening. All he needed was a leg up. At the same moment there was a crash of glass as a window exploded inwards and his pursuer appeared inches from him. Kovic rammed the pole into his chest and put him on the floor, a specimen pinned for display.

He saw a second skylight, with a stove beneath it. He vaulted on to it, hit the window with his fist and lifted himself through. The fresh air was wondrous after the thick gluey fug of the workshop and the tickling rain refreshingly welcome. He scrabbled across a few rooftops to the end of the row and looked down into the street. There was no sign of Wu. He lifted himself over a parapet and found himself in a rooftop garden, filled with pot plants and green plastic turf covered in fresh dog shit. Suddenly the rooftop thundered with the vibration of something heading towards him – a roaring, growling, squat muscular dog at a ferocious gallop. Kovic fell back and saw the dog abruptly arc into the air as it was wrenched up and back by its chain. He scrambled to his feet and moved wide of the leaping dog which was on its hind legs, its bark strained by the choke chain. Kovic mounted the parapet and worked his way round to where the chain was anchored, the dog following him leaping and snapping at his feet. It got his boot in its mouth and tore it off which distracted it just long enough for Kovic to reach the door next to the chain post. The dog paused, undecided between the whole human and the boot. The bike guy then dropped on to the turf, beyond the reach of the dog, giving Kovic his chance. He jumped down and unclipped the leash. The dog leapt on the biker and they rolled over together until the dog gave out a squealing whimper and fell into a heap as the biker pulled a long bloodied blade from its neck.

Kovic was through the doors now and flying down the stairs, past a roomful of vacuum cleaners, in the middle of which a man and woman stooped over one, as if performing resuscitation.

'Emergency exit?'

The man nodded at a large aperture in the back of the room with a cargo jib for hoisting stuff up from the street. Kovic looked out. The alley was strung with washing lines, a few damp items that hadn't been taken in before the rain. Below them, several pig carcasses hung from hooks, a bucket under each to collect the remaining drips. From behind them came the sound of chopping, and to the right was a dumpster from which came a rhythmic hissing, like a miniature steam engine. He could just make out a crouching figure beneath it, his shirt bloodied. To his left, two men were coming up the alley. They had seen the croucher; it was Wu, hiding, gasping for breath.

'Hey! Guys! Up here,' Kovic yelled down at them.

They both looked up. The adrenalin surged through him, the aches and pains from the border incident anaesthetised. He was pumped, ready to take on the world, and in this mode he knew he was also apt to do stupid things. But what else was there to do?

He flung himself off the ledge and dived towards the lead guy, who broke his fall. Kovic went blank for a few seconds, coming to just in time to roll out of the way of a blade that swept down towards his eyes. Wu emerged from behind the dumpster. He was limping, wounded and exhausted. The second man was on him. Kovic summoned another burst of energy and lunged at the knifeman. They both collapsed on Wu. Kovic scrambled for the knifeman's arm, wondering when the other guy was going to run him through. He looked round to see a rotund man coming out from the rear of the butcher's with a basin full of animal parts. Knifeman two crashed into him and they both tumbled, spilling the meat and bone over the cobbles. Furious, the knifeman slashed out at the rotund man as he rose and a great red fissure opened up in his vest as he sank to his knees. The sheer wanton senselessness of this filled Kovic with fury. He snapped knifeman one's wrist backwards and wrenched the weapon out of his flailing hand. It clattered on the ground. Wu seized it, as Kovic kicked his remaining boot into the ex-knifeman's face. Knifeman two bore down on them. Kovic could see the poor butcher clutching his guts as he rocked forward and fell face first into a puddle. He dodged the knife and smashed his forehead into the knifeman's nose. He staggered back, still slicing the air with the blade. Kovic kicked him in the chest but lost his balance, his feet sucked from under him by some slimy offal underfoot, and he was down on his back, the knifeman on top of him. Wu sprang on to him but the knifeman, wild with rage, flung him off. The blade bore down towards Kovic's face, quivering a couple of inches above his eyes. Evidently his assailant wanted to savour the moment. This was Kovic's chance. He found the feeling in his arms and clamped his hands round the knifeman's. For a long half minute the knifeman fought to drive the blade into Kovic's face while Kovic tried to force it upward and away from him. He could see the lethal intent in the other man's eyes as they fought for control of the weapon.

'I hope you've got a good pension, pal. Your family's going to need it.'

The knifeman spat something back but with all the blood and saliva accompanying his words it defied translation. Agonisingly slowly the blade started to turn, but Kovic could feel his strength going. Wu, finally free of the other guy, grabbed the man's head and lifted it. At last Kovic had control of the blade even though it was still in the knifeman's hands. He forced it towards his assailant until it was pointed under the chin. With perfect timing, Wu thrust the head downwards. The tip of the blade entered the soft tissue just between his throat and his Adam's apple. Wu drove the head down until the knife was embedded right up to the hilt. Blood bubbled out of his mouth as the knifeman went limp and rolled over on to the ground.

Kovic slowly got to his feet. Wu knelt, his chest heaving from the exertion, wiping the palms of his bloody hands on his thighs. Kovic unpeeled the dead man's fingers, which were still wrapped round the knife, and with the tip of the blade lifted his coat cuff. The tattoo went halfway up his arm. Three snake heads on a trident clutched by a flaming fist.

Wu leaned over and looked.

'Any ideas?'

Wu shook his head.

'Think I'd like to show that to someone.'

Several men had emerged from the butcher's to help their colleague. Kovic went up to one who was holding a cleaver.

'May I?'

Something in Kovic's face decided the owner against protesting. He handed him the cleaver. Kovic went back to the knifeman and with one decisive swing, severed the forearm below the tattoo. He passed the cleaver back to his dismayed owner.

'Thanks, do you have a bag?'

# 15

## Shanghai Old Town

The room was smoky and the yellow paper shade round the low single bulb projected a warm golden glow on to the scrubbed wooden walls. Xiang reminded Kovic of a new-born baby. The wisp of hair, the sheen on his forehead and sparkly inquiring eyes. Kovic was momentarily propelled back to a nativity scene at his elementary school. But there wasn't anything holy about Xiang in the ninety-seven years that had passed since the occasion of his birth.

After toasts with sorghum liquor, which Kovic likened to a liquid firecracker, he unwrapped the forearm and laid it on the table like an offering. Xiang didn't show the slightest alarm, which said a lot about the world he had inhabited and why Kovic was consulting him.

Xiang looked round to the boy standing in the doorway.

'My glass, please.'

The boy disappeared then reappeared holding the largest magnifying glass Kovic had ever seen.

Xiang slowly raised it to his face and bent over the arm. He moved it up to the three snakeheads and back down to the flaming fist.

He let out a series of hen-like clucks, which Kovic eventually deciphered as laughter.

'You Americans, your appetite for trouble is insatiable.' He clucked some more, put down the glass and nodded. Kovic started to wrap up the arm. Xiang gestured at the tattoo, then took another pull on his long, thin pipe and exhaled.

'Very showy.'

'I'm sorry?'

Xiang swatted the air gently with his fingers, then tugged at his sleeve and revealed a simple cross with splayed ends, faded almost to invisibility on his leathery walnut coloured skin.

'Very simple, you see.'

Kovic knew better than to hurry the old man. They were seated in the back room of the bar his grandson now ran on Danfeng Lu Street. Xiang had been born in the room upstairs, had formed his first gang from this room in 1931, killed his first man, a rival gang leader, on the front step while he was still a teenager, severed his head with a machete to show who was boss, and also brokered a truce with the four main Shanghai gangs right here as the Japanese were bombing Pearl Harbor. As well as being a distinguished member of the resistance, Xiang was also the CIA's first Chinese recruit. Kovic only knew all this because he had sought out the old man's archived file in Langley.

'They gave me my own aeroplane, very generous. A German Junkers Ju 52 with floats so we could land on any water. And fuel. We did a regular run to Hokkaido to pick up arms and opium. Terrible shortages after the war. We did what we could to stop the Reds but—'

He let out a sigh so long that Kovic worried for a moment it was his last. Perhaps he was silently mourning the passing of Shanghai's previous crazy era before Mao came in and spoiled all the fun. The city had been the vice capital of the East and gangs like Xiang's passed for legitimate businesses.

'We had our own notepaper; we used trained accountants. It was very professional.' There was something almost touching about Xiang's badges of respectability.

Curiosity had originally brought Kovic to Xiang's door. He had assumed the legendary gangster turned CIA asset had rotted away in some gulag decades ago. Just out of curiosity he had tracked down the bar, only to find Xiang alive and well in this back room. How he survived the worst of Mao's purges was a miracle. Not only was he a criminal, he had backed the nationalist Kuomintang in their losing battle against the Reds before they retreated to Taiwan, never to return. Even worse, Xiang was in the pay of the Americans, surely another death sentence.

'What was your secret?'

'Simplicity,' Xiang told him. 'Simplicity is a great asset.' He tapped the tattoo on his wrist and waved at the scrubbed walls around him. 'Many of my rivals acquired the trappings of success – elaborate cars and mansions. Examples had to be made of them. While I've always lived more like a true Communist than any of the real ones.'

He laughed for some time at this insight. Kovic laughed too.

There was no rushing him. Xiang moved at his own pace. He would answer the question when he was good and ready – and maybe not at all, at least not directly.

He sucked again on his pipe.

'When the Reds came, we were doomed. Many of my rivals were put to the sword. Almost all the gangs simply became extinct. Those who had not been executed starved to death or were broken by hard labour in the camps. A very few of us were lucky. We just withdrew like tortoises into our shells.' He made a shrinking gesture with his neck.

Kovic shifted his weight. He longed to climb into a deep bath and soothe his battered body, but Xiang and his mysterious forgotten world fascinated him.

Xiang tapped the tattoo with the end of his pipe.

'This is more than one.'

'There was more than one today.'

Xiang laughed and shook his head. 'No, no, you misunderstand. This symbol means that two gangs are in alliance. The Flaming Fist, they were most lucky. They were not purged. Instead, they were absorbed into the People's Liberation Army. Mao needed his personal people he could call on to deal with – difficulties, like an acolyte becoming too big for his boots, a local commissar who had not shown appropriate respect—'

'And the snakehead trident?'

Xiang put down his pipe. 'They were purged, gone. None are left.'

He turned to his left, spat generously into a nearby spittoon.

Kovic sensed a change of atmosphere. 'Looks like they've made a comeback.'

Xiang reached out a gnarled hand and laid it on Kovic's shoulder.

'You know I have always been careful. I choose my battles after much deliberation. So should you.'

Kovic nodded. Xiang was winding up the conversation.

'As a friend of America, a critic too but a friend at heart, my message is this: whatever your business is with these people, drop it. Because you will not win, not with all your might.'

'How do you know?'

He clucked again. 'I'm ninety-seven. I know.'

He tapped the package, still on the table.

'Bury this deep. You won't want to be found with it. I sense you are an impetuous man, Kovic. Don't let this be your downfall.'

'Sir, I feel there is more you could tell me. If you could just give me something on the other gang.'

Xiang blinked slowly and drew in a breath.

'We have arrived at a crossroads. Old and new must fight it out. Luckily for me, I have finished my battles.'

He turned away and waved to the boy. 'Show the gentleman out. He is ready to go.'

Then he fixed his gaze on Kovic one last time. 'It was pleasant to see you again, Kovic. But don't come back.'

Xiang slowly closed his eyes and leaned back. The meeting was over.

# 16

Kovic threw the arm in a dumpster and went in search of Wu. He found him at the repair shop that belonged to his cousin, bent over the battle-scarred X6, moving his hands over the destroyed bodywork like a physiotherapist feeling for bruised vertebrae. The front bumper and lights were completely gone, the hood was riddled with bullet holes. The rear and two side windows were shot out and the tailgate that had been rammed was hanging drunkenly by one hinge. And all down the nearside, bright metal grinned through deep scores, as if it had been clawed by a huge monster.

'I'm sorry, pal, I really am.' Kovic put his arm round him. 'But it's just a car.'

Clearly that wasn't going to work. He was no good at this kind of moment. He groped for something positive to say.

'Your cousin's a skilled panel beater. I've seen his work. Incredible.'

Wu said nothing; his normally buoyant optimism levels were flatlining.

He looked at Kovic, his eyes hollow.

'I did good today, yes?'

'More than good. And so did the car – it saved our asses. Look, I'll see what Uncle Sam can do.'

He would just have to delve into his slush fund.

'Will there be more like today?'

Kovic took a deep breath. 'You want out? I'll understand.'

'Is it going to get badder?'

'*Worse*. Yes, it is going to get worse.'

'*Ai ya!*' said a voice from behind them.

Wu turned and faced his cousin who was staring at the X6 in disbelief.

88

A short exchange followed in Zhujinese, the local dialect that Kovic was glad he couldn't follow. Wu's crest fell even further.

The cousin turned to Kovic and addressed him in English.

'Explain – this is totalled. Goodbye car.'

'Easy, pal,' said Kovic. 'This is a difficult time for him.' He moved closer to the cousin, like a desperate relative beseeching a doctor. 'Is there nothing you can do?'

The cousin walked round the car slowly, assessing the damage and shaking his head.

'It's gonna cost you big dollars.'

'Whatever it takes.'

The cousin mentioned a sum in yuan that sounded uncomfortably far away from $10,000 – on the wrong side.

'What about the family discount?'

'That's *with* family discount.'

'Okay. You got a courtesy car?'

'Maybe. Come back in the morning.'

Kovic led Wu away.

'It's going to be okay, buddy. And look at it this way; when you get to the States you'll get yourself a whole new car.'

He knew the hint about a future in America would cheer him up – even though Kovic had yet to figure out how he was going to swing that for him.

They went to a favourite food stall of Wu's in Fanbang Lu and ordered Snow beers. Up on the wall, the TV was on. Wu squinted at it a moment then suddenly cheered up.

'Jin Jié is back!'

'Well, deck the halls,' said Kovic.

He was aware of the young politician, but had dismissed him as just another celebrity star burning brightly and briefly in the New China firmament. They watched the screen. At Pudong airport, on a small podium set up in front of the aircraft from which he had just disembarked, the young man with the improbably innocent face was waving at the crowd and throwing his arms in the air in a very un-Chinese manner. Each time he punched the air a fresh roar of delight rose from the crowd, followed by more chanting of his name.

'So?' Something about the spectacle irritated Kovic.

'Very good man, very good for future.' Wu's English always took a nosedive when he was excited.

'He's a kid with a degree from MIT and good dental work.'

Kovic knew that wasn't quite fair. Jin Jié had just been named *Time* magazine's Person of the Year. His book on the new global economy was a bestseller. America seemed to have taken him into their hearts. What did interest Kovic was how this American adulation would play back here, especially after what he had seen this morning.

Kovic noticed some of the diners paying attention. '*Jin Jié! Jin Jié!*' several tens of thousands of ecstatic fans chanted. Between the semi-continuous chanting of the crowd and the hyper-excited commentator a few phrases from Jin Jié's speech floated through …

'*know that we can achieve whatever we put our mind to.*'

'*… pursue our individual dreams but still come together as one nation …*'

'*… keep, in the twenty-first century, promise alive …*'

And then he paused, and spread his hands to quiet the crowd.

'*… Our government should work for us, not against us, listen to all voices …*'

And at a reference to the thousands of dissidents banged up in China's jails, the crowd broke into a rapturous roar. Kovic looked across at Wu, gazing wide-eyed at the screen. 'Well that's gonna go down like a cup of cold sick in Beijing.'

Wu was oblivious to Kovic's warning tone.

'The man's a visionary. We never had nothing like this before.'

Kovic pondered the contrast between the protest earlier in the day, the angry mob on the point of lynching an American, and this upstart wowing the crowd having just come from the US where he was feted. Xiang was right: China was at a crossroads.

# 17

**French Concession, Shanghai**

A cab dropped Kovic at his gate. He told the driver to keep the change and eased himself gingerly out of the back seat. He stood for a moment as the car moved away. It was night, the sky a smoky purple. The sounds of evening were in full flow: a mash up of TV, radio, Western pop, Chinese folk, advertising jingles and a heavy reggae beat under a shrill trilling falsetto.

He was exhausted, and his whole body felt like a punchbag. The effort required to get through the gate and up the steps seemed overwhelming. He wondered about Louise. Maybe he should track her down, make amends. In theory he had the time now he had been laid off by Cutler, if he could just get to the bottom of what happened on the border.

A black Mercedes SUV screeched to a halt beside him and two heavies emerged. They weren't gangsters – their suits were too cheap. They stood to attention by the vehicle while a young Chinese woman stepped out from behind the wheel. She was slightly built, in a black leather jacket and fatigue type pants. Under the look of stern officiousness was a face of austere beauty. A pair of piercing black eyes were trained on him, cold and glittering. She came to-wards him. It was a pretty safe bet she wasn't looking for a date.

'Agent Kovic?'

She held up an ID: Ministry of State Security.

'I was just going for a shower. Care to join me?'

Before he could gauge her response, she raised an arm and he was on the ground, his head in something damp. One of her point-ed boots pressed on his lower abdomen and then everything went dark as one of the heavies slid a hood over his head. Another pair of hands clamped his wrists together with a zip-cuff. Then he was bundled into the back of the SUV and the tailgate slammed shut. Alone or otherwise, that shower was going to have to wait.

Kovic was both furious and confused. The MSS routinely questioned him but usually he was politely invited to take a ride and the whole process was little more than a charade, a reminder that they were watching. This was definitely abduction. The choice of vehicle, a Benz SUV, suggested some kind of inflated status, or that someone inside had for some reason started throwing money around. It was decidedly unpatriotic, indeed positively decadent. Maybe the local Mercedes dealer imagined it would be good for the brand if MSS operatives rode around in their product and had been loaning them out. And as for the woman, while her heavies were standard government issue she definitely was not. In fact he had never encountered a female MSS agent.

He heard her speak into a phone.

*'Target on board: ETA twenty minutes.'*

The pedantic monotone struck Kovic as somehow ludicrous. He realised it was a measure of how worn out he was that he had felt no inclination to resist. The Benz had a siren, which confirmed that he was in the hands of the authorities. Maybe that was a good thing – the devil he knew, rather than strange criminals with mysterious tattoos. He tried to find a comfortable position but with his hands cuffed behind his back it was impossible. A day that had already gone on for far too long was suddenly getting even longer, but there was no point in protesting; it wouldn't change anything. He decided to try and grab a short nap. He had the ability to sleep anywhere, no matter how uncomfortable – well, almost.

The journey was short; they were still in town. That meant he probably wasn't being taken out to some wasteland to be shot, which was nice. Judging by the distance it was probably to the Golfball, the MSS's Shanghai HQ. The SUV made a sharp descent, the engine noise bouncing back off walls that were very close, the tyres squeaking on a smooth surface: another underground car park, oh great. They stopped, the doors opened. No smell of piss though, so definitely a better class of car park than the CIA's. Then he was out of the vehicle, through some security doors and frogmarched along an interminable corridor into a lift and down more levels. That wasn't good. The deeper you were taken, the deeper the trouble you were in, he had generally found. He heard a door being unlocked, another bad sign, and a strong smell of disinfectant, also not good. Then he was manoeuvred into a sharp left and made to sit on a hard flat chair with only a bar for a back, so at least his wrists had somewhere to go. No one said anything. They seemed to be leaving him here so he decided to try again and have that nap, but each time his head dropped someone roughly pushed it up. He really was way too tired for this.

'Hey, leave me the fuck alone, will ya?'

And then he was on his side on the floor – the chair clattering away as it was kicked from under him. He felt a sharp pain in his neck and was instantly strangely happy.

'Okay, here is good,' he murmured gratefully as he slipped away. 'I'll just stay here …'

His dreams were a toxic mix of the executions in the snow, the chase through Shanghai and the encounter with Cutler; all three playing in a continuous loop in his head.

Later, maybe much later – he didn't know when because they had taken his watch and all his belongings – he regained consciousness. The hood was off, and he found himself on a hard wooden chair with arms. The room was all done in Interrogation Grey: floors walls and ceiling. There were no windows. This was the Golfball all right; the Ministry of State Security's recently made-over Shanghai HQ, so named because of the large concave indentations in its concrete exterior. The air still smelled the same, as if it had been breathed in and out by generations of halitosis sufferers going back to the Cultural Revolution.

Whenever there were demonstrations, or bombs, or the political tension was heightened in any way, it was standard practice to pull in foreign station agents for a routine conversation. The intelligence game in China was just that: a game. And whenever he was pulled in, the FBI did the same with one of theirs in Washington or LA. Kovic had cultivated an image, which Chinese Intelligence seemed to have swallowed. To them he was a middle ranking CIA asset, a typical American abroad, lazy, with a reputation for drinking and occasional brawling, who gathered low to medium level intel that seemed to please his bosses enough to keep him in post. He knew this because he had hacked their file on him. And when they hauled him in for questioning he always made sure he looked suitably troubled by their findings – even though he had already read them.

The worst aspect of these Q&As, Kovic found, was the boredom. A hundred pro forma questions would be asked to which a hundred stock responses would be given. It wasn't about the content of the answers, it was the fact of the event itself; the MSS needed to show Washington it knew who its agents were. It was just a formality, a bit of low level sabre-rattling, since their own hackers would be doing their best to keep them up to date with all his activities: emails, phone calls to and from Langley, and, of course, all his traffic with Cutler in Beijing. With this in mind, he made sure to keep these channels appropriately active with carefully selected intel, some of it mildly sensitive, or sensitive enough to convince the MSS that they were efficiently keeping tabs on him, but all of relatively low grade, to suggest he wasn't that good at his job. He had even created a series of fictitious moles inside the Party whose fake communiqués to him were littered with government gossip he had gained access to from other sources, to be pored over by their analysts. This material caused them to waste hundreds of hours trying to uncover his fictitious sources.

Kovic noticed he was now zipped into a GITMO style boiler suit that had definitely not been washed since the last wearer had had it on, perhaps even the first. The red-brown stains and another, less vividly coloured, crunchy patch were testimony to that. He had nothing on his feet and the floor seemed artificially chilled. Beside him there were two identical metal bowls. One had a liquid in that he hoped was water; at least it didn't seem to smell of anything either human or deadly. The other was presumably his toilet.

There was no point in speculating about what was coming, it was a waste of time and brainpower. 'Know this,' a grizzled instructor at the Farm told his group as they were about to go out into the world as fully fledged agents, 'however many billions of dollars they spend on you and however many thousands of hours you put in to figuring what your friend or enemy's next move is, only one thing is for sure – it ain't gonna be what you predicted. From the Iran hostages to jets slamming into the Twin Towers, the shit that happens will be the last thing you expected. Never underestimate how little you know.'

He heard steps outside – not heavy, lumbering, goon steps but the light, well balanced tread of someone who hadn't been hired for their muscle. The woman was back.

She strode in, sat and opened a fat file. In English, he recited the standard pro forma he was required to when detained by in-country officials.

'I am a US Government public servant and I demand to know on what authority you are acting. I must protest in the strongest terms that under the—'

The woman was standing over him. She seemed to be somewhat agitated.

'Just shut the fuck up, okay?' she said in English, her voice barely an inch from his ear. Something hard landed on the side of his head: a fist.

'I insist on speaking to my—'

'We have already informed your office of your detention.'

She sat down and reached for a table lamp that was by her chair, set it on the table, switched it on and trained the light in his face. He started to laugh. Suddenly his face was stinging again. He hadn't even seen the slap coming.

'What is this, step two from the MSS interrogation manual? Train light on prisoner to maximise discomfort. Or are you gonna give me a facial? Or a new nose – I sure could do with one. Are you a plastic surgeon? Or just a make-up artist? I know – it's Shanghai's municipal clean up foreigner day.'

She ignored him and continued to study the file in front of her.

'No, honestly, why am I here? And I didn't catch your name.'

She started to read from the file.

'Kovic, Laszlo—'

'No one calls me that.'

She continued to read: 'United States Central Intelligence Agency Directorate of Operations, Shanghai Station.'

'I am not and have never been an employee of any organisation of that name.' Technically this was true. On his paperwork he was simply 'Government Servant'.

'Your lies are futile.'

'Your L's are excellent. Where'd you go to college?'

She continued to examine the file as he watched her. This was new to him. Just by her movements he could tell she'd spent time in the West. Her English was fluent and natural. The MSS he was used to was an all-male machine and Chinese ministerial paranoia dictated that all MSS agents had to be purebred products of the system, uncontaminated by pernicious outside influences. Family devotion to the Party was a prerequisite for admission, which meant they didn't necessarily get the best or the brightest. The only MSS women he knew of were either the clerical staff or the honey traps, run by a totally separate division to ensure no contagion spread to the core.

She continued to read from the big file.

'You have resided in Shanghai for six years following transfer from Afghanistan.'

'As I said, your English is excellent.'

'It's better than your Mandarin.'

'How would you know?'

He cleared his throat, and recited in Mandarin:

*'Who is lovelier than she?*

*Yet she lives alone in an empty valley.*

*She tells me she came from a good family*

*Which is humbled now into the dust ...'*

A small frown, otherwise her face was blank.

'Du Fu – "Alone In Her Beauty". I know the whole poem.'

He drew some satisfaction from the fact that his refusal to take this too seriously was irritating her.

'Do you realise how much trouble you are in?'

'I'm always in trouble.'

'Try not to brag.'

'I'll work on it. Is this going to take long?'

She ignored this and smoothed out the page in front of her.

'Recruited 1999, after flunking out of high school in Detroit.'

'It was no place for a young man of ambition.'

'Your principal concluded that your only memorable character traits were deceitfulness and a disregard for authority.'

'They always stood me in good stead.'

'You failed Basic Training at the Farm.'

'Actually I think they were threatened by my brilliance.'

'Your previous tour in Afghanistan was marked by controversy.'

'I think you skipped some of the good stuff there.'

She sighed heavily. Good, he was getting to her.

'Your purpose here is to lure citizens into the corrupt practice of betraying their country by stealing secrets in return for monetary gain. Do you deny it?'

Her exasperation was starting to show in her voice. She was new to this, he could tell. It was time to try another tack.

'Of course I don't deny it. It's what we both do, you know that.'

'In addition to being involved in espionage,' she said, her voice becoming shriller, 'you are a corrupt degenerate. You have been consorting with criminal elements. You are not only an embarrassment to your country but a menace and a danger to ours.'

It sounded like a textbook denunciation from the time of Mao's Cultural Revolution.

'Oh stop, you're making me blush.'

'Are you intoxicated?'

'Sadly not, but I could use a shot of something. What say we go on over to Danny Tang's and get—'

She slapped his face again, hard.

Her indignation seemed genuine. Either that or she was putting on a pretty good act for her superiors who might be watching, which in practice amounted to the same thing.

She opened a laptop, fired it up and turned it round to show him a video: a compilation of CCTV footage, the chase, first in Wu's car, then on foot and on the rooftops, all lovingly edited together like a trailer for an action movie.

'Nicely paced. Your leading man is quite a hunk, isn't he?'

'You caused thousands of yuan of criminal damage, committed violence against numerous other persons, showing a flagrant disregard for public safety—'

'I was fleeing for my life. If you examine the footage more closely – the unedited version – you might notice some of your comrade citizens were trying to kill me.'

'They are criminal degenerates with whom you had been consorting, presumably with the intention of procuring narcotics.'

'I don't do drugs: it's in my contract.'

'Or prostitutes.'

'I am happily, serially monogamous.' *Or I was.*

She raised a hand, as if stopping traffic.

'Agent Kovic, America may think it can trample all over other countries with impunity, leaving a trail of destruction and – chaos.' She took a deep breath and almost hissed into his face. '*Not China!*'

She paused, lowered her tone and rebooted herself.

'For the last six years your purpose here has been to lure citizens into the corrupt practice of betraying their country by stealing secrets in return for monetary gain. Your presence has been closely monitored and many of the traitors who have collaborated have been punished appropriately.'

It was true. Some of his more expendable sources had been found out, usually because they were careless with the money he paid them. Instead of being parsimonious, as it certainly was with its own salaried employees, the Agency allowed agents to be generous towards their assets, so he could splash out hundreds and even thousands of dollars on intel that was frequently low level or unprovable and sometimes obviously false.

He stared at her, puzzled. 'You know what? I don't think you really know why I'm here. I think you've been told to bring me in, but you don't know why. I think this whole interrogation is a sham. You've got your file and your video, but this is just a denunciation.'

She didn't move, didn't even blink, but her sudden stillness said it all. He was right. What did she know about the border incident? Did she even know he'd been there? Or about Vaughan's involvement with the demonstration, why he had had to run for his life?

'What do they want? I'll give it to you. I want to go home.'

She stared at him as if she was at a loss to know how to answer.

Kovic felt his patience running out. 'Look, where is all this going? Despite the chemically induced nap, I'm seriously tired. It's been an extremely long day and I'd like to go home and have that shower.'

She stood up and glared at him, a flicker of satisfaction lifting her expression. 'You are going to get your wish.' She closed the file.

'You are going home.'

It took a moment to sink in.

'You are booked on the Delta flight to Washington DC at 8.30 a.m. tomorrow.'

# 18

## French Concession, Shanghai

This had to be some kind of mistake. Cutler would have to intervene, smooth it out. Chinese agents in the US were frequently in trouble for crossing lines. But expulsion ... Surely this whole charade was just a slapped wrist. The metal door swung open and the two suited heavies from the Benz appeared and began to un-cuff him. One had his clothes in a plastic bag. The woman got up and started towards the door. Suit One hauled Kovic to his feet and started pulling off the jump suit.

He yelled after the departing interrogator.

'Hey! You can't do this without notifying the US Consulate.'

She turned and smiled thinly.

'We already did. Before we picked you up.'

Shit. Few things got to Kovic like the thought of going home. He wasn't ready. He had stuff to do.

'You have to allow them the opportunity to make a formal objection.'

'They confirmed no objection was being raised. Perhaps your behaviour today was an embarrassment. You seem to make trouble and draw attention to yourself wherever you go. Hardly the correct behaviour of even a mediocre agent. They must be very disappointed to have wasted all those tax dollars on your training.'

That cunt Cutler had hung him out to dry.

'You will be escorted to your place of residence where you will be permitted to collect essentials for the journey. Then you will be taken straight to Pudong airport and on to the flight for Washington DC. You will never return to China.'

This wasn't right. There were always deals to be done. Nothing was ever final and in Shanghai there was always the option of the

100

cash offer, even to the most upstanding zealot. Even on the tarmac, at the bottom of the airline stairs. He stared at her. She was resolute, something unflinching in her determined look, as if compromise had never been in her vocabulary. Perhaps his cover as a crap agent had been too convincing. She didn't know what he had.

'Can we talk?'

'We just did.'

She turned away and disappeared out of the room. The suits frog-marched him out and they retraced their steps to the Benz. This time they put him in the front passenger seat and cuffed him to the grab rail on the dash. They hovered outside the vehicle, smoking and spitting, splinters of their exchange floating towards the car.

'... *fucking Daddy's girl ...*'

'... *Chief was overruled, forced to take her on ...*'

'... *fuck up sooner or later and then ...*'

'... *back to Harvard ...*'

Kovic shut down his thoughts and strained to listen. Between bursts of sadistic laughter they swapped descriptions of the inde-cent acts they wanted to perform on their colleague.

'... *how much more I can stick ...*'

'... *like to stick it right up her, show who's boss.*'

They both thought this was hilarious, their blubbery chests shaking.

Kovic's mind went into hyperdrive. Maybe there was an arrange-ment he could come to with the suits to help them get rid of her, like if he escaped in such a way that it was her fault and he gave them some financial inducement; operatives at their level were always susceptible to a bribe. The lift doors opened and the woman strutted towards them.

They were back on the street. The clock in the Benz said 02.35. The woman was driving; the heavies were in the back. All Kovic's exhaustion from the day had been extinguished by the surge of adrenalin at the prospect of his fate. He had to think of some-thing, make something happen. He couldn't jump for it, but maybe he could head butt her and cause a traffic accident, create some mayhem, get free and make a run for it. The guys in back didn't have their belts on. A decent impact would deploy the airbags, but she'd be crushed by the guy behind.

Despite the late hour, the streets the traffic was solid. Even with the siren there was no way their path would clear. This city never slept. He looked at her behind the wheel, the men who hated her sitting in back. Was she really such a hard-ass? What had she done to deserve such hostility or was it just because she was a woman?

Then it came to him.

'Huang Shuyi.'

There was no reaction.

'Daughter of Han Zaiohong. Hannah to your friends in Cambridge.'

Two years earlier, Langley had forwarded a request from the FBI who were examining a group of students from Shanghai suspected of espionage. He had done some background checks. Two were part of a complex hacking operation that Kovic argued should be allowed to run in order to trace whoever they were working for. Huang Shuyi was one of them. They all shared a house in Cambridge, Mass. The Feds had bugged it but were having trouble deciphering their dialect. Kovic was asked to listen in. What he discovered was one of the household, a kid named Rai, had contracted AIDS. Much of their communication was about how to get him help without tipping off his family. The shame of exposure was literally a fate worth than death.

'I'm sorry for what happened to your friend at Harvard.'

Again no response.

'By the way, you should change the meatloaves on the back seat there. They were saying some pretty disgusting things about you back in the car park.'

They passed by People's Square. The protest was still going, with fewer people now, carrying traditional candlelit lanterns on poles.

'Looks like it isn't America's week.'

What did she really know about the border incident? He pressed on.

'Guess we really screwed that one up.'

She shrugged. 'American stupidity plays into the hands of reactionary elements.'

Interesting response, thought Kovic. 'Reactionary? Surely those kids are the true patriots.'

He had nothing left to lose; she had shone a tiny light into her own thoughts.

'I was there, on the border; the only one who survived. Your bosses must know that – how come they didn't tell you? Don't they trust you? That's probably the real reason why you're deporting me.'

She didn't answer. He had gone too far. His thoughts drifted away to his home. The stuff he had accumulated.

'Do I get to pack?'

'Just your hygiene requirements. The rest will be confiscated.'

He thought about Louise; they had parted on a bad note. He should at least say goodbye. Hell, she'd be better off without him, she had put up with so much. Without him she'd be able to get on with her life, get married, raise a couple of mortgages. He was just holding her back.

A couple of fire trucks whooshed past, sirens blaring. In the distance he could see a helicopter searchlight beaming down less than a mile ahead. Hannah swerved into their slipstream.

They were heading in the same direction, towards the French Concession. The way ahead was clearer now and she made a good job of keeping up with the emergency vehicles. If he could cause some kind of accident. This could be his last chance. When they stopped, whoever opened his door could be put out of action for a few moments but with all three of them it would be pretty hopeless. But as they got nearer the plan ceased to matter. The helicopter's searchlight was playing on a column of brown smoke funnelling up into the equally smoky night sky. It appeared to be coming from the area where he lived.

One of the suits spoke up.

'We should leave this – go straight to the airport.'

But Hannah didn't answer.

Fires weren't unusual in the French Concession. Cramped accommodation, the fashion for paper lanterns, the common proximity of laundry to gas rings and – even more popular – bad electrical connections with several appliances run off a single light socket all made the whole place a bonfire waiting to be lit. But this one was bigger than he had ever seen. Shanghai's firemen were notoriously inept when it came to dealing with domestic blazes and none too willing to risk their lives for some careless citizen who'd left the gas on.

Hannah pulled up a block short of the narrow street that led to his building. It was clogged with fire trucks, a large crowd pressed up against them, paying no attention to a cop shouting at them to disperse. The car door on his side now opened and one of the suits unlocked his cuffs from the dash. He should take advantage of the mayhem. But his desire to flee was fading, overtaken by curiosity and a rising sense of dread. It was now clear that the smoke was coming from his courtyard. As a clutch of firemen in hi-vis green jumpsuits were attempting to manoeuvre a ladder into the cramped space, a flash of flame shot into the air from an exploding gas canister. The firemen retreated.

Two policemen were restraining someone who was trying to enter the building. Kovic recognised him as Ren, the son in law of one of the old ladies. He was screaming and gesticulating wildly. The cops who were restraining him pushed him back and he fell, slipping on the paving that was awash with fire hose water.

This was his chance. He whirled round. One of the suits lost his grip and he slammed his free fist into the face of the other. Hannah gripped him by the collar with both hands but he knocked her sideways using all his weight. The crowd engulfed her. But he didn't run. Instead he threw himself at the gateway into the courtyard, kicking out at a cop who tried to tackle him, and dashed into the smoke. He could hear one of the old ladies screaming from one of the inner rooms. The door was jammed from the heat. Where the fuck were the firemen? Probably consulting the manual. He shouldered the door four, maybe five times before it gave, his lungs bursting, his eyes streaming. He plunged into the smoky darkness and tripped over a soft mound: his elderly neighbours, huddled together below the smoke.

'Get up. Come!'

He scooped up one of them but she could barely stand. He hitched an arm over his shoulder and dragged her forward as he reached for the other. Both of them collapsed back on to the ground. He bent low to take a lungful of the least smoky air just inches from the ground, then grabbed one of the women by the shoulders and dragged her out of the door and into the courtyard, coughing and yelling to the firemen to help. A group of them rushed forward as he dashed back through the door, retraced his steps and brought out the other woman who was now unconscious.

Through the smoke he glimpsed his own door. This morning he had locked it. Now it was open.

# 19

There was no question where the fire had started. Fires, like explosions, left telltale burn patterns that could be deciphered, ugly shapes he remembered all too well from his time in Afghanistan. It had started in his bedroom, right on his bed in fact, the remains of which still reeked of gasoline. Despite the cramped conditions, he was a hoarder of books and magazines, thanks to an old fashioned weakness for print on paper. This was deliberate. Someone had made a pyre of papers on the bed. Although the fire was out now, everything sodden from being hosed down, the base of the bed was still warm, the jet-black charred wood frame incongruously reminiscent of the glistening coat of his parents' black Labrador. Nothing much of the mattress remained. With mounting apprehension he parted the damp clumps of ash.

Most people would not recognise what he now saw. But Kovic wasn't most people. He had seen things that he was glad most people hadn't. He had entered freshly bombed and burned dwellings in search of crucial intelligence, methodically working through the pockets of the dead when their bodies, sometimes in pieces, were still warm, coolly focused on the job in hand, not thinking about the horror of what surrounded him. Today his head was in another place, not primed to receive the horrible truth of what he was now looking at.

He turned towards the scorched bedside table, and a pair of sunglasses, melted and fused with the surface as if they had been cooked on a hotplate. And something else caught his eye beside the table, on the floor, too low to have been caught by the flame and almost intact but for a scorch mark; side by side, bright as day, the earrings.

Louise had come back.

# 20

**Hotel Majesty Plaza, Shanghai**

Hannah refilled the glass. The Scotch seared his throat, then dulled the throbbing a little. Rage and remorse jockeyed for control of him.

He had let her escort him away. At first he had resisted, giving her the brunt of his rage at the horrific sight of Louise's remains. But all his strength and the will to resist had ebbed away.

'She always slept curled up right under the duvet. They must have shot first and not even bothered to check who was under.'

'Did she know about your work?'

He shook his head. 'But it was getting to be a problem, the sudden disappearances, changes of plan. It couldn't have lasted; things were coming to a head. She deserved better.'

Each of them had known the other had stuff they didn't want to unload. Louise was a fugitive from an unhappy life in London. Once in an idle moment, Kovic had started to run a character check on her. Langley demanded that 'significant others' were all vetted and declared. He was equipped to retrieve every email, all her phone history, every search she had made. But then he stopped; instead he submitted a whole load of data harvested from a stranger who roughly fitted her profile. She would choose when to tell him stuff, when she was good and ready. But now that would never happen. His life with her had existed in a compartment all of its own, completely separate from his work. Now one had spilled over into the other in the most lethal way.

Hannah, respectful of his grief, avoided eye contact.

'I am sorry for your loss and after your courage saving the two women—'

He cut her off with a wave of his hand.

She had taken him to a hotel and got a room for him where

he could shower. She sent one of the suits to get him some new clothes; his own were smeared with soot and stank of smoke. When he was cleaned up, instead of continuing the journey to the airport, she took him to the hotel bar. The goons were gone.

'I can't keep up. Few hours ago you were smacking me about, now I feel like I'm on some kind of … date. Is this a new MSS tactic?'

She was very still. The shrill patriot-dominatrix had been replaced by a more sombre persona.

'I am very sorry about your friend. Do you know who might have started the fire?'

He pulled a paper napkin towards him and made a sketch of the snakehead trident tattoo.

'Mean anything to you?'

She stared at it blankly.

'Why should it?

'You don't know Shanghai, do you?'

'It's where I live and work.'

'Yes, but you don't *know* Shanghai. It has many layers. This is a tattoo.'

She shrugged. 'We don't deal with gangsters; that's for the police.'

'But you're dealing with me.'

'You are a spy and therefore under my jurisdiction, even though you appear to be involved with criminal gangs.'

'In my world there's a fine distinction between involvement and running for your life.'

She was silent for some time, looking down into her Coke.

'You sure you don't want any Scotch?'

She shook her head, lost in thought. He stared at her until she met his eyes.

'Here's what I think you're thinking: behind all that righteous indignation about what I was saying being such a terrible slur on your proud Ministry et cetera, you're thinking – what's this guy on about? He's got no reason to be making this stuff up. Maybe he's on to something. Maybe he knows stuff I could do with knowing too, which could further my career.'

She showed no reaction to this, so he pressed on.

'You and I, we both want the same thing: stability and harmony between our countries. Without that the whole world suffers. China's come a long way since the Cultural Revolution. All those intellectuals, denounced by their own students, then sent out to break rocks to make them better Communists, that's all in the past. China's relationship with America is crucial to the future – and someone's trying to throw a wrench into it.'

Again, no reaction, but she was listening. He pressed on. 'We barely know each other – we've only just met. I guess in the MSS manual of how to deal with degenerate foreign spies, rule one is to deport them, ship them home, but that doesn't alter the fact that things are happening here which you appear not to even know about – which frankly doesn't say much for the state of your Ministry of State Security.'

'Why should I believe you?'

He gave her his version of the incident on the border. She was dismissive.

'An example of foolish imperialist aggression, typical of the arrogance of your leaders. China would never involve itself in such a mission.'

Kovic sighed. 'Ah, don't go all Little Red Book on me, just when we're starting to get along.'

'Why would they shoot the others and not you?'

'They didn't see me.'

'You're invisible?'

'I was under the snow. Look, this was billed as a joint mission, mounted from Chinese territory. I witnessed, with my own eyes, wounded suffering Americans pleading for their lives. Shot in the snow like dogs. By people from your side.'

'How do you expect me to believe any of this?'

'Take out your phone. Check out the border photos.'

She found the image that had been on the flier.

'This is supposed to have been taken on the North Korean side. See the flag; it's hanging westward so the wind is in the east. If you check the weather records for the last three days the wind had been coming from the west. That photo is taken on the Chinese side of the border. Someone in China set this up.'

She was silent, absorbing what he had told her.

He moved his glass to one side, put his elbows on the table and leaned forward.

'Whoever murdered Louise almost certainly thinks they killed me. They don't know they screwed up. You could put me on a plane home and wash your hands of me. But how are you ever going to find out the truth? And I'm never going to get to the bottom of who killed Louise. You saw her remains. I know you're a compassionate person because I know what you went through to help your friend in Cambridge. I go home tomorrow and you're going to be left sitting here, wondering what the hell just happened. And I'll bet your masters are going to want to bury this, just as mine do.'

Her eyes narrowed.

'What are you suggesting?'

He downed the contents of the glass.

'Don't send me home. Declare me dead. Let the CIA think I'm gone too. You've said yourself they'll probably be glad to be rid of me. Let me find out who did this and I'll share it all with you, whatever I discover.'

She looked at him, incredulous. Her mouth tightened so that her lips almost disappeared, her head slightly lowered.

'You're asking me to recruit – you?'

His pulse raced. Into the pause he poured all his hope.

'What makes you think I would trust you?'

'My bosses just cut me loose. They don't want me hanging around. Sending me home – you're doing *them* a favour. Why does Cutler want rid of me? Because I'm an embarrassment, because I don't toe the line, because he's probably sharp enough to know that if I stay, I won't sit by and pretend what I saw never happened.

'I thought most Americans hated China.'

'I'm not most Americans.'

At that moment there was a commotion at the entrance to the bar. A crowd of excited people thronged around a young man. Kovic saw Hannah's eyes widen a fraction then look away.

'Friend of yours?'

It was Jin Jié, the returning superstar that Wu had got all excited about on the TV in the bar. He was surrounded by bodyguards, but they weren't doing much to beat back his admirers who were either trying to photograph him with their phones or thrusting paper and pens at him for autographs. He paused, so they could all get what they wanted, and politely bade them farewell, then, seeing Hannah, detached himself from his companions and strode towards the table, arms wide.

'Hello, stranger.'

He beamed down at Hannah who could no longer ignore him. She smiled back – her face completely altered. She rose slightly. He pecked her on the cheek and she blushed.

His broad grin made him look even younger. He exuded vitality and youth, all of which made Kovic feel even more battered and tired. He bent, took Hannah's hand and kissed it, then turned to Kovic, expecting to be introduced but Hannah hesitated. Kovic put out his hand. 'Congratulations on the success of your book.'

'Why thank you,' Jin practically genuflected at the compliment, taking his hand and shaking his hand vigorously. Boy, could he exude enthusiasm.

'Seems like the timing of your return is most auspicious.'

He smiled. 'How so?'

'With this trouble between our two countries, maybe you can be a corrective.'

He nodded, digesting Kovic's words.

'Thanks – I'll give it some thought.'

He turned to Hannah. 'Don't disappear now I'm home. We've got so much to catch up on.'

They watched him go back to his crowd.

Kovic lifted his glass. 'The West loves him; that must piss off a few people here.'

She didn't respond.

'Good friend of yours? Bit high profile – thought you people preferred to creep about in the shadows.'

She looked a little sheepish.

111

'It is important to maintain contact with a broad spectrum of individuals.'

'That what it says in the manual? Then I'm honoured to be in such celebrated company.'

She fixed him with a firm glare. 'How will you manage?'

'I can call in some favours. Plus I've put a bit by in case of emergencies.'

She let out a deep sigh. 'I know I'm going to regret this.'

'We got a deal?'

'Bring me names. You have forty-eight hours.'

He put the last bit from the bottle into her glass.

'Let's drink to that.'

She got up.

'Better get started, don't you think?'

# 21

The rain lashed the deck, cutting visibility to no more than fifty feet. Beyond, the grey sea was completely obscured by the downpour. Garrison was waiting. He wanted to be there in person when the Sea Hawk made its descent. Above all he wanted the crew to see him out and about, on the case. This was no time to hide.

He heard the helo circling before it came into view. It hovered, the blades feathering before it dropped on to the apron in front of the control tower. The door opened. He knew CIA people came in all shapes and sizes. Just the way he descended the steps, cautiously, shielding his head from the rain, it was clear that Cutler wasn't a field man. The briefcase said it all.

Garrison took Cutler's arm and steered him to the stairs and straight up to his private suite where they could be alone. He would have preferred the formality of the command room and a table between them in case he needed to bang his fist on something – in the circumstances a distinct possibility – but all the systems were down and he didn't want to draw attention to it with a bank of blank screens.

Even so, Cutler was aware. 'Too bad about the glitch,' he said, as he shook off his damp raincoat.

Garrison shrugged. 'We should have it back up in a few hours.'

He handed him a coffee. In fact, he had no idea how long it would take. He needed to change the subject.

'It's good of you to make the trip.'

Garrison was genuinely surprised that Cutler had chosen to fly in personally. Agency people usually preferred to communicate electronically. Perhaps he felt some personally delivered TLC was necessary.

'The least I could do, under the circumstances.'

Cutler glanced around the room as if checking for microphones.

'I thought it best if we spoke privately.'

Garrison sat back as Cutler launched in.

'There's no getting around it. We fucked up bad.'

The novelty of hearing someone take responsibility almost put Garrison in shock, but he kept his face free of amazement; he'd had years of practice.

'Beijing and Washington are both putting a brave face on it but there's no question this is a game-changer.'

'Meaning?'

Cutler looked faintly irritated.

'The fallout! The Chinese people don't seem to like us as much as some of us thought.'

Cutler spread his hands as if carrying a giant tray.

Garrison reached for his coffee.

'So, how did you get it so wrong?'

Just because the guy was grovelling didn't mean he was going to get an easy ride.

Cutler took a deep breath and let it out slowly.

'I know this name has – uh, troubled you, before.'

Garrison sighed.

'Kovic.'

'If I'd had the slightest idea—'

The commander wafted his contrition away.

'That's in the past; let's concentrate on what just happened.'

Cutler sighed.

'The guy's been in-country six years. That's a long tour. Kind of plays with your perspective.'

Garrison looked at him for a while, then leaned forward.

'So let me get this right. You're saying—'

'Obviously I can only say so much, you'll understand.'

'He wasn't in the photographs.'

Cutler looked away, as if there was something he couldn't find the words for.

'Yeah, he survived.'

Garrison stiffened.

'You're saying he was complicit? Where is he now?'

Cutler's expression was grave.

'Well, he got back to Shanghai but – it seems it was all too much for him.'

'How so?'

'Looks like he chose to end it all.' Cutler stared into the distance, chewing his lips. 'In his residence, if you can call it that. Set fire to the place. I'd seen him that morning, told him I was standing him down, pending inquiries. And the Chinese wanted him out of the country. I think that was likely the last straw. Maybe what with everything that haunted him …'

He shot a meaningful glance at Garrison. '… it had all got too much to handle.'

'Son of a bitch.'

Garrison sat back and digested the news. What did he feel? Quiet satisfaction? No, nothing like that. A sense of justice having been done? That wasn't it either. Blankness – he just felt blank.

He studied Cutler's face.

'So can you take me through what actually happened? I don't want to be giving those Marines' families any bull.'

'We're working on the detail of it now. But without Kovic's input …'

His demeanour suddenly changed.

'But Commander, you have my word we will keep you in the loop. Whatever we come up with. But right now we've got one hell of a shitstorm coming our way: Shanghai's going crazy, protests against America; Beijing doesn't know which way to turn.'

He glanced at his watch.

'I want to thank you, Commander, for giving up the time to hear me out.'

He got to his feet. Garrison rose too.

'Well, I appreciate your taking the trouble to come all this way just to brief me – especially at this difficult time.'

They shook hands. Garrison saw him back to the Sea Hawk. Cutler used his briefcase to cover his head as he mounted the steps.

He gave the Commander a sort of apologetic salute as the door closed behind him.

Garrison watched the helicopter rise into the cloud and disappear. He stood there staring into the clouds. Whenever he was in conversation with Agency people Garrison could never shake the feeling that he was being played. Cutler had done all the right things, the personal visit, the admission, the contrition. But something else was going on, something he couldn't put his finger on.

# 22

**Hotel Majesty Plaza, Shanghai**

Kovic slept fitfully through what was left of the night and much of the next day, plunging into deep unconsciousness then being jolted awake by the images of Louise's remains. He'd seen dead people before, burned, shot, dismembered, detonated, and pretty much anything else that could happen to a person in a riot, insurgency, famine or war. But never someone close to him. He turned the TV and radio on low, to fill the room with noise and jam the memories while he slept. He had to rest. He would need all his energy and all his wits for what was ahead.

He surfaced at three in the afternoon, focused and horribly alive. A rainstorm had temporarily washed the air clean and the city stood out in high definition against a rare blue sky reflecting off the still slick pavements. He ordered room service and took a shower, trying to get rid of the persistent smell of smoke. Even afterwards, his hair still smelled singed.

He ate a traditional rice soup with eggs and dressed in the kit that Hannah's goons had got him. They fitted. Maybe they had his measurements on file. Courtesy of Hannah, he had the room for one more night. What happened after that – who knew?

For Louise he felt a kind of numb grief, but at least the memory of her was part of who he was, or had once been, the man inside Kovic, who joined the Agency with a good deal more hope for the human race than he had now. But with everything else destroyed, he was in a vacuum. He was used to being other people, had inhabited eight different aliases in his life so far. But now, hollowed out by the madness of the last three days, he felt like no one at all. On the up side, he was officially dead, which for his purposes couldn't have been more ideal. The question almost amused him: now that he was dead, how long could he stay alive?

He dived into a VW Santana taxi and headed for the Hong Kong & Shanghai Safety Deposit Company. By now word would have gotten back to Cutler either that he had been successfully deported, or that he had died in the fire. Whichever he believed, it meant the CIA wasn't about to go looking for him and getting in his way, at least not right away. And with the trident boys thinking that they'd nailed him in his bed, he had more than a good head start. All the same, the less time he spent on the streets the better.

He got the driver to stop first at a luggage store, where he bought a standard white collar salaryman's 'Dream' briefcase, then at the side entrance of the bank, where he moved quickly through the revolving doors, the lobby and up to the security desk. He picked up a pad, wrote a name and a number on it and passed it to the blank-faced assistant. It helped that he didn't have to say anything, and that they didn't want him to. Coming from a world of *And just how are you today, sir?* and 'knowing your customer', the absence of grovelling was always a relief. Give me Chinese service industry surliness any day, he thought.

The assistant took the pad and directed him to the eye scanner that boasted an error rate at one in ten million. But since China had a population of one point four billion maybe it was just as well they also required a palm scan, plus a good old-fashioned signature.

A minute later he was riding the elevator deep into the bowels of the bank. Another attendant met him at the lift door, handed him a key and pointed him to the wall of slim metal doors. He inserted the key, opened the door and slid out the shallow, drawer-shaped box. Just as a final touch he had added his own double combination padlock. He was shown to a small curtained cubicle with a chair and a small desk where he could lift the lid in privacy.

'Hello, John Richards.'

John Richards' passport photo did have him looking a bit younger, less frayed; a man who hadn't yet had to look on the charred corpse of his lover. But then Americans seemed to age faster in Shanghai; maybe the pollution eroded their collagen, and deciphering the two or three thousand characters needed even to read a news report screwed their eyes.

He pulled out another: Ray Nyman, South African, physical instructor. His current physique may not have quite fitted the bill but at least his scars did. And now was not a great time to be an American in China. He decided to take both, together with their matching drivers' licences. Into his Dream case also went a fat wad of around a million yuan, nearly two hundred thousand US dollars and two debit cards, from Deutsche Bank and Credit Agricole: nice solid European institutions, each with a deposit behind them of fifty thousand dollars. Underneath those was a Sig Sauer P220 Combat TB with a couple of clips. Kovic hadn't had much need of a weapon since he hit Shanghai, nor had Langley authorised him to keep one, but he had added it to his kit when a friend in the ATF skipped town in a hurry and left it in a drawer. He knew if he didn't help himself someone else would, and the day might just come when he would need it. Today was that day, and probably tomorrow was too, and beyond that – maybe forever, who knew?

Even in the Tribal Area badlands of the Af–Pak border or on the mean streets of Baghdad, Kovic had had the comfort of knowing he was part of a machine, that the CIA would watch his back, and even when he got into deep shit, even though they might deny all knowledge of him, they would try to get him out. Now there was no one. Never in his whole time in the game had he felt like a fugitive. And yet this wasn't the US or Lebanon or Afghanistan. Packing a weapon in Shanghai could land you in big trouble. He held it in his hand. It was comforting. He felt in the drawer for the suppressor and screwed it into place. It wouldn't make that *foof* sound that Hollywood liked, but it would turn the volume down from an ear-splitting crack to something that wouldn't frighten the horses. He checked the clips: standard eight rounds. Okay to be going on with.

The phone still had some charge in it. The service provider was Hong Kong registered, a popular one with private security operatives as it automatically erased the call log and couldn't store contacts. It was a device that required the user to have a good memory. Fine: he wasn't planning on organising a party with it.

He put it all into the briefcase and headed for the exit. John Richards, aka Ray Nyman, was on his way.

Wu was waiting for him, parked across the street in his cousin's pickup. Kovic examined the badge and burst out laughing.

'For real that's what it's called, a Great Wall *Wingle?*'

Wu's face was blank, his humiliation complete.

'Guess you won't be bringing one of these with you to America.'

The Chinese might be on their way to making more cars than anywhere else, but they had a way to go with naming them.

Kovic got in and turned the radio on low: a traditional music station, playing classic songs for the older generation.

'No, no, I got Springsteen. Or you want James Brown? "Sex Machine"?'

'Really. This is okay. So, what do you know?'

'That there was a fire in your building. I was relieved to get your call. I thought maybe you—'

He told him about Louise. Wu looked horrified.

'I don't know what to say.'

'So if I come over a little vengeful you'll know why.'

'You think it was—?' He patted the back of one hand with three splayed fingers like the trident.

Kovic shrugged.

'Fire up the Wingle; we need to go find ourselves a posse.'

The pickup's cab smelled of brand new plastic.

'Where do you want to start?'

'By getting rid of this smell. Open the windows, for God's sake, and let the smog in.'

# 23

Kovic sat on the roof terrace of the Wooden Box cafe, waiting. It seemed an appropriate venue for a dead man. He'd had enough bad coffee for one day so stuck with green tea. Wu sat at another table by the door, keeping watch. The blue sky had gone and purple grey cumulus was rolling in over the city like a giant roof, pressing the day's pollution back down on its inhabitants. Maybe he should take up smoking again, just to give his lungs a change of poison.

Kovic stared at the table in front of him until he became aware of a presence, lingering nearby.

'Hey, don't sneak up on me like that, okay?'

Zhou's eyes almost disappeared, enveloped by his grin.

'Sneak up on the spy!'

His gaspy laugh was straight out of *Beavis and Butt-Head*; that and the grin were his only distinguishing features. Otherwise, he prided himself on his blandness; when his face was still it became impossible to remember. It was a brilliant cover, especially for a burglar. Zhou had done Kovic's dirty work for several years, specialising in theft and safe breaking, which he conducted with meticulous care bordering on the obsessive. Frequently his victims never realised they had had an intruder, believing they had mislaid the missing items themselves or blaming family members or staff. Most of his jobs were carried out in broad daylight. 'By day I am much less conspicuous,' he explained to Kovic.

The suit he had on was an anonymous grey, but Kovic could tell it was seriously expensive.

'Tailor made in Savile Row. I flew there specially.'

'Maybe you should slow down.'

A thief since he could walk, Zhou had grown up on the streets of

Shanghai after his parents abandoned him to avoid the punitive fine for having more than one child. First he stole to survive, developing such a gift for it that he soon graduated to ever more sophisticated and daring thefts, culminating at the age of twelve in spending weeks studying how to fly online and stealing a light aircraft. He crashed the plane, but managed to escape from the emergency services by feigning concussion. Briefly, he worked for casino owners, stealing money from their own safes so they could avoid taxes. But after a bloody argument over his rate he resolved never to work for criminals again. He came into Kovic's life when they chose the same moment to break into a Singaporean arms dealer's penthouse. Kovic had set off the alarm and Zhou switched it off. From then on he outsourced that part of his work to Zhou, who also proved to be an expert at scaling buildings, as well as claiming to have an inbuilt sonar-like sixth sense for infrared motion sensors.

Kovic told him about what he had in mind to begin with.

'There will be more once we've achieved stage one.'

Zhou shrugged. 'Sounds good to me.'

'Beyond that it may turn ugly. I think the people I'm going up against may make life very hard for us. You going to be okay with that?'

The *Beavis and Butt-Head* laugh suggested he was.

# 24

Vaughan's eyes fluttered open, closed, then opened again – wide. He jerked his head to the left, but there was no sign of – what was his name? A blond anyhow. He was supposed to stay the whole night, that was what he had paid for. But the boy appeared to have untied himself and gone. Something wasn't right. He could hear music drifting from the ambient entertainment module under the window. 'Strangers in the Night', it sounded like. Sinatra? This wasn't on his playlist. He felt for his glasses: not there. He reached further for the remote that controlled the light and pressed it, but nothing happened. Something gripped him by the wrist.

'Allow me,' said a disembodied voice.

The lights in the room glowed and brightened. Vaughan twisted his head round to glimpse a blurred face inches from his. Another hand brought his glasses on to his nose and Zhou's face came into sharp focus. How could this be happening? His security system was state of the art. Then he saw another face – one he recognised instantly but hadn't expected to see ever again.

'Jesus Christ.'

'Not quite, though we are both risen from the dead.'

'Steig!'

His voice was hoarse. He had been sleeping with his mouth open again.

'Steig's taking a nap,' Kovic explained from the sofa.

The improbably named Steig, a Thai boxer, was curled up in a foetal position by the bathroom door. Wren and Sparrow, the other two members of Vaughan's security detail, were conscious, trussed together by Wu with thin wire round their necks. Very painful, even just to swallow, he had warned them, before stuffing their mouths with some of Vaughan's socks. Vaughan tried to raise his head but Kovic pressed it down.

'What have you done with the boy?'

'How touching to see your chivalry hasn't deserted you. He's on her way to his next appointment. I gave him an extra fifty for the nasty marks your chains made. You really are a nasty little pervert, Victor.'

Vaughan's indignation suddenly rose to the surface.

'You've got a bloody nerve, you know.' His jowls shook when he spoke.

Kovic smiled.

'Yes, I know. So! Let's pick up where we left off in your office, before we were inconveniently interrupted by – let's see, a car chase, arson and murder.'

Vaughan's face was now a deep red.

'Look here, I haven't the foggiest idea—'

Behind the bluster, Kovic could read his fear.

'Your people forgot to look under the bedclothes. That was my girlfriend you murdered and torched.'

Vaughan's voice rose half an octave.

'I can assure you I had nothing to do with it. I don't even know what you're talking about.'

Kovic got up and sat on the edge of the bed, closer. Vaughan saw something shiny catch the light, something shiny and pointed. Zhou and Wu held him while Kovic laid the knife against Vaughan's upper lip, the blade resting on the inner edge of his left nostril.

'Who hired you?'

Vaughan blinked several times but did not reply.

'Perhaps you didn't hear me.' Kovic bent closer. 'Who hired you, you upper-class paedo cunt?'

'Look, I don't know anything. I'm not – I'm not important, you know that.'

'It's a pretty good job they did, excellent reconstruction.' He glanced at Zhou. 'Silicon septum wrapped in skin from the thigh or upper arm; sorts out the ravages of early cocaine use. He was a bit of a wild boy in his youth, weren't you, Victor?'

Kovic pressed the blade a little; a millimetre more and the septum would come away from its moorings.

There was a girlish scream from the bed, followed by the honeyed tones of Ol' Blue Eyes.

'Think we've exhausted the Sinatra, now we've all got to know each other. Take your pick, Wu.'

Wu found a remote and skimmed through the selection before settling on a robust house beat.

'Please! I beg you!' Vaughan was hyperventilating now, in danger of passing out. Kovic moved back.

'Please, there must be something – we could help each other!'

The words tumbled out in an undignified babble, the urbane imperiousness of their previous meeting long gone.

'I mean I didn't really want the job; it's not what I do, you know that. Though it wasn't really a *job* – it was more a favour than anything. You know how it is here, you get into these situations, they run rings round us Westerners. Before you know what's going on, you've agreed ... they're so *tricky*.'

Kovic glanced at Zhou, his expression showing a flicker of amusement at the Englishman's frantic explanation. He glanced at his watch.

'We really need to get moving. Got to cut this short, I'm afraid.'

Two things Kovic had learned about torture. If you're going to use it, get on with it. Spin it out and they start making stuff up. Databases in Langley groaned with interminable, improvised confessions, admissions and denunciations, the product of long drawn out 'enhanced interrogations'.

He pressed the blade down again. Blood spurted from Vaughan's nose. He tried to move his hands but Wu had tethered them with wire.

'Shall we try a name?'

Vaughan tried to swallow.

'It, well, it's not that easy to say. It's all done through intermediaries; you know how it is. You never know who's behind who. Chinese whispers, and all that.'

Kovic looked wearily at Zhou, who rolled his eyes theatrically. Kovic turned away.

'Guy's a time waster. Unzip him from the nose down.'

'No, no! Please!' Vaughan's eyes bulged and his whole body shook violently, his protests slurred by the blood running into his mouth.

'Oh God, no. Please. If we … if … could your government guarantee my safe passage? In return for my cooperation?'

You had to hand it to the guy. Even in his darkest hour, his chutzpah never failed him.

'I think, let's see – oh yeah, the murdered Marines might somewhat count against you.'

'Look, all we did was prepare the artwork and arrange the protest. The rest – that was—'

'I'm about to take apart your face. What name can you be so scared of coming up with?'

His mouth was open, trembling.

'Tsu Yuntao.'

Kovic repeated the name, and looked at Zhou and then Wu. It meant nothing to them.

He moved the knife from under Vaughan's nose and placed the point just under his bulging left eye. It would have given him some grim satisfaction to continue, but he knew he'd be wasting it on the wrong man.

'There, that wasn't so hard.'

Kovic lifted the knife away, wiped the blade on the pillow and slipped it into Vaughan's pyjama pocket.

'In case you want to slash your wrists after we're gone. Where will I find Tsu?'

'Please believe me when I say I don't know. Where Tsu's concerned the less one knows the better.'

Kovic reached over and switched off his recorder.

'When I find him, which I will, I'll make sure he gets a copy of this.'

Vaughan's voice was practically soprano. 'Please! I gave you what you came for. Have some mercy, for God's sake.'

'I'm all out of mercy. We need a location.'

Kovic nodded to Zhou who pulled off the quilt. In the king-sized bed Vaughan looked diminished, deflated by fear and the loss of his prime characteristic, his hubris. He sat up in the patch of his own urine and tried to dab his nose with his sleeve.

'Can you at least take off the wire? Please?'

China's a big country. Where is your client?'

Kovic led Vaughan towards the open window. He undid the wire and put a hand on his shoulder.

'Where?' he whispered.

'Look – there's no point. You'll never get to him. He's up in the mountains somewhere.'

'China has a lot of mountains. Which ones?'

I don't know! He operates remotely – never appears.'

A wisp of breeze rippled the curtains.

'We'll see you out,' said Kovic.

Vaughan looked from one to the other.

'What? What d'you mean?'

Kovic nodded at the open window.

'They say most people black out before they hit the ground.'

# 25

Qi Linbau's operations room was concealed behind his father's stationery store. Access was via the kitchen and through a narrow door that looked as though it led to a latrine but opened on to a very steep and lopsided wooden stairway. At the top was what looked like a dead end – a slab of metal. Kovic mounted the stairs as far as they went and gave a half wave. Qi's voice floated out of an unseen speaker.

'You're supposed to be dead.'

'So I heard.'

The metal door slid back and revealed a cross between a TV studio gallery and an electrician's workshop. Qi was facing a bank of screens, some of which were filled with numbers, others that played soundless newsfeeds. He twirled round and grinned.

'In trouble again.'

'No more than you.'

'Is this the day?'

'What day?'

'The one you turn me over.'

Kovic laughed.

'Oh no, we're not done. How dead am I exactly?'

Qi gestured at his screens.

'MSS internal communiqué; the same message was conveyed via police to the US Consulate but not listing you as CIA, just US public servant. Someone covering your tracks?'

Hannah had come good. At least no one would be on his tail – for now.

'What do you need from me?'

There was a wary look in Qi's eye. Kovic guessed he was fretting

128

that his CIA handler's sudden change of status – from alive to dead – could mean the same for him, only for real. It wasn't the Chinese authorities that were after Qi, it was the Americans.

'How about you make us some coffee and I'll tell you what I need.'

Qi slid off his revolving stool and moved towards a brand new coffee maker and began spooning beans into it.

To the intelligence community in the US Qi was only known as *Armistead*, the notorious international cyber terrorist who had harvested vast quantities of US Government data for Chinese Intelligence, yet couldn't be traced. It wasn't even confirmed that he was operating out of China. What particularly got to Washington was that he had also hacked into the White House's electrical system, causing lights to go on and off at unscheduled times, creating not only chaos but widespread embarrassment. The magnitude of Washington's indignation at this breach was out of all proportion to the crime. When Kovic narrowed *Armistead*'s location down to 'somewhere in Shanghai', Langley granted Kovic leave to have him 'neutralised' if and when he tracked him down.

Qi had covered his tracks so well that finding him would have been impossible but for the carelessness of his MSS handler. Kovic traced the harvested material to a middle ranking MSS operative who had failed to appreciate the quality of his work and simply filed it on a database where another of Kovic's assets inside the MSS found it, and therefore was able to identify who put it there. After that it was simply a matter of keeping the handler under surveillance until he hooked up with Qi.

This could have been the coup that made Kovic's career. But the more Kovic looked into Qi the more he realised that it would be far better to leave him in place, but turn him and put him to his own use. Kovic laid on a discreet 'bust' that wouldn't come up on the MSS radar, but was heavy enough to convince Qi that he was toast if he didn't cooperate. Langley should have appreciated this opportunity, but such was the ill feeling towards *Armistead* in Washington that Kovic decided to keep him under the radar and made out that he was still on the loose.

'This is the deal; I cut you loose – for good after this one last job. But it's a big one, likely to be dangerous, and may involve some travel.'

Qi came towards him with a coffee. He was painfully thin, his chest concave, the tips of his collarbone poking up in his too-big *Family Guy* T-shirt. A wisp of beard hung from his chin like an unswept cobweb, and his upper lip had sprouted the beginnings of an adolescent moustache. His high cheekbones and heavy lidded eyes betrayed his Mongolian heritage.

'The prison diet's not done you any favours.'

Luckily, a recent spell in jail had not blown his cover. Kovic took a sip of his coffee. It was unexpectedly good.

'I thought you people hated the stuff.'

'I've been shorting coffee futures; thought I should sample the product.'

'Enjoying your freedom?'

'I made some good contacts in jail. They put me with a bond fraudster from the Shenzhen Stock Exchange. Very interesting. While we were inside we bought and sold five million acres in Wyoming. I like to keep my hand in. Plus it kept the boredom at bay.'

'Did you do well?'

Qi shrugged.

'Go on, how much did you lose?'

'It wasn't my money.'

'Because you don't have any.'

Theoretically Qi's online expertise should have made him a yuan trillionaire, except that it was the chase that interested him, rather than the money.

'Honestly. Did you make a single buck?'

'Not really, but it was a good challenge – we did it all from a guard's mobile phone.'

It was on a job for Kovic that Qi got busted. He hired him to help peel open the inner workings of an arms dealer's online transactions with a terror group based in Bali. Qi had hacked deep into their business, posing as a customer and then making a payment with a worm embedded in the code that burrowed deep inside their offshore bank accounts and sucked out all their assets. But the arms dealer's network spread into the procurement section of the Chinese Ministry of Defence, and in order to save face the MoD's investigators needed a scapegoat. Qi was pressured to take the rap. To soften the blow, Kovic arranged for a large sum of the seized assets to be channelled into Qi's family's stationery business. The CIA didn't know it but it was technically the proud owner of Wanjoo Paper and Card Supplies of Shanghai.

The coffee grinder shattered the eerie soundproofed silence. For his work the structure had to be both bombproof and surveillance proof.

'Okay, so where do I start?'

'Yesterday I left one of your chewing gum receivers in an office in the Jin Mao Tower. It'll have picked up all kinds of crap but I want anything that locates a guy named Tsu Yuntao.'

He jotted down Parnham Vaughan's address and then sketched out the trident-flaming fist tattoo.

'What's that?'

'I want to know what the significance of this tattoo is and how it connects with Tsu.'

Qi shrugged, as if he'd just been asked to pick up some dry cleaning.

'That it?'

'I want to know everything about him, where he operates, who his associates are, what his assets are, where they are – and how I find him. And when you've located him, I'll need all the security data on getting under his radar, how he opens his doors, who gets in and when.'

'No problem. And then what you going to do?'

'I'm going to go and meet him, and then probably I'll kill him. Okay?'

Qi stared at him.

'You okay?'

'Sure, why not?'

Kovic dictated his new phone number then got to his feet.

'One more thing; I need this guy's private cell number. You should find it somewhere in the Pentagon's HR database.'

He picked up a pad and wrote down: Commander Garrison, USS *Valkyrie*.

# 26

Huang Shuyi, Hannah to her friends but not her family, waved to her father, stepped out of her family home off Fudan Road and walked towards her Mercedes.

'Be careful, it's not good out there.'

The old man had a sixth sense about trouble. He had been glued to the TV watching reports of the protests. 'Just keep it down today.'

She knew what he meant. Ever since she had come back from America he had worried about her manner, her new-found tendency to argue back, to forget her place.

'Just for your own good,' he told her. 'There are times and places where cosmopolitan behaviour is inadvisable.'

The only result of this advice was to turn her into a grumpy teenager all over again. 'Cosmopolitan behaviour' was his euphemism for assertiveness, for treating men as equals, doing all the things she'd gotten used to in America, things that came naturally to her now. She had changed. She wasn't going back.

But she could also tell by the way he looked at her that he knew something else was wrong. Part of her wished she had confided in him about her encounter last night but she didn't dare. Her disobedience would have frightened him.

What had she been thinking? How had this rough edged, beaten up, probably alcoholic, seemingly failed CIA agent with a gift for Mandarin persuaded her to disobey her masters? She must go and explain to the director, take responsibility for her actions before he found out. She had turned him, she would explain, *he's my asset now*. Surely he would be impressed.

But now she was starting to regret the whole thing. She should wash her hands of Kovic.

She opened the door and climbed behind the wheel. She felt better inside the car. It was her own private APC and an instrument of rebellion. She refused to go around in the government-issue Cherys. All of them smelled of disinfectant with a hint of body fluids that had more to do with their misuse as mobile fuckstops than any actual espionage. She took out the key.

Something wasn't right.

There was someone in the rear-view mirror – Kovic.

'I thought you might want an update.'

She whirled round.

'How the fuck did you get in here?'

'One of my people, he's good with locks.'

'Why—?'

'I wanted to catch you before you got to the Golfball, in case you had a change of heart.'

'What makes you think I would?'

'Because it would be entirely understandable.'

He rubbed his eyes. Hannah thought he looked like he had had no sleep.

'And because it's getting uglier out there. Just this morning some guys jostled me off the sidewalk.'

'Do you mind if I drive? I'm late.'

'Sure, go ahead, you can drop me at Chifeng Road Station. I've got a name for you.'

'What is it?'

'Tsu Yuntao.'

Kovic observed no reaction other than a mild flicker of recognition.

'So you've heard of him. You're ahead of me there.'

'I didn't say I had.'

'Come on, Hannah, we're both trained at this. What do you know about him?'

'All I know is that he runs a private security operation for public figures.'

'Jin Jié's?'

'No, Jin Jié prides himself on no bodyguards. It's part of the image he likes to project.'

'Well tell him he needs to be careful. Some of this anti-America shit may rub off on him since he's such a hit over there.'

Kovic fixed his eye on her in the rear-view mirror.

'Is our deal still good? I worried it mightn't seem such a good idea to you in the cold light of day.'

She didn't want to give him the satisfaction of knowing he had read her mind.

She took a deep breath.

'No, no, we're still good.'

The Metro stop came into view.

'I'll update you when I know more.'

He opened the door and was gone.

# 27

'You want my advice?'

'No, just the information.' Kovic was impatient. Time was passing.

Qi looked at Wu and Zhou and then back at Kovic.

'Go home. Now. On the next plane.'

Kovic smiled at the idea. Qi let the tablet he was waving as a fan drop out of his hand. He clutched his head.

'You're playing with fire, man. Nobody crosses this guy, not even the most powerful.'

Kovic signalled with a finger for him to shush.

'Duly noted. Now, just gimme the facts.'

Qi sighed. He had lost a good few battles with Kovic before and knew when to quit. Kovic also knew that Qi loved nothing better than to be the oracle, especially in front of an audience. For a solitary hacker he was surprisingly gregarious.

'C'mon, do your stuff. You know you want to.'

'First of all Tsu is not technically Chinese. He was born in America but don't get the impression he has any attachment to the stars and stripes, except when he wipes his ass with it.'

'Interesting. Keep going.'

'His father took off for LA in the late 1940s after getting caught on the wrong side of the Revolution. He did good there – became a big fish in Chinatown. Tsu grows up with every luxury, wanting nothing, but he's a loner, incapable of bonding with family or friends. He's given a hard time at the flashy school he's at, so he starts exhibiting anti-social traits that even by his father's standards are way out of order. He doesn't target the bullies themselves, he goes for their *mothers*. Believe me when I say you won't want to know the details. LAPD called it aggravated rape, but for what he did that's a hell of a euphemism. Before the cops could connect the crimes, dad sends son into exile – to Shanghai. Timing couldn't have been better. He arrives in 2000, just as things are taking off. So he tries to revive his dad's old gang.

'The trident part of the tattoo.'

'Correct. He tracks down sons of his father's fellow gang members, but what they're into, the traditional stuff – armed robbery, racketeering, extortion, smuggling, drugs trafficking, gambling, prostitution – is old hat to him. Then he gets a visit from an old guy who says he belongs to something called the Flaming Fist.'

'I know about those guys, they were Mao's super-secret guard.'

'They were all old, but having been part of the party apparatus they had great contacts and had been both feared and revered even by big deal politicos. The Fist guy gives Tsu a better idea. Being raised in America Tsu already knows all about wealth, understands what comes with it, how complicated it makes people's lives. Fist guy tells him how they kept Mao's people in line, while seeming to offer them protection.'

Wu raised his hand as if he was in class. 'You're talking home security, right?' He pointed at Zhou, 'To stop people like him.'

'There isn't anyone else like me,' Zhou said reproachfully.

'Security – but at a much more sophisticated level. What's the point of being worth a fortune if you're scared the whole time someone's going to steal it from you? Paranoia is a major headache for Shanghai's new super rich. So Tsu, the son of a criminal, pioneers the business of crime *prevention*. He offers a twenty-four-seven three-hundred-and-sixty-degree service to Shanghai's first generation millionaires – he supplies their drivers, their minders, their housekeepers, people to walk their dogs, take the kids to school. He sources them their home security systems, and has them wired up to a central command centre that monitors properties, cars, secret apartments for the mistresses round the clock. But the twist is by doing this he gets to know *everything* about them. Very fucking powerful. If he wants he can control their lives. And because he's cornered the market, no one dare do without him. And don't even think of terminating your contract.'

Kovic shook his head.

'A private secret police; how come I'm hearing this for the first time?'

'Because what Tsu also learned from the Fist guy was the advantage of invisibility. It's like a secret society. Gangs are all about making noise, cool wheels, turf wars. Tsu's the opposite. He's not really in it for the money, just the power.'

'So answer me this, what's he doing getting involved in a border skirmish with North Korea?'

Qi shrugged.

'Pass.'

'Why is there no visibility? Is he some kind of a recluse?'

'Correct. Only if there's something messy to be done he sometimes appears. He likes to show his guys who's the toughest. He gets off on it.'

Kovic let out a long breath. 'That might be his weakness.'

They all looked at him.

'Suggests he's not got complete control of his blood lust. It could work against him.'

He glared at them. No one looked convinced.

'Just an idea. So Qi, where did you get all this?'

'I pulled it off an archived MSS file I harvested. The guy who wrote it was a counter-terrorism officer – he was poisoned the week after he submitted it. His replacement wisely filed it away on his first day and no one's touched it since. That was three years ago.'

'And where do we find him?'

'We?'

'I did warn you.'

Qi touched his head with his hands, as if holding his brain in.

'No, no, no. You don't get it. He missed you on the border – his men came after you here in the city. They burned your house down and your woman.'

'Lucky then that he thinks I'm dead.'

'He finds out you're not, he'll go on and on and on until he gets you.'

'No, I'm going to him. Show me where he hangs out.'

Qi turned to his screens.

'You won't find it on Google Earth.'

He punched up a page that said *this image is no longer available.*

'He's had all the photographs deleted or destroyed, except for this one I found from 1992 which was incorrectly catalogued. Here.'

He tapped his keyboard. A grainy image in monochrome appeared on the screen. It wasn't so much a mountain as a giant funnel of rock, as if something molten had burst through the earth's crust, soared upward, and then frozen. Qi enlarged the picture. The base and the surrounding hills were covered in thick forest. At the summit was a wall and behind it a few buildings that looked like ruins.

'This isn't much help.' Kovic's fuse was particularly short today, he noticed.

Qi held up a hand, like a medieval messenger with important news from the front.

'Behold.' He tapped away and the huge screen above his desk sprang into life to reveal a satellite image of forested mountains threaded with sinews of cloud.

'The Huangshan mountains: three hundred miles from Shanghai as the missile flies.'

Seven hours' drive.

Qi magnified the image.

'The structure was a martial arts school dating back to the fifth century. It carried on right up to the 1920s when it was briefly occupied by a warlord. Most of the wooden part was destroyed in a battle with a rival, after which it was rebuilt by monks. But in the Cultural Revolution it was attacked again, this time by Red Guards who hung the monks on long ropes from the edge with signs round their necks proclaiming their supposed crimes against the state. They used them for propaganda films – it's the only moving footage of the rock.'

He hit a key and another screen lit up. The scratched monochrome footage showed three of the unfortunate monks as birds pecked at them.

'That's a bad omen,' said Wu.

'Never mind that, check out the ladder going up to the top.'

Kovic got off his stool and pointed. 'See?'

He punched up two more pictures, stills taken from the ground. Just visible through the foliage was an immensely long, thin bamboo ladder with two ant-like figures making their way up it.

'Who took these?'

'Someone on a student exchange programme, thirty years ago. They produced a magazine. Guess what it was called? *Open China*. Funny, huh?'

None of them spoke. They could all guess what was in his mind and hoped they were guessing wrong.

Another screen lit up. Qi moved a small wand on his control panel. The image zoomed on the pillar of mountain growing out of a sea of cloud. Tsu's lair from above.

'Nice. How are we seeing this?'

'A Russian weather satellite. I've overridden the controls. The guys in Vladivostok just think it's a power failure – pretty common with their equipment, so they won't even think it's abnormal.'

'It looks different.'

'The walls have been rebuilt and a whole new complex added under a layer of shrubs, a lot of it carved out of the rock. The court-yard serves as a helipad. See the Z-8?'

Just visible was the shape of a large military helicopter.

'Whose is that?'

'Registered to a cargo firm in Guam. He doesn't directly own any aircraft.'

Qi moved his cursor in a circle over an area where the foliage was even denser.

'He has a staff of twenty running it, but there's room for another fifty so it's much bigger than it looks. Then his own quarters have space for six guests. There's a separate kitchen, pool, gym and hydroponic vegetable garden. Up there he can cut himself off from the rest of the world. It's got a dedicated hydroelectric power source and they stock enough food for a year. It's like a space station, basically, but on Earth.'

'Who uses the guest quarters?'

'Not known. This is a log of all helicopter flights in and out over the last six-week period. Doesn't tell us a lot as there are no registrations captured, but they are all big fat privately registered Z-8s. Since the only way in is by air it could just be supplies.'

'Is this for real? Or has he just been watching too much James Bond?'

'This is real all right. He controls everything from here. He has a private satellite channel, a dedicated private cellphone network that only connects with his people. He has direct personal contact with all his people on the ground. They are his eyes and ears. When they meet clients they have receivers so he can hear the conversations and he can give them orders in real time. When you work for Tsu, you are never alone. He's always in your earpiece. You go off air, you're toast. He sends another man in to replace you.'

'Can we listen in, get a feel for him?'

'Sure, if you've got six weeks to spare. He uses a different encryption every day – never the same sequence twice in a year. There are 365 of them; by the time I've cracked one, he's moved on to another. He's also got a further communication set-up with an entirely alien set of protocols.'

'Can you describe it?'

'Other than it looks like a jamming signal, just a fog of interference, it lasts less than a second so it can't be captured and examined, it just dissolves into the ether. But here's a thing. Twenty-four hours ago, a radio operator on the USS *Valkyrie* forwarded a dispatch to the NSA in Fort Meade reporting an identical signal coming from guess where?'

Kovic felt his pulse quicken.

'The North Korean border?'

Qi nodded. 'And coming right into China.'

Kovic got to his feet. 'He's our man then, no question. When shall we start?'

Each one was frozen in their place as if time had stuttered to a halt. Kovic patted Zhou's shoulder.

'Zhou, you've gotten in to some unusual places.'

He looked at Kovic, incredulous. 'You want to actually go there?'

'That's where he hangs out.'

Kovic's gaze moved to Wu. 'After yesterday, I think you're ready.'

Wu looked at his boss. He had never refused him, but this was not like anything he had been asked to do before.

Qi was looking quite cheerful, as if his work was done. Kovic put a hand on his shoulder.

'Your box of tricks fits in a backpack right?'

His face fell. 'Man, I work on the inside.' He gestured at his screens. 'This is my battlefield.'

'I can't get in without you. Their security will be state of the art. I'll need major disruption as well, security system, power supply.'

The other two were concentrating hard on the floor. If one of them agreed, Kovic reasoned, the other two would follow. The loss of face would be more unbearable than any thousand-foot drop.

Qi spoke up. 'You're a mean son of a bitch asking us like this in front of others. I mean, that's not how it's done in our culture.'

'Don't pull that "our culture" shit on me, we're way past that. I've got the whole of Shanghai out there; young men desperate to prove themselves, earn some serious cash, maybe a free passage to the US—'

# 28

Qi's text with the number and encryption code for Garrison's secure phone came through. Kovic stared at it for some time. If the *Valkyrie* sent that message about the unusual signal to the NSA, then the Commander would have sanctioned it. What was also on Kovic's mind was that since it was Garrison who selected the Marines for the mission, he would be wanting answers too. He would have seen the photographs; he would be making the calls home, fielding the questions he couldn't answer because doubtless Cutler wouldn't be giving him anything but Agency spin.

But calling him was a risk, breaking his useful cover of being officially dead. And then there was the matter of Garrison's son, the dedicated young Marine who had died in Afghanistan under Kovic's command. Garrison's opinion of him couldn't get any lower. He could just pick up the phone to Cutler and Kovic would be blown. But if there was anyone else in the world who might share Kovic's desire for retribution it would be him. And if something happened to him, if this mission failed and he didn't survive, well then at least there was someone on the US side who could do something with the knowledge other than bury it – which was what Cutler was most likely to do.

It rang only once.

'Sir, this is Kovic.'

There were several seconds of silence at the other end.

'Holy mother of fuck. What in goddamn hell's name are you doing on this line? How come you're even alive?'

Kovic could hear his sharp angry breaths, the breaths of a 200lb, underslept, sixty-two-year-old naval commander on his sixth cup of coffee, being telephoned on his private cell by the man apparently responsible for the deaths of six of his Marines, not to mention his own son. He could feel the anger from fifteen hundred miles away. It didn't feel like nearly far enough.

'I am deeply, profoundly sorry for the loss of your men, sir.'

'We've been here before, Agent Kovic. Haven't we?'

More than once, Kovic had tried to contact Garrison after Tommy's death, but he had refused to take the calls so he had written him a personal note. They had only ever spoken in the run-up to the *Highbeam* mission and Garrison had kept that conversation extremely short.

'I guess so, sir.'

'I just got off the phone to Sergeant Olsen's mother. She wanted me to explain why her son's corpse is appearing on photo sharing sites and why the US government can't stop it.'

There wasn't anything Kovic could say about that so he remained silent. If Garrison needed someone to sound off at, why not him? Whether it would have been any different if someone else had led the mission he couldn't say, but that was irrelevant now. The Commander was properly warmed up now, a man who would have fielded a hundred questions from the Pentagon and another hundred enquiries from the US Navy's press office, trying to nuance a statement that wouldn't increase America's humiliation any more than absolutely necessary – while the CIA stayed silent.

'Do you want to tell me how come you're alive? Your boss thinks you're dead.'

If that was what Cutler was saying, fine.

'It may only be a matter of time, once the people who killed your men find out I'm still in circulation.'

He explained about the fire and Louise.

'That's some track record you have for dodging bullets. What makes you think I won't pick up the phone and tell Cutler you're out there?'

'Because my guess, sir, is that you are as suspicious as I am about what really happened, that whatever explanation Cutler gave you it left as many questions as it answered.'

Garrison was silent while he processed this. A good sign.

'You ran into a DPRK patrol. The CIA is holding you responsible, you aware of that? As far as they're concerned, *you* screwed up.'

'I believe it's a lot more complicated than that, sir.'

He let out a long sigh. 'Do I want to hear it?'

'The short version is we were blown. They knew we were coming. Either it was a set-up from the start, or there was a leak and they ambushed us. Either way the intel was contaminated. Whichever it was, it falls on Langley's shoulders. So that guarantees only one thing.'

'What?'

'You'll never get the truth from them.'

'And what are you going to do about that?'

'I'm going to ask for your help.'

'Kovic, I'll say one thing for you. You've got one fuck of a lot of chutzpah.'

'I have a name.'

He told him about Tsu and his plan to find him. Saying it out loud, it sounded preposterous and they both knew it.

'You're right, you need help all right but I'm no psychiatrist.'

He could feel Garrison wanting to hang up.

'Your ship reported an unusual signal to the NSA.'

'How do you know this?'

'The signal went from the NK border to somewhere in the Chinese interior.' He quoted the grid reference. 'That location is Tsu's mountain HQ. He's our man, sir. I'm going to ask you if your people can look out for any similar signals – capture coordinates for the origin and destination of each dispatch. We may not crack the content but where they're going might tell us something.'

'You're clutching at straws here, Kovic.'

'Straws are all I have right now.'

'And that includes my private family cell number.'

'Yes, sir, and I'm going to need you to take the SIM card out and destroy it after we're done.'

'Oh, I think we're done.'

The line went dead.

# 29

'Kovic, wake up. There's a problem.'

Wu, at the wheel, was slowing down.

In the back next to Qi, Kovic woke grudgingly from a deep and grateful sleep.

'Big or small?'

'Could be big. There's a checkpoint up ahead. They're searching vehicles.'

Qi shut the laptop and slid it into the compartment under the front seat.

'Army or police?'

'Neither. These guys don't seem to have any insignia.'

'Welcome to Tsu's fiefdom.'

An hour before they had turned off the Hangrui Expressway that taken them almost due west from Shanghai. As it curved south they left the smooth freshly laid blacktop and turned north on to progressively less well tended roads, hemmed in by thick forest, with the first peaks of the Huangshan mountains rising behind.

They took their place in a line of vehicles, mostly trucks and minibuses. Inside the cab, each of them prepared for their first encounter with a potentially hostile authority. Wu and Zhou were dressed in blue work overalls. Their story was that they were coming to provide Wu's 'aunt' Mrs Chen with a much-needed running water system and connection to the municipal drains. Mrs Chen was one of Kovic's former assets who had retired to her home village inside Tsu's territory. In the back of the pickup were pipes, U-bends, spanners – even a toilet; everything needed to convince even the most suspicious guard that they were genuine plumbers. Qi's cover was that he was a student who had missed the bus taking his class to the mountains for a field trip and was having to hitch-hike. His story would account for the climbing gear. He had also created the necessary paperwork for each of them.

As for Kovic, he was Ray Nyman, physical instructor, former Special Forces operative and now freelance security contractor. For the Chinese authorities, Africa was a neutral place where their country was doing lots of business and was zero threat. To smooth the way he also had a hundred thousand Yuan on him, some of it sewn into his clothes.

When they pulled up it was almost dark, slanting rain running down the windshield. From somewhere up the line came the sounds of a scuffle and shouts of 'On the ground, now!' which didn't bode well.

'Better get in the coffin,' said Wu. 'Sounds like they're in a bad mood. Don't think they'll take kindly to a foreign face.'

The least enjoyable part of Kovic's training at the Farm had been abduction survival, specifically being confined in cramped spaces like the trunk of a car and driven to other parts of the grounds to be yelled at and accused of being an infidel, imperialist CIA pig and so forth at wearisome length. He could stand extreme levels of interrogation, but the being shut in a trunk part brought him out in a cold sweat. He never admitted it, naturally, or he would have failed that part of the course, rendering him ineligible for the best postings. And in all his tours he had never had to do it for real. He hadn't bargained on having to do it in China, with his own team.

In the cab of the Great Wall Wingle, Wu's cousin had installed a hidden compartment under the rear seat. Qi's surveillance kit went into it, along with the semi-automatic QB-88 sniper rifle with telescopic and night sights that Kovic had procured for Wu, plus four QSZ-92 pistols. And now, so did Kovic.

Wu called it the 'coffin,' a word Kovic wished he hadn't bothered to teach him, but which Wu found hilarious.

'Think of it as payback time,' suggested Qi.

'For what?'

'In advance, for what you are making us do.'

Qi lifted the seat and Kovic got in. It was hot, dark and stank of diesel and fresh spray paint. Thoughtfully the cousin had added two air holes.

'How many of them can you see?' Kovic said from his hideout.

'Only two, plus a small minibus, empty. Looks like they're just making it clear who's boss.'

'They heavy looking types?'

'You planning on taking them on?'

'If they're gonna give us a hard time, we may have to. Their uniforms might come in useful – and the bus. If Wu can let go of his Wingle.'

It was crass and childish, but it took his mind off being folded up into the equivalent of a carry-on bag.

'They're armed,' said Zhou. 'One's got a Hawk semi-automatic slung over his shoulder. The other's just taken a revolver out of its holster.'

Mrs Chen had already warned Kovic what to expect from the local police, that the chief was effectively Tsu's puppet and ran the force like a private army on his behalf.

'They are bullies,' she had warned him, 'but since this is China, they should respond to cash.'

'Okay, the people they searched are moving on. They're starting on the car in front.'

'The driver's passed his ID out the window,' said Zhou. 'They're opening the trunk.' He started to laugh.

'What's going on?' The coffin was heating up and he could feel his balls sticking together like badly packed fruit.

'Three goats. In the trunk. Oh, now they're pulling the driver out. He's waving his papers. The cop's just ripped them out of his hands. And the goats are trying to escape!'

There were three sharp cracks, and then silence. These weren't your average officious cops.

'Goat stew anyone?'

'I think we need to be very, very careful here,' said Qi.

The shocked driver was pushed back into his seat and waved on. The cop holstered his revolver.

Wu moved forward and stopped by the outstretched hand of the

148

cop who had done the shooting. He passed out the papers for all three of them.

'From outside the district.'

The cop's face was frozen with disapproval.

Wu went into overdrive. Despite the unpleasantness of his confinement, Kovic couldn't help smiling at his refusal to be cowed by bureaucracy – even when it came with a gun.

'My aunt is much respected in Fenju, and it is a matter of concern to the community that a person of her standing does not have proper sanitation.'

'Shut up, I don't give a shit about that.'

'No, listen. She said that if we had any problem we should insist on speaking to the Superintendent.'

Kovic could hear more trucks pulling up behind. With any luck this might induce them to lose interest and move them on.

'Stop talking. Pull over here and get out – all of you.'

Wu continued to remonstrate while doing what he was told. Kovic wondered how long this was going to take. Already he was finding it difficult to breathe and the fumes were giving him a raging headache.

'Okay. Easy now, guys, let's keep it cool,' Kovic whispered, more to himself than anyone else. This was Tsu's private army – answerable only to him. A dead goat or a dead man wasn't going to cause a fuss round here. While Wu kept up his barrage of indignation, Zhou gave Kovic a whispered commentary.

'They are both young, one with the semi looks quite weak, bad acne too. They're examining all the pipes in the back.'

Kovic could feel the equipment being rearranged, uncomfortably close by.

'Careful with those, don't get them scratched.'

Wu sounded suitably indignant. The guard showed his contempt by dropping something hard that banged an inch from Kovic's ear.

Qi, who had said nothing so far, now piped up.

'Would it be permissible to make a supplementary payment in order to expedite the processing of our papers?'

Nicely put, thought Kovic. Prison had rubbed some of Qi's natural arrogance off him.

Kovic could hear fumbling, and a safety catch coming off. So much for 'a soft answer turneth away wrath', but then the Bible never was much of a training manual.

'Stay where you are! Attempting to bribe an officer is an extremely serious offence! You will accompany us to our headquarters.'

The way this was going, Kovic thought he might as well have stayed in his seat where at least he would have been more use, and been able to breathe.

'Get in the vehicle – all of you in the front where we can see you. You will drive to our headquarters now! Feng, in the back with me where we can watch them.'

Shit, thought Kovic. The good news is we're going in; the shit news is I'm still under the goddamn seat. Wu fired up the engine, the fan blasting Kovic with hot air through his breathing holes. At this rate he wouldn't make it to headquarters. He tried to visualise the map, and calculate how far they were from the mountain. Where their base was he had no idea. He was going to die of asphyxiation in this improvised tomb, with two assholes on top of him – literally.

Wu was driving fast – figuring that the sooner they got where they were going the sooner Kovic could get out. Kovic felt the tail slide on some gravel, which was followed by a sharp rebuke from above him and a hard slap.

'Don't drive so fast.'

Kovic had had enough. He scrabbled around, feeling for the weapons. He could feel himself becoming hazy, intoxicated by the heat, and the fumes. His hand closed round one of the QSZs, and he tried to move his head as far away from it as possible while he took aim.

# 30

'My cousin will *not* be happy about this,' said Wu, as he surveyed the damage to the interior of the truck. They had turned down a rough track into the forest to regroup and dispose of the dead guards. The rain had stopped and the fresh damp woodland air smelled almost fragrant.

Kovic was taking deep breaths to clear his system.

'In Beirut there used to be a guy and his wife who called themselves Crime Scene Steam & Clean. Did great business in the old days.'

'Yeah, well we're not in Beirut now.'

The back seat was shredded, and the headlining and sides of the rear doors were splattered with blood and other bodily matter.

'At least we have the top half of the uniforms. Too bad about the pants, though.'

Kovic had set about digging a shallow grave for the guards with a plumber's trenching tool. Zhou was struggling to remove the tunic from one of them. Qi, standing further away from the corpses, was fiddling with their radios. He hadn't spoken since the shooting.

'Not quite what you expected, huh?'

Qi shrugged. 'With you I try not to expect anything.'

'That makes two of us.'

Kovic saw the need for a little empathy. 'If you decide to bail, I'll understand.'

Qi nodded, but they both knew that wasn't an option. This was payback for Kovic's protection from the long arm of US law.

Zhou was methodically working his way through the guards' pockets, collecting the contents. He jangled some keys he had found.

'Must be for the minibus.'

Kovic examined them.

'Okay. Wu and Zhou, put those tunics and caps on and go get the minibus. I'll finish dealing with these guys.'

He could see from their expressions how well all this was going down. For him the shooting was simply a means to an end, and a reminder of how far he was prepared to go. For them it had moved the mission into another gear. All three looked at him now.

'I never said this was going to be fun.'

He also knew he was doing them all a favour by taking charge of the burial.

'Qi, you go with them. Take the radios, try and figure out a way of jamming their network, something to give us some cover and buy us a bit of time.'

Kovic watched as they piled into the pickup and drove away, leaving him alone in the woods with the dead guards. I wouldn't blame them if they didn't come back, he thought, as he hacked at the earth. What a strange job this was, alone in a Chinese forest burying a couple of corpses. And then he remembered he wasn't actually in a job any more. He wasn't on anyone's payroll; he had no idea if his mission would be a success, if indeed Tsu was at home in his mountain lair, or even if he was, whether he would get near him. And even if he succeeded, what would he do after that?

Digging the grave reminded him of the funeral of his mother, an elaborate affair that his father insisted on, way beyond his means, which Kovic had stumped up for, to try and atone for having been such a disappointment to them. They had despaired of his way-ward ways, his lack of respect for authority, his tendency to hang out with the wrong sort of crowd. His father's only ambition for his son had been that he would keep up the family tradition and follow him into the Rouge, Henry Ford's sprawling factory complex where his dad assured him there would be a job waiting for him. But it didn't take a rocket scientist to see that Detroit's future was bleak and he wasted no time in joining the exodus that more than halved the city's population in a couple of decades. His father was in a home now, waiting to die. All he knew about his son was that he was somewhere in China doing government work he couldn't understand, let alone brag about to his fellow retirees. Had he failed his father and mother? Was that what he did with all the important people in his life? He had failed Louise; she was the best thing that had ever happened to him and yet he had let her down so many times, and then finally, put her in mortal danger.

Going after Tsu was his chance to make amends, to right some wrongs. Campbell, his predecessor in Shanghai who drank himself out of the job, said that the trouble with the CIA was that most of the work was just a game played out between powers to keep each other's security services occupied and none of it made a scintilla of difference. Well someone had now broken the rules of the game and Kovic knew he would die rather than lie back and accept the consequences.

# 31

'Put the blue light on and step on it. Mrs Chen is waiting for her new bathroom.'

They were in the minibus that Wu and the others had retrieved. It was night and the road was quiet. The atmosphere was lifting now they had left the dead guards behind. It was night and the road was quiet. Qi had wired the guards' radios to his laptop and was busy on the keyboard.

Kovic caught sight of some images of what looked like parts of very fat people on the screen: naked.

'What the fuck is *that*?'

'It's called "Big Ass Party",' explained Qi. 'Very popular Russian porn. Everyone on their network will stop what they're doing to watch, no one will have the balls to refer it up, and it'll postpone any response to our guys' disappearance.'

Kovic was relieved to see that Qi was back to his old self. He gestured with one of the radios.

'Also from here on I'll be able to monitor all their radio traffic, if and when they start to get curious. I can get a fix to within five hundred metres of how close they are.'

'You're a genius, Qi. We couldn't have done this without you.'

Qi shrugged. 'I never saw anyone get killed before, that's all.'

'It gets easier. Whether that's a good thing—'

Until a few days ago, Kovic had been on a long vacation from killing. But Louise's death had catapulted him back into business as usual, and reminded him of his true purpose. It felt as if that precious time which had elapsed since Afghanistan and all his other wars had collapsed in on itself. This was the norm; Shanghai and Louise had been an aberration. But he knew that this was the life he lived for, the sense of danger and uncertainty was something he thrived on, thinking on his feet, making plans on the run, taking risks. He had taken a huge risk confiding in Garrison, and had acquired an unlikely and sceptical sponsor in the form of Hannah, another potentially risky presumption of trust. Around him he had a team whose loyalty he was about to test to the limit. However mad or dangerous it was, this was what he was made for. Live for the moment and let tomorrow look after itself.

They raced through a checkpoint without even slowing down. The guards dealing with a long string of vehicles just looked up and saluted. They were on their way.

# 32

Hannah sat at the briefing table in precisely the way she had been trained: hands on the surface, not flat – that was too emphatic – not fists – too aggressive – but somewhere in between, as if holding imaginary tennis balls. Shoulders back as if standing to attention, even when sitting, to show respect. Make no eye contact with the Director even when speaking, yet look focused, concentrating on a space between one and two metres ahead. Feet flat on the floor, legs not crossed – to avoid any body language which could be construed as suggestive.

*Fuck this. Fuck this right up the ass. Fuck the boss's mother and his sister and his philandering bitch wife,* came a voice from somewhere deep in her head. *What am I doing here?*

'Huang Shuyi, I trust that you are thinking constructive thoughts.'

Director Guo Hua-fe paused in his monologue about the current situation and let his cold gaze drift towards Hannah. He wanted her. He should be able to have her. He was her superior after all. Other women on his staff were his for the taking, but they were all lowly clerks. This one was different: an enticing challenge with her American education and confident, individualistic Western ways. All independent thought in women was disturbing; in one with Western influences it could be positively dangerous. Another reason she needed to be tamed.

She snapped to attention.

'Most assuredly, Director. May I share one with you?'

He waved a hand, which indicated he didn't much care either way.

'My proposal, sir, is that the while the police are dealing with the

156

protesters we should be investigating those forces fomenting the current unrest.'

Guo cocked his head on one side.

'An interesting suggestion, Agent Huang. What makes you think such "forces", as you put it, exist?'

He implied by his tone that her suspicion was faintly ridiculous, but he let his eyes linger on her. Hannah felt a cold shudder run through her. He was not an ugly man, but he exuded the institutionalised lack of empathy of one who had seen and done things in the name of his country that had eaten into his humanity; someone who would never feel for anyone but himself. The three agents sitting opposite shared a smile under their bowed heads. She knew they deeply resented her presence, the way she drew attention to herself and poisoned the previously convivial, smug relationship they had enjoyed with their boss, whom they worshipped.

The Director kept his eyes on her as he awaited her reply. Her appointment by all appearances had been his. However, her father's standing as one of that diminishing number of untainted heroes of the Mao era meant that there was useful political capital to be gained by giving her a role. *Not* to have hired her would in all probability have resulted in some disfavour. But he wanted her to see it as his gift, not her father's, and therefore something she owed him for. So far she had shown little sign of gratitude. If anything, she seemed bent on causing him problems. She would have to learn her place.

She met his gaze.

'To quote an old English axiom, Director, there is no smoke without fire.'

She watched for a reaction. Did he even know about the fire at Kovic's apartment? Did he know what an axiom was? He had passed on the directive to deport him as if it was a shopping list, a trivial task of no significance. Strange, then, that he hadn't asked her if she had carried it out.

'Agent Huang, you have spent considerable time outside the country, under the influence of alien value systems.' He never missed an opportunity to remind her of her time abroad, as if it were some kind of truancy. 'You must beware of becoming detached from day to day realities. Do not underestimate the patriotism of the Chinese people.'

'All I would suggest, sir, is the possibility that reactionary elements may be capitalising on the events on the North Korean border to further undermine Sino–US relations.'

She chose her words carefully, using the same soulless ministry-speak that she had become horribly familiar with. The other agents, seated at the table in identical poses, kept their eyes firmly fixed on their hands. Questioning the Director's procedure or even his interpretation of events could put you on the fast track to oblivion. But then she was a woman; she didn't have that much to lose.

The Director looked at her with a disquieting mixture of lust and contempt.

'And what evidence do you have for these "reactionary elements", as you describe them?'

The other agents all nodded gravely: how fortunate they were to have such a wise Director.

'None, sir, which is why I am proposing that we establish if there are any.'

She could feel herself sliding irrevocably back into a void of incoherence, like a car on an icy road with the wrong tyres. At Harvard she had wowed her tutors with her steely insights, and they had hung on her every word as she dismantled the intricate moving parts of China's governing politburo and laid them out like the pieces of a clock for them to examine.

*I have made a terrible mistake,* she thought. I am being anaesthetised by this job. They don't want my insights or my suggestions. They just want a woman they can humiliate. *And I am powerless to change this. I am trapped.*

She blushed at her own frustration. How long could she keep her true feelings to herself? The mistake had been in joining up at all, in letting herself be persuaded by her father. But to have denied him this would have been a rejection of all he stood for, and a personal humiliation tantamount to proof of the deepest ingratitude. If they were an American family ... but they were not, so why waste mental energy on futile speculation? Then he had been diagnosed with cancer and given four months to live, so she had abandoned her studies and come home.

'Harvard was your wish, now it's my turn to fulfil a wish,' he had said, and – seeing the longing in his eyes, how could she have refused?

The Director was in full flow again, expounding on the natural tendencies of the simple yet admirably patriotic populace. She knew from experience that these monologues could go on for as long as an hour, as he went on, enraptured by the sound of his own voice – while her life ticked away.

Her father's intentions had been entirely good, which made it all the more impossible for her to deny him his wish. '*The MSS needs new blood, people who have been out in the world. You must enlist,*' he had told her. In fact *he* had done the enlisting before she had even come home. One call to an old comrade and she was on the fast track programme for cadets of exceptional ability – but all of them the offspring of Party high-ups.

And then there was his illness. 'He's slipping away,' her mother had warned. 'He needs you at his side – he needs you to fulfil your destiny while he can live to see it.'

But that had been two years ago and the General had shown no signs of deterioration. He still walked three miles a day, spent at least one morning a week at the firing range and did the super fiendish Sudoku in eight minutes flat.

'*Your return has lifted him into remission,*' said her mother, and Hannah discovered the unexpected benefit of making her other parent happy as well. When she caught up with her Harvard friends on Facebook – their travels, their engagements, careers starting in Wall Street, London, Hollywood – she replied politely, unable even to admit what she was doing. She knew what they would be thinking, that she'd given in to tradition and gone home to be married off.

Some of the MSS she had enjoyed: weapons training, in which she excelled; the gruelling water and climbing challenges at which she came top in her year, and, of course, languages, at which she was truly gifted. But the job itself had been stultifyingly boring as all the more demanding assignments were handed out to her male colleagues, with the sons of the most influential cadres getting the plum jobs. She soon realised that a mediocre man had twenty times more chance of getting a promotion – or even just escaping the office – than even the most brilliant woman. This had sharpened her determination to rise up the ranks and prove the system wrong, to get out in the field and grab some of the action – somehow, no matter what it took.

From early childhood, her father had been her mentor, challenging her to stretch herself, not settle for just good enough. Now, whenever she was at home he asked her to read to him – Winston Churchill's *History of the English Speaking Peoples*. Even being allowed to read such a book would not so long ago have been unimaginable, he reminded her. He understood English well enough but had trouble reading it now his eyes were failing.

'*To fight imperialism you must understand the mind of the imperialist,*' he had told her with a twinkle in his eye, as if to say, *well, that's my excuse*. He had lived for the Revolution. What was happening today troubled him, but not as much as what he had discovered in his later years about his erstwhile hero, the Great Helmsman. Even when exiled and put to work in a paper mill, inhaling the poisonous wood pulp purifier that would destroy his lungs, he still exalted Mao Zedong as the great leader who had brought the country into the modern age, and rationalised his own period of internal exile as a necessary sacrifice for the cause of progress. When he had been brought out of the cold by Premier Deng and given new duties, he showed no disillusionment with the system that had starved over sixty-five million people, punishing him and millions of others just for having 'incorrect thoughts'. He simply took up the reins again and rejoined the next stage of the Long March. Hannah admired his stoicism and his resolve, but try as she did to model herself on him, she knew it wasn't working.

The Director was still talking, enumerating the threats to China in a speech that they all knew off by heart. She looked round the table at the others, their heads bowed in reverence. *Did they all believe this crap?* Her father had wanted her to experience the world, to know and understand things that had been way beyond his reach in his own youth. But the price of that knowledge was the realisation of how far China had to go if it was to root out the backwardness and corruption that was holding it back. These stupid drones with their BlackBerries and iPhones, thinking they were just like Americans; it wasn't the machines that mattered, but what you did with them.

Her thoughts turned to Kovic. At first he had infuriated her. Superficially he was just the sort of American she despised: cocky, arrogant, a smart alec know-it-all, showing off his admittedly excellent Mandarin which was, she conceded, almost as good as her English. Worse, he had seen right through her, realised that she knew nothing about the border incident and ridiculed her for not interrogating him about it. The humiliation! She had also been forced to realise how wrong she had got him, how literally she had taken his MSS file that masked what an impressive job he had done of building up a cover as a so-so spook with nothing in his track record to suggest exceptional initiative or draw attention to his ability. What had also surprised her was his reaction to the prospect of deportation, when most Americans she knew always longed to go home. Then his bravery at the fire came as a complete surprise. Rescuing those two women showed a surprising concern for the welfare of others when there was nothing to gain for him personally, not an attitude she had usually associated with either his nationality or his profession. Finally, there was the terrible discovery in his own property of the remains of his girlfriend. His barely concealed grief and his passion for revenge had been completely unexpected – almost as unexpected as her own response to his plea to stay. Dare she examine her motives for that? This was treachery on her part to help an agent of a power seen increasingly as hostile … She blushed again at the shock of what she had done.

But as quickly as this thought came, another overtook it. Had she been tricked? After all, his own people had registered no objection to his deportation. Was he just a rogue element, a menace to both countries who had pulled the wool over her eyes?

She came back to consciousness. The agent sitting opposite was complimenting the Director on his speech.

'What very perceptive insights you have given us into the situation, sir.'

*Kiss-ass.* She glanced at the Director who was basking in the praise like some moronic pet who would no doubt beg at the feet of his own bosses for a morsel of approval. The others round the table began to clap. She had no choice but to join in.

Kiss-ass was emboldened by this. 'Perhaps, sir,' he ventured, 'the appearance of Jin Jié on TV tonight will provide some balance to our appraisal of the situation.'

Immediately the Director frowned. The agent went bright red, aghast that he might have displeased his superior. Hannah smiled to herself. At least she wasn't the only one in the room to feel ostracised. But the feeling was short-lived.

He turned to her.

'Agent Huang, since you are so interested in investigating the "forces behind", perhaps you could give us an insight into who is "behind" this individual?'

That she knew Jin Jié was no secret. They had met at Harvard and a Chinese gossip magazine had recently unearthed a photo of them together at a fraternity ball: 'General's daughter dates golden boy' was the headline. In Europe or America that would have been seen as a normal acquaintance; in China it was suspect, and for the woman – always for the woman – an excuse to denigrate her.

The Director started to laugh, and right on cue so did the other men in the room. She looked from one to the other and then finally at him. She would find a way to shut them up.

# 33

## Huangpu District, Shanghai

All day she had felt it – something oppressive in the city: not just the smog, or the sticky heat that dusk had done nothing to dissipate. It was not just the increased police presence, but a change of tone, as if people were choosing sides. If she was going to understand it she had to experience it for herself. The occupation of People's Square had been bulldozed by the police but instead of squashing the protest, their action seemed to have spread it around the city, like spores. On street corners there were huddles of people with banners: *Death to America … Americans Go Home* – not just on hand-painted banners but professionally printed T-shirts, which was new. She stopped a youth walking past, grabbed him by the sleeve.

'You believe in this?' she said, gesturing at his T-shirt.

He shrugged.

'Where did you get it?'

'Some guy gave it to me.'

'So you just wear it? Take it off. It's not appropriate.'

'Get lost. He paid me to wear it.'

'Who?'

'I dunno. Ask them.'

He pointed at a group of student age youths with similar shirts on.

Hannah approached two girls with a banner and asked the same questions.

'Someone has to pay for this crime,' said one.

'The Americans think they can just go into places and shoot people,' said the other. 'China should stay away from America. It's a bad influence.'

Hannah looked at their clothes and shoes: Nike, Converse, Hollister, Gap ...

'Yeah, they're taking us over. We must resist.' The girl's iPhone buzzed and she looked at the screen. 'Gotta go. Bye.'

The girls moved off and were enveloped by the crowd, which had begun to surge forward. Hannah felt compelled to follow. There were hundreds of them, all headed back to People's Square: mainly students, but also young salary workers. Some instinct told her to hang back. Another told her to get right in there to talk to more of them, to see if she could discover how they were being organised. They must have all received a second message because they all speeded up, as if there was an urgent reason to get to the square. Three hurrying girls crashed into her and apologised.

'Hey, how do you know?'

'Know what?'

'Where to go, what it's for?'

One of them waved her Galaxy in the air. Hannah had made a grab for her hand so she could read the message when a streak of white light flashed skywards between the buildings. Even though the sound was muffled by the wall of people, the rush of air knocked her to the ground along with everyone around her – an invisible tsunami breaking over them, lifting them en masse and propelling them half a block from where they had been standing.

When Hannah came to she was in a shop window, face down and covered in shards of glass. A cacophony of a hundred burglar and car alarms rang and hooted, and behind them came the screams and moans of the injured and dying.

She got to her feet and gently brushed her eyes. She had been lucky, shielded from the full force of the blast by the sea of people in front. She stepped out of the trashed shop front, like a mannequin coming to life. A young man was lying a few feet away. He raised a faltering hand. There was a blade shaped splinter of glass several inches long protruding from his chest. She bent down to help him. His eyes pleaded with her. He grabbed her hand, gripped it hard and then let go, his gaze losing its focus as the life drained out of him. From his other hand slipped his phone. Hannah's was gone, separated from her by the blast. She scrolled through his last few messages: *Mum, don't wait up*, and the seemingly innocuous, *See you all in the Square*. She tucked the phone into a pocket and turned to see where she could help.

# 34

'*The tectonic plates of our great nation are shifting. On one side, the progressive – on the other, the reactionary. They must not split apart. They must join together ...*'

Jin Jié made a gesture like breaststroke, as if pushing two large objects apart, and concluded with a hugging motion. The approving audience broke into spontaneous applause as a crane camera swept over the cheering crowd. The host joined in the clapping briefly, taking care that her immensely long nails didn't collide.

'*Jin Jié, thank you very much for sparing the time in your busy schedule to talk to us today.*'

Mrs Chen flipped the remote and the picture vanished.

They were seated round the table in the kitchen at the back of her house. The wood and thatch structure had been in her family for several generations, barring a period during the Cultural Revolution when her parents were hustled off to atone for having incorrect thoughts. She waved a long wooden spoon at the TV.

'That guy is headed either for stardom or a labour camp.'

She turned back to the pot of pork and steamed greens.

'I know which side my money's on,' said Kovic, gesturing with a length of cabbage between his chopsticks before he twirled it into his mouth.

'Hey! You're supposed to wait for the others. You have no manners.'

'That's good, coming from a Chinese.'

She clouted him on the head – to the amazement of her servant, who was resting on a blanket by the fire.

Mrs Chen had been useful to Kovic. Every so often, for the equivalent of a year's salary, she would deliver product to him from

166

her lowly but invaluable position as a filing clerk in the Ministry of Procurement. If there were orders for helicopters from Russia, or negotiations with the French for missiles, he got to hear about it. He fed the information back to Langley sparingly, to ensure the security of his source. And he paid her over the odds because he liked her and she was a widow. The relationship soured a little when her husband turned out not to be dead but merely absent for bureaucratic expediency, but Kovic came to admire her for her deft subversion of China's suffocating bureaucracy. When she left the city for her home village he made a point of keeping in touch, always maintaining his assets for a rainy day – such as today.

She was shaking her head doubtfully.

'He makes it sound so simple. China's not simple; it's very complicated.'

Kovic couldn't help but agree with her homespun wisdom. And there was something about Jin Jié that irritated him, with his relentless optimism and fresh-faced born-again smile. He looked at Mrs Chen, her greying hair tied up in a bun, her features as weather-beaten as those of any village peasant, as if the sum of all her ancestors' pain and struggle was etched into the filigree of lines on her ageing face. She possessed more than her fair share of wisdom about the political temperature of China. So he paid attention to what she had to say.

'You must listen for the sound of marching feet; listen for which way they are moving.'

Kovic knew she was a fatalist, one of the generation that had yet to come to terms with the new wealth. Drilled into them from such an early age was the anti materialistic message, that the fruits of capitalism were a mirage.

Guessing what she was about to say, Kovic nodded at the flat screen TV and her smartphone.

'All this stuff, you didn't have anything like this before. What's not to like?'

'It makes people uneasy, like they've got it on false pretences, not by following the correct values but only by money. Look at the riots in Shanghai – it's all too much for some of them, they want to slow things down.' She thrust a thumb in the direction of the TV.

'That boy, he's going too fast for them.'

She shook her head slowly. She was enjoying her audience's attention. Kovic was thinking about Vaughan and his protesters. Were they just a PR stunt, or a reflection of something bigger? The China he knew was moving so fast, maybe it was hard for some to keep up. But here in the country something else was going on that reminded him of the warlord era of old. He knew which he preferred.

'So tell me about Tsu.'

Mrs Chen shrugged and let out a long sigh.

'Round here they don't talk about him. We never see or hear from him. He keeps the roads maintained, there's no crime. Security: that's what makes people content.'

'And freedom?'

'You Americans, always on about freedom. What freedom do you really have? These people wouldn't know freedom if it bit them on the ass.'

They all laughed.

'Besides, no one knows much about him. He stays in the shadows. There are stories of course—'

She narrowed her eyes and fell silent, waiting for him to coax more from her.

'Go on. Like what?'

'Staff who fall from favour.' She made a downward spiralling gesture with a forefinger.

'Literally?'

'Some bodies have been found at the foot of the mountain. Every bone broken by the fall—'

'Nice.'

'And the prison. He has his own cells up there.'

'What for?'

She shrugged.

'As a reminder of the consequences of disobedience.'

'Doesn't that scare the hell out of everyone?'

She gave him a wry smile.

'We lost sixty million people in the famines and the camps

– probably more. We don't scare that easily. But I tell you what does scare me.'

She sat down and faced him.

'Agent Kovic, we have done good business in the past, and I have taken risks on your behalf for which you have rewarded me most handsomely, but this plan to ...'

Kovic nodded his acknowledgment then gently raised a hand.

'It's okay, I know. The men with me have in their own way said the same. But I have committed myself to this mission and there is no going back for me – even if I have to do it alone.'

In the politest way he could, he needed her to shut up now. He gestured at the door.

'Would you like to see the new toilet we've brought you?'

# 35

For several hours Hannah worked with the emergency services, helping the injured and, once they were stabilised, moving them to a makeshift ER tent that had been set up on the square. Her own injuries were slight, her face peppered with small glass cuts that were painful but not deep. The area around the square had been cordoned off. The of the downtown district was swarming with police, moving the remaining people off the street, stopping vehicles and being generally officious to make themselves look useful. She took out the dead man's phone and examined the text that had brought him to the square. The name of the sender was blocked.

The first three cabs she tried looked at her face and drove away. In the end she forced one to take her by flashing her MSS ID in the driver's face and grabbing him by the collar.

When she reached the Golfball it was almost deserted. She found just the guards on the desk who buzzed her in and went back to their screens as she passed through. Neither remarked on her appearance. She went to her workstation, unlocked her desk, took out the SIM reader and inserted the dead man's card. Then she extracted the blocked number, typed it into the MSS command directory, and waited.

Surely that couldn't be right? She retyped the number twice and each time got the same response: the People's Liberation Army's Naval Force. It was a generic number and the navy's bureaucracy was huge, but there was no question from where the text had emanated. She called the Director on his emergency number.

'We shouldn't discuss this on the phone. Meet me here, as soon as you can.'

He gave her an address. On her way out of the building she stopped at the restroom. Her face was now covered with tiny scabs, some with flecks of glass still embedded in them. She removed as many as she could, dabbing her face with a towel dipped in hot water, washed off most of the dried blood and combed her hair, which was also full of glass. Then she stopped and looked at her expression: not the dead eyed woman who had gazed dully out at her every morning for the past six months, but a new version – alive, engaged, fired by the sudden focus and sense of purpose her discovery had given her.

The address the Director had given her was an old building on the Bund with a small brass plate by the door, which said simply '66'. She rang the bell and a tall European appeared, dressed in tails like a traditional English butler. Through the door wafted a strong aroma of cigar smoke and scent. He looked her up and down with disdain before reluctantly letting her through the door. Along with the cuts on her face, her shirt and trousers were torn. She hadn't noticed this. She must still be in shock.

'Wait here,' he said, without a trace of politeness.

She sat in one of several large wing-backed chairs in a wide hall that had been elaborately renovated. Chandeliers glistened above her, festooned with tiny lights. Western paintings adorned the walls. After she'd studied them for a minute it occurred to her they were all nudes.

'My dear child.'

The Director stood in front of her, with two of his security men not far behind. He looked pleased to see her. That made a change. Then he noticed the cuts on her face.

'My goodness you have been in the wars.'

Concerned, attentive – human; this wasn't the man she was used to. She took out the dead man's phone and showed him the message. He took it from her and examined it closely, frowning. Then he looked at her with another expression she had not seen before.

'Good work. You must have shown great courage tonight. Come!'

He set off down the corridor. Part of her was elated. This was the first praise she had ever received from him. A set of double doors swung open. On the other side was a nightclub, lavishly decorated in the style of a 1920s American speakeasy. A floorshow was underway, featuring tall Western dancers scantily clad in costumes decorated with feathers.

Hannah stepped back.

'Please, I'd prefer not.'

He looked irritated, then his expression softened.

'Of course. What was I thinking? In fact, I have a much better idea. Let me get you away from here.'

He snapped his fingers at the guards.

'Car! Now!'

As they reached the door a black Audi lurched to a halt at the bottom of the steps. The guard who had run ahead opened the rear door for them. As soon as they were inside, Hannah turned sideways to engage his full attention.

'Sir, I am convinced that this was no spontaneous gathering. The people who went to People's Square were summoned by this text.'

She launched into a vivid description of what she'd seen. As she talked he nodded slowly. Finally, she thought: he appreciates what I'm doing. She moved on to her discovery of the source of the message.

He looked at her, his face full of concern at this revelation.

Then he laid a hand on her knee.

'And you've told no one else of this?'

She shook her head.

'Of course not – it was something I could only refer to you.'

'Then be absolutely sure that it stays that way.'

Inside she couldn't help being thrilled at having done something of value at last.

'What should be our next move? Whoever sent the texts, if they had prior knowledge of the bomb—'

'Good work. I'm proud of you. And I'm so glad you found a reason to track me down at this late hour.'

A reason?

His eyes shone in a disturbing way she had never seen before. Of course, he had been drinking. But he had seemed to have taken her discovery very seriously.

'Where are we going?'

'Somewhere quiet, where we can talk and relax. I imagine you could do with a drink, after all you've been through.'

He pressed a button on the armrest and the glass partition rose between them and the guards in front. He felt her knee tense under his hand, which excited him. He had dreamed of this moment since the first day he set eyes on her, and now she had come to him, dropped right into his lap like a ripe peach.

Her instinct was to slap his hand away, but she forced herself to bide her time. She was in a moving car with three men. And he was a bit drunk; many women would forgive this attention, even find it flattering. Try to be a bit more Chinese, she told herself.

'I am sure that your father would be very proud of your actions tonight. I shall be sure to congratulate him personally for having produced such a heroic daughter. I'm also sure that he would agree with me when I tell you that what you have learned we must keep very much to ourselves.'

Why did she have this feeling his sense of urgency was about something other than finding out why the Chinese Navy was organising protests? And the mention of her father made her feel weaker. This wasn't right. She fixed her eyes on the road ahead. She had to get out of this.

# 36

The Audi swept through a set of gates and up to a large mansion. She had hoped it would at least be a downtown hotel with lots of people around: no such luck. She allowed herself a glance over her shoulder, and saw the gates closing behind them. The car came to a halt and the two guards leapt out and opened the door on the Director's side.

'Welcome to my official residence,' he announced.

She tried to open her door but it was locked. Suddenly she felt like a prisoner. He reached in to help her. There was no escape. Maybe she was overreacting. Perhaps he did want to get her to somewhere comfortable so they could properly discuss what she had seen and learned. If she was wrong, the best she could do was behave in such a way that he might let his guard down.

She accepted his hand, smiling thinly as she emerged from the car.

'This is a fine house,' she managed.

He didn't reply. The brief glimpse of charm earlier was all it was – brief. He took her by the arm and led her up to the house.

The room was panelled and grand in a bland sort of way, like the house occupied by the dean of her school at Harvard. He opened a huge drinks cabinet and poured out two large tumblers of Scotch. She needed that drink, but she had to remain alert. Then he signalled to the two guards to leave them. He turned to her and grinned, revealing uneven, nicotine-stained teeth. In America no one could have got to his position with those teeth.

He lifted his glass to her. She nodded, tilted her glass briefly in his direction and drank. She could have downed the lot in one gulp

174

but that would have been unwise. He took a sip and put his glass down.

'So, here we are at last.'

He grinned again then his face became serious.

'Your future depends on the outcome of this evening.'

Did he mean what she had witnessed, the information she had discovered? If only. He gestured for her to join him on the large leather Chesterfield.

He made a space on the glass table beside her, took out a small packet and emptied out a little mound of white powder.

'You've been in America so you'll be well acquainted with this.'

She wasn't. She had never had any drugs in her life. Not even weed. Her sorority friends had tried many times to initiate her, to no avail. She decided to make one last attempt.

'Sir, I thought that we were going to discuss the—'

He cut her off.

'Yes, yes, naturally. First things first.'

He chopped and sorted the powder into three lines and took out what looked like an antique silver propelling pencil with the pencil part removed.

'Much more stylish than a rolled-up banknote, I'm sure you'll agree. It's a relic from pre-war Shanghai, when people really knew how to have fun.'

He took off his jacket.

'Shuyi, we've always understood each other, haven't we?'

This felt far too intimate. Only her parents called her that.

'I – I am keen to do my utmost for the department, sir.'

A tiny emphasis on the 'sir' was all she could do to remind him that their relationship was strictly professional.

'Very good. I'm glad to hear it.'

He leaned closer and looked her up and down.

'You've got great potential. Your commitment to the work is a credit to you. Don't pass up any opportunity for advancement.'

'I understand, sir.' She even managed a smile, before the true meaning hit home. She cursed her naivety.

He grinned again.

'Good, I'm glad that is clear to you.'

Before she had registered it, his hand had reached out towards the buttons on her shirt. Two had been broken during the explosion.

'I should think you'd like to get out of those torn clothes, wouldn't you?'

She smiled again, forcing her facial muscles to comply. She could feel her heart hammering, yet she couldn't move a muscle. What could she do?

He bent over the powder and inhaled deeply. Her eyes swept the room, the solitary door with the guards outside, the heavily curtained windows on the first floor: too high to jump. She watched as one line disappeared up the tube. A terrible sense of defeat engulfed her as if the dead weight of generations of women who had reluctantly submitted to the unwelcome advances of men was bearing down on her, saying *oh, just let him have his way*. He lifted his head, his eyes closed, and let out a satisfied sigh. Then he looked at her again, his eyes bulging.

He angled the tube towards her.

'I hope you aren't going to disappoint me, Shuyi.'

She noticed that with his jacket off he looked much more powerful, that far from being the 'desk jockey' she'd dismissively assumed, he had thick upper arms and strong looking wrists. She had also noted his quick reactions. His reflexes were excellent.

She sat frozen in the chair, rigid with a mixture of fear and disgust. She had no idea what to do so she cocked her head on one side and smiled.

The first line had made him eager for more. He looked at her and when she shook her head, shrugged and bent forward again. She watched closely as he positioned the tube at one end of the second line, bent down and inserted the other end in his left nostril, with the tip of his forefinger pressed against his right. Stay calm, she told herself: wait for the right moment. She would only get one chance and she had to get it right. Her only advantage would be surprise.

She reached out, grasped the crown of his head as if it were a basketball, and with all the strength she could find, slammed her hands downwards, pushing and pushing with everything she had. It was as if all the months of humiliation and ridicule had been fuelled into one powerful, devastating gesture of vengeance. There was a gluey tearing, crunching sound as the silver pipe drove up the nostril and buried itself deep in his head. She let go. He staggered back, half rising; eyes swivelled, then focused on her, his mouth a distorted outline of dismay. Then he fell back and slumped to the floor, his limbs twitching as blood bubbled out of the silver tube.

She looked at him with cold unblinking eyes, then started towards the door. But then she stopped. If she didn't put on a show the guards would suspect her. She put her hands up to her face and screamed as loudly as she could manage.

They rushed into the room. She stood frozen in her place clutching her mouth as if she was about to throw up.

'One moment he was fine and then – oh my God, I think he's had a brain haemorrhage.'

One of them put his arm round her and steered her out of the room.

'I need to go home—'

He held her a little too tightly. *Jesus, she thought: they're all the same.*

'I think I can manage now, thank you.'

Once they were out of the room she shrugged him off, bowed her head slightly and started down the stairs.

'You need to contact Internal Affairs, not the police. They will handle this, appropriately.'

The second guard frowned.

'As a witness you need to stay—'

But she was already moving past him.

'Hey, stop—!'

She ran out through the doors, down the front steps and on to the drive. There were two more guards standing by the car, smoking. Where the hell had they come from?

'Quick! The Director's had a stroke!'

They hesitated. She whirled round, spotted the Audi's keys still in the ignition.

'Go now! You may be able to save him!'

She dived into the front seat, turned the key, rammed the stick into Drive. She headed straight for the gates. They looked very solid but there wasn't much choice. She closed her eyes and floored the gas.

# 37

Huangshan Mountains

It was almost dawn. Kovic arched backwards, training the binoculars almost vertically in the direction of the peak. On Qi's screen it had looked forbidding; now he was standing at its foot it was like no mountain he had ever seen, a vast column of volcanic granite. Its sheer sides were flecked with vegetation and pockmarked with holes preserved from the time it was forced upwards by the subterranean power deep in the Earth's core, glowing a fiery orange. The top was shrouded in cloud. He felt an unfamiliar stab of concern for what he was about to subject his crew to. Any other time common sense would have prevailed. But he was all out of that particular commodity.

'How's it look?'

Qi, laying out the ropes and clips, was making an extra effort to be positive.

'No idea. Thanks to the cloud I can see zip.'

Even though it was only just light, it was already stickily humid. They had left at 5 a.m. and driven deep into the forest to a makeshift dam where they were to meet the guide Mrs Chen had arranged. Zhou had stripped off and was swimming. Wu sat on the edge of the logs, dangling his feet in the cool, clear mountain water. Among the trees surrounding the dam was a tiered patchwork of tiny fields of tea, ginseng and other crops. Wu looked uncharacteristically charmed by this unexpected Eden.

'Still sure you want to go to America?'

Kovic hoped he was changing his mind, since the chances of his making that happen for him were slipping away by the day.

Wu nodded at the base of the mountain.

'Ask me again after this.'

Qi was sorting through the equipment: a harness each, soft rubber soled shoes, chalk to increase hand grip, Kernmantle nylon rope, the most expensive he could find, carabiners to hold the rope in place, nuts to drive into the rock to secure the rope, descenders and belay plates to run the rope through.

He gestured at their surroundings.

'Incredible to think that a hundred million years ago this was under the sea.'

'Yeah? Well it's still not dried out.' The humidity was already getting to him.

The first thousand metres was thick vegetation, mostly pines, some of them growing straight out of deep fissures in the rock. Above the treeline, where the vast granite plug emerged, it bristled with small shrubs and ferns that clung stubbornly to its vertical surfaces. Stone steps carved by the monks who were the first to inhabit the peak over a thousand years ago were still visible in places, but notably absent in others. And for the last ten years it had been a no-go area. Finding the way up would be impossible without help.

Qi moved on to his laptop, which he had connected to a small antenna attached to a tripod beside him. Kovic peered over his shoulder. 'This is a map of the electrical system, which gives a pretty good idea of the layout. Combined with what I got via the spectral imaging from the weather satellite I can confirm that the perimeter wall has a high voltage line round it that acts as both a deterrent and an alarm.'

'Work on how you can disable it. Any indication of ways in or out through the wall?'

'Seems as if the only conventional way in is via the helipad.'

Almost right on cue the sound of a big twin rotor helicopter pounded the air, unseen above the low cloud collaring the mountain. Qi looked at Kovic.

'We could do with one of those.'

'Maybe we'll borrow one to get out. Look out!'

A tiny man came trotting briskly towards them over the dam, grinning and waving, wearing the hat and clothes of a country peasant. Slung over his shoulder was a small canvas knapsack, out of which stuck the head of an ice axe. His agility and his face, a network of deep creases, did not match.

'My God,' said Kovic. 'It's the goblin of the rock.'

'Welcome to our country!' He saluted Kovic and then wrapped a claw-like hand around his. 'My name is Heng. I hope you are taking pleasure in the many wonders of our land.'

They all stopped what they were doing and looked at him. Seriously – this was their guide?

'Absolutely: I am a great admirer of your country,' said Kovic. What had Mrs Chen told him? That they were harmless hikers hoping to take in a spot of bird watching and guerrilla warfare?

'He's older than my grandfather,' whispered Wu.

The man looked at least eighty, and Kovic felt a twinge of responsibility. They were prepared for danger, but this guy looked as though he might expire before they'd even fired a shot.

'Mrs Chen has given me strict instructions not to ask you about the purpose of your trip, nor to repeat any words I hear exchanged between you. On this you have my word. There is no time to waste. We need to be above the treeline by sundown.'

'How long to the top?'

He looked at them like a new teacher discovering he'd been stuck with the duds.

'I have done it in a day. You, maybe two – if you make an effort and don't waste time. Don't worry, I will wait for you!'

At this he let out a weird, staccato sound as if imitating machine gun fire: he was laughing.

'Let me see your equipment.'

Qi showed him the pieces he had laid out. The old man examined each item and frowned, then shook his head and wagged his finger at each one.

'This – no, this – no, these – no.'

Qi looked aghast. He had spent hours researching the best equipment for such a climb. Heng kicked the high tensile ropes dismissively.

'No point in these. There are plenty of ledges to grip with your fingers.'

This supposed reassurance fell like a dead weight between them. Wu looked particularly sick.

'Adds bulk – loses you balance …'

Kovic looked afresh at the old man's claw-like hands with new respect – the perfect implements for clinging to a rock face in a gale.

'What about those nice old ancient steps?' asked Zhou.

Another burst of machine gun fire.

'They are long gone. The current inhabitant had them destroyed.'

He resumed his critique of their kit.

'Much too much. You will have enough trouble just hauling your own body weight up the sheer face. Only the most essential items must come with you. Open your backpacks and throw out anything you can live without. Look.'

He opened his own frayed canvas bag.

'Water, food and blanket. That's all. And the axe, for putting the injured out of their misery.' More gunfire.

Kovic wondered how much Mrs Chen had actually told him. He nodded, curtly hoping he wouldn't say anything else that exacerbated the mood of despondency.

None of them had moved so Heng snatched up one of the bags and started rummaging through it. As well as the climbing kit there were the weapons, one gun each, ammunition, explosive packs for detonating doors. At the sight of the arsenal, Heng's expression changed. He admired the guns, nodding gravely. He'd got the message all right. Mrs Chen had insisted they could trust him. Let's hope she's right, Kovic thought.

'Okay, maybe we take the ropes to help you with all this.'

There was a collective sigh of relief. Heng examined the ancient watch on his wrist, its face almost opaque with years of cracks and scratches, like his own.

'Well, let's not stand around scratching our arses, eh!'

# 38

Kovic inched forward. Above him, the wall of rock disappeared into cloud; below, between his feet, perched on a ledge no more than a foot wide, the sheer face dropped into the world they had left. To his left a few yards behind was Zhou, ashen. Wu and Qi stayed close behind him, their faces against the rock, tears glinting on Qi's anxious face.

He looked away to the right at Heng who gave him a broad grin. When he had first seen the old man skipping across the log dam he had instantly dismissed him as a joke. Now he was in awe.

They had been climbing for six hours. At first it was relatively easy. Some of the ancient steps carved centuries ago by monks were still there. But after a few hundred feet they petered out. Kovic wondered if it had been Tsu's deliberate joke to leave the first few steps intact.

'Just close your mind to what is below,' Heng said, cheerily. 'Focus on each step, grip and think: *I am going forward.* You will feel very alive at these moments, more so perhaps than ever in your life before.'

Heng had been a mountain guide for twenty years, he had told Kovic. Before that he had spent twenty-five in a work camp, mining asbestos.

'All I have to do is remember those days, deep underground: the dust, the coughing, rats swimming in the great vats of rice soup they fed us. People dying all around me. This is the life!'

The old man's eyes sparkled as he spoke.

# 39

'Here is good.'

Heng swung round and put down his pack. The ledge they were moving along had narrowed, and the darkness that had settled around them was almost a blessing as it shrouded the ever-increasing drop below.

'We can have a few hours' rest and be fresh for the dawn.'

Kovic looked at the others. None of them returned his gaze. Their eyes were fixed either on the rock face to their left or the ledge immediately under their feet.

'I told you you'd get into the swing of it,' Heng added cheerfully. He unrolled his thin mat and lay down gratefully, as if on a king-size four-poster at the Hyatt.

It was 2 a.m. They had been on the move without stopping for five hours. Kovic lay down and the others followed suit. Qi fell straight to sleep without even removing his pack.

'Sleep well, gentlemen,' said Heng. A few moments later he was snoring loudly, his tiny frame vibrating, his mouth wide open to the elements.

'I hope a large insect flies in and chokes him,' said Zhou.

'He *is* an insect,' said Wu. 'He's *The Fly*.'

'He's not normal. Have you noticed he never has to piss?'

'Hey, cut it out. Do like he says. Get some rest.'

Kovic felt his phone buzz in his pocket and twisted himself round to try and pull it out without plummeting to his death. It was certainly one way to put you off checking it too often. It was a text from Hannah. *We need to speak. URGENT.* His time was up. She was back on his tail. He turned it off and concentrated on trying to get to sleep without falling. He found a rock about the size of a melon to put in the narrow space between him and oblivion, to discourage his tendency to roll over in his sleep. Then he closed his eyes and dreamed of Louise.

# 40

The bright beam of light prised Kovic out of his slumber. His dream had shifted location. He was back in the Sea Hawk – but not over North Korea, he was peering out of the door looking down on Tsu's hideout. He opened his eyes and found he was looking straight down the thousand-foot drop. All that had prevented him from going over was the rock he had used to wedge himself in. He recoiled, twisting on to his back, and realised the helicopter was no dream. A big twin-rotor Chinook was overhead, commencing its descent on to the mountaintop.

They were all awake now, and in different states of alarm. Heng turned and greeted them, water bottle in one hand, a date bar in the other, legs crossed casually.

'Good morning, gentlemen. A fine day for the last leg of your journey.'

The temperature had dropped dramatically in the night. The others looked grey and underslept.

'How far now?' Qi asked in a small voice.

'Well, that was the easy bit—' Heng announced. He was enjoying his role as team sadist. 'Today the ledge disappears. There is also a fissure.'

None of them felt like asking him to elaborate.

'Come, I'll show you. It's just around the corner.'

They all edged forward. Heng crouched down so they could see past him. The rock face was split open in a vertical crevice about ten metres deep.

'We used to sling a rope and winch across. The alternative is to go straight up. Since you have been quite slow I suggest the latter. Also there is a weather system coming in which means high winds.'

He delivered this news like it was another twist in an exciting game he had arranged for them.

'I don't think I can do this,' said Qi. The other two looked at Kovic. Wu cleared his throat.

'The fact is – we had a discussion in the night, while you were asleep—'

'We came to a decision.'

Zhou chipped in.

'Even if we made it over the wall, what then?'

'Why say this now?'

'It's one thing to look at it on a laptop—' He gestured at the vertical face of the mountain.

Kovic looked from one to the other. Any sense of adventure or challenge had drained from them. He couldn't blame them. It was his project. They didn't have the same investment in it. He had exploited their loyalty, their disinclination to refuse a mission due to their own pride. But somewhere on the punishing climb this had ebbed away.

'You're right. It's madness.'

Kovic got to his feet. Relief swept across their faces.

'I'll go on alone – with Heng. It's probably for the best. You guys head back. I'm sorry to have brought you this far.'

Kovic could see the unfamiliar expression of pure hatred on Wu's face. Going back without Heng would be suicide. Kovic knew it. They all knew it.

Zhou spoke up again – the first time he had sounded negative.

'Even if you get in, how will you get out?'

'If I ever asked myself that question, I wouldn't have gotten into this game.'

Up ahead they could hear a low humming sound.

'What's that?'

Heng beckoned. 'Look past the crevice – you'll see.'

At first it looked like a giant birdcage slung from a cable that reached the summit, inching its way up.

'It's a new addition.'

Qi spat. 'Now you tell us.'

'It can only be operated from the mountaintop end. The station at the bottom is unmanned and remotely locked.'

Kovic raised his binoculars and examined it.

'There's someone on board.'

Inside the cage they could see three people. Two were in uniforms similar to the checkpoint guards, and kneeling between them there was a third person, shackled and hooded.

He turned back to Heng. For the first time on their journey Heng's face failed to radiate any joy.

'The transports are becoming more frequent.'

'How come?'

'It is known that Tsu has an appetite for pain – other people's. I've heard it said that he makes them fight each other for their lives while he watches.' Heng shrugged. 'Anyway, what's it to be?'

# 41

Heng secured the rope, and Kovic went first. There were points where the face leaned outwards and he was clinging on only with the edge of his fingers. And, as Heng had warned, a wind was getting up. He had promised the others that he would get them out either by the cable car or by commandeering a chopper. But he knew that it was the thought of trying to get back without Heng that had swung it. What none of them knew was Kovic had not thought beyond his encounter with Tsu.

Zhou came next. He seemed to have passed through a barrier of fear and recovered some of his cat burglar's head for heights and was now approaching the rope task with steely determination. Wu, following in his wake, was soldiering doggedly on but Qi, so far out of his hacker's comfort zone, had tears running freely down his face, and to add to his sense of shame, he had wet himself. The others pretended not to see.

Heng hauled Kovic over the last rock and there it was: Tsu's domain.

'Holy mother of fuck.'

It was nothing like Qi's grainy photographs. The entire wooden structure and pagoda roof was gone. In its place the granite perimeter wall had been raised another ten feet, with a series of narrow apertures, like arrow slits in a mediaeval castle, spaced about fifty feet apart, too narrow for any human to fit.

'Come.' Heng beckoned them forward. At the base of the wall was a five- or six-foot-wide ledge. 'This goes all the way around.'

'What about the gate?'

'It's blocked up. There is just one opening for the cable car.'

'No other way in other than over the wall?'

'There's a storm drain. It travels deep under the structure then climbs vertically to a grate in the south-west corner of the courtyard.'

'Are there any cameras? Is it patrolled?'

Heng shrugged. 'What for? They don't expect anyone to be mad enough to make the climb.'

Heng put out his hand.

'Well, good luck. You know the way back. I'll leave the rope in place in case you decide to come down the slow way.'

He gave one last burst of laughter.

Kovic embraced him. The old man's spirit had sustained him and was a useful antidote to the falling morale of his crew. He wished he would stay, but he didn't want to involve him in what was coming.

Heng shook each man's hand. They were all of them in awe of him, and Kovic knew that without his example as well as his knowledge, they would never have made it.

Kovic watched him disappear over the ledge and down, then looked at the other three, each of them in different states of exhaustion.

'What's the plan, boss?' Zhou seemed to have gotten his second wind.

'We make a base while Qi gets his kit set up and gives us an update on activity inside.'

The ledge sloped down to the east, close to where a small clump of bushes clung to the edge of the wall.

'There.'

After the endless balancing act in so little room, the space felt like a football field. They dropped their bags. Qi got out his equipment, set up the tripod antenna and adjusted his screen.

From out to the east, skimming the surface of the clouds, accompanied by a deep throated thrumming, a large heavy-duty helicopter came into view.

'Aha, what do we have here?'

'That's a Chinese AC313, based on a 1960s French Aerospatiale Super Frelon. Carries twenty-seven passengers, and four to five tons of cargo.'

'Way past its sell by date then.'

'Not exactly,' said Qi. 'The rotor blades are composite, it's got digital avionics, it's certified for high altitude – over 4500 metres above sea level, plus it's fully equipped to work in extreme weather like blizzards and as low as minus 46C.'

'I'll check the registration.'

Kovic raised his binoculars but there was nothing visible on the polished black surface of the machine. It made a circle of the mountaintop before starting its descent, disappearing behind the wall.

'Okay, thanks to our friends the Russians' misbehaving weather satellite I have eyes inside the wall—'

'And?'

'Oh fuck. Look at this.' Qi turned the laptop toward Kovic. He used his hand to give the screen some shadow while he peered at it. He hadn't known what to expect and the jumbo-sized chopper should have been a hint. The inner courtyard also contained two smaller helicopters, one a standard executive carrier, the other a two-seater with open sides. But what really caught his attention was the number of men in military gear exiting the AC313: at least thirty, fully tooled up with armour and guns. His half-baked plan to storm the battlements was rapidly evaporating.

'For a recluse, he sure likes company.' Kovic looked at the wall. 'I need a better look.'

A fresh plan started to take shape in his head. He glanced at the others. Wu was already asleep and Zhou not far off. He turned back to Qi.

'Wire me up.'

'What, right now? Don't be crazy. You need to rest like us mortals.'

Kovic wasn't listening. He felt energy coursing through him. He had come this far. Something big was happening over the wall and he couldn't risk missing it – or worse – missing Tsu. He unrolled the grappling hook and the gas-propelled launcher. It could also fire stun darts, of which he had brought a generous quantity, as well as a couple of smoke canisters. He hesitated then decided against taking any of them with him.

Qi was watching him closely.

'This is just a look, yeah?'

'Yeah, 'course.'

There was a lack of conviction in Kovic's tone that Qi found worrying. He gave him a micro-receiver, which he pushed deep into his ear. 'This is the same model you use on surveillance and stings, but it's modified for altitude and has a bigger range. These walls might cause some distortion and if you go underground you're incommunicado, remember that. It's technology, not magic.'

Qi switched on his end.

'Receiving?'

Kovic nodded.

'Copy.'

Qi grasped his shoulder.

'You be careful. Don't get carried away, okay.'

He spread his arms. 'Like this? I doubt it.'

Qi wasn't convinced, but he wasn't in a position to argue.

Kovic attached the grappling hook and line, aimed and fired. It caught the top of the parapet. He pulled on it with all his weight: it was firm. He tensed the line and started to climb, looping it round his fist as he went. It was punishing on his arms, but something else was driving him now that blotted out the exhaustion. He reached the parapet, grasped the edge with both hands and hauled himself up, flattening himself along its surface. A flag on a pole fluttered in the wind, bearing the snakehead trident and flaming fist.

'Holy shit,' he whispered to himself.

Qi picked up the whisper loud and clear.

'*Talk to me!*'

'Another group of men are disembarking from the chopper, camouflage dress, no armour, just cases and laptops. They look like command staff. But there's blue in that camouflage. They're not private security, they're navy. What the fuck is this guy up to?'

He took out his phone and ran a burst of video for Qi to work with as he built up a plan of the facility and ID'd the uniforms.

Qi's computer sucked up the video.

'*Okay, got that. You coming down now?*'

Kovic didn't answer. Still crouching on the parapet, he pulled up the rope.

'*Kovic?*'

Qi was waving up at him.

Kovic waved back. He knew it was madness, but the whole venture was. Why stop now?

He patted his top pocket, checked for the South African passport. 'I'm going to offer him my services.'

# 42

Kovic lay face down on the helipad, surrounded by guards, their rifle muzzles inches from his head and a boot pressing on the small of his back.

'Give me a freakin' break, guys – I'm hardly going anywhere.'

None of them showed any understanding of what he was saying. He couldn't see because they had forced him to face the ground but he could hear more men being rushed towards him.

'Find someone who speaks English, quick.'

A minute passed before the English speaker was found.

'State your name and business.'

He waved the passport.

'Ray Nyman, from South Africa. I heard Mr Tsu is recruiting.'

He was banking on this being more plausible than most covers he could have chosen, now the world was awash with former South African Special Forces looking for private security work.

'*Okay, I'm hearing you,*' came Qi's voice in the receiver buried in his ear.

'Look you guys, go easy on me, okay? It was a lot harder getting in here than I bargained for and I'm as good as dead so you can do pretty much what you want with me. Lock me up if you have to, but a bowl of rice wouldn't go amiss, or better still, a nice juicy ostrich steak to remind me of home.'

They hauled him to his feet.

'Thanks. You gonna take me to the boss?'

Without a word they frogmarched him towards a small metal door that didn't look like the visitors' entrance. As they got near, another guard on the inside opened the door and they entered a dank, dark tunnel, which had been carved out of the mountain itself. The only light was from a series of naked bulbs attached to a cord that was pinned to the roof. Through another door was a row of cages. The stench of human waste caught in his throat. At first it seemed that none of them were occupied until he noticed what appeared to be a bundle on the floor of one which moved slightly.

'Hey, I wanna see Mr Tsu. I've got serious skills here, man. Hey—!'

'Be quiet. Stay here.'

They pushed him through the mesh door into a cage and locked it behind him.

'Hey, how about some of that famous Chinese hospitality?'

The guards turned and left. He whispered to Qi but, of course, there was no answer.

'Well at least I'm in,' he said to himself. He examined the cage. There was a bucket, and a bunk made of the same mesh as the cage. The floor was disturbingly sticky. He wasn't sure which category this mission came under: impressively courageous or just stupid. Right now it felt like the latter. For all he knew Tsu might not even be here. But what other options did he have? What sustained him was the thought that he could very easily be sitting at a desk back in Langley, just at the moment a very attractive thought, but not once he had replayed the events of the last few days. Eight thousand miles wouldn't have taken him away from the reality of what had happened to the men on the border, and to Louise.

He remembered something he was once told by a Vietnam vet who had survived four years in a Vietcong prison camp. At first the idea of getting back home sustained him; he felt motivated to hang on in there and when he got back to marry the girl who was waiting for him and take up the job that was lined up for him in her dad's auto repair shop. But, as time wore on, something in him knew that future was receding. The war and imprisonment had killed that part of him. So to fend off despair he focused everything on vengeance. And when the opportunity came to escape, instead of getting the hell out and going home, he went rogue, and with a couple of fellow inmates wreaked revenge on their captors. If Kovic needed any further inspiration, it was in that story.

After an hour the lights went out. There was nothing to do but try and sleep, but after about three hours all the lights came back on and two guards appeared. They marched him to a shower room, gestured for him to strip and wash. He pretended not to understand in the hope of picking up some useful comment. The water was tepid but welcome. He dried himself on a small, stained cloth and they gave him a green jump suit to put on and some rope-soled slippers.

'Do I get to eat?'

Neither of them replied. He made an eating motion but there was no reaction. He was seriously hungry. They marched him out through the tunnel and into the courtyard. It was dark outside; cloud shrouding the mountain fogged the floodlights so they cast ghostly rays. This time he was unshackled and allowed to walk without being held, but when he glanced at the watchtower to his left a hand reached out and gripped his neck, turning his head away.

'Okay, washed and dressed for dinner,' he mumbled as if to himself but in the hope Qi was listening.

'*Thank God: where were you?*'

'Taking a nap.'

They paused at a huge pair of varnished dark wooden doors, knocked and waited. Kovic heard automated bolts slide back and one of the doors opened. They passed down a stone-floored corridor decorated with fabulous ancient tapestries, Han Dynasty depictions of warriors on horseback, worth millions. Through another pair of heavy doors was a room that seemed to be constructed entirely out of grey marble that reminded Kovic uncomfortably of a tomb.

A lone figure stood with his back to him, smoking. Without turning round he waved the guards away. Kovic stood and waited.

'What do you want?'

'Just looking for work, sir.'

'How did you get here?'

The voice was so low it was almost inaudible, the English fluent with an American accent.

'Climbed, sir. It's a hobby.'

'South African?'

'Born and bred, sir.'

'Speak some Afrikaans?'

*'Daar was eendag 'n woud*
*aan die kant van die son,*
*die maan is 'n flou olielamp*
*saans brand honderde kersies …'*

'What's that?'

'"*Hansie en Grietjie*" – Hansel and Gretel. First poem I learned at school. And the last.' Kovic gave a little chuckle, which Tsu didn't share.

Slowly he turned; Kovic felt his innards go cold. He hoped to be in the presence of the man who had sent his killers to the border. But the profile was unmistakable. Tsu himself was the assassin – no question. His profile, the slight stoop as if his neck had been broken some time ago and had never fully straightened, and the tattoo on his left, not his right wrist like the others he had seen. He must have descended from his mountain retreat especially for that mission. He gestured for Kovic to sit, exposing the tattoo under his cuff as he did. Kovic sat. It was all he could do to keep his composure – and his cover.

'You don't look white enough.'

'My father emigrated to Jo'burg from Athens. My mother's Cape Coloured.'

'What would I want with a *lǎowài*?'

'I've seen guys in Hong Kong with white muscle: drivers, minders. It's a fashion statement.'

'The fashion is for Anglo Saxons. You're too dark.'

'I can speak the lingo a good deal better than most.' He recited a few lines of Mandarin.

Tsu's gaze hovered somewhere above his head. Despite the lack of eye contact, Kovic could feel himself being sized up.

'Ever killed anyone?'

'A few.'

'Where?'

'Soweto. Then Liberia, Sierra Leone, all the shitholes in Africa.'

'So you think you are capable of serving me. Would you kill your fellow man – to order?

Kovic shrugged.

'It's all the same to me.'

Tsu came up very close and peered into his eyes. He wasn't all Chinese, that much Kovic could tell. His features were too pointed. It was a hollow stare that emitted supreme confidence and deathliness all at once. Kovic wondered for how many this look had been the last thing they had seen.

Tsu turned away. 'Show me what you can do.'

He snapped his fingers. A door opened and one of the guards entered, dragging what Kovic thought at first was a large animal on a long chain. It tried to move on all fours but its limbs wouldn't work properly. It was a grey brown colour; its back was mottled and scarred. The guard carried a whip in his other hand and with this he lashed the creature's back with the whip so it jolted upright. Then Kovic realised – it was human, a naked, horribly beaten male, grey with dirt, the hair on his head caked and matted, with pinkish bald patches where tufts had been wrenched from his scalp. Judging by the length of his beard and the way his long hair was matted into semi-dreadlocks, he had been imprisoned for some considerable time. The remnants of shirtsleeves clung to his back, the cuffs of which flapped emptily at the end of each arm. If the man still had any hands Kovic couldn't see them. The guard, oozing contempt, put on a show for his master of kicking his prisoner hard in the stomach and wrenching the chain as he shouted something indecipherable. The man convulsed; a dribble of bloody spit hung from his half open mouth. He made no noise except hoarse breaths. The guard jerked the chain and dragged the man to a point about fifteen feet from Kovic.

Tsu came round the table and stood beside Kovic. From his tunic he took a Glock and raised it to Kovic's temple.

'Stand and face them.'

Kovic stood, his heart smashing at the inside of his ribcage. Tsu kept the Glock pressed against Kovic's head. With his other hand he produced an identical gun and handed it to him.

'There's one bullet. Let's see what you're made of.'

The guard tugged the chain again and the man knelt upright. His eyes swam in Kovic's direction but they didn't focus. Now that he knew it was Tsu who had administered the fatal shots on the border, Kovic knew he would not hesitate to pull the trigger. Kovic had been in a few firefights, but had only killed in what he reasoned was self-defence. *I should put the poor bastard out of his misery,* he thought. *And anyhow, what choice do I have?*

He clicked off the safety and raised his arm. The prisoner slumped a little and the guard lashed his back with the whip so he jolted upright. Without moving his head, Kovic glanced at Tsu whose eyes were focused on his face. No chance of swinging round and taking a shot, no matter how quick his reflexes were. He aimed at the slouching figure. The guard jerked the chain that was attached to a metal collar round the man's neck and whipped him again on the back. Kovic looked at the prisoner, who was barely conscious, and the guard who was frothing with hate. He aimed, squeezed. His hand jolted with the recoil. The guard's head jerked sideways as the bullet burst open his neck just above the Adam's apple, his cap tipped back off his head and he sank slowly to his knees as if the life were ebbing out of him feet first.

Kovic turned his gaze back to Tsu to leave him in no doubt which man he had aimed at.

'What's the matter? Didn't I get the right one?'

# 43

Tsu's mouth stretched wide. His eyes lit up like a kid at Christmas and he let out a long hyena-like laugh that was like nothing Kovic had ever heard before. Eventually the laugh subsided.

'Interesting choice.'

Kovic said nothing. He gazed at the poor prisoner, who was trying to comprehend what had happened. Tsu took the empty Glock from him and pressed a button on the wall.

'Amusing, but also very revealing.'

Two more guards rushed in, then slid to a halt when they saw their dead comrade.

'Your cover is absurd. I can tell that you are an American. You're fatally compromised; you've allowed yourself to be infected by a naive sense of fair play, hence your siding with the victim, the little guy. You want to help the downtrodden, bring liberty and justice for all, blah, blah, blah. You've come to the wrong place. I don't help the downtrodden; I help the powerful become more powerful.'

Tsu was right; he had blown it. Kovic turned and faced him. There were many things he had done in the line of duty that he wasn't proud of, that he would prefer to forget if his mind allowed it. He had bent and broken the rules and made up some of his own along the way. But he had never killed a defenceless man. He levelled his gaze at Tsu.

'And you can shoot a man in the head when he's lying wounded in the snow. What kind of "helping the powerful" is that?'

Tsu snorted contemptuously, but when he looked at Kovic again the lofty disdain had faded from his face. The retort had hit home. He could see Tsu's thoughts whirring.

Well, Kovic thought to himself, at least I've got in front of the monster. But he knew the truth was he had fucked up.

Outside, the courtyard was filled with the sound of another helicopter preparing to land. Floodlights came on and a landing crew moved into position. Tsu pressed the button. Two more guards rushed in.

'Clear that away,' he barked at them. 'And take this one back to the cells as well.' He picked up the gun he had given Kovic and smashed him across the face with the grip. 'Have him prepared for questioning.'

# 44

'Qi, you clocking this?'

There was no reply on the transmitter at first. Then Qi's voice, low. *'You okay?'*

'Been better. I'll be out of range for a while but try to stay online. You got eyes on the arrivals?'

*'Yeah, captured on camera, checking the IDs. Some VIP and his entourage. How are you going to get out of this?'*

'No idea yet. If I don't make it out, take everything you have to Huang Shuyi at the MSS. Record everything you can. Wu should recce the cable car, see if it's viable for exfil.'

Qi signed off.

There was no point in alarming them and the last thing he wanted right now was rescuing. He wanted to see who had arrived on the helicopter, but just as the door was being opened, with two of Tsu's henchmen in attendance, his head was twisted away from the view. All he caught was the gleam of the highly polished finish on the machine and a carpet being rolled out across the rain swept courtyard. A guard hustled him forward.

'Hey, easy, okay?'

The butt of the guard's gun slammed into the side of his head and he blacked out.

He came to, trying not to focus on the phrase 'prepared for questioning'. He was in another cheerless, windowless room, again with one bare bulb for illumination. In the centre was a thick wooden pillar that looked like it had been part of the original structure. On it were several metal rings of the sort found in a stable. There was a metal band round both of his wrists that was attached to a chain that tethered him to the pillar.

Alone in this dank cell, doubt began to gnaw at him. What had he achieved? He had risked the lives of three good men on this crazy mission. He had gotten access to his adversary's hideout and come face to face with him. But that was it. Now he was powerless and about to be tortured by a sadistic killer. Self-doubt, an alien sensation he barely recognised, engulfed him. He cursed his own impetuousness. He remembered some comments of his instructors at the Farm. *Too headstrong, can take things to extremes, drives too fast at obstacles, a reckless appetite for risk that needs to be reined in.* It was all true, and he hadn't changed. For all those reasons he was here now gambling with his life – and those of his crew – on an encounter with an adversary who would almost certainly destroy him.

He thought of Cutler, his head propped up on his fingertips, shaking his head in dismay. Glad to be rid of him no doubt, relieved – even happy – in the misguided assumption that he had died in a fire.

Then he thought again about the shootings on the border, re-membered his promise to Garrison, and then thought, painfully, about Louise. What did he have left to live for? It was as if all his life he had been jumping into the fire, propelled by some death wish or an insatiable need to challenge himself, to live as close to the edge as he could. Only in Shanghai had he found a kind of peace – and now even that was gone, forever.

His thoughts drifted on to Hannah. She had surprised him. He had detected something of the maverick in her, and the misfit, as if she knew her destiny lay somewhere other than in the MSS bureaucracy and was just looking for a good enough reason to rebel. She had believed him – against all odds, against her better judge-ment. She had staked her career on him. He had better not let her down. As he thought about her the sense of doubt and defeat began to dissolve. Perhaps he was not done yet.

A low metal door opened and Tsu stepped through it. He had changed uniforms, from loose fatigues into a dark formal tunic. He was carrying a brandy glass. He held the door open and an-other figure came in. This man was older: fifty-something, bald, unusually tall for a Chinese. His whole bearing exuded authority. The brilliant-white uniform stood out in such dazzling contrast to the dank grime of the room it almost glowed. The sight of this figure in these surroundings was so strange and unexpected that for a few seconds Kovic didn't register who it was. The naval dress was a give-away, but it seemed hardly possible. As he came closer, there was no doubt – Admiral Chang Wei, Commander-in-Chief of the Chinese Navy. *What the fuck was he doing with Tsu?* The two men circled the pillar he was chained to, studying him as if he was an exhibit at a show.

Eventually Tsu spoke, in Mandarin.

'The one who escaped from the border: Kovic. The CIA claim he's dead. Quite why he's here is a mystery. Maybe we can – encourage him to tell us.'

Chang came right up close and peered at Kovic. He smelled of aftershave and liquor. His voice was hard edged from decades of barking orders.

'One less American running around our territory can only be a good thing. It was remiss of the bureaucrats in Beijing to have let so many of them in. How much does he know? Has he talked?'

Tsu grinned.

'I haven't applied myself to that yet.'

Chang turned to Kovic, addressing him in English.

'Your people have polluted the minds of our young generation. Your values are not our values. Our spineless politicians have been seduced by your toys, let you offer the people Buicks for their bi-cycles, fooling them into thinking they were getting some fanciful idea of freedom by buying your goods.'

He waited for some response from Kovic. None came.

'Do you know how many people there are in China, Agent Kovic?'

'One-point-three-four-three billion. Give or take.'

'Good.'

'If you don't include Taiwan.'

The Admiral's face registered irritation at this perennial bone of contention, but he pressed on.

'Four times that of the United States. And the average American consumes *fifty times* more of the earth's resources than a Chinese. Imagine what would happen if we allowed every one of those Chinese to consume at the same rate. Your so-called values will kill our nation. I'm not going to let that happen. You've fooled our politicians into letting the capitalist genie out of the bottle. I'm going to put it back.'

Kovic stared ahead, silent, trying to get to grips with what was happening right in front of him: one of China's most powerful military men in league with its most notorious criminal. But he absorbed every one of Chang's words. The pieces were slowly starting to come together.

'Modern China was forged in the furnaces of sacrifice, and honourable toil – something America lost long ago. Now you seduce and corrupt us with your poison, of the body and the mind.'

His voice was getting louder; this was his worldview, the mantra that drove him, and it told Kovic just what he had walked into. The border incident, the riots – it all amounted to nothing less than the preparations for a military coup engineered by Chang himself. This lunatic was planning to take over the biggest nation on earth.

'Democracy is an illusion! A dream you use to sell refrigerators and French fries. The real rulers of your world are corporations, not your precious Congress.'

Kovic felt he should show he was paying attention.

'So you want to turn the clock back? That'll be popular.'

Chang's reply started as little more than a whisper.

'Agent Kovic, do you know how old our civilisation is? When your continent was still overrun by savages with feathers through their noses, China had invented gunpowder, the compass, the clock, the printing press. Before Western meddlers came and corrupted us with their opium, China had bestowed a good living on a fifth of the world's population.'

Tsu was nodding and grinning. He was enjoying his party. Kovic felt a lifetime's worth of hatred and bitterness trained on him. Tsu addressed Chang in Mandarin.

'Is there anything specific you'd like me to get from him? His career was completely compromised by the border incident. His bosses seem to have dispensed with him and he must be sore about that. I doubt there's much there. The MSS regards him as low level.'

Was this designed to provoke him into talking? And who had Tsu had got that from – Hannah or her bosses? How deep did his links to the MSS penetrate?

Tsu glanced at Kovic and continued, slipping back into English.

'He's unimportant but quite slippery. He left his whore in his bed as a decoy so he could pretend to be dead and escape.'

Kovic felt the tenuous hold he had on his anger break apart.

'You mean your goons were too stupid to check under the bed-clothes before they shot and burned her.'

Tsu brought his face up to his and pressed a finger under each of Kovic's eyes, pushing into the sockets.

'Be careful or I might give in to my natural tendencies.'

The Admiral turned away, a look of disgust on his face, murmuring in Mandarin.

'See what he has on Jin Jié and his associates – elements among the elite who support him. Then do what you want with him.'

Tsu relaxed the pressure and Chang headed towards the door.

'What's your problem with Jin Jié? He seems pretty harmless to me.'

Both men turned and looked at him, surprised by his grasp of the language. Chang's response was full of venom.

'Jin Jié represents everything that is sick and corrupt in this country. His so-called "progressive" ideology will destroy what's left of our system. His weak will has allowed him to be seduced by the mirage of American superiority. He's just another instrument of Western humiliation. It is time to turn back the clock, to bring order back to our society. America is a threat and must be treated as such. *You* are the enemy.' Chang's voice became shriller with each sentence until he was shouting into Kovic's face, spraying him with his sulphurous saliva.

He turned to Tsu.

'Squeeze everything out of him and then post the remains back to the White House.'

And with that, Chang strode out of the room.

# 45

Kovic opened his eyes but could see nothing. Had his eyes been gouged out as well? He had a vague memory of Tsu knocking him about the face after Chang had left the room. Every part of his body stung as if he had been attacked by a swarm of hornets. What had he told him? It was coming back. He had recited random names from his extensive knowledge of politburo apparatchiks until Tsu realised that they were just that – random names.

'That's the problem with torture, isn't it, Tsu – you may get answers but how do you know they're the truth? We know all about the pitfalls of torture. We spent thousands of hours chasing leads from rendered detainees who gave us the first thing that came into their heads to stop the pain.'

Tsu hadn't liked that answer much and Kovic expected not to make it to the end of the session. But apparently he was still alive.

He felt his eyes. They seemed to be intact. He was just in complete darkness. Then with his fingers he explored the area around him. The rough rock surface was slimily damp. There was a foul smell of human waste. He tried to raise himself a little, but his head hit hard rock. He was in a crevice no more than thirty inches high, deep inside the mountain rock.

Now it was all starting to make sense – in a mad kind of way. Chang was Tsu's client. If Tsu was working for Chang when he killed the Americans on the border then Chang must have been the architect of the whole *Highbeam* set-up. He would have had the clout to get the North Koreans to cooperate. His aim must have been to disgrace the current Beijing administration for its collaboration with the US, and create the opportunity to foment anti-American feeling. But to what end? He had focused his hostility on Jin Jié, but he was just one man – influential, yes, but an outsider. Chang had talked grandly about putting the capitalist genie back in the bottle, turning the clock back. Then the border incident was just an appetiser for what he was cooking up. It was as if he wanted nothing less than a new cold war – or even a hot one.

As he recovered his senses, Kovic realised he wasn't alone. Someone, or something, was sharing his cell. He felt something nudge his hand. Something cold and soft: a rat? He moved it away. A minute later he felt the nudge again and a slurping sound. The sound was a word.

'Here.' The voice was no more than a lisping whisper. 'Follow.'

Kovic let his hand be nudged and didn't move it away this time. He was pushing it in a direction where the floor met the wall. But he was at the extremity of what the chain attached to his wristband would allow. He forced his arm forward until the band cut into his flesh.

'Feel – under.'

There was a slot-like gap where the wall met the floor, no more than an inch wide, just enough for Kovic to insert his little finger. He felt something smooth, a blade.

'I made – can't use now.'

Kovic withdrew it from its hiding place. It was no more than half an inch wide but a promising six inches long.

'Hey, thanks. Who are you?'

But there was no answer.

Kovic slid the blade under his right cuff. Then he drifted back into unconsciousness.

# 46

Kovic came to again to find himself being pulled from his crevice by the chains attached to his wrists. He struggled to shield his eyes from the blinding torchlight coming from the two guards who were manhandling him. They tried to stand him up, but under his bare feet it felt as if the ground was covered in broken glass. As his eyes adjusted to the light, he looked down and saw that the soles of his feet were a bloody mass, and remembered Tsu beating them. Then they put a blindfold over his eyes and tied it fast and dragged him out into the open air.

'*Kovic. My God, what have they done to you?*'

It was Qi. He must be looking right at him.

He didn't want to risk talking so he just nodded an acknowledgement, then moved his head around as if trying to focus after his time in the dark.

'*Okay, there's twenty-plus in paramilitary kit, all carrying Uzis. Looks like they're waiting to board the chopper.*'

Kovic nodded a response.

'*Something else you should know – all hell's broken loose in Shanghai: eighty-plus killed by a bomb in People's Square. No one knows what the fuck's going on.*'

The guards dragged Kovic further into the centre of the courtyard. He felt the sun on his back, so reckoned he was facing north. He tried to blank out the searing pain in the soles of his feet.

'*There's a scaffolding on the north face of the perimeter wall, with a long plank of wood on top, which sticks way out over the edge. They put it up overnight, next to the steps.*'

Before Qi had worked it out, Kovic guessed.

*Oh, fuck.*

'Tsu?' He said the name aloud, figuring the guards would assume he was asking them.

'*No sign. Wait! Some big doors opening on the south side. That's him. Same para gear as the others. Coming towards you now.*'

They were outgunned as well as outnumbered. Even with what they had, Wu and Zhou would be no match for the guards with their Uzis. Kovic needed a Plan B but there wasn't much time to dream one up. He knew this had been a suicide mission, so he deliberately hadn't thought too much about the outcome. He wanted to find Tsu and he had. He wanted to confirm that it was he who killed his team on the border and who else was behind it, which he had. And now he was about to pay the price with a fast trip back down the mountain. With his fingertips he felt for the home-made blade in his sleeve. It was trapped behind the metal cuff on his wrist. He could feel Tsu's breaths near him now, short, quick, excited. He addressed his men.

'Before we embark, a little appetiser. And a reminder of what the consequences are if any of you arouse my displeasure.'

Tsu whipped off the blindfold.

'You smell disgusting.'

'Guess that's what happens when I get near you.'

Tsu struck him across the face. A ring on his forefinger cut a furrow across his cheek and he felt the blood run.

'Up the steps, you worthless piece of shit.'

'That would be a whole lot easier if you hadn't beaten the crap out of my feet.'

'You don't shut up, do you? Maybe you will when you understand what's happening.'

'Yeah, yeah, the old walk the plank routine. Thought you'd be bored with that by now, but maybe you don't have the imagination to think of anything new.'

Kovic reasoned that if he was going to go, he wasn't going to give Tsu the satisfaction of seeing any flicker of fear. He continued in Mandarin for the benefit of his men.

'*No wonder you were such a reject at high school. Is it true that your dick is as thin as a pencil? Is that why all the girls laughed at you?*'

211

Kovic saw a couple of the guards exchange astonished glances, trying not to laugh. His hands were still shackled, about thirty inches of chain connecting the metal cuffs, with a similar arrangement around his ankles. All the time he kept his hand pressed over the cuff on his wrist, wary that the blade might drop through. He needed Tsu to come close again so he could use it.

The guards were filing into the helicopter as the pilot started the engines. He could see Qi, the top of his head just visible over the parapet on the south side. Beside him was Wu, half hidden behind the gun-sight. Kovic shook his head. Even with his level of marksmanship, it was too risky a shot and doubly disastrous if he missed and alerted Tsu to their presence.

'Up the stairs. Get on with it.'

Kovic refused to move.

'*Is it true you are so sexually perverted you can only do it with a chicken?*' To this Kovic added a stream of orgiastic clucking.

Tsu came forward, grabbed him by the chains and hauled him up the steps. A stiff wind was blowing from the east and Kovic felt it tug at his clothing. Tsu prodded him forward.

'I'm through with you, Kovic.'

'Just as I thought we were beginning to get along.'

Tsu kicked him hard and Kovic fell against the planks. He was beyond the edge of the parapet now, nothing beneath him except a few thousand metres of crisp mountain air. Tsu pulled him back up on to his feet. Kovic worked at the blade furiously, but it was jammed in the metal band. It was now or never. Below, some wisps of low cloud hung damply, waiting to receive him. Suddenly, the blade came free, too fast for him to catch it. He watched in despair as it pinged off the granite wall and flew downwards, glinting in the sun.

It was gone.

Tsu, surprised, looked down – and Kovic saw another chance. He yanked his fists upward so the metal cuffs hit Tsu under the chin. Then he pushed forward with all the strength that his exploded feet would allow so that they both fell. He didn't care if they both went over; at least he would be sure of finishing the job. But they didn't. Tsu landed on the stone of the parapet, Kovic on top of him. Tsu writhed and struggled to free himself. He was in much better shape than Kovic after his night of torture and was soon on top, bearing down, trying to press his thumbs into Kovic's eyes. Kovic tried to fight him off, but his movements were limited by the metal cuffs. Then he saw one last opportunity, stretched his arms out and raised them as high as he could. He couldn't see any more, he could feel thumbnails almost piercing his eyelids. As Tsu pressed down, Kovic swung the chain so it wrapped around Tsu's neck and with what strength he had left he crossed his fists and kicked out at the same time. Tsu was now half off the parapet, his arms flailing. Kovic could hear someone coming up the steps.

'Take out the chopper!' he yelled, in the hope that Qi would pick up the order and pass it on to Wu. For a second nothing happened. Only Wu had the marksman's skill and knowledge of the right place to hit an aircraft. Then it came – the shot – followed by a massive blast as the machine's fuel tank erupted. The rush of air nearly sent them both over the edge. But it was Tsu who slipped. He scrabbled desperately to get some purchase on the stone. Kovic kicked out again and Tsu's weight dropped. Now he was suspended by the chain, his own weight tightening it around his neck. His body twitched and jerked, his fingers scratching at the chain and his legs flailing, but there was nothing he could do. All Kovic had to do was hold on just long enough.

'This is for Olsen and all the others.' Kovic gave the chain an extra tug. 'And for Louise.'

Tsu's tongue hung out of his mouth like it was trying to escape. His eyes bulged in dismay. He was trying to speak but Kovic didn't care. He had heard enough.

Gradually Tsu's strength ebbed away and his body hung limp. Kovic couldn't hold on much longer. It would be too cruel if Tsu's dead weight carried him over. Wu was running towards him along the parapet.

'Get me out of here!'

He stopped, twenty metres away. 'Head down.'

Kovic turned and Wu fired. The explosion stunned him, but the bullet did the job. The chain sprang apart and Kovic looked up in time to see Tsu's corpse smash into the wall and then bounce out again and fall down and down and down, head twirling over heels until it was engulfed by the clouds.

# 47

There was no one else to tell. Hannah didn't spare her father any details and after she had finished, he sat in silence processing what he had heard. They were in his study, surrounded by memorabilia: photos of him with Mao, Deng, his staff, and his medals. His patriotism was undimmed by the years in exile. He was the one she measured herself against, his stoicism and forbearance she tried to live up to, but lately she had started to question whether those fine values were relevant to her now – especially today.

'I'm sorry I had to burden you with this. And I hope you will understand I had no alternative.'

She was braced for his reaction. She knew that as an exemplary Communist he had always cherished the sanctity of the state and respected its authority, despite the past. How would he respond? Surely he would accept it was self-defence, though she was under no illusion that she would have a hard time convincing a court of that.

To her surprise, the old general's mouth curved into a small smile. He wiped a strand of silvery hair from his brow.

'Your method of dispatch shows great ingenuity, I will say that for you. And the fact that he was in the act of ingesting an illegal substance does leave his reputation somewhat compromised.' Then the smile vanished. 'But I've always warned you, dearest Shuyi, your impetuousness would land you in trouble.'

She let out a long silent sigh. How many times had she heard this before?

'Of course, I will make some inquiries and see to it that you are not implicated. The chances are that the powers that be will wish this sorry incident to be hushed up. Such an ignominious demise does nothing to help the reputation of the MSS.' He let out a small hoarse laugh. 'And based on what you've told me it sounds like he could have – slipped.'

Then his brow furrowed again. 'For the time being you must take great care not to upset anyone. Further unusual acts could focus suspicion on you and cause people to suspect you. As we used to say, keep the peak of your cap pulled down and your eyes low.'

'But how can I, knowing what I know?'

She had told him about the bomb in the square and the call-to-action text.

'Really, my dear, it could have been from a friend in the Navy Ministry to that poor boy.'

'It's an official internal Chinese Navy number and the text was broadcast to over two thousand people!'

He wasn't hearing her. The fate of the Director of the MSS was one thing, but he wouldn't hear of the navy's good name being brought into disrepute. It was one thing to have exposed a single bad apple at the MSS, but his respect for the armed forces, as for all state institutions, remained inviolable.

'My advice is to let that lie. Especially in these times of heightened tension with foreign elements.' He tapped the chair arm with a gnarled finger. 'And also with the return of your friend Jin Jié—' He shook his head as if the mere thought of him was distasteful. 'You don't want any – how shall I put it – repercussions from your association with him.'

He wrapped his gown around him and stood.

'I must return to bed. You get some sleep, my child, and we'll talk about it some more in the morning. I'm sure it will all look a bit different by then.'

He stooped to kiss her on the forehead and walked slowly out of the room. She watched him go. All her life she had looked up to him as the fount of all wisdom. Now he seemed deaf to her, deaf to what was happening in his beloved China.

She went to her old room and lay down on the bed. But what exactly *was* happening? The sight of young people dead and horribly wounded ... It was as if the country was unravelling and she didn't

216

know why. Then a horrible thought occurred to her. The Director had been deaf to her concerns, just like her father. Were they *all* in denial? Why?

She thought again about Kovic. She hadn't breathed a word about him. Turning him loose was a classic example of what her father called her impetuousness. Anyway, it didn't much matter now. He had ignored all her texts. She would be surprised if she ever heard from him again. Maybe it didn't matter now. Her own future was in jeopardy. She took out her phone. She needed to call Jin Jié and see that he was safe. Then she saw all the missed calls and the text.

*For fuck's sake call.*

It was from Kovic.

# 48

**USS *Valkyrie*, South China Sea**

Garrison stared out at the vast, jet-black expanse. It was a strange thing to do, to spend months away from home, trapped on a gigantic floating metal city, surrounded only by sea and sky. Not for the first time, he was asking himself what made him do it when the personal price had been so high. Sure, he wanted to serve his country – to be a role model, even a hero. But the effect on his own life had been a cruel reversal of that dream. He knew what it had done to his marriage. As for his son ... Tommy had said that he had followed him into the navy to get closer to him: his exact words. He was killed in Afghanistan at nineteen. And Marcy had never explicitly blamed him but it was there in her eyes. The deaths of Olsen and his team and then the conversation with Kovic had brought back memories of that terrible day. And now Kovic was back on the satphone, with more crazy stories.

Only this time something was different. Against his better judgement, he found himself believing every word.

Garrison had met Admiral Chang Wei only twice; once on the first Sino–American joint manoeuvres, a pointless exercise that had nothing whatsoever to do with naval matters and everything to do with politics. There, he had been respectful but aloof, barely able to hide his disdain for the whole venture. The second time was more purposeful, to flesh out the strategy for their anti-piracy campaign here in the South China Sea. Then, Garrison had noted a disturbing change in the man, as if his arrogance, barely restrained before, had burst out and taken charge. His opposition to the mere idea of the US policing waters so close to China was something he made no secret of. There were many orders Garrison had had to follow regardless of what he thought of them, but that was all part of military life. Without obedience the whole proposition was blown. Chang had done his part, gone through the motions of cooperation, but all the time Garrison couldn't get it out of his mind that there was another agenda driving him. And although the sea looked empty from the command bridge, he knew damn well that over the horizon the Chinese Navy – Chang's fleet – was watching his every move, just as he was watching theirs. Something about the way Chang was positioning his fleet bothered him. And then there was the unrest in Shanghai. Two separate things – until Kovic put them together.

'You still there, sir?'

'I was thinking.'

'Are you aware of the implications of this, sir?' There was an impatience in Kovic's tone.

'Naturally I am. You sound like hell, Kovic. You looking for exfil?'

'Negative, sir, attractive as that sounds. There's more to be done here.'

'So what is it you want me to do?'

'Raise the alarm about Chang with the Pentagon.'

'You briefing your people – Cutler?'

'Not till I'm back in Shanghai. I want to do that face to face. It's going to be difficult for him, accepting the idea that he was set up by Chang. When you speak to the Pentagon don't use me as the source. It will be dismissed as ass-covering.'

'How you gonna get off that mountain?'

'I'm working on that now, sir.'

Garrison thought he could hear gunfire in the background.

'You under attack?'

'Kind of.'

'You better watch out, Kovic. If what you're saying has any substance, any substance at all—'

'Absolutely, sir, will do.'

And with that he was gone.

# 49

Kovic dropped the satphone into his pack. A second later, the cable car jolted to a halt.

'Fan-fucking-tastic.'

At least this time he wasn't to blame. The auxiliary battery power was Zhou's discovery; it kept the cable car going if the mains electricity was cut, which thanks to Qi it was. He had blacked out the whole complex, plunging all the subterranean rooms into darkness. And for good measure he had also jammed their backup systems. The whole mountaintop was literally powerless. The cable car was the only moving part left – until now.

The helicopter explosion had taken out a substantial number of Tsu's men and distracted many more. The survivors, thinking there was more to come, had taken cover underground, which gave Kovic and his crew some time to organise their escape with only limited resistance. And as Zhou had also managed to disable the security system, all but a few stragglers were locked in. Kovic was delighted. His team had all come good. But now they were suspended on a tiny platform, a thousand feet from the ground, unable to move.

Eventually Wu spoke up.

'So, what we gonna do?'

There was a definite change of tone towards their leader. Just the state of him saw to that. Every part of his body whipped, beaten or slashed. The soles of his feet were now huge scabs from being flogged, and he had lost a couple of teeth when Tsu smashed him over the face with the Glock. He glanced sideways, causing a new increment of pain to shoot across his jaw.

'See that rope?'

A large coil of cord was tethered to the side of the platform cage,

220

quite long, but almost certainly not long enough. He tried to infuse his voice with optimism.

'Do a quick measurement; see if it reaches ground level. If it does, we fast-rope down.'

'Without gloves?'

'We'll use our clothing.'

The others tried not to look too obviously at the rags he had left.

'And if it doesn't reach the ground?'

'The tree canopy down there's quite thick. We fast-rope – and pray.'

Wu went first, as he was the only one of them who had been trained to do this. Zhou, whose head for heights had been severely tested on this mission, followed. Whatever misgivings he had, he kept them to himself.

'It's like this. Either you try or I'm gonna have to leave you behind and you can hope someone switches the power back on, but I wouldn't fancy your chances after that.'

Qi took his time, knowing there was no alternative but unable to bring himself to commit to the rope. His face was streaked with fear and sweat but this was no time for pity, in fact there was no time for anything. In the end he made quite a good job of it, trapping the rope between his feet, benefitting from his low body weight. Kovic watched him disappear into the foliage. Like the captain of a ship, he insisted on going last.

Then he bound his hands with strips of what was left of his shirt, and was preparing to go when something knocked him on the head. Whatever it was floored him, and he lost consciousness for at least a minute. A bullet must have grazed him because when he came to, blood was oozing down his forehead into his eyes. But the car had lurched forward. The power was back on. He was going up, not down, and someone was shooting at him.

Another shot twanged off the cage. Kovic had to get off the cable car – now. Already it had ascended at least five hundred feet. He had survived to this point, and there was no way he was going back up the mountain. There was nothing else for it. He gripped the rope and kicked out. The rope immediately chewed through the makeshift bindings on his hands and his feet failed to get a proper purchase on the cord. He was falling, falling, the air around him soothing, cooling his wounds, even as the rope burned his hands. Another shot zinged past him as he hurtled towards the tree canopy. After that he blacked out again.

# 50

*Always in the right place at the wrong time.*

It had been said about him more than once. In Lebanon, searching the room next door to the one that was booby-trapped; in Iraq, in the seat behind the Humvee driver who took the bullet; in Afghanistan, in the one part of the base where the suicide bomber's blast didn't reach.

And now, after losing his grip, freefalling towards the earth and crashing through a network of branches, he had splashed down harmlessly, in a deep narrow lake. If he was religious he could have said it was God's work, giving him a break after the night's indignities.

He was wet and winded, but unmarked by the fall. He looked around at the tranquil woodland scene, an unspoiled pocket of the world not yet desecrated by man. Maybe someone was on his side after all. He was filled with euphoria. He had gone up the impossible mountain and come back down in one piece, having done what he set out to do. And the water cooled all his injuries wonderfully. But as he swam to the edge of the pool he knew that there was no time to waste, that events were gathering pace. Tsu had been thwarted, but Chang was unstoppable. The whole world order was under threat.

From his backpack he took out the satphone. He prayed to God, if he was there, that it still worked.

# 51

**MSS HQ, Shanghai**

Hannah moved swiftly through the subterranean corridors of the Golfball. More than ever, she felt like a stranger, an interloper. People stared at her. She was used to that, being one of so few women in the Ministry, but there was also the damage to her face from the bomb, which she had made no effort to cover up. She wanted people to know that she had been there and took some grim pride in the fact that unlike the rest of them she had first-hand experience of what was going on. So far no one was talking about the Director. That was expected. The shameful circumstances of his demise would already be a closely guarded secret. But how long did she have? No one had seen what she had done, but his guards had been close by, had known she was in the room. There would be questions. And even if they couldn't prove it, she, an American-educated woman, in this time of paranoia, would make a perfect scapegoat. But all of this was blotted from her mind by what she was hearing now, the phone pressed to her ear as she headed for the parking garage. Surely Kovic had got it wrong.

'Admiral Chang Wei is one of our greatest military heroes. He is revered for his devotion to the Party.'

'For fuck's sake, Hannah.'

'Please can you lighten up on the profanities? He is one of my father's oldest comrades.'

'Yeah? Well your old man's got great taste in friends.'

'What's more, he's regarded as a standard bearer for all those who reject corruption.'

'Okay, try this: Chang made no secret of his loathing of your pal Jin Jié as the shining example of everything he hates about the way China's going. So if he wants to deliver the country from evil, he should get the hell out. Tsu turned out to be Chang's go-to guy for all his dirty operations; neutralising him isn't going to stop the Admiral from world domination.'

She slammed her pass down on the card reader and pushed through the double doors. Chang Wei, of all people. Was it possible? Did her father know anything about this? Was that why he wouldn't listen to her?'

'Are you still there? Look, I know the MSS only hears what it wants to hear but I thought you were above that. Or are you gonna tell me that in the daylight you're just another of those drones sucking dick for preferment?'

She held the phone away in disgust, but she didn't hang up. She would have completely discounted Kovic's claims, but for the one small but terrifyingly significant detail – the texts that had emanated from the navy bureaucracy. Kovic was effectively telling her she was right. Now she felt completely alone, except for Jin Jié and this uncouth American barking down the phone.

'So, anyway, you gonna get me outta here or what? Because the remainder of Tsu's men are going to be crawling through the forest looking for us.'

'Stay out of sight. Text me your location and give me six hours.'

She killed the phone and pointed the remote at her car.

# 52

There was just the two of them in his quarters: Bale and Commander Garrison, his eyes fixed on the young radioman.

'This stays in the room. No one outside is to know. *No one.*'

Bale nodded vigorously, his eyes shining with excitement. When he enlisted he had been told to keep his expectations low, just do what he was told and not to expect recognition. His MAIN-COMM supervisor on the *Valkyrie* had chewed him out more than once for asking too many questions. And he had nearly fallen in the shit again for daring to speak to Garrison. But hey, look where it had got him. And now his supervisor was under strict orders to leave Bale alone to concentrate on his special project. Garrison had even given it its own codename – *Armature*.

Spread out on his desk was a large map of the Chinese mainland.

'Okay, Bale, do your thing.'

'I can input it to your laptop, sir.'

'Just draw it in good old fashioned pencil, please.'

'Yessir.'

Bale bent over the map and positioned Garrison's parallel rule, a family heirloom from his grandfather's sailing days. The first line he drew followed the path of the first stream of 'noise' he had picked up – from the North Korean border to the point in the mountains west of Shanghai. Garrison hadn't shared the significance of this; in fact all he knew himself was that it conclusively linked the scene of his Marines' annihilation with the mountain hideout Kovic had just called from. His first thought had been to communicate this straight to Washington, but some instinct kicked in which stopped him. The CIA would get to hear about it and however he played it, it didn't look good for them. If what Kovic was saying was right,

Chang had led them into a trap. Langley might try and spin it or squash it. He wanted Bale to help him put some more flesh on it first.

'Sir, you understand we don't know what its content is unless someone in the NSA can decode it. And you gave me strict instructions not to forward it to them.'

'Yeah, let's not worry about that right now. Let's concentrate on where it goes. See where that takes us.'

Bale consulted his notes and drew another line.

'This starts in the same mountain location and goes out to Zhanjiang.'

'The base of the South Sea Fleet of the PLA Navy.'

'Yessir.'

'Can you be more specific? Zhanjiang's a big base.'

'Well, sir, there are two streams with an interval of about five minutes between them. The first starts on land—'

'It's mobile?'

Bale nodded. '—and the second finishes on water.'

'Okay, let me ask you this – how big a device would it need to be to generate this kind of stream.'

'Sir, I don't have that information.'

Garrison smiled.

'I'm asking your opinion. Give me your best guess.'

'It could be as small as a laptop.'

'So the device is portable. Possibly carried by an individual?'

Bale wasn't given to speculation but Garrison was pushing him. He nodded. 'I guess so, sir.'

'Okay, this is good. Where else?'

Bale unrolled a large street map of Shanghai.

'I've collected three streams coming from Zhanjiang.'

'Coming into the city?'

'No, going out – and from three different locations.'

Bale consulted his notes again and carefully drew three small crosses.

'Let me look.'

Garrison bent over the map. The first he recognised. It was the

Navy Ministry. The second he didn't know but the third ... He felt the blood drain from his face. He looked away so Bale wouldn't notice, kept his voice matter of fact and level.

'Okay. Double-check those coordinates?'

He turned back to Bale and fixed him with a deathly gaze.

'Absolutely no one else is to know about this, Bale. You come direct to me, as soon as you're done. Doesn't matter when, day or night.'

'Understood, sir.' Bale saluted and left.

The door closed. Garrison was alone, listening to the blood pulsing in his temples.

# 53

**Hangrui Expressway**

The road was slicked with rain, but Hannah drove like a bat out of hell. Not just because Kovic needed exfil ASAP; she was filled with the need to get out of the stifling atmosphere of Shanghai – fast, as if it would engulf and suffocate her if she didn't hurry. There was something gratifying about the thunderous power of the Benz, her domination of the fast lane, wipers on high swatting the slanting rain, as if bearing down on slower vehicles, lights ablaze, all but pushing them out of her path, gave her back some sense of control over her destiny. One of the compensations about her country was that you could drive like a madman and not get stopped.

In her head, she still didn't know what to make of Kovic. He was a type that just didn't exist in China. He was more like a character out of Wild West mythology. A loner, blazing his own trail, taking the law into his own hands, making more enemies than friends along the way. Since his appearance, her life had turned upside down. She had done things she would never have imagined herself capable of. He was nothing like her father and he was the polar opposite to the only other significant male in her life, Jin Jié, the visionary, the believer, who looked for the good in everyone with whom he came into contact. It shocked her how Kovic had got under her skin, as if he had detected that underneath her armour of reserve and respectability was an inner core of rebellion. And he had willed it to the surface. Now it came back to her. As she was facing the Director's advances, desperately working out how to react, she had asked herself, what would Kovic do? She looked forward to telling him.

A BMW she had blasted past was giving chase, the driver evidently infuriated at being overtaken by a woman. She pushed her foot down further, hearing the supercharger kicking in. The BMW shrank in her rear-view mirror as the needle edged past 200kph.

She and Kovic were in much the same position, fugitives from their own organisations, in pursuit of a truth to which their masters were either deaf or actively against them finding out. But still she was wary. He was clever, probably a highly skilled manipulator, a con man; he needed to be to do the work he did. Was he using her for his own dubious ends?

And his claims about Admiral Chang Wei … the man was a legend; he commanded almost universal respect, her own father's closest comrade. She had intended to put off telling Jin Jié what Kovic had told her until she was able to interrogate him face to face, but as she put more miles between her and the city, she started to doubt the wisdom of that. She selected the phone on the car's computer and speed-dialled Jin Jié's number.

'Hannah, what a pleasant surprise.'

He was always so fucking cheerful. Nothing seemed to faze him, no matter what his detractors threw at him, but up to now that had just been words. She told him what Kovic had said.

'You've got to take precautions. You need a proper security detail, people you know you can trust.'

He laughed.

'So thoughtful of you to worry about me. Please don't. What's happening is just the inevitable knee jerk against progressivism. It's to be expected.'

'Chang wants to eliminate you. My sources for this are impeccable.'

She didn't tell him it had come from the uncouth looking American he had seen her with the other night.

'All right, I'll lock the door and keep the curtains drawn, if it makes you happy. I've got to go; my lecture's about to start.'

He rang off. Hannah fumed to herself. Why didn't anyone want to take her seriously? Couldn't they see what was happening?

# 54

**Huangshan Mountains**

Keeping directly under the cable car's wires high above, Kovic slowly navigated his way through the forest; following them would surely lead him back to where the others had fallen to earth. The undergrowth was thick and the rain had made it boggy underfoot. Not much light filtered through the canopy above and the forest was filled with the strange sounds of exotic wildlife. Tsu had certainly been good for one thing – the land around his mountain had been almost untouched by humans.

Kovic's body still hurt like hell, but surviving the fall had restored his energy, that, and the grim satisfaction of having wreaked his revenge on Tsu. He plodded forward. The others had better have survived.

He found Zhou first. He was sitting on a fallen tree barely awake, keeping watch. Qi was with him, asleep behind a curtain of foliage. Zhou had found him curled up in a foetal position, frozen in shock from the descent. Qi was so convinced he wasn't going to make it Zhou had spent some minutes persuading him that he was still alive and intact. Thanks in part to luck, and his own light weight, Qi had hit the ground without injury. It was Zhou, the accomplished burglar with a track record of jumping off tall things, who had broken his leg. In spite of this, the joy of having survived had lifted his spirits. Kovic shook Qi awake. He looked up and eyed him with a mixture of relief and dread.

Kovic read his mind.

'The worst is over – that's a promise. You did good. Real good. Get some rest.'

Qi's eyelids closed and he sank back into sleep.

'No sign of Wu?'

He was missing. They had disabled their phones, removing the batteries when they were on the mountain. Perhaps he had forgotten to put his back together, though Kovic doubted he would overlook something so basic. Maybe he was lying unconscious somewhere. The rain was coming down harder. They were all soaked, dazed and hungry. Kovic texted Hannah their location from the satphone. The best they could do was wait for her rather than go looking for Wu.

'Get some sleep. I'll keep watch.'

Zhou fell immediately into a deep slumber. Kovic watched his sleeping comrades. In the last forty-eight hours they had explored the limits of their capability, and risked their lives over and over for him and his crazy cause. It was his job now to get them back where they came from. Shanghai might be in a state of unrest, but at least it was their home turf; they knew how to go to ground there. Word would have come down from the mountain about them and their escape. But now that Tsu was gone, would anyone be bothered to come after them? About five metres away there was a narrow path through deep undergrowth that ran parallel with the fallen tree. Kovic kept watch on it, turning his head each way every few seconds so there was no chance of being surprised.

It was inevitable. He hadn't slept for thirty-six hours. Only jumping up and down on the spot could have kept him from following the other two and being sucked into a deep and all-consuming sleep. It might only have been for fifteen minutes, but it was deep enough for the search party to form a tight circle around him before they prodded him awake. There were five of them and five guns and no possible means of escape.

# 55

They stared at him down their gunsights for several seconds. They all looked young and inexperienced. Always a bad sign. Youth usually went with an inclination to shoot out of sheer nervousness. None of them looked at all calm. Mind you, their great leader was lying dead somewhere in the foothills of his own mountain. Maybe after the head had been guillotined, the body soldiered on.

Eventually the tallest, who also appeared to be the leader, murmured in Mandarin.

'He's a real mess. Must be the one. Call it in.'

Kovic slowly raised his hands. He figured at least giving himself up on the spot might distract them from searching for the other two still asleep just a few metres away. He hoped the guards hadn't found Wu, but that would explain his silence.

The leader prodded him to get up. Kovic rose, keeping his movements slow and deliberate. They patted him down and then grabbed his bag, with the satphone back inside. Unless they destroyed it, the GPS signal would lead Hannah to him, he hoped.

The leader studied the screen. Kovic had emptied its call log. He dropped it in front of him and stamped on it.

'You, come. Hands – on – head,' barked the leader, in an apparently exhaustive demonstration of his English.

'Sure thing.' Kovic cursed himself for this lapse of concentration. After all he had been through in the last forty-eight hours, what an inglorious apprehension. The guards were whispering to each other as he staggered forward. What punishment had Tsu decreed for whoever took his life? Perhaps his hubris was such that he never legislated for such an event.

It was a short march to an identical minibus to the one they had commandeered two days before. A guard sat either side of him. Since there was no possibility of escape at this stage he tried to relax, and conserve some energy for a moment when he might be able to use it. Did they even know the fate of their boss? Knowing the Chinese phobia about shame and ignominy, attempts would certainly have been made to hush it up, or at least spin it into a courageous death in combat. He wondered if they had found the body.

As they drove off, the leader, who was seated beside the driver, turned to him, his face full of venom.

'You pay – you die, same as him.'

Kovic didn't respond. So they knew. Well, at least he had accomplished this part of his mission.

The leader, perturbed by the lack of reaction, reached out and slapped his face. But the force of the blow was minimal, because just at that moment the driver slammed on the brakes. The bus slewed to a halt. Broadside on the track ahead of them was a Mercedes Benz SUV.

# 56

Hannah stood in the middle of the path, her ID at arm's length in front of her, her legs apart. Her Chang Feng sub-machine gun was hanging from her other hand.

'MSS. Here to receive your prisoner.'

The guards looked at each other. She was doing and saying the right things, but this was clearly the first time they had ever encountered a female MSS operative – or perhaps any armed female.

'This American scum is wanted on suspicion of mass murder and I have orders to bring him in.'

Nice touch, thought Kovic. But the fact she was alone, and the fancy SUV; they would take some convincing.

The leader stuck his head out of the window.

'Well you can suck my dick, cunt.'

Oh dear, thought Kovic, simultaneously appalled and fascinated by how this was going to play out.

Emboldened by their leader, another one chipped in.

'Yeah, get ready to receive my cock.'

What a shit country to be a woman in law enforcement. Hannah's eyes widened.

Now they all had to have a go.

'She can do us two at a time.'

'Yeah, one at each end.'

Hannah shifted her weight slightly and raised the barrel of the Chang Feng. There was that resolute look in her eyes that he remembered from when she had first arrested him.

'She's way out of her depth,' one of them said to another.

The leader leaned towards the driver and said, 'Go forward. And if she doesn't move, run her down.'

Hannah put away her ID and for a moment Kovic thought she was giving up. The driver revved the engine as if to warn her what he was about to do. Then instinct told him to duck – now.

# 57

'You don't think you're burning your boats here?'

Kovic shoved one of the dead guards out of the door and climbed out.

'Not at all. It was a simple matter of self defence in the face of insubordination.'

She threw the sub-machine gun on to the passenger seat of the Benz. The burst of fire had almost sliced the roof off the bus. The remains of the guards were scattered about the interior. She was utterly calm.

'First time I killed a man I threw up over him, couldn't stop myself.'

She eyed him coldly.

'Who said it was my first time?'

She didn't let on how shocked she was by the state of him, caked in dried blood and grime. He looked and smelled like something primeval.

'You need to get yourself smartened up.'

He put out his hand. It seemed strangely impersonal but he couldn't think of a more appropriate gesture.

'Thank you – you just saved my life.'

She didn't shake it. Instead she took his hands in hers and looked at them briefly. Her touch was cool yet somehow comforting.

'What about these guys?'

'They'll think you did it.'

Suddenly she grabbed her gun and shoved him aside. His ears were still ringing from all the rounds she'd fired so he didn't hear what had distracted her. Another vehicle approaching from inside the forest. Hannah raised her weapon.

'Wait.'

Lurching over the rough ground towards them was the Great Wall Wingle, with Wu at the wheel, and Qi and Zhou sitting alongside.

# 58

The rain hammered on the roof of Hannah's SUV as they slowed for the toll. On the outbound side, cars and minibuses jammed all the lanes, many of them weighed down with luggage. The exodus from Shanghai had begun.

The inner city streets were eerily quiet. Only the police were out in force, swishing hurriedly through the rain on bikes and in vans. Kovic considered his options. Officially he was still dead. He could check in with the CIA, brief Cutler on all he knew and face any consequences of his insubordination. Or he could disappear, reinvent himself and start over. He had the means and the cash to keep himself afloat for a good while, and boy, did he need a break. Hunting Tsu down and sending him to his death had brought him some grim satisfaction, but he was just the means, not the end. Chang was calling the shots and the thought of him out there threatening to blow up the world felt like unfinished business. If he didn't stop him, who would?

He had given Hannah a detailed account of his experience on the mountain, majoring on his encounter with the esteemed Admiral. She had listened without comment.

'You're not getting it, are you?'

'Admiral Chang is a great patriot. He has also fought against corruption in the political elite. The people love him for that.'

'Yeah, and it's all great cover for his plans for world domination. He's the reason for all that's going on – all this.'

Kovic gestured at a convoy they passed of minibuses laden with fleeing citizens.

'Lady, I just don't get you. One minute you're the gun-toting

239

freedom fighter, all for changing the world, next thing, you're the blind patriot toeing the party line.'

'We're just not as simplistic as you Americans with your good guys and bad guys. I thought you of all people would have learned by now that China has many layers. There's far more to it than you Americans will ever understand.'

'Then I'll be very clear,' he said, unable to mask his rising irritation. 'Chang has your boy Jin Jié in his sights. He's the next target, I guarantee it.'

'He's not "my boy".'

'Whatever. Look, it's fine if you want to believe his schtick. He's young, he's cute and he's got a way with words. But to Chang, Jin Jié's an American puppet, spreading the twin evils of democracy and materialism. Your great patriotic Admiral's too smart just to take him out. My bet is he'll use him in some other way.'

'Like what?'

'That's what you and I need to figure out, while Jin Jié goes underground.'

'He won't do that; it would be an admission of defeat. He'll stay visible no matter what.'

Four military helicopters swooped over them, headed for the centre.

'Good luck to that.'

She pulled up at a traffic light and looked over at him.

'You really are a mess.'

# 59

**Hotel Majesty Plaza, Shanghai**

It had been some time since Kovic had looked in a mirror, and what he saw looked like something that had risen from the dead. In a way it was perfectly appropriate, because that was exactly what he was going to do next. He was going to go and see Cutler and relay the news about Chang. He wanted to watch his face as he listened.

He attempted to shave but it was a challenge inserting the razor between the swollen cuts, bruises and fresh scabs. When he was done he wasn't sure there was any improvement, but at least he was clean and had made full use of Hannah's medicine cabinet.

Her apartment was small and austerely furnished, the kitchen evidently little used. This was the home of someone who didn't do much with her spare time other than sleep. What exactly was there between her and Jin Jié? Had they been involved at Harvard? Why should he care? When she bade him goodnight he thought he detected a different look in her eyes. She had let her gaze remain on his tattered face for a second longer than necessary, as if to imply – were he to ask, she might not refuse. But maybe he was flattering himself. And besides, the timing was all wrong. Louise still haunted his thoughts.

When he woke in the morning she was gone and there was no message. So maybe that was it, their brief partnership was over.

He put on a grey shirt and lightweight blue suit that she'd left out for him. She'd got the right size; maybe she had looked at him pretty closely – if only to take mental measurements. She had even found him some shoes that were well padded to house his flayed feet. He felt smarter than he had in a long time – almost human again – and renewed, ready to step back out into the world and rejoin the living.

The security presence around the US Consulate complex was heavier than usual. There were local police outside the gates, armed with sub-machine guns, and inside was a detachment of Marines in fatigues who looked extremely nervous. You should be, he thought to himself. The eye scanner and hand print reader confirmed his ID and he was waved through.

Mrs Chan was emptying a filing cabinet into aluminium boxes. She let out a piercing scream when she saw him, leapt from her seat and cowered in the corner of the room as if he was the Grim Reaper himself come to announce that her time was up.

'Good morning! Hope I'm not interrupting anything.'

He smiled in what he hoped was a reassuring way and made for the doors of Cutler's office.

'Th-the Chief is in conference,' she squeaked from her refuge. 'He said to let nobody disturb him.'

'Well that's okay then, because that's exactly what I am: no-body.' He let out an exaggerated Dracula-style laugh and opened the door.

Cutler looked up, and the colour drained out of his face. He swiftly glanced at the other person in the room, closed the file in front of him and got to his feet, by which time he had recovered his composure and spread his arms.

'Kovic! Thank God—'

Kovic glanced at his visitor who was leaning back in his chair. He looked vaguely familiar.

Cutler grasped Kovic's hand before he could offer it and clapped him hard on the shoulder right on one of Tsu's blows. He winced.

'Senator, this is Agent Kovic. Kovic, Senator Hiram Metzger.'

'Jeez, what've the Commies done to you, boy?'

Kovic glanced at Cutler.

'Got a little lost in the woods but I'm all right now, thank you, Senator.'

He rifled through his mental files trying to recall what he knew about Metzger. All he came up with was that he was a hawk and that he represented some Midwestern state, one of those in deep financial shit with a lot of shuttered factories that built the tanks and planes that won World War Two. Not someone he would expect to see in China, even on a good day. In fact as far as he could recall, Metzger was an outspoken critic of Chinese imports, who had publicly warned about the consequences of their being allowed to continue undercutting American products. He was a big man in his mid-sixties; one of those classic American males who was once military-grade fit but never stopped eating soldiers' portions. His shirt buttons strained over the mound of his gut and his neck rolled over his collar, but the eyes that peered out from under fleshy brows were still blue and sharp. What was he doing here?

'Well, I guess that wraps it up for now,' the Senator growled. He looked faintly irritated by the intrusion. He struggled to his feet. 'You know where to find me, Ned. But don't turn up unannounced – I may be sampling some local delicacy.'

Cutler forced out a laugh.

'Sorry if I interrupted something,' said Kovic.

Cutler was still in bonhomie mode.

'No, no, we're done. Take a seat while I show the Senator out.'

They were gone about thirty seconds. Kovic looked round the room. There were none of Cutler's workaholic stacks of paper on the desk, not even his camo laptop. More aluminium boxes were stacked in a corner, and parked behind his chair was a large American Tourister trolley suitcase. Cutler reappeared, closed the door, came back to the desk. His mood had changed.

'So, this is unexpected.'

Kovic smiled.

'I'm glad to know you're so relieved I'm still alive.'

'Well, of course we are; the authorities told us you'd died in a fire.'

Kovic studied Cutler's face closely as he replied.

'Yeah, it looked that way, but the body in the bed was my girl-friend. They got the wrong person.'

Cutler frowned.

'Who's they?'

Kovic helped himself to the chair Metzger had just vacated.

'I need to bring you up to speed.'

He outlined the highlights of his encounter with Tsu and Chang and what he had learned about the border incident.

As he listened, Cutler went pale. He put his hands together in his habitual way, as if hoping for divine inspiration, and pressed his fingertips against his lips. When Kovic had finished speaking, he was silent for several seconds. Eventually he spoke.

'You realise the incendiary nature of what you're saying.'

'Damn right.'

'This will have to go right to the top – the *very* top. You know what I'm talking about, don't you, Kovic?'

'Sure I do. That's why I came back. But where does this leave you, Chief?'

Cutler looked suddenly indignant.

'I'm not sure what you mean by that.'

'*Highbeam* being your pet project and—'

He shook his head and swatted the idea away.

'Kovic, this is the business we're in. I shouldn't need to tell you this. We have to take things on the chin.'

'Yes, sir.'

Kovic wondered if the murder of the Marines and Louise was something he needed to take "on the chin".

'I'll send this up the line right away. There are sure to be further questions and for your own safety stay in the compound from here on. Get some rest.'

Cutler got up quickly and marched towards the door and opened it. Then he put out his hand and arranged his face into a smile.

'Good to have you back, soldier.'

# 60

## Pudong District, Shanghai

Hannah rode the elevator up to her apartment. Her life was spinning out of control, her future in jeopardy. Disposing of her boss, the exchange with her father, the efficient dispatch of Tsu's men – she barely recognised herself. And yet she had never felt so alive. Though she hadn't admitted it to him, Kovic's claims about the Admiral's treachery added credence to her own suspicions, that the texts emanating from the Navy Ministry were not some rogue act, but part of a well orchestrated conspiracy.

She reached her door and turned the key. There was a strong smell of cigarettes. Was Kovic back? She hoped so.

There were at least six of them waiting for her, slouched over her furniture. Three more dressed in forensic suits were sifting through the contents of her bathroom. Instinctively she turned back towards the door, but another of them slammed it shut before she could reach it.

'Who are you?'

Their suits were too good for MSS. Could they be Tsu's men? One who was wearing tinted glasses held up a smartphone.

'Watch.'

She looked at the small screen. Frozen on it was a picture of her father, trussed up in a chair, a wide piece of tape over his mouth. The screen came alive. A hand ripped off the tape. His eyelids fluttered and then he focused.

'*Hannah, dearest. Please help ... please do what they say ...*'

There was a pause while he took several breaths as if just those few words had exhausted him. He looked anxiously to his left as if someone out of shot was directing him. '*Give them the American or they will kill me.*'

The screen went blank. Hannah lunged at the man with the phone but two others grabbed her from behind and held her.

'Do you get the message?'

She didn't move.

'We know about him and you.' He glanced at the two in the white suits. 'His DNA is all over this place. You are not only a traitor but a whore. Do it. Summon the American, or the old man will suffer – and so will you.'

# 61

Kovic gazed at the text: somehow it wasn't what he had expected.

*I want you – now. Come to me.*

Well this was an interesting turn, he thought. His mind had been elsewhere, digesting the events of the last few days, the first time he had actually stopped. He was beginning to wonder if his work was done, that there was nothing more he could do. He had dealt with Tsu, discovered who was behind him, convinced Hannah of the danger to Jin Jié, communicated with Garrison—

No, he wasn't finished at all. He went over his meeting with Cutler and the encounter with Metzger. What had brought the Senator to his office? He paid Mrs Chan another visit. She had recovered herself. Nevertheless he brought flowers, made profuse apologies for upsetting her, asked after her family and even made her blush with a reference to how lonely he would be having to stick around the compound. By the end of this he had established which downtown hotel Metzger was staying in, and had the personal numbers of his chief of staff and PA as well as the Senator's cellphone.

He spent some time online, studying Metzger's history. Over the last couple of weeks he had been globetrotting in his capacity as a member of the Senate National Security Committee. Kovic also YouTubed a couple of his more recent speeches back in his home state, strident denunciations of the Chinese for sucking business out of America's heartland, causing the loss of factories, and blaming them for the devastation of communities with their cheap crappy goods. The man was definitely no friend of China.

He hadn't decided how to reply to Hannah's text. Ten minutes passed and there it was again, with the additional message: *I know what you want and I want it too. Don't let me down.*

# 62

Qi took his time counting the money. Kovic had seen him do this a hundred times, and each time it irritated him more.

'Come on. Surely you trust me after all this time.'

Qi frowned at him and continued to count.

'I trusted you to bring me back alive.'

'Well I did, didn't I?'

He held up his bandaged, blistered hands from the rope descent.

'After this, we call it quits, okay?'

'Okay, sure, whatever you want.'

Qi finished counting and put the money in his safe – insisting, as he always did, that Kovic look away while it was opened.

'Okay, let's get to work.'

He plugged Kovic's cellphone into his system, put on the headphones and stared intently at a screen full of digits and characters that made no sense to Kovic. But that was what he was paid for, his ability to read and interpret intel that even other IT geeks couldn't understand. Worryingly, he was now looking confused. Confused was not good.

'I don't like this. I don't like this at all.' Qi shook his head. 'It's completely dead, like the whole building's been jammed. This is something new, okay? I may need some time.'

Kovic got up.

'Time is what I don't have.'

# 63

Kovic rang the bell and waited. When she opened the door he was lost for words.

She was dressed in a long strapless dress that stretched to the floor, in silver, with a hypnotic pattern that resembled fish scales. Her face was made-up so she was almost unrecognisable, her mouth painted a lustrous deep red that shone almost as much as the dress. She put up her arms as she came towards him and pulled him to her, burying her face in his neck.

'They have my father,' she whispered.

He held her, because it was all he could think to do.

He looked at the men in the room. They looked very like the ones who had chased him and Wu through Shanghai, their tattoos visible. You had to hand it to Tsu; he had organised his private army so well it continued to march on without him. They pulled them apart and frisked him roughly. There was no point in offering any resistance. If he went quietly, perhaps they would leave her alone, though he knew that was unlikely. They pushed them toward the door and frogmarched them both out of the apartment into the elevator. At this stage, his priority was to do what he could to protect her. What guarantee was there that they would release her father anyhow?

As they rode the elevator down to the parking garage, Hannah choked back tears of rage and shame. She felt weak and helpless. She had given in. She had compromised her only asset. They told her that her job might require appalling decisions, that people she cared for might have to be sacrificed; it was part of her training. She had been instructed that in such situations, loyalty to the Ministry, and ultimately to her country, came first. Where was her loyalty

249

now? A true professional should not have buckled at the sight of a parent in distress as she had. She hoped that Kovic had at least recognised her text for what it was – both a plea and a warning. He had looked so pleased to see her. Had she overestimated him? Just at that moment he gave her hand a small squeeze as if to say, *it's okay: I know.*

But that made it all the harder. He had come, knowing something was wrong, knowing that her text was out of character, and therefore that he would be walking into some kind of trap.

The doors opened onto the underground car park. They were moving toward a large highly polished black Cadillac Escalade SUV. A metre from the vehicle, she stopped.

'I want to see him.'

None of them spoke.

'I got you the American. Give me my father.' The leader had taken off the tinted glasses. He appeared to have one drooping eyelid.

'You want to see him? Here.' He pulled out his phone.

He dialled and waited, then said something none of them could hear. He held up the phone and they all turned to watch her as she looked. The screen suddenly lit up and there he was, her father, still sitting in the chair, but blindfolded now.

'*Shuyi? Is that you? Are you there?*'

'Father!'

She tried to grab the phone, but they held it away from her. The old man appeared to be able to hear her. Someone ripped off his blindfold.

'*Shuyi! I love you—*'

Then something wafted through from the left-hand edge of the screen and the old man jerked back as a spurt of blood shot from his right temple – everything else was drowned out by the volcanic roar of sound coming from Hannah.

Kovic hoped that she would have prepared for this, though looking at the long tight dress he couldn't see how. She didn't even have a bag in which to conceal a weapon.

The dress must have been specially made because the thin blade, about twenty centimetres long, appeared to come out of nowhere.

It must have been hidden in a secret pocket sewn into the seam that ran down her thigh. It was very narrow, less than a centimetre, the grip just slightly thicker. He watched with a mixture of dismay and admiration as she wielded it with such speed and precision, it was as if she had trained with it all her life for this moment. She didn't go for the chest; she went for the face and neck. So quickly did it drive into the team leader's droopy eye and out again that for a second he looked as if nothing had happened, until it came, a thin jet of blood. But already she had slashed it across the neck of the next man, down the face of the face of the third, and finally into the open mouth of the fourth. And all the time the sound, chilling and inhuman, came from her.

The fourth man was still clutching his weapon but Kovic's foot smashed into his balls and the gun fell from his grip as he doubled up in pain. A shot zinged over them from a fifth man in the vehicle but Kovic grabbed the fallen gun and took him out with a burst of fire.

The dress, the blade, the rage, all in the enclosed space – it was as if Hannah had morphed into some mythical beast. Now almost methodically, but suffused with anger, she revisited each one with the blade to ensure that none had any chance of survival. He hung back. This was her show, her grief. He knew all about that and what this would mean to her. He remembered Louise, what there was left of her and his own grim satisfaction at watching Tsu's body twirling helplessly as it plummeted from the mountaintop.

When she was done, she stood there and looked at him, blood dripping from the blade that was still in her hand, her fish-scale dress spattered and sprayed like a Jackson Pollock painting.

'Okay,' she said in a quiet voice. 'What now?'

# 64

Garrison's call came in before Kovic could think of a reply.

'I've got something for you.'

'Go ahead, sir.'

'Chang's location – he's in Shanghai in a downtown hotel. The Pudong Royale. His private chopper's on the roof. The place is pretty much in lockdown. We don't know why he's there or who he's seeing. But I thought you might like to know.'

Kovic reached out to Hannah and drew her in, held her close, while he continued the conversation.

'That's unless you want out. That exfil offer still stands.'

He held Hannah against him, as her body shook with grief.

'I'm not done here. What's the overview? What's the Pentagon saying?'

'The overview is that China's southern fleet is pulling in around us, and the Pentagon's telling me to do zip lest it inflame things further. Which for them is somewhat out of character.'

'Are they hearing what you're telling them about Chang?'

'I'm telling, but I can't guarantee they're listening.'

'And Langley?'

'Not a peep.'

'And you're certain about Chang's whereabouts?'

'I only have eyes from above but I'm looking at a live image of his machine on that hotel roof.'

'Thanks.'

Kovic slipped the phone back into his pocket.

Hannah straightened up, moved away from him, and wiped a hand across her face.

'I look like shit, right?'

'Under the circumstances I'd say you look pretty tremendous.'

'I'm sorry I had to involve you.'

'I think we're way past that.'

'I tricked you.'

'It was clear from your text that you were – not yourself.'

She managed a faint smile.

'You couldn't believe I'm – I was attracted to you?'

'Let's say I try to be realistic.'

She looked at him for several seconds, some indecipherable signal arcing between them. Eventually she spoke.

'My father's dead, my job's gone, I've just killed a bunch of men – I don't even know who they were. It's just you and me now.'

Kovic started to form a sentence in his head: *I can get us out of this right now – we could be on a US aircraft carrier in forty minutes ...* But the words stayed unsaid.

She took a big breath and slowly let it out. She looked small and vulnerable, but after what he had just seen, he knew that was highly misleading.

'Jin Jié's having a rally – the theme is "unity". I should be there with him.'

'Jeez, he doesn't give up, does he?'

'He feels it's his last chance to bring together the progressive forces in a show of numbers that will convince any doubters that there really is a future in China for freedom and democracy.'

'He has no idea—'

She cut him off.

'Ideas are what he's all about. Ideas and being able to express them. If he doesn't, who else will? The others—' she shook her head in disgust, '—are too afraid to step out of line and take a stand; too scared, and too corrupt.'

She stepped over one of the corpses.

'I'm going to go to him. The least I can do is show him some support – and watch his back.'

She started towards her car then looked down at the state of her dress.

'Perhaps I'll go upstairs and freshen up first.' Then she paused again. 'You could come too?'

Kovic smiled. 'Thanks, but I think you've got better things to do.'

# 65

Kovic made no comment on Wu's latest wheels, a sure sign that his mind was elsewhere. He didn't even ask him if he was rested after their ordeal up the mountain. All he wanted to know was that he had brought his spare ID. There was no point going in armed, they would never get past security. Wu drove at speed through the deserted streets.

He glanced at Kovic, who was deep in his own thoughts.

'What's the plan, boss?'

'You know me, I don't like plans. I'll figure something out when we get there.'

Kovic got as far as the main desk of the Pudong Royale Hotel, waving one of his South African passports.

'Where's my bags, hey? I left my luggage here only last week and now you're telling me it's gone? What kind of a show are you running here? You get the police on to it now. RIGHT NOW, do you hear?'

The women on the desk looked embarrassed. This kind of behaviour could get them into trouble with their bosses. Wu, standing beside him, pleaded to be allowed to look through the left luggage closet.

'Only for a moment, just to be sure – we're not going to touch anyone else's stuff. It's just, he's a bit upset, you know.'

'Upset!' roared Kovic. 'Of course I'm freakin' upset! D'you know what's in those bags? My wife's anniversary present, that's what!'

'I'm sure they will let us look,' said Wu. 'Just calm yourself.'

'Don't tell me to calm myself!'

So far so good. A young male receptionist took the initiative and led them to the inner lobby, where Kovic started to breathe strangely and stagger about.

'Oh Jesus, oh God! It's my heart!'

They were beside the main lifts.

'Get help!' yelled Wu. 'Get a doctor! Now!'

As soon as the guy's back was turned, they slipped into the express lift that took them to the top floor.

'If only everything in life was that easy.'

'I thought I was the one who gave the Oscar winning performances.'

'You are, but heart attacks require someone more—'

'Worn out looking?'

The top floor, the seventy-ninth, had been shut off. Kovic exited on the seventy-eighth and Wu pressed Down, then just as it started, flipped the Emergency Stop. Kovic forced the doors open and stepped on to the roof of the car. Wu then released the button and pressed Up. The car ascended as far as it would go, just far enough for Kovic to reach the doors of the seventy-ninth and force them open. As soon as they began to part, two guards peered at him from behind the muzzles of their QSZs.

'Guys, there's been a hijacking. I don't know what's going on but they're trying to … could you give me a—'

Kovic seized the barrel of the nearest guard's weapon and rammed it against the other guard's outstretched hand. The first guard's trigger finger instinctively squeezed and a bullet went at almost point blank range into his comrade's forearm. Kovic then grabbed the second gun, fired, and both men were down. He climbed on to their floor and shoved the guards through the gap in the doors on to the roof of the car, before letting them close.

Now he was armed and alone.

He set off down the hall and turned a corner into more guards who immediately closed round him.

'Hey! The fuck you think you're doing?'

They weren't buying the indignant guest act. Any unannounced individual, no matter what their nationality, was bound to be a source of suspicion. Their comrade's gun would be a dead giveaway and it was too late to get rid of it. He had to think of something else.

'I've brought a message from Jin Jié. It's an urgent request for talks. I need to speak to a member of the Admiral's staff—'

'From Jin Jié? Where's your proof?'

'He realises it's all over. He wants to do a deal.'

*When you improvise, be plausible.* That was what he had been taught and it had stood him in good stead. He had the nagging feeling he sounded ridiculous, but then he could almost believe Jin Jié actually was potentially naive enough to try and negotiate with Chang. A more senior official appeared wanting to know what was going on.

'He claims he's been sent by Jin Jié.'

'Trust the jumped-up little prick to send a foreigner. He's too late anyway. Cuff him.'

Suddenly the doors opened behind them and an official in navy uniform shouted at them to stand to attention. *Shit, I've really fucked this up,* thought Kovic. Over the shoulders of the guards he could see a huddle of naval uniforms sailing toward them. *Chang will be with them and he'll see me, and I can't do a fucking thing.* He couldn't move forward or back. He was surrounded, so he bent his knees in the hope that he would make himself less visible and bowed his head. As the entourage approached, he heard the engines of a chopper powering up on the helipad overhead. He felt the bodies around him straighten as the entourage came past. He kept his head down, and heard a muffled exchange of pleasantries. The bodies around him relaxed and parted, just enough to reveal who had just bid the Admiral farewell.

It was Senator Hiram Metzger.

# 66

The guards holding him hesitated. Surely they couldn't be taking orders from Metzger? It was impossible, yet he seemed to hold some sway with them.

'Hey, cut that guy loose – he's with me,' he barked.

Kovic shook them off and, and stepped towards the Senator.

'Thank you, sir.'

'They're a little jumpy right now, with what's going down out there. Come and have a drink.'

Metzger strode down the corridor as if he owned the place. Fighting to hide his incredulity, Kovic followed.

'Too bad you missed the Admiral.'

Kovic digested this. Indeed, he had come so close to Chang and yet couldn't do a damn thing except hide. But what was Metzger the Sinophobe doing with him?

'Yeah, it was too bad, sir.'

The best he could do was play along.

Metzger laughed as he strode ahead.

'The guy's a piece of work, I'll tell you that. But we don't have to like him, so long as he plays ball. Tell you something, Kovic; wouldn't hurt us to have a few more like him in our military. The guy knows how to bust a few balls.'

'Yeah, I guess,' said Kovic, thinking, *What the fuck—?*

Metzger steered him into a banqueting room with a spectacular view of the skyline. He pointed at a magnum of Pol Roger on a table. The champagne glasses strewn about suggested that he, or someone, had already been celebrating.

'Warrior's nectar – Churchill's favourite apparently. Help yourself. No point leaving any for Cutler, the man's teetotal.'

'He's on his way?'

Metzger frowned. Kovic's heart skipped a beat. He turned away, found a clean glass and poured. It was the last thing he wanted right now but he had to buy some time to work out what the hell was happening here. *Improvise.*

He raised his glass to Metzger.

'The Station Chief plays his cards close to his chest sometimes.'

Metzger shrugged, looked at his watch.

'Yeah, well, we're past that point, now.'

'Well here's to—' *To what? Betrayal?* For a second Kovic couldn't finish the sentence. He came up with a suitably meaningless word. '—to progress.'

Metzger nodded, approvingly. Kovic took a swig. It was warm and sickly. He put the glass down. What the fuck was going on? He had to know.

'Maybe you should bring me up to speed, sir. Anything – more from Chang?'

Metzger waved the question away.

'Cutler has all the details. All I care is that I'm outta here before kick off.'

Metzger walked over to the window and stood there, surveying the vast nightscape of light.

'Tell you one thing, when Chang gets his hands on the controls it's gonna be a whole lot darker down there.'

He gave another of his guttural chuckles.

'You know what he said? He stood right here and said, "These are going off. Night is for sleeping." Boy, do they have it coming to them.'

Kovic's mind was in overdrive. Nothing made sense. He stared down at the city.

'Sir, I gotta say, I never had you down as a friend of China.'

Metzger wheeled round, frowning. *I've blown it now*, thought Kovic.

'Friend? I hate the little yellow fuckers. They've closed down half the factories in the States, flooding the market with all their cheap shit.'

'Yeah, right.'

Still barely able to believe what he was hearing, it was all Kovic could think of to say.

Metzger turned towards him, eyes ablaze.

'What you did for us on the border. That was good work. We needed that. Too bad we had to lose a few good men but – that's how it goes sometimes. You lit the fuse for us.'

Kovic felt a cold, sick feeling deep in his gut. He had been played – by his own side. He summoned all his mental energy to suppress his revulsion. He needed more from Metzger.

'Cutler's a clever operator, sir.'

Metzger snorted.

'Yeah, well he can take the credit if he wants, but you and I, we both know it's been Chang all along. He's one evil genius.'

Metzger was in full flow now, the truth spilling out of him. Kovic's mouth had gone completely dry. He looked round for some water. There wasn't any so he took another swig of champagne.

'So how's the Pentagon taking it? So far.'

At first Metzger just glared. Had Kovic gone too far?

But the Senator just shrugged. 'Cutler sure does like to keep you in the dark, don't he!'

Kovic laughed. 'You can say that again, sir.'

'The Pentagon don't know shit. They're gonna look like pricks when this goes up in their faces and you know what? They're gonna come crawling to us for hardware and I'm so gonna enjoy that.'

'You're going to be very popular back home, sir.'

'On the button, Kovic. And if I play this right—'

'The White House?'

'Well, it had crossed my mind ...'

Metzger's eyes were shining with hubris. The guy was completely out of control.

The door opened and in came Cutler, wheeling his case with one hand, his fat briefcase in the other. He stopped in his tracks when he saw Kovic, as if he'd been shot.

Metzger advanced on him.

'So, we all done?'

Cutler's forehead reddened. He let the briefcase slide to the ground.

'Relax, Cutler! I've just been bringing our hero here into the tent. Are we good down there?'

He turned to Kovic.

'You better be off the streets when Chang starts telling the world we iced that whack job Jin Jié.'

The pulsing throb of a descending helicopter filled the air. Metzger's security detail entered the room, two jarheads with high-and-tight cuts. They stood to attention and held the door open.

'Senator?'

'I guess that's my ride, gentlemen.'

Cutler picked up his case; his hand was trembling.

'I'm gonna need to come along with you, Senator.'

'Sorry, Ned, no can do. We'll catch up in DC.'

Cutler glanced at the security guys who stood either side of the door. They had heard what the Senator said all right.

Metzger picked up his coat, came up to Kovic and pumped his hand.

'Good work, son. For some kind of foreigner you make quite a passable American.'

He chuckled at his own brilliance and swept out of the room.

Kovic and Cutler were alone.

# 67

Cutler was still clutching his briefcase, his other hand flapping at his thigh like the futile motion of a flightless bird. Eventually he broke the silence.

'We don't have much time.'

'Metzger filled me in on what's in store. He didn't specify what you had in mind for Jin Jié.'

Cutler laughed awkwardly.

'That's Chang's play.'

'And we get the blame.'

'Too late to stop it now.' Tiny drops of sweat dotted Cutler's forehead.

Kovic took a step closer. 'It was good of you to credit me for the border incident. Metzger practically gave me a Congressional Medal of Honor for it on the spot.'

Cutler sighed wearily. Treason was tiring.

'Kovic, you know how it is. The job we do ... as the world gets more complicated, it gets harder. We face difficult choices.'

Kovic felt a tsunami of rage building up inside him.

'Yeah, guess I wasn't in on the "choices" bit of that.'

He moved round the table to the door, cutting off Cutler's exit.

'Don't do anything stupid now.'

'Depends on your definition of stupid. I've been doing stupid stuff all my life. It's too late to change. What's the plan for Jin Jié?'

'I can't tell you that.'

Kovic closed in on him.

'Kovic, remember you're an American public servant.'

'Don't go there. The plan – tell me.'

Kovic picked up a champagne glass and tapped it lightly on the table so the end of it shattered and broke off.

'What's Metzger promised you? He gonna make you Director when he hits the White House?'

Glass in hand, he took a step nearer.

'Kovic, you have a choice. I know you've been under a lot of strain. But we have to get out of here before—'

'I don't have a choice, Cutler. You've seen to that.'

Cutler reached into his coat but Kovic's kick came before his weapon was even out of its holster. Cutler's training should have prepared him, but something, maybe his own hubris, his own belief in his plan, had weakened his guard. As he went down, Kovic pressed his foot hard on his balls and ground them so he arched and writhed like an overturned cockroach trying to right itself.

Kovic bent over him. 'Jin Jié: just tell me where, and when.'

Cutler's gasps smelled faintly of vomit. Kovic lowered the broken glass so it pressed against his neck.

Cutler could barely speak. The words came out as hoarse little whispers.

When he had got what he wanted, he reached into Cutler's coat and pulled out the Sig 226.

'That's a big toy for a desk man.'

He straightened up and checked the clip. He was standing over Cutler just like Tsu had stood over the Marines on the border. There was a noise from inside Cutler's pants as he soiled himself and a sharp sweet smell wafted from him. Kovic aimed.

'This is how it was for Olsen.'

He fired once, low.

Cutler flinched, tried to haul himself up with a chair but slipped back down.

'And Faulkner.'

He fired again, higher.

Cutler's torso arched. 'You must understand. I did it for America.'

'Not my America.'

'And this one's for Price.'

All the pent up rage welled up inside him.

He fired, and fired again. And again, until the chamber was empty.

263

# 68

Either Hannah's phone was off or she couldn't hear it. Kovic cursed himself for letting her go to Jin Jié's rally. As he descended in the lift, Kovic left a message and sent a text: *Get out now – BOMB.*

Wu was waiting outside as Kovic burst through the cordon round the hotel and dashed for the car.

'Continental Centre – NOW!'

'Sure, boss.'

He had never seen Kovic like this, tearing towards him, gun in his hand.

'Where did you get that?'

'Souvenir. Hit it, Wu! We have about zero seconds to save Jin Jié's ass.'

The Continental Conference Centre was less than three blocks away but the route was jammed with military vehicles.

'These all arrived in the last hour. Bi-i-i-ig build-up.'

'Gimme the satphone.'

Wu threw the car into reverse, inserted it between two army trucks and nosed it into a narrow alley clearly not designed for traffic.

'This better be the right way.'

Kovic dialled Garrison. He picked up before it even rang.

'You want to tell me what in hell's name is happening down there?'

Kovic told him, all of it. There was no point holding back.

'Cutler knew. What happened on the border, the ambush. He cooked it up with Chang.'

'Holy mother of fuck. You absolutely sure about this?'

He outlined his encounter with Metzger.

'He thought I was in on it as well. I wish I could be there when you tell the Pentagon, sir.'

'Where's Cutler now?'

'I'll leave you to draw your own conclusions. Sir, that exfil we talked about – how soon can you get airborne?'

'We'll need clearance, what with the heightened tension.'

'I might be dead before then.'

He killed the line.

Wu skidded to a halt outside the Conference Centre. Kovic was out before he had come to a stop.

'Stick around – somewhere I can find you. Jeez, this guy can pull a crowd.'

The plaza outside was packed with young people watching on two big screens. A line of TV satellite trucks were parked down a side street. Over the cheering crowds, Jin Jié's voice boomed out from the speakers.

'*...And I believe that for all our shortcomings, we are also full of decency and fellowship, that what divides us is not as strong as what unites us ...*'

Kovic battled his way through the crowd, which was in a state of mass euphoria, thousands who had turned out to show their support. There was no visible security, even though the city was crawling with police and military. In the foyer, Kovic smashed the butt of the SIG into the first fire alarm he saw. No one took any notice. Jin Jié was in full flow, the audience rapt. Kovic dodged through, into the auditorium.

It was completely packed. People filled the aisles and stood on seats. Some had tears running down their faces. Kovic elbowed his way towards the front.

'*I see the task of shaping the future as one we can all share. I want our democracy to set new standards for the world. To become the benchmark for this young century ...*'

He searched for Hannah in the group surrounding Jin Jié but she was nowhere to be seen. The audience near the stage was tightly packed, pressing forward. He tried to fight his way through but there was no way. In desperation he raised the Sig and fired into the air.

'Get out now!' he yelled. 'There's a bomb.'

The crowd around him shrank back and a path to the lectern opened up. The bullet had hit a chandelier above and showered them with glass. Several people screamed. Well maybe that would get them moving. Jin Jié stopped speaking and glared at Kovic. Who was this madman?

'Jin Jié, we gotta go. Now. Where's Hannah? Where is she? HANNAH!'

Kovic grabbed him with both hands, pulled him down on to the stage and dragged him towards the wings; all the time he kept yelling for Hannah.

The giant flash erupted from somewhere close to the lectern, the blast that came with it sweeping them off their feet. Kovic lost his grip on Jin Jié as they took flight. For a second he blacked out, coming to again as he landed in a heap of bodies. The lights went out, plunging them into complete darkness. Blasted by the explosion, his ears barely registered the thousands of screams coming from all around him. He struggled to free himself and tried to take a breath but the air was thick with dust. An emergency light flickered into action, glowing a sickly yellow. Gradually his eyes adjusted. A thick fog of dust swirled around them. Those who could move looked grey, like half-exposed images in an old photo. Kovic took a step and stumbled over a body at his feet, a young woman lying face down, inert. He bent down and turned her over. Two eyes stared up, wide, unseeing, her torso a mass of blood. It wasn't Hannah. He surveyed the scene around him and caught sight of Jin Jié, bleeding from his shoulder and the side of his head. He was trying to get up.

Kovic grabbed him by the collar and hauled him out of the mass of bodies piled against the wall. He was moving but his eyes were unfocused. Kovic groped his way towards the flickering emergency exit sign. The sprinklers came on, drenching them and turning the dust that had settled on them into a slippery paste. He slapped Jin Jié's face but his head lolled to one side. Kovic inspected the wound. It looked deep. Again he looked left and right and behind him, hoping to see Hannah. Surely she would have been here, but that would put her near the blast ...

'You fucking naive bastard. You brought all these people here—'

Jin Jié's gaze wandered his way, uncomprehending. Kovic glared at him, half inclined to leave him where he was and get the hell out. His head jerked up and his eyes came into focus.

'Please—'

'No.'

Kovic was damned if Chang was going to get his way.

'C'mon.'

He hauled him forward until they encountered a stairwell. In the dust it was impossible to tell whether the exit was down there or not. But the walking wounded were now pressing forward and Kovic lost his footing and fell, taking Jin Jié with him. The others, propelled by what was now a surge of fleeing people, tumbled after them, burying them in another human heap.

Winded and suffocating under the mass of writhing bodies, Kovic felt himself slipping into unconsciousness. This can't happen, he told himself, not now. He had lost his grip on Jin Jié. His strength ebbed away as he felt himself drowning under a human wave.

# 69

Garrison climbed the stairs heavily. He'd missed breakfast and his energy levels were dropping. By the time he got to his quarters he was feeling faint with hunger and fatigue. An hour had passed since he sent the communiqué, encrypted and marked with the Secretary of Defense's codename, *GAUNTLET – Eyes Only*, along with the exfil request. What was taking so damn long?

He patted his tunic in search of the granola bar he thought he remembered pocketing sometime in the night. Then the red phone sounded, and obliterated all sensation of exhaustion. A female voice asked him to confirm his ID.

'I have *Gauntlet* for you, Commander – please hold.'

While he waited, Garrison flicked on the large LED screen across the table. Furious rioters were setting fire to a Chevy Suburban while a mob cheered them on. Behind them, militiamen were standing by, pointedly not intervening. The shot changed to an image of Admiral Chang in full naval dress behind a bank of microphones. Subtitles flashed up on the screen.

'*Today we mourn the murdered Jin Jié; tomorrow we will retaliate. The foreign perpetrators will face the full force of our wrath.*'

It was just as Kovic had warned; Chang was blaming America. Out of the corner of his eye, he glimpsed a half-flattened pack of Luckies that someone must have dropped. It had been nearly eighteen months but he still felt the magnetic urge.

'Roland?'

Garrison muted the TV and cleared his throat.

'Good morning, Mr Secretary.'

His breezy manner sounded horribly false.

'Are we good to talk?'

'There's no one else in the room if that's what you mean, sir.'

'Good.'

'You received my request, sir?'

'We'll get to that.' The Secretary let out a long guttural sound somewhere between a cough and a sigh. 'What you're saying – this is fissile material, Roland. Sure you want to put your name on it?'

Garrison watched his free hand curling into a fist. He was damned if he was going to take the rap for delivering news they didn't want to hear, but he wasn't afraid to stand by Kovic.

'You know, sir, I've gotten to an age where my own ass is not the first thing I'm thinking of.'

'Yeah, that's a fine sentiment, Roland, but no one's gonna take this sitting down over here, you realise that.'

'Well, it's playing out just how Kovic said it would, sir. Chang's declared martial law, Shanghai's in uproar and we're in their waters. If this escalates and Chang tears up the non-aggression pact, we're at DEFCON ONE for World War Three and no one's gonna remember how it started.'

'Okay, okay, let's not go there just yet.'

Was he getting through? Where was the urgency – the outrage?

The Secretary lowered his voice almost to a whisper. 'You shared this with anyone else?'

'Just you, sir.'

'Keep it that way, okay?'

Garrison tried not to broadcast his exasperation. 'Sir, do I have clearance to go get our man?'

The Secretary took his time to reply. Garrison reached for the Luckies; there were three left inside, squashed. He pushed them away.

'This should be Langley's problem, not ours.'

'Sir, he's gone out on a limb for us. We owe him.'

'Yeah, I know all about Kovic. And your capacity to forgive and forget is all very noble. But right now he doesn't have a whole lot of friends in this town.'

Garrison could feel the rage rising up his throat like bile. He was having trouble swallowing. 'And none of us want any more of our own men's blood on our hands.'

The Secretary was silent for a few seconds. When he spoke again, his tone was softer.

'Roland, we go way back. We've both made a lot of tough calls in our time; that's the job – what they pay us for.'

Garrison didn't like where this was heading.

'If you attempt exfil and Chang gets wind of you in his airspace, he's gonna call it an act of war. You'll be playing right into his hands. Let's hold back here for a minute, shall we, and think before we act.'

Garrison's hand reached for the crumpled Luckies, and felt the willpower drain out of him as he shook one out.

'We're way past that point, sir. Chang's already pinning Jin Jié's killing on us.'

The Secretary let out a long grumbling sigh.

'Sorry, Roland: permission denied.'

The line went dead.

Garrison lowered the receiver into its cradle, then because he could hold it in no longer, swept the phone off the table. It crashed against the wall. Then he lit up. It felt like the last request of a condemned man.

# 70

**Continental Conference Centre, Shanghai**

Something stung Kovic's cheek. He felt it again on the other side and a third time … a sharp slap. He took a great gasp of air – he could breathe. He was awake, alive. He opened his eyes. Hannah was bending over him, grey with dust like a beautiful statue, almost invisible in the semi-darkness. What was more, she was unhurt. He felt a surge of relief.

'How—?'

He grasped her arms. She shrugged. 'Just luck. About time I had some, wouldn't you say?'

The space under the stage was full of people, crying, screaming, feeling their way up and over each other, stumbling as if blind. She took his hand.

'Get up. Hurry.'

'Where's Jin Jié?'

'We need to get him to a hospital.'

Jin Jié was still alive but deteriorating. The front of his shirt was wet with blood. Kovic got to his feet and together they hauled him up, each with an arm over their shoulder, and dragged him towards what looked like an exit.

'He goes to hospital now, he'll never come out. Chang's people will find him and kill him.'

'There's shrapnel in his neck and shoulder. He needs surgery.'

They reached an emergency exit, and walked in small steps, agonisingly slowly, up a shallow ramp that led to the plaza. The Conference Centre was on fire, blue grey smoke billowing upwards into the night sky. Kovic lowered Jin Jié while he surveyed the scene, looking for Wu. The plaza outside was in chaos, emergency services rushing forward with stretchers as survivors spewed out of the doors, many of them clutching wounds or each other. Behind them, armed soldiers were descending from trucks.

'Jesus, it's already begun. We have to get him out of here.'

There was no sign of Wu.

'C'mon, we're wasting time.'

He hauled Jin Jié on to his shoulder and together he and Hannah moved him towards the line of TV trucks. In the mêlée they were less conspicuous; the dust from the explosion had coated everyone in the same uniform grey. All the same, Kovic kept his head down as they moved through the throng.

'You, stop! Turn round!'

A soldier in full body armour grabbed Kovic by the arm. Hannah lunged forward and landed a kick in the gap below his armour, karate chopping his neck as he went down.

'Okay, let's keep moving.'

The militia were forming a cordon round the building to corral Jin Jié's supporters within the plaza. A group trying to flee the area were tussling with some soldiers. Three shots rang out.

'Jesus.'

Another soldier spotted them and started pushing toward them through the wounded. Then he suddenly put his hand up to his throat and dropped to the ground. Kovic scanned the crowd and saw Wu holstering his gun.

Never had Kovic been so pleased to see him. Despite the dead weight of Jin Jié hanging limply from his shoulder, he speeded up, Hannah struggled to stay with him as he surged forward.

'Where's your vehicle?'

'Blocked in; I can't get back to it.'

Jin Jié groaned. The blood was still dripping off him. They had to stop the blood loss and try and stabilise him. But with the shrapnel still in him, Kovic knew his chances were slim and getting slimmer. He eyed the TV trucks, their dishes beaming pictures of the chaos to the world.

'I got an idea.'

He pointed at one of them. 'That one, come on.'

He hammered on the door. 'US Government: open up.'

The door opened an inch. Kovic wrenched it wider. Inside was the young TV technician he had rescued from the mob only a few days ago. He looked as terrified as he had been then.

'Hey, remember me?'

The technician was frozen with fear.

'Hey, buddy, we're on the same side. It's okay, we just want your help. What's your name, son?'

'Hal.'

'We need your van, Hal.'

'Sir, um, I'm not allowed—'

Kovic pushed his way inside and eased Hal out of the way. Wu and Hannah followed, manoeuvring Jin Jié with difficulty through the narrow door. There was another technician inside with head-phones on. He jumped up off his stool.

'Hey, you can't come in here! Get the fuck out—'

He stopped when he saw Jin Jié's blood soaked shirt.

'Oh my God— Is that who I think it is?'

Kovic swept everything off the counter – coffee cups, pens, bottles, notepads and mobile phones – and beckoned Wu and Hannah.

'Lie him on there so I can get a look. You guys got any first aid?'

The headphone guy reached into a small cabinet and pulled out a tiny pack of antiseptic and some small bandages.

'Not exactly warzone-prepped, are you?'

Kovic ripped open Jin Jié's shirt. A jagged piece of shrapnel had torn into his neck and travelled along his shoulder, carving a bloody trench before embedding itself under the collarbone.

'Oh God.'

The headphones guy staggered and leaned against the bank of TV screens. He was turning pale.

'Hal, take your buddy and go sit up front in the cab for a minute, okay?'

Hal's eye caught the TV monitor. Chang, surrounded by microphones, was still addressing the world.

'Shit, Jin Jié's dead.'

Kovic probed Jin Jié's wounds.

'And if that's what Chang's saying, it must be true. Now let us do what we need to do.'

'But—'

The headphones guy was still staring at the patient on his counter. He seemed to have recovered and now had that *world exclusive* gleam in his eyes.

Kovic grabbed him by the throat.

'Don't even think of it, okay, or I'll have to kill you both. Anyhow, Jin Jié's not a story outside China. But I got something much better for you: get down to the Pudong Royale right away. On the top floor you'll find a dead American spy, who's been shot for treachery. His name is Edward Cutler. You break that story; it'll make you as famous as Woodward and Bernstein.'

The two looked at each other, then moved to the cab. Kovic started opening hatches, sifting through equipment, looking for something he could improvise with. He glanced at Hannah who was cradling Jin Jié's head.

'We're gonna have to clean him up a bit so we can move him.'

Hannah pointed at where the shrapnel was lodged.

'We have to get that out.'

Kovic shook his head.

'Negative. First rule of field care – strap it up and leave it to the professionals. Biggest problem we face is he bleeds out. Best we TQ and get the hell out of here.'

Jin Jié stirred and groaned. He didn't look good. Hannah patted his brow with some tissues.

Hannah was insistent. 'The shrapnel's going to be grinding away inside. If it travels deeper and hits an artery …'

More blood was seeping out from under him.

'We should turn him over.'

Kovic eased him on to his side. There was a large dark patch on his back. Hannah ripped the shirt away.

'Oh shit,' said Wu.

An exit wound under Jin Jié's arm. Another piece of the bomb had travelled right through him.

274

'Jesus, what a mess. Okay, we're going to try and take out the biggest lump.'

'What with?'

Kovic scanned the contents of the van, and found a bottle of vodka. Thank God for the drinking habits of journalists.

'That's a start.'

Hanging up on the door on a coat hanger was a hi-vis yellow jacket. He pulled it off and let it drop it on the floor, then worked fast, bending the hanger into something resembling barbecue tongs. He held them between his thumb and forefinger, adjusting the jaws until they met.

'Not exactly a precision instrument but it'll do.'

'Have you done this before?'

He smiled in a way he hoped looked confident and reassuring.

'There's always a first time.'

Hannah shook her head.

'How is it you're so sure of everything?'

Kovic tried to keep the smile going.

'I'm not: I just want this to work.'

He emptied some of the vodka over the wound and the tongs.

'Hold him. Wu – grab his other side. This may sting a little.'

He leant down with the tongs and probed the wound with them. Jin Jié's body flexed as if he'd been shot through with electricity. Hannah gripped his arm.

'That's a good sign, means he's still with us.'

He worked his home-made forceps round the dark, jagged object lodged in the flesh of Jin Jié's shoulder, submerged under a rising ooze of blood. Then, praying inwardly, he tightened his grip and eased them upwards.

'Eureka.'

He held the tongs aloft, clasped in them a dripping golf-ball-sized lump. With his other hand he tossed Hannah the bandage.

'Okay, now we TQ him and he'll be good to go.'

'Go where?'

'We got to get him out of Shanghai to the coast. Between Maojia and Tanglu Port there's plenty of easy landing for a seaborne exfil. We've got warships a few hours away by RHIB.'

'What's that?'

'Rigid hulled inflatable – a fast rescue boat, the Porsche of the seas.'

Hannah tore up what remained of Jin Jié's shirt and made it into a thick pad which she used as a pressure dressing on his wounds, then she wound the bandage round his shoulder and under his arm. He winced at the pain as he sat up.

'I'm sorry but I'm not leaving the city. I cannot desert my people. My destiny is with them. Isn't that right, Hannah?'

Kovic looked from Jin Jié to Hannah. Why did she hang on his every word?

He folded his arms and leaned against the counter.

'Jin Jié, having just risked my life – and that of my friend here – to save yours, I'm not going to listen to any more of this idealistic crap. Right now Chang's telling the world you're dead and that it's all our fault. He finds out you're alive, he'll fry you and invite the world's media to inspect the remains. Do you get that?'

'My mind is made up.'

They both looked at Hannah.

Kovic sighed.

'If you stay she's going to want to stay too. You can throw yourself to the wolves, but not her too.'

Jin Jié shook his head and gazed dejectedly at Hannah. There was something of the lost puppy about him. Did she love him? He wrenched his mind back into focus.

'Okay, think about this: when the Nazis invaded France, what did General de Gaulle do? He got the hell out and regrouped with the help of the Brits. Couple of years later he rode back into Paris, victorious, on the shoulders of the Allies.'

Jin Jié shook his head.

'But look what happened to Chiang Kai-Shek. He abandoned his fight with Mao and retreated to Taiwan. He never came back.'

So much for history. Kovic glanced at the screens. A military official was issuing instructions.

'*All foreigners are to report to the Zhi You Tower complex in preparation for evacuation.*'

Kovic let out a long sigh and looked at Wu, who'd diplomatically remained silent.

'Fine, we'll do it your way. Wu, let's get out of here.'

He flung open the door, blasting them with the full volume of the mayhem outside. There were more gunshots. As he stepped down from the truck he felt a hand on his shoulder. It was Hannah.

'Please.'

'Please what?'

All the force seemed to have drained from her. She looked small and vulnerable and alone.

He grasped her by the shoulders. 'I just don't want to see you die because of him.'

She looked hard at him, projecting all her charm. 'I'll make him leave. Just let me do it my way, okay? He has too much pride to do what you tell him.'

# 71

They crept between the TV vans, and found they were surrounded by a ring of military trucks. Hannah had put the rest of the bandages round Jin Jié's head to disguise him, and Wu steadied him protectively as they moved cautiously through the crowd.

'He's very weak. He shouldn't walk too far.'

'We need some wheels. We need to get away from here.'

'Through another militia cordon – how?'

Kovic quickened his pace, moving noiselessly under the cacophony coming from around the conference centre. As they neared a young soldier on guard between two of the trucks, he bent low and rammed his shoulder into the kid's stomach, snatching the Chang Feng sub-machine gun from him as he buckled and slamming the butt down on his temple. Kovic swung open the truck door.

'No one's going to stop us in this.'

Together they hauled Jin Jié up into the cab. Kovic fired up the engine and shoved the gearshift into first.

They were crammed into the cab, four abreast, Jin Jié only upright because there was no room for him to slump down. Kovic manoeuvred the truck out of the line.

'Just keep your heads down – if you can.'

The road on the other side of the cordon was clear. Kovic floored the gas and the vehicle gathered momentum. Up ahead, the junction was blocked by a couple of motorcycle cops.

Wu gripped his arm.

'Boss, slow down – just drive normally. No one's going to chase an army truck.'

'Okay, okay.'

A motorbike cop stepped out and waved them to stop.

'He looks into the cab, we're done for.'

The cop turned and signalled to whatever was coming down the cross street. A pair of tank transporters rumbled past.

'It's for the cameras,' said Hannah. 'To show they mean business.'

'Maybe it's more than show.'

The cop waved them forward, to follow the transporters.

'Uh uh, that's not the way we want to go.'

Kovic ignored the cop and started to turn left, but a second jumped in front of them gesticulating furiously. Kovic swerved even harder left. The first cop's bike crunched under their wheels.

'Oops.'

'He won't like that.'

There were more oncoming tanks. Kovic whizzed through a gap in the convoy and sped up the road. This thing was faster than it looked. In the mirror he saw the second cop coming after them. They hadn't gone a block before he was level with them and taking aim. He swerved to avoid another oncoming truck and, just as the cop started to overtake, wrenched open his door. The cop smacked into it head first, came right off the bike and went rolling into the gutter.

'I've only ever seen that in the movies. Never thought it would work in real life.'

Wu looked up from his phone. 'They're shutting off all the exit routes from the city. No one's allowed to leave.'

'Whatever.'

They were on the slip road that joined the Hushan Expressway flyover. It was solid with traffic, even the emergency lanes; cars and minibuses crammed with people and luggage, some with trailers stacked with boxes, even livestock.

'Only one thing to do here.'

Kovic slammed on the brakes, made a multi-point turn and roared back down the slip road, to the consternation of drivers coming the other way.

'Wu, see if the satphone's got any reception.'

Wu fiddled with the controls.

'Only a very weak signal. A text may get through.'

'Okay, you steer while I type.'

Kovic snatched it, tapped out a message and pressed Send.

# 72

Garrison stared at the message.

*No exit S'hai. Exfil RV roof of Zhi You Towers. Have JJ intact so no excuses.*

He smiled to himself. Kovic had figured correctly that they wouldn't okay his exfil, but having Jin Jié put a whole new spin on it. He hadn't any of this information yet, but he was already scoping out options for bringing Kovic out. He was damned if he was going to bend over for the Pentagon. Like the Secretary had said, tough calls were what they paid him for – well, this was one right here, and he was going to do the right thing.

'Duncan, show me the Zhi You Towers.'

Lieutenant Duncan tapped at her keyboard and the screen on the wall, which had been playing mute CNN images from the city, switched to an aerial of the Towers. The three Marines who were round the table examining the map looked up.

Recker whistled.

'Those are big motherfucking skyscrapers.'

Garrison coughed and glanced at Duncan, who was oblivious.

Recker looked at the floor.

'Er ... excuse me, sir.'

'Apology accepted. It is an accurate description.'

The three soldiers stared at the screen. None of them was even half his age. Was he about to send more able young men to their deaths? How much longer could he keep this up? This game needed someone younger, with less imagination.

Pac shrugged. 'Too bad we can't go in airborne.'

Garrison leaned over the map and drew a circle with his finger round the city.

'We enter Shanghai airspace, we're dead. My recommendation, gentlemen, is you focus on the positives. There's enough chaos on the ground to afford you some useful cover. The Zhi You complex is less than a mile from the shore. You'll be in civvies and since it's the mustering point for all foreign nationals, you won't stick out like Christmas trees if you have to enter the building.'

Irish was thinking ahead; thank God somebody was.

'Sir, will they be able to RV with us at ground level?'

'If we can still communicate with them, but don't assume anything. Also he's got a couple of VIPs with him, so chances are they'll be having to hide out somewhere in the building.'

There was silence while they all absorbed the enormity of what they were taking on. Irish raised a tentative finger.

'Sir, Kovic was with Olsen – on the North Korea mission?'

They all looked up, waiting to see how he would respond. So they all knew. Well what did he expect? Stuff got around – even on a ship this big. He looked at each of them in turn.

'I'm not gonna mess with you: this mission is off the grid. It's not authorised by anyone above me. I want Kovic out of there because he's put his life on the line to get to the truth about what happened to Olsen and the others. That's worth a lot to me, to all of us.'

None of them spoke.

Pac raised a hand.

'Shoot.'

'Sir, how come Kovic was the only survivor on that mission?'

Garrison's gaze drifted off to the picture on the desk of his son Tommy.

'Some people travel with more than the standard complement of luck. And my guess is that right now, he's wondering just exactly when it's going to run out.'

# 73

The Zhi You Towers, a hundred and forty storeys each, were Shanghai's tallest buildings. Above the fifth floor all the lights had been extinguished, so they loomed like a pair of giant tombstones.

'How are we going to do this?'

Hannah surveyed the scene on the forecourt in front of the main doors. A long queue of foreigners had formed, some trailing luggage, several with children. Half a dozen soldiers were keeping them in line.

'Wu, lose the truck and make your own way in. Steal a uniform and get us a couple of weapons. Meet us by the elevators.'

He turned to Hannah.

'We're going in the front door.'

'How are they not going to notice us?'

'Because we're going to hide smack in plain view. I'll do the talking. Just play along. You're my wife, and he's your brother. We're Canadians. Put your weapon in his pocket. They're less likely to search him.'

Hannah looked at him. Was he brilliant? Or insane?

He squeezed her hand.

'Trust me ...'

Jin Jié did not look good. His eyes were half closed and his head tilted awkwardly as if he didn't have the strength to hold it upright.

Kovic raised his chin.

'Okay – no greeting your flock. Just pretend you're not a celebrity for a while. See if you can get the hang of it.'

Jin Jié nodded feebly, evidently without the strength to argue. But Hannah looked desolate.

'I don't see how we're going to do this.'

283

He gave her his winning smile.

'I promise you, just go with it.'

Kovic was already getting into character, remonstrating as he struggled towards the front of the queue, an arm round the heavily bandaged Jin Jié, and Hannah on the other side. Righteous indignation flared from his every pore.

'Who's in charge here? I *demand* to know *right now*. You see what your people have done? Look at her brother, for God's sake. That's one of *your* drivers did this. Goddamn maniac. Don't they teach you people how to drive? I've got pictures on my phone to prove it. I demand to speak to someone in authority. Well?'

A young militia guard stepped forward and frowned at the blood on Jin Jié's front.

'Passports?'

Kovic waved his free hand and turned as if to engage his audience.

'Passports? *Passports?* Oh ha ha, yeah, that's great. Sure we *had* all our documents, we *had* luggage, we *had* my wife's jewellery. You wanna see what's left of our hire car?' He gestured at Hannah and Jin Jié with his free hand. 'This is all there is. The rest went up in flames under one of your freakin' *trucks*.'

The guard was looking embarrassed: a good start. Kovic waved at the entrance.

'So – if it's not too much *trouble*, we'd like to get in there and get my brother-in-law here some help. Unless, that is, you want to deal with a *stiff*.'

Kovic knew that the young soldier probably didn't understand a word of this but he was getting the point. He stepped forward.

'I – help?'

'Yes, you do that. You help.'

The soldier took one of Jin's arms. Kovic glimpsed Hannah's face, then turned to a sullen looking family at the front of the line.

'Excuse us for butting in like this, folks, but we're all the family he's got.' He turned to Hannah. 'You see, honey? A uniform is a uniform, wherever you are. And you got to make them see reason.'

Another soldier held the door while they struggled through with the bandaged Jin Jié as the whole queue looked on.

They were in.

The smart formality of the lobby had been submerged under the flotsam of refugees. People of all nationalities – Arabs, Africans, Indians, Europeans, families and servants – sat or lay alongside piles of luggage, waiting for they knew not what. The helpful soldier, not wanting to involve himself any more than he already had with the difficult foreigners, swiftly unhooked himself from Jin Jié and disappeared back the way he'd come.

There were no staff at the desks. Soldiers wandered through the crowds clutching their rifles. A couple of officials with clipboards were gathering details and checking documents. A nurse was handing out bottles of water. At the opposite end of the foyer by the elevators was Wu, transformed, in military gear. He had also acquired a sub-machine gun.

Some wealthy-looking Arabs had commandeered a porter's luggage trolley. Kovic pointed at it and gestured at Jin Jié.

'Could we?'

The Arabs looked unmoved. Then the youngest, no more than about ten, jumped up and started unloading a mountain of cases, evidently castigating his parents for being so selfish.

'I'm much obliged to you, my friend: I truly am.'

Hannah lowered Jin Jié on to the trolley and they started pushing him toward the elevator.

Then, out of the corner of her eye, Hannah saw a hand waving in their direction. Kovic pressed on, pulling her firmly with him. A pretty blonde woman in a smart trench coat detached herself from her partner and jumped to her feet.

'Hey, Hannah! Over here! It's Katie.'

'Oh no—'

Kovic whispered. 'It's okay, play along. Be friendly, keep moving.'

Hannah waved back. 'This is bad.'

The woman called Katie bounced up to Hannah and kissed her. What did she think this was, a class reunion?

'Gaad – of all the places! If I'd known you were back here.'

Katie's face moved from joy to dismay as she glanced at Kovic and Jin Jié.

Hannah smiled back and nodded. *What would Kovic say?* She was determined not to let him down. Besides, their lives depended on it. 'Yeah, a – a lot's happened.' She gestured at Kovic and let out an uncharacteristically girlish giggle.

'My husband. From Canada.'

'Oh my *Gaad*! And not a word on Facebook. You dark horse, you!'

She grinned fixedly at Kovic who grinned back. 'Yeah, just married. Ain't that somethin'? Well, nice meetin' you.'

Hannah pressed on. 'So, yeah. And this is my brother – we got into a – er, a bit of a problem out there.'

But Katie had stopped listening. She waved at the man she was with.

'Hey, Chip! Over here!'

Katie looked back at Hannah and then to Kovic.

Chip strode toward them, frowning. His trench coat was streaked with mud. He glared at Hannah, oozing Sinophobia.

'Hey, how come she's in here?'

Katie looked embarrassed. 'She's married to a Canadian citizen, that all right with you?'

'Yeah, but what about him?'

Chip was pointing at Jin Jié, inert on the trolley. Kovic had the measure of him; patrician WASP hard-ons were the bane of his life. *You know you want to kick him in the balls – but just stay cool,* a voice inside him urged.

Other people were now starting to stare. Katie was now looking down at Jin Jié, inert on the trolley. The bandage over his face had slipped. She put her hand to her mouth.

'Oh my God.'

Kovic bent down and pushed the bandage back into place.

'Yeah, he's pretty bad. Car crash on the way here. We got to get him upstairs – to the doctor.'

Kovic started to move the trolley again, but Chip was in the way, frowning at his wife who was staring wide-eyed at Jin Jié.

'Honey, what is it?'

Kovic glanced at Wu, over by the elevators. Wu gestured at one of the clipboard officials who was now moving towards them.

Kovic's voice was low but emphatic. 'Look, guys: just let us get to where we're going, okay? We all keep our cool, we all get outta this in one piece.'

Katie whispered something to Chip, whose face puffed up with indignation. He looked down at Jin Jié and up again. They knew who he was.

Kovic gripped him by the arm, hard, and hissed into his ear.

'Listen, *Chip*. It's like this. You take care of Katie here and I'll look after my friend on the trolley, or there's gonna be bullets flying. Got it?'

He hadn't. His face turned red and his eyes bulged with indignation.

'How dare you threaten me? You're jeopardising the safety of innocent people.'

The clipboard man was now a few feet from them with a soldier in tow, frowning at the trolley. Kovic looked over at Wu, who had raised his weapon. Clipboard man wheeled round and barked something at the soldier.

Kovic nodded at Wu. The bullet passed through a five-inch gap between Chip and Katie and hit the clipboard man smack in the middle of his forehead. Katie screamed and Chip pulled her down. The whole foyer erupted in screams as the crowd cowered.

'Yeah, you stay down, Chip, or you're next.'

Kovic dived for the soldier's machine gun as he barged Chip out of the path of the trolley, forcing his way toward the elevators. Several soldiers returned Wu's fire but he had retreated into the express elevator and with his foot keeping the doors a few inches apart, picked them off one by one. A bullet ricocheted off the trolley and grazed Kovic on the side of the head. He stumbled and lost his balance. Hannah caught him and grabbed the trolley, and forced it into the mouth of the elevator.

'Okay, beam us up.'

Wu closed the doors and they shot skywards.

# 74

Kovic was slumped on the floor beside the trolley. The only light came from the glow of the control panel.

'Nice of them to leave the elevators working.'

'They were off. I switched this one back on.' Wu handed him one of the sub-machine guns he had lifted. 'I got this too.' He showed Kovic a grenade, and grinned.

Hannah was trying to catch her breath. 'You know for sure they're gonna take us off the roof – right?'

He shrugged. 'No other way.'

That didn't look like the answer she was expecting.

'I hope you know what you're doing. That was pretty close down there.'

'Sure, but we're here now, aren't we?'

Kovic's calm was infuriating, but she needed one of them to be.

He felt his phone buzz. His signal had come back. He looked at the screen. It was from Garrison, sent over an hour before.

*Negative on airborne. Ground exfil.*

Kovic stared at the text, his heart sinking as fast as the lift rose. He had gambled on being lifted off the building. The entire ground floor was now enemy territory. Jin Jié had been recognised; it would be only a matter of time before Chang got to hear and then – they'd be toast.

He called Garrison back.

'*This line's not secure.*'

'Fuck secure. Where are your people?'

'*Approaching ground level, thirty minutes.*'

'I'm already headed to the roof. Ground level is hostile. Our package is damaged.'

'Jin Jié?'

'That's right, so fuck clearance, come in airborne. Put some Super Hornets up.'

'*Negative. This mission is already way off the grid. Sit tight. We'll come and find you.*'

Kovic was almost hissing now. 'For fuck's sake, Jin Jié needs medical attention like yesterday.'

There was silence for a few seconds.

'*I'll get back to you.*'

Kovic threw the phone down and avoided Hannah's gaze.

'There's a problem?'

'No, no – just a logistical thing.'

He'd spent his whole career lying, and now suddenly his heart was no longer in it. But he knew he had no choice.

The lift slowed to a halt. They were at the top.

'Okay, get ready. We don't know what's out there.'

He turned to Hannah. 'Wu and I'll go first. Jam the doors with the trolley. Make sure that elevator stays where it is. Do not let it go. You wait with Jin Jié till I say we're clear.'

Hannah gripped Kovic's arm, her faith in him ebbing. She had let him take the lead and look where it had got them.

'What did he say, your guy on the phone?'

He grinned inanely, Garrison's pay-off echoing in his head. Right now he couldn't think of anything to make her feel better.

'We're good. Now let's get this done.'

The doors parted and Kovic stepped out into the pitch darkness. Even the emergency guide lights were out. And with the air conditioning off the atmosphere was warm and sticky. There was no sound other than the wind in the elevator shaft. Wu produced a torch from his newly acquired uniform.

'Glad someone's come prepared.'

Kovic examined the nearest door and listened. He turned the handle; it was locked. He kicked it open.

One side of the room was all glass, part of a VIP suite with white leather sofas arranged round a huge black glass coffee table. Below lay the city, several sections of which had been plunged into darkness. Plumes of fiery smoke rose from several places. The devastation outside made a surreal contrast with the luxury in the foreground. Two different realities – both fragile. Kovic beckoned Hannah forward.

'Leave the trolley jamming the doors. Get in here with Jin Jié and put your feet up while I recce the roof. Wu will stand guard in the corridor.'

He pointed at Jin Jié, 'Keep him conscious, check his dressings.'

Her face was explosive. 'What is this? I don't take orders from you.'

'Okay, swap with Wu if it makes you feel any better.'

He passed her one of the guns. But she wasn't finished. 'Kovic, if you think this isn't going to work, the sooner you share this with me the better. Do you have a plan B?'

He gazed at her. Why was he being such a prick? Louise used to say it always happened when he was in the shit and wouldn't admit it. What a long way away their life was now. But there was no time to reflect, even to think. He picked up one of the weapons Wu had got from the conscripts and checked the magazine; it was full. He racked the slide to chamber the first round and slowly opened the door. The corridor was quiet.

Behind the elevator shaft, a flight of stairs led to the roof. Kovic felt his way up, listening all the time for any activity above. He could hear the wind whistling outside. The door had a big wheel attachment like an air lock. He turned it slowly anti-clockwise and inched it open.

Now he was alone, he was suddenly conscious of his own exhaustion, and worse, the rising tide of doubt about the outcome of his mission. Yet again, he had allowed himself to become intoxicated with hope, relying on some deluded inner belief that he could will things to somehow come right, that if he just kept his eyes open and his wits about him, a solution would ultimately present itself.

But it was a losing battle. He had not been straight with Hannah about their chances and now the extent of his failure to deliver was out in the open. Stabilising Jin Jié had bought them a bit of time, but not much. He had committed himself to getting him out – but he knew full well whose survival he cared about most.

He stepped out on to the roof. The night sky was dull and smoky: no moon or stars. The cloud cover pressed close, a dirty purple. The top of the building was far bigger than he'd expected: a large, flat expanse with a chest-high perimeter wall – a perfect LZ for a helicopter or even an Osprey. In the south-east corner was a forest of air vents. West of that, a single storey concrete box housed the elevator winding gear, on top of which were several antennae and three huge satellite dishes. He walked up to the nearest part of the parapet that ran round the perimeter, hauled himself up and looked down at the streets below. Even from this height convoys of tanks and other military vehicles were visible, along with the red and blue flashing lights of emergency vehicles.

He couldn't kid himself any longer. He had made a mistake. They would be trapped up here. How would Garrison's guys get into the building and all the way up to them? He looked around for something that would give him a last burst of inspiration. Parked next to the air vents was a pair of small cranes from which was suspended a window-cleaner's gondola. It was far too slow and too conspicuous, but maybe by adapting the cables he could create some kind of fast-rope system, like with Tsu's cable car. He looked over the parapet at the concrete a hundred and forty storeys down. But even if he could, how would Jin Jié manage it?

He knew he was clutching at straws.

He examined the cranes. They moved on a rail round the perimeter of the building so the gondola could be deployed on any side. He tore off the tarpaulin that covered it, reached in and found the wireless console that controlled it. He pressed a red button; it lit up. He felt an almost childish burst of joy. He reached in and tested each control in turn until he had worked out which ones operated the cranes' travel and rotation, and which of them moved the cables that raised and lowered the gondola. He did a mental calculation of the location of the suite they had taken over and trucked the cranes round to roughly above where he thought it was. Then he lowered the gondola over the side until it was level with the suite window.

Through his feet he felt a dull thud from somewhere inside the building. He pocketed the handset and started back for the stair-well. Wu was coming up it towards him.

'Someone's in the other elevator. It's back on! They're coming up!'

But before Kovic could reply, he was distracted by another sound, a deep, shattering pulse coming from the north of the building. He felt a twinge of hope: had Garrison come through for him after all? Rearing up from behind the parapet came first the rotors and then the fuselage of a large military helicopter. For a second he hoped irrationally it was from Garrison.

It was a Z–9 one of Chang's.

# 75

Kovic ran for the door, slammed it behind him and turned the wheel; yeah that should stop them for a good two and a half seconds.

He and Wu dashed back down to the suite. In the gloom, Jin Jié was lying on one of the beds, Hannah beside him trying to give him water. She glared at them.

'His temperature's gone up and he's not making any sense.'

He clearly had a fever; the wound must be infected or there was something else he hadn't spotted. He went to the window. He could see the gondola a few metres to the left of them.

'That's the least of our problems right now. We've got enemy on the stairs.'

He scanned the room wildly, looking for an idea. Directly above the door was an air conditioning grille. He leapt on to the counter adjacent to the door and reached up to it, working his fingers under the frame until it popped out and landed on the carpet.

'Can we get him in there?'

'How?'

'I don't know, but we have to try.' He hauled a chair over to the door. 'Wu, get over here.'

Together the three of them lifted Jin Jié. Kovic got on the counter and lifted his shoulders.

Jin Jié stirred drowsily.

'What's happening?'

'Hide and seek. Preferably without the seek. I need you to squeeze yourself into that air duct.'

He looked very pale. 'Do I have to?'

'If you want to live.'

Kovic and Hannah lifted him together. Jin Jié reached out and pulled himself into the shaft.

'Nothing like the proximity of death to give you that extra spurt of energy.'

He held Hannah's shoulders. 'Now you. Feet first. You need to be facing the grille.'

'How many are there?'

'I don't know. Could be twenty, could be fifty.'

'We don't have enough ammunition.'

'We'll have to make it stretch – no missing. Take this.'

He handed her the sub-machine gun he had taken off the soldier in the lobby. She squeezed into the shaft beside Jin Jié and turned on to her stomach. He replaced the grille.

'Wait until you have a clear shot. Don't waste bullets.'

'How will they know to try this room?'

'We're going to lure them in.'

Wu had his ear to the door.

'They're in the corridor. Here.'

He handed him one of two sub-machine guns he'd brought up on the luggage trolley.

Kovic went into the bathroom, turned on the shower and drew the curtain, then came back out. The noise might distract them. Opposite was a locked connecting door to the next suite; he forced the handle. On the other side was a second door to the next room. The gap between them was less than two feet deep. He beckoned to Wu. They stepped into it and shut themselves in between the two doors.

In the cramped space their breaths and heartbeats sounded deafening. They heard the main door open, then a mumble of hushed voices. There was no guarantee that they wouldn't make straight for the connecting door. Kovic had to believe that the sound of the shower would attract enough of them to make Hannah's shot worth it.

A torch beam swept along the gap at the bottom of their door. There were more muffled voices. The room was filling with men. One was so close to them on the other side of the door that they could hear his breathing. Come on, Hannah – do your thing.

Just as he was beginning to think there was a problem, a sharp burst of fire splintered the air, and then a second, followed by several shouts and groans. Wu and Kovic burst through the door. Several men were down and Hannah's fire had sent the others crouching for cover by the window. Kovic aimed and with one short burst, the entire wall of glass crazed and dropped away into the night. Together they raked the area with fire until all those who were huddled by the window fell away too.

The firing stopped. Kovic helped himself to one of the dead men's weapons and signalled to Wu to stay in position. For the second time that night he saw himself as if he was in a movie, two machine guns at his hip ready to blast away. Even now, there was still something intoxicating about a firefight. But his elation was cut short. One of the fallen men lifted a weapon and aimed. A huge red hole appeared in Wu's chest. He slumped to his knees. Kovic leaped towards him as Hannah took down the shooter with a burst of fire.

Kovic eased Wu to the ground, cradling his head. There was nothing he could do. The exit wound was a six-inch crater, exposing his heart.

'Jesus, fuck, no!'

Wu gripped his arm.

'Guess I'm not going to make it to America.'

Kovic stared into his friend's eyes.

'That road through Big Sur, Route . . .'

'Route 1.'

'You make that drive for me.'

'You know my driving – you sure about that?'

Wu smiled and then the light went from his eyes.

Kovic blinked away the tears and looked round. The door to the corridor was open and he had no idea how many more there were out there.

He ran towards the door and kicked it shut. Then, as an afterthought, he picked up the grenade that Wu had lifted and set it between the door and the frame, ready to blow if anyone entered the room. He looked up at the grate, now shredded by Hannah's fire, and gestured for her to follow him. Together they lowered Jin Jié down and then moved quickly across the suite, through the connecting door into the second room. They waited. There was almost total silence, except for the howl of the wind.

The blast of the grenade shook the room, showering them in plaster. Kovic motioned for Hannah to stay put, then cautiously moved back into the suite. There were dead Chinese soldiers everywhere, just visible through the smoke. No one moved. He thought he heard a creak of boot leather. If there were more out there, he wanted them where he could see them before he fired. He waited. What was left of the door moved an inch and then another. In the smoke and dust he could make out one figure holding a small firearm in his outstretched hands.

The man stepped into the room. He had no uniform, just jeans, jacket and ski mask. Then Kovic recognised the weapon. He breathed out.

'What took you so long?'

Garrison's Marines.

# 76

'C'mon in, boys. Check out the room service.'

The three Marines, Irish, Pac and Recker, filed into the room. Kovic imagined the gleam that would have been in Wu's eye as America came a step closer. As they exchanged handshakes, the Marines gazed at the corpses, at least ten, spreadeagled across the floor and over the white leather.

'Man, you really cleaned up here.'

'Yeah, you missed a great party.'

They tensed as they heard the door to the second room move. Hannah emerged.

Kovic stepped back.

'She's with us. There's another one in there; he's injured.'

'These your VIPs?' Hannah looked at the Marines.

'Affirmative, they have priority check-in.'

Together they helped Jin Jié into the room and set him on his feet.

'Jeez, this guy's pretty smashed up. Can you walk okay, buddy?'

'It's a long way down the stairs, or we could risk the elevator.'

Jin Jié tried to straighten up.

'It's okay. I'm good.'

He smiled, then swayed and collapsed against the wall.

Kovic steered him to a chair.

'We'll never make it out that way. They know we're up here.' Kovic pointed at the floor. 'And there are hundreds more of these guys where they came from.'

Irish shrugged. 'They our orders – seaborne evac. We go out the way we came in.'

Hannah looked at him, confused. 'What d'you mean? That wasn't your helicopter we heard?'

Her face clouded. Kovic hadn't said anything to her about the Chinese machine on the roof.

Kovic and the Marines exchanged glances.

She gestured at the ceiling. 'So what was that, then?'

Still Kovic didn't speak. Hannah looked thunderous. 'That's how we're getting out. What's wrong?' She grabbed him by the shirt and pulled him towards her, screaming.

'You said Jin Jié shouldn't stay in Shanghai – that you would get us out. I went along with it. Now we're fucking screwed. I trusted you, you – bastard!'

The building shuddered with another explosion.

Kovic went over to the hole where the window had been, the wind blasting his face, threatening to suck him out right out of the room. He took out the handset for the gondola, prayed that it still worked. The cranes whirred towards him. The gondola moved closer, but stubbornly stayed more than a metre adrift from the floor of the room. He turned to the others.

'You coming?'

Pac gasped and looked at Recker, who shook his head.

'You're kidding, right?'

Jin Jié's eyes widened. He clutched on to Hannah.

'I don't know that I can do this. I suffer from vertigo.'

'Just leap. You can do it.'

Kovic was all out of patience.

'You'll be suffering from death if you don't. If you can save China you can get into this thing. Just don't look down.'

Kovic went first. He stepped back and took a couple of running steps. But as he jumped, the wind swung the gondola towards him, closing the gap, so he overshot. His legs crashed into the base but the rest of him from his hips up was over the far side of the gondola, winding him as the weight of his torso tipped him out the other side. He was staring down at the concrete and flashing lights a hundred and forty floors below. He dropped his weapon as he tried to grab hold of the side with both hands, too late. He went head first over the edge and ended up dangling from just one hand.

'Has this guy got some kinda death wish?' said Pac. He jumped, made a perfect landing in the gondola and grasped Kovic's arm. Then he hauled him up, seized his belt and tipped him back into the gondola where he landed in a heap.

'Okay, good.'

'I know,' said Pac. 'You were just showing me how *not* to do it.'

Irish followed. As he landed, the cable holding one end of the gondola dropped a couple of feet so they were now hanging at an ungainly angle.

'Jeez, how many's this thing hold?'

'Two, more or less.'

Recker grabbed the gondola. 'This like the *Titanic*, man.'

'Hold it steady, for fuck's sake!' screamed Hannah as she positioned Jin Jié. Together with Pac, they manoeuvred him in. Hannah went last with an expert leap.

Kovic put up his hand.

'No one speak.'

All they had to do now was pray none of the incoming soldiers looked out of the window.

Kovic worked the remote. The gondola shuddered, then started to rise.

Hannah looked at him again in dismay.

'I thought we were going down?'

'Give me a minute, okay. I want to see what we got up there.'

Pac and Irish trained their weapons on the window as they rose. Kovic stopped the gondola just before it came level with the parapet. He peered over. The helicopter was an aging Z-9, its long rotor blades hanging low around it like huge drooping petals. His pulse quickened. Out of the corner of his eye he saw a guard patrolling the perimeter turn the corner to come towards them.

He turned to the Marines beside him and whispered.

'Anyone got a blade?'

Irish handed him a KA-BAR combat knife.

Kovic waited, watching the guard approach. It seemed to take forever. When he was almost upon them, he sprang out, threw an arm round his neck and took him down silently with a well-aimed thrust of the knife. Then he dragged him over the perimeter wall and let him drop.

Irish looked at the Z-9. 'You think you can get back to the *Valkyrie* in that?'

Hannah saw the gleam in Kovic's eyes as he briefed them.

'Whatever we do, we take the crew alive. I don't have time to read the manual. There are three guards: Irish, take the one at the rear, Pac, the one near the nose, I'll take the centre one and for fuck's sake don't hole the bird. Don't let anyone come through. Jin Jié, stay here till we have the aircraft secure.'

They scrambled out of the gondola and charged across the roof, shooting. As soon as the pilot saw them he fired up the engines. The rotors stirred from their slumber and slowly swept the area. Irish missed the rear guard who let off a burst that sent them running for cover behind the head of the stairwell.

The rotors were gaining speed. The downforce was almost overwhelming. The rear guard dashed behind the tail rotor.

'Don't let him leave!' He turned to Recker. 'Take out the pilot.'

Recker grinned as he aimed, relishing the challenge. For a second he was dead still.

His single shot pierced the Plexiglas and the pilot fell forward. Recker turned and gave Kovic the thumbs up as the tail guard emerged from behind the craft.

'Over there!' screamed Kovic, pointing frantically. Recker whirled round and took out the guard.

The stairwell door opened. Jesus, thought Kovic, they just keep coming.

'Hold them off!'

Pac emptied a mag down the stairs.

Hannah reached Kovic, pulling Jin Jié with her.

'Load him in.' He looked at Recker. 'You wanna ride?'

Recker shook his head. 'We'll hold them off for you. That crate's got no weaponry.'

Kovic climbed aboard, grabbed the dead pilot, took off his headset and heaved him out of the cockpit.

Hannah scrambled in, hauling Jin Jié with her.

'Have you flown one of these before?'

'Sure.'

'When?'

'It's been a while.'

More than a while. And it had only been a training run. He scanned the controls, a mass of dials and lights blinking at him, all a blur. He felt for the controls and it started to come back, the collective down to the left of the seat, the cyclic in front of him. He put his feet on the pedals. The instructor's words drifted back to him. *Think of it as like ballet, every limb keeping you moving, keeping you balanced.* Kovic didn't feel very balletic right now. He twisted the throttle grip and heard the whine of the shafts climbing as the rotors tensed, clawing at the air. He heaved on the collective, depressing the right pedal to counteract the torque from the increased pitch of the blades. Gradually the machine started to struggle into the air. It was nothing like the nimble little TH-67 he had trained on, more like a truck. He needed as much altitude as he could get before he moved out from above the building or gravity would have its way. He pushed the stick forward, and the nose dipped. He pulled back – too much – and the tail scraped the roof, nearly taking off the rear rotor. After what seemed a lifetime he got it level and continued to rise. Three metallic cracks warned him of fire coming from below. He looked round at Hannah who had found herself a headset and managed to strap Jin Jié into a seat. He switched on the comms.

He pushed the cyclic further forward and the nose tipped again.

'Come on, baby—'

He willed it forward but the Z-9 was taking its time. They were now right over the perimeter wall, Kovic striving to find both the lift and the speed to move into full forward flight and escape the rotor wash into clean air. He skimmed the parapet round the perimeter of the roof, almost catching the gondola cranes. The tower and the machine seemed to drop like a stone towards the city below. He twisted the throttle up to full revs and yanked the stick back in an attempt to pull out of the dive. Nothing happened. They were dropping and gaining speed. Then he remembered – stick forward, drive out of the dive. He thrust it forward and prayed. It was touch and go in the battle between the rotors and gravity. The machine levelled and then began to ascend.

The comms in his headset crackled. It was Hannah. 'Sorry I doubted you.'

Kovic turned and grinned at her. 'No problem. I had it covered. Now get up here and make the radio work. Find out where the fuck we're supposed to be headed.'

# 77

Kovic jolted awake and sat up. For a few seconds he had no recollection of where he was. He felt a strange swaying sensation as if
there was something wrong with his balance. Then he looked over
to where the light was coming from. A porthole – he was on board
the *Valkyrie*. He had made it.

They should have crashed. Once he had levelled out they headed
due south for the sea and none of the other craft in the sky noticed
them, just an old Z-9 chuntering along looking for all the world
like it was on a milk run to the Chinese fleet. His navigation skills
were zero and Hannah had made the most of that. She also claimed
it was her idea to take the helicopter. In a way she was right. She
had shamed him into it, though they both knew there was no other
way, not with Jin Jié in the state he was. But they hadn't bargained
for the fuel level. Either the engines drank like a dying man in the
desert, or one of the tanks had been grazed in the firefight. The
warning light was blinking at them before they had even cleared
land. And then there was the sea mist, lying like a deceptively soft
fluffy mattress, so successfully concealing the *Valkyrie* that they
had to be talked down by the Command Tower. Somewhere on
this descent, he had gone blank for a second so they came in hard,
smashing up the landing gear, which left the Z-9 leaning on the
remains of two of its rotor blades.

He remembered turning to Hannah whose face was a mask of
disdain.

'Did I pass?'

And she had leaned over and kissed him.

'I'll get back to you about that.'

\*

303

There was a soft knocking at the door.

'Come in.'

A young steward stood at the door with a tray.

'Good morning, sir. Commander Garrison would like to know if you would care to join him for breakfast.'

'What time is it?'

'Seven a.m., sir.'

Kovic frowned. It had been almost dawn when they landed. He waved the crewman in.

'How long have I been in here?'

'About twenty-six hours, sir.'

No wonder he felt so rested. The steward put the mug of tea on the bedside table and indicated a set of clothing folded over a chair.

'There's some fresh kit for you, sir.'

It was an officer's khaki shirt and pants. He looked at them doubtfully. He had never worn a uniform in his life. The idea of putting one on now made him feel like an impostor. But wasn't that what he had always been?

'Give me ten minutes.'

Showered, shaved and dressed, Kovic followed the steward to Garrison's quarters. The vessel was alive with activity as he travelled up near vertical stairs and squeezed along narrow corridors. Overhead came the throb of helicopters and Ospreys; on deck, hooters blasted. There were shouts from crew and coded announcements blared over the PA.

'So it's started?'

'Looks like it, sir.'

He took a deep breath and knocked.

Garrison was standing with his back to the door. The first thing Kovic noticed was the photograph of his son, Tommy. Garrison slowly turned and followed his gaze. He looked older than his age, his eyes tired from seeing too many men go to their deaths.

'It's a good portrait, isn't it? Taken just a few weeks before—'

Kovic reached to shake Garrison's hand and the two men's eyes met for the first time.

Kovic struggled to work out what was going on in that head. Maybe he would find out.

Two stewards appeared with trays: eggs, bacon, toast and hash browns. Suddenly Kovic realised how long it was since he had eaten an actual meal.

'I figured you'd be hungry.'

Garrison gestured for him to sit. They both wired into the food.

'Did the Marines make it out okay?'

Garrison tried to answer promptly, but without chewing at the same time.

'They brought out a whole boatload of Chinese nationals with them.' He shot Kovic a glance. 'One of the advantages of seaborne evac.'

'They could have come out on the chopper. They had the option. But we might not have made it off the roof if they hadn't covered our exit.'

Garrison chuckled. 'Well after the mess you made of landing it I guess they made the right decision.'

'They said they couldn't figure out why there was no airborne exfil.'

Garrison nodded, his mouth full. He made no attempt to explain or justify it.

'How are the others? Is Jin Jié—?'

Garrison swallowed and took a swig of coffee.

'Alive? Sure. He's doing okay. They cleaned up his wounds, gave him some blood. His – er – wife's keeping an eye on him.'

Kovic flashed him a look.

'Well that's who she's claiming she is but she's being pretty tight lipped with us. MSS, I assume. I wouldn't want to cross swords with her. You – er, think she's got some other agenda going there?'

Kovic shrugged.

'Well, I wouldn't fancy Jin Jié's chances without her watching his back. He's going to need some good people around him if he's ever going to be a credible alternative to Chang.'

Garrison pushed his plate away and put his knife and fork neatly together, fixing Kovic with his tired grey eyes.

'After my son – after Tommy was killed, I'll be honest, Kovic, I wanted you dead. I wanted someone to pay; a life for a life.' He shook his head.

'Sir, I—'

Garrison raised a hand.

'Now you're sitting right here in front of me – boy, am I glad you made it out.'

'Thank you, sir. Thank you for changing your mind. I don't need to tell you that Tommy was a fine Marine.'

'You know he'd been thinking about going over to the dark side.'

'Sir?'

'The CIA. You made quite an impression.'

Kovic held his gaze until Garrison glanced at the portrait once more and let out a long sigh.

'Do you ever ask yourself what the fuck we're doing – what all this is for?'

It felt like a relief to hear his own doubts echoed.

'The past few days – more than ever.'

Garrison got up from the table and took a step towards the porthole.

'It's happening. They're gonna get their war.'

'Shouldn't you be on the bridge, sir? I mean, it's good of you to give me breakfast, but—'

'Kovic, I've been here a hundred times before. You can sit up there in the big chair, being important, barking orders and generally making a noise – but there's a whole mess of guys out there who know just what to do.'

'What happens next?'

'Chang seems to have come to some agreement with the Russians. We expect an engagement anytime in the next twenty-four hours.'

He refilled their cups and leaned forward.

'I wanted this time with you before we go our separate ways.' His face brightened, though there was still a faraway look in his eyes. 'So it's game over for you. You're all done.'

Kovic drained his coffee.

'How do you mean, sir?'

'There's an Osprey due in at 1400 from Guam. Seems like they're giving you the VIP treatment.'

There was an odd expression on Garrison's face as he pushed the printout towards him.

'A nice stretch of R&R, maybe a gratitude posting to some fine, civilised place like Paris or Rome, promotion maybe?'

Kovic felt a strange sensation moving through his gut as he studied the message. He put it down on the table and passed it back.

'It says for your eyes only, sir.'

Garrison raised an eyebrow.

'Does it now? I must have overlooked that.'

'And it's from the CIA's Inspector General's office.'

Garrison said nothing. Kovic put his fork down and pushed his chair back a little.

'Did it surprise you, sir, that the exfil request was denied?'

They both knew the answer. Garrison's face reddened. Kovic feared for a moment he was going to have a heart attack.

'Cutler was a goddamn traitor. And that bastard Metzger. When they did a deal with Chang they signed my men's death certificates.'

Kovic looked at the document again. 'And when I blew the whistle on them, I signed my own.'

*'Commander to bridge. Commander to bridge.'*

The message blared out from a speaker on the wall.

Garrison was on his feet.

'Looks like this is it. Wanna tag along?'

'Thanks, sir, but I should get round to see the others.'

Garrison nodded and was gone.

# 78

Jin Jié was sitting up in his bed sipping a can of root beer. Hannah was beside him staring into space. She also had been given a set of khakis to wear, which only served to enhance her air of businesslike sexiness. They both looked up as he approached.

Kovic nodded at the root beer.

'I see you're sampling the local delicacies.'

Jin Jié raised his can.

'I always loved this stuff.'

He put out his hand. 'Kovic – how do I begin to thank you?'

Kovic took it in his. It felt damp and fleshy.

'No need. It was a great pleasure to fuck with Chang's grand plan. Now you'll be the thorn in his side that he can't get his hands on. You need to get fully well so you can muster the opposition.'

'So you think the forces of progress will prevail?'

Kovic shrugged. How the fuck did he know? And as for Jin Jié's chances – well he never got what Hannah and all the rest saw in him. He was waiting eagerly for an answer. He glanced over at Hannah.

'I never speculate about the future. I leave that to the fortune-tellers and the politicians. Plus I seem to have made a career out of telling people stuff they didn't want to hear.'

Hannah turned to Jin Jié and got to her feet.

'You must rest now.'

Jin Jié sighed.

'I suppose so. Don't go far, will you.'

Hannah took Kovic's arm and propelled him out of the room.

On deck the wind swirled around them. A Super Hornet screamed overhead. It was a crisp clear day.

'Where were you? I thought you'd disappeared.'

'Catching up on a little sleep. Anyhow, I thought you'd be glad to see the back of me after the last few days.'

She gave him one of her thunderous looks that said otherwise. A couple of ratings jogged past and gave her the eye. Kovic stepped closer.

'Don't you think you should have some security around you?'

She pursed her lips and hissed at him.

'Jin Jié seems to be on the mend.'

'Oh, he's going to be fine. You almost certainly saved his life digging that shrapnel out of him. The surgeon said it had grazed the subclavian artery. Any more aggravation, it would have ruptured and he'd have bled out.'

Another aircraft screamed overhead.

'He wants me with him; he's asked me to be his second in command.'

Her face gave nothing away.

'Is that – solely a day job?'

She pulled him close. She smelled heavenly.

'Is there somewhere on here we can be alone – just for a while?'

# 79

Kovic checked the time: 13.48. She was looking at him, her beautiful dark eyes full of sadness. In less than fifteen minutes an Osprey would arrive to take him away.

She reached up to him.

'What will you do now?'

'Eh – I'll get back to you on that.'

He held her for a second, then rose and reached for his clothes.

Outside the cabin the air was thick with the sounds of the carrier moving to battle stations.

'Let's go on deck. See what's happening.'

They had only gone a few metres when Recker shouted up to them from below. He was in full kit, about to deploy.

They descended the stairs. Irish and Pac joined him, also kitted up.

'What's happening?'

'The *Titan*'s been hit. There's a whole bunch of intel that we can't let fall into Chang's hands. We're gonna RHIB over and claim it before the ship goes down.'

As he spoke, Kovic saw the Osprey descending, its rotors tilted in preparation to land.

He looked at Hannah, trying to smile at him through the tears. He looked at Irish and Pac, then Recker who was carrying a spare kit. Then he noticed Garrison on the balcony of the bridge, looking down at them.

Garrison caught his eye, then gave him a nod.

Recker held out the kit.

'We should get going, sir. Commander's orders.'

The Osprey was down, its doors opening.

Kovic grinned at the Marines.

'Then what are we waiting for?'

# Acknowledgements

For invaluable specialised advice, Brad Auerbach, Rita Auerbach and Dean Morris in America, James Thorniley in Shanghai and Karen Stirgwolt in Dulwich.

For such diligent and enthusiastic copy-editing, Julian Flanders, and proof-reading by Jane Selley.

For all round support, Sophie Doyle.

For making it happen, Jon Wood and Jo Gledhill, the team at Orion and my wonderful agent Mark Lucas.

For inventing such a fertile universe to work from and giving me the freedom to play with it, my thanks and respect to the creators of Battlefield – DICE and EA.

And lastly, thanks to my wife Stephanie who read, re-read and never held back.